# Thirty-Five
## *and a*
# Half Conspiracies

A ROSE GARDNER MYSTERY

# Other books by Denise Grover Swank:

*Rose Gardner Mysteries*
(Humorous Southern mysteries)
TWENTY-EIGHT AND A HALF WISHES
TWENTY-NINE AND A HALF REASONS
THIRTY AND A HALF EXCUSES
FALLING TO PIECES (novella)
THIRTY-ONE AND A HALF REGRETS
THIRTY-TWO AND A HALF COMPLICATIONS
PICKING UP THE PIECES (novella)
THIRTY-THREE AND A HALF SHENANIGANS
ROSE AND HELENA SAVE CHRISTMAS (novella)
RIPPLE OF SECRETS (novella)
THIRTY-FOUR AND A HALF PREDICAMENTS
THIRTY-FOUR BONUS CHAPTERS

*The Wedding Pact*
*(Contemporary Romance)*
*THE SUBSITUTE*
*THE PLAYER*
*THE GAMBLER*

*New Adult Contemporary Romance*
AFTER MATH
REDESIGNED
BUSINESS AS USUAL

# Thirty-Five
## *and a*
# Half Conspiracies

A ROSE GARDNER MYSTERY

## Denise Grover Swank

Copyright 2015 by Denise Grover Swank

Cover art and design: Damonza
Developmental Editor: Angela Polidoro
Copy editor: Shannon Page
Proofreaders: Carolina Valedez-Miller and Cynthia L. Moyer

# Chapter One

They say sitting in a jail cell can make you reevaluate your life.

As I sat in Fenton County lockup—charged with my own momma's murder—I was definitely learning the truth of that statement.

I sat on the lower bunk of a bed while the three women who shared the cell eyed me liked I'd just announced I was from the planet Jupiter. Of course, their reaction might have had something to do with the fact that I hadn't stopped crying once in the last hour.

One of the women sat down next to me. She had long blond hair and looked to be in her late twenties. If it weren't for her rotten teeth, she would remind me a little bit of my best friend, Neely Kate. "I'm Rhea, and these two are Tawana and Janie."

The dark-complected woman sitting cross-legged on the bed across from me lifted her hand at Tawana, and the older gray-haired woman standing in the corner nodded at Janie.

"I'm Rose."

Rhea patted my hand. "Is it your first time getting arrested, honey?"

I nodded and wiped my cheeks with the back of my hand. I considered telling her I'd been locked up before. But I was pretty sure neither time counted since this was the first time I'd been put in full lockup in a bright orange jumpsuit.

"What were you arrested for?"

"Murder." I broke down into tears again, thoroughly disgusted with myself but unable to stop.

This was bad. Very bad. I wasn't sure my boyfriend, Mason, could get me out of it now that he'd lost his job as the Fenton County Assistant District Attorney.

The other two women eyed me with new respect, and Rhea moved away a few inches. "You don't say."

"I didn't do it, though," I gushed out. "I was framed."

Tawana tsked as she crossed her arms and shook her head. "Ain't we all, baby girl. Ain't we all."

"Was yer man beatin' ya?" Rhea asked. "So you killed him in self-defense?"

"No." I shook my head. "It was my mother."

"*Damn*," Tawana said, shaking her head. "That's cold."

"But I didn't do it," I protested. "Daniel Crocker did it. But J.R. Simmons made it look like I paid him to do it."

All three women were now openly staring, and it occurred to me that I should probably have kept all of that to myself.

"Let me get this straight," Janie piped up from the corner. "You paid Daniel Crocker to kill yer momma?" She scrunched up her face. "*And he did it?*"

"No. He killed her, but I never paid him to do it. In fact, I'm pretty doggone sure he intended to kill me instead."

"Rose." Tawana snapped her fingers and pointed at me. "Well, I'll be damned. Yer Rose *Gardner*, ain't ya?"

I wasn't sure admitting *that* was a good idea either.

Janie gave me a long cold stare. "Yer the one who killed him."

There was no use denying it. I'd killed him in self-defense, but I'd long since learned that quite a few people in Fenton County had practically worshipped the man. They liked to ignore the fact that he'd been a sadistic sociopath.

Janie began to stalk toward me. "I worked for him. At least I did until you killed him."

"So why don't you work for Skeeter Malcolm now?" I asked. Hopefully my question would distract her from physical violence.

She laughed, but it wasn't a friendly sound. "What does a Mary Sue like you know about Skeeter Malcolm?"

A whole lot more than she'd ever suspect. "What did you do for Crocker?"

She released a bitter chuckle. "What? You conducting a job interview?"

I shrugged, happy that I'd been distracted enough to stop crying. "I've got nothing but time, so why not tell me?"

She crossed her arms over her chest. "I worked in his greenhouse. Used to grow his pot."

"Maybe I can help you get a new job. What are you willin' to do?"

Janie started to speak, but Tawana leaned forward and whacked her on the arm. "What are you doin'? Don't you know who she is?"

Janie nodded. "Yeah, she's Rose Gardner. The woman who killed Daniel Crocker."

"She's also Rose Gardner, girlfriend to the assistant DA."

The woman's eyes widened in fear.

"But he's not the ADA anymore," I said. "He lost his job tonight."

"I still wouldn't trust her," Tawana harrumphed. "She also used to date the chief deputy sheriff."

"Damn, girl," Rhea said a little wistfully. "You get around."

There was no denying I'd dated both men, but I was fairly sure they didn't want to hear that my former boyfriend had taken a front-row seat while that witch Deputy Hoffstetter arrested me.

Tawana crossed her arms. "They put her here to spy on us."

"No." I shook my head. "I'm not spying on anyone."

Janie closed the distance between us. She grabbed my arm, hauled me to my feet, and slammed me against the bars. Grabbing my jumpsuit in her fists, she leaned in until we practically stood nose to nose.

"I don't like snitches," she snarled.

And that's when I felt the beginning of a vision.

I would have groaned if I had been capable of it, but once a vision got its hooks into me, it wouldn't let go until it was done. The visions only lasted a few seconds, and I looked kind of zoned out when I was having one. That was easy enough to explain, but the fact that I would uncontrollably blurt out a description of whatever I'd seen? Not so much.

My vision grew fuzzy and the jail cell disappeared. I was standing in a kitchen next to a man in a white tank top and basketball shorts. He had a respirator mask in his hand.

"I don't want to do any more jail time, Titus," I said in Janie's voice. "Next time I'm going back for good."

"Then get the hell out," he said. "I ain't gonna quit a six-figure job to save your sorry ass."

When the vision faded, Janie's eyeballs were inches from mine.

"He ain't gonna quit to save your sorry ass," I said. "He told you to get out."

Her eyes flew open and her fists tightened on my jumpsuit. "What did you just say?"

"Makin' friends already, I see," a man said in a dry tone. With great hesitation, I took my gaze off the threat in front of me to assess the possible threat beyond the bars.

Carter Hale gave me a sardonic grin as he hooked his thumbs on his belt. "I see you've met Janie. She's a gentle spirit."

I wouldn't have used that phrase to describe her, but who was I to quibble when she was about to strangle me?

Carter gave her a frown. "Janie, would you be kind enough to take your hands off my client?"

"*Your* client?" both of us screeched.

Janie dropped her fists from my jumpsuit and scowled at the defense attorney. "You defending this white bread bitch?"

He gave her an apologetic shrug. "Looks like it, and I'd like her to show up for her arraignment on Monday without a bruised face, so I'd appreciate it if you kept your hands off her."

"She's gonna snitch to Simmons about what we've done."

"I'm pretty damn sure she has enough of a beef with Chief Deputy Simmons that she has no plans to talk to him any time soon. Which means your secrets are safe."

Janie grumbled as a guard approached the cell door.

He scanned the room and his gaze landed on me as he opened the door. "Gardner, I need you to step out."

"Do I get to go home now?"

Janie laughed. "She don't know shit, does she?"

Carter's smart-ass grin softened as I walked through the opening. "Sorry, that's not likely to happen until Monday. This is just a chance for you and I to have a little get-to-know-you chat."

The guard led us down a hall and into a small room with a table and two chairs. Once we were alone, Carter gestured to one of the chairs. "After you."

I took a seat and waited as he pulled his legal pad out of his bag and placed it on the table in front of him. He glanced up and shot me an ornery grin. "It looks like you needed that get-out-of-jail-free card after all."

Before I was arrested, he'd handed Neely Kate and me a business card, telling us he had a feeling we'd need it. It was hard to believe it had only been the day before.

"Where's Mason?" I asked.

His shoulders shifted in a lazy roll. "Hell if I know."

I blinked in surprise. "Didn't he hire you?"

He looked me over and leaned his forearm on the table. "Here's the thing, I'm not supposed to tell anyone why I took this case . . . including you. But that hardly seems fair considering you're trusting me to represent you." He shifted his weight as his eyes pierced mine. "And I confess, my curiosity is piqued. So how about I answer your question with a question of my own: How do you know Skeeter Malcolm?"

The blood rushed from my face. "How *would* I know Skeeter Malcolm?"

A lazy grin lifted the corners of his mouth as something flickered in his eyes. I realized that while Carter Hale oozed the persona of laziness, he was anything but.

"I suppose it's not important who convinced you to take my case," I said, hoping to distract him. "Just that you took it."

He nodded and cocked his head, fiddling with the pen in his hand. "I guess we should start with the obvious question. Did you do it?"

"Are you kidding me? Everyone and their dog knows Daniel Crocker killed my momma."

He stopped playing with his pen, and his mouth puckered. "That's not in dispute. The question is whether you paid Daniel Crocker money to do it."

"No."

"So why does the DA think you did?"

What should I tell him? I'd kept so many secrets for so long, it was hard to know what to keep quiet now. But this man was supposed to help keep me out of prison, which meant he needed to know everything there was to know about my case.

So I told him almost everything.

I started off by telling him about dating Joe—how I'd met him while he was working undercover to bust Crocker. And how Joe had kept the information about his family secret for fear they would destroy us. And how they ultimately *did* destroy us when Joe's father, J.R. Simmons, the richest and most powerful man in southern Arkansas, fabricated evidence against me to blackmail Joe. And I also told him about all the dirt J.R. had gathered about my family—my sister Violet's affair with Henryetta's mayor, Brody MacIntosh, and the business mistake made by soon-to-be-ex brother-in-law. And I told him about Hilary—Joe's ex-girlfriend—who'd shown up in Henryetta a couple of months ago, pregnant with Joe's baby. And about Kate, Joe's sister, who'd come to town after Christmas following a mysterious two-year disappearance.

After a moment's hesitation, I told him about my visions too. I didn't usually volunteer that information willingly, so it was at once frightening and liberating. He gave me a weighing look, but he didn't question me or call me crazy. He just kept scribbling down notes.

I *didn't* tell him about how I'd started working for Skeeter Malcolm. Or how I'd used my gift of sight to help Skeeter win the Thanksgiving Day auction that had granted him the right to run the Fenton County criminal world. And I most definitely did not tell him that I was the Lady in Black.

After I had talked myself breathless, Carter released a low whistle. "You could write a book about all of this. I bet it would be a bestseller."

I shook my head, embarrassed. "I assure you, Mr. Hale. *No one* wants to read about my life."

He smirked. "I bet you'd be surprised."

"You believe me about my visions?"

"Trust me, I've heard stranger things in this room.

And besides, it fills in a few blanks you didn't bring up."

Oh, crappy doodles. He'd guessed the truth—I could see it in his eyes. And if he'd made the connection this quickly, how long would it be before Mason did too?

But before I could say a word, Carter's expression changed. He looked down at his notes and then lifted his face, wearing a grim expression. "I'm gonna shoot it to you straight, Rose. J.R. Simmons is not a man to be trifled with. He never does anything half-assed. This case is as thin as the ham they put on the sandwiches at Tucker's Deli, and I suspect the evidence is flimsy at best. If he weren't involved, I'd count on getting it tossed out before trial. But Simmons *is* involved, so you can bet he has all his ducks in a row."

He wasn't telling me anything I didn't already suspect.

"He got Deveraux out of the way so he could set this in motion, which means he's got the DA, and most likely a judge, in his back pocket. Not to mention his son's involvement." He set his pen down and leaned back in his chair. "The trial's gonna be a waste of everyone's time because there's no doubt whatsoever what the verdict will be."

"Guilty." It wasn't a question. I already knew that too.

He pushed the notepad away, his forehead wrinkling. Finally he sat up. "There's no use fighting this in court when every last one of them is probably on his payroll."

"So what are you sayin'?" I asked, my anger rising. "That I should just plead guilty and expect to live out the rest of my days in the state pen?"

"No. But I'm warning you that short of a miracle, you're gonna be convicted." At least he didn't look too happy with his declaration.

"I think I want a new attorney."

He chuckled, but he stayed firmly seated in his chair. "I assure you that no one else wants this case. Hell, I didn't even want it. When your boyfriend showed up at my door a few hours ago, I told him no."

"Mason asked you to take my case?"

He frowned, looking displeased. "It doesn't matter who asked me or why I took it. The fact is that I'm the only one who's willing to take it on."

"And that's supposed to make me feel better?" I could see he was holding back information, and I was sick to death of people hiding things . . . including me. "If I'm expected to tell you everything, then I need you to tell me everything too."

His eyebrows lifted in mock reprimand. "Oh, but you haven't told me everything, have you?"

My blood ran cold. "There are things that don't seem pertinent to my case."

"Yet they seem pertinent to the reason why I'm here."

I was in deep trouble. He knew, all right. I might as well be wearing the Lady in Black's veil right now.

He released a sigh and picked up his pen, twirling it in his hand. "How about we go at this another way?"

"And which way is that?"

He stopped to ponder his words for a moment, then said, "I have a client who keeps me on retainer. We have an . . . understanding."

I sat up in my chair. He was talking about Skeeter.

"I take the cases he requests that I represent. Some seem hopeless—not as hopeless as this one, mind you," he said with an ornery grin. "But hopeless nonetheless."

I wanted to reach over and slug him, but I suspected that wouldn't help my situation.

"I'm very good at what I do, Ms. Gardner, a trait that has earned your boyfriend's dislike—and that's putting it mildly. But sometimes even I can't make the law work the way I need it to."

I leaned forward and rested my hand on the table. "Mason's been workin' on finding something to use against J.R. Simmons. If he finds it, that should help, right?"

"It depends on what he finds and how quickly your case goes to trial. Once you're convicted, it'll be a helluva lot harder to get you out. But every piece of information will help, and my client seems determined to do everything in his power to keep you protected." His eyes narrowed and a grin tugged at his lips. "And that has me very curious. Why's he so interested in keepin' you out of jail?"

I kept my mouth shut.

He grinned. "Not to worry. I was always good at puzzles. And I've already got this one mostly figured out."

"Then I guess you don't need anything else from me," I grumbled.

Carter sat up and slid his notebook back in front of him. "Since we seem to have everything else wrapped up, how about we move on to personal matters? Any messages you want to give to your family? I doubt anyone will be able to see you until Monday at your arraignment."

"What about Mason?"

"*Especially* not Mason." When I shot him an angry glare, he lifted his hands in defense. "Not my rules. Your boyfriend could be Charles Manson for all I care. We love who we love." He didn't sound too happy about the last part. "But if they went to the trouble of kicking him out of his position, I suspect they won't want him communicating with you."

"But I can see him on Monday at my arraignment?" When he nodded, I asked, "So what happens after my arraignment? Will they put me back in jail?"

He grimaced. "It depends on if they give you bail. With a case as hopeless as this one, Simmons and the judge who's handling the arraignment are probably worried you're a flight risk. But I'll assure them you're a productive member of society—that you've sunk all your money into your businesses and are dedicated to making them work."

"How do you know all of that?"

He rolled his eyes. "Rose Gardner, owner of RBW Landscaping, has an office right across the square from mine."

My face burned with embarrassment. Yes, of course he knew. Neely Kate and I had practically barged into his office the other day while we were trying to duck one of Skeeter's guys.

"In the arraignment, I'll do all the speaking on your behalf, including entering your plea."

"You are going to plead innocent, aren't you?"

His gaze held mine. "If I pled guilty—even if you asked me to do it—I suspect I'd face repercussions that would haunt me to my dying breath, which no doubt be much sooner than I'd like." His mouth twisted into a condescending smile. "So the answer to your question is yes, I will be pleading innocent."

I nodded. I wasn't sure where his sudden hostility had come from, but if he really was the only one willing to take my case, I couldn't afford to alienate him.

"So," he drawled, tapping his pen on the tablet. "Any messages?"

I had more messages in my head than he had paper to write them down on, but I felt awkward about sharing my soul with Carter. Especially after his latest display. "Could you please tell Mason not to worry? That I'm okay."

He nodded.

I shifted in my seat, worried about the next one. "I need you to give Neely Kate a message too." I paused. "But it must remain completely confidential, even from Mason. Can you assure me of that?"

His eyebrows lifted, but he nodded. "Yes."

"Ask her if she'll make sure my closet is clean."

His head cocked to the side, and his eyes narrowed with curiosity. "Most women aren't concerned about housekeeping when they're sitting in jail for murder."

I shrugged. "Call me a neat freak, just make sure she gets the message. Do you need her number?"

He gave me a half-grin. "No. She put her number in my speed dial and told me to call her after I saw you."

That caught me by surprise. "When did you see her?"

"Right before I came here to see you." He grimaced and absently rubbed his arm. "She can be *very* persuasive."

I couldn't help grinning, but the smile slipped off my face when I realized a hard truth: Carter was about to walk out of this room, which meant I was going back to that jail cell. Where I'd sit for the next sixty hours or so. If Janie didn't decide to add to her sentence by murdering me.

"Any more messages?"

I shook my head.

"Chin up, Rose Gardner. You've got people in your corner, me included. And you don't have to worry about Janie Parsons beatin' the shit out of you. You'll be gettin' your own cell when you walk out of here."

My head jerked up. "What? Why?"

"Let's just say I used my own powers of persuasion to convince them your safety was at risk given your personal connections and your past with Crocker." He winked, then stood. "I confess, you've piqued my curiosity for some time, Rose Gardner. I'm looking forward to peekin' behind the curtain." He walked to the door and rapped with his knuckles. The door opened seconds later. Carter glanced back at me with a grin. "See you Monday morning."

It was gonna be a long weekend.

# Chapter Two

On Monday morning, my stomach cramped as the sheriff cruiser that was transporting me pulled up to the side entrance of the Fenton County courthouse. Deputy Randy Miller opened the back door, took one look at me, and frowned at the driver.

"Shackles, Abbie Lee?" he asked in disbelief. "Is that really necessary?"

Deputy Hoffstetter shot him a glare. "I wouldn't be surprised if her blonde bimbo friend showed up and tried to make a break for it with 'er."

In all honesty, I wouldn't have been too surprised by that either. And after all the evasion maneuvers we performed the day of the fire at Gems, the strip club Neely Kate's cousin had worked at and disappeared from, I wasn't all that surprised Deputy Hoffstetter was being so cautious.

Deputy Miller's face reddened. "Well, I'm not walking her in like this, so hand over the key."

"She'll take advantage of ya, Miller."

He searched my eyes. "Rose, if I take these shackles off, are you gonna make a break for it?"

I shook my head. "Not only would it be a foolish move, I think you're fast enough to have me recaptured in less than five seconds."

He gave me a grin, but his statement was addressed to the redheaded deputy in the driver's seat. "There you have it. Give me the key."

She started to protest until the usually mild-mannered deputy gave her a look that would have curled paint. Grumbling, she handed it over, and he squatted next to me, unlocking the wrist and ankle shackles.

When he stood, he reached down and gently took my arm and tugged me out.

"You better put cuffs on her!" Deputy Hoffstetter yelled as Deputy Miller started to lead me through the side entrance—handcuff-free.

He slowed his steps as the cruiser pulled away. "Mr. Deveraux's inside waiting for you. I've arranged for him to meet you in the elevator before you go into court."

My stomach fluttered with nerves. "How's he doin'?"

"Honestly, Rose, not that great. I think seein' you will help."

He took me through security, then stopped in front of an elevator bank at the rear of the building I hadn't even known existed. When the doors opened, Mason was waiting in the elevator car. I lunged for him, and he pulled me against his chest, his arms holding me close. "Rose."

I wrapped my arms around his neck, burying my face into his chest as I fought to keep from crying. "I've missed you."

Deputy Miller followed us into the elevator, and the doors closed behind us. "I can stall the elevator a minute, tops," the deputy said. "Then they'll get suspicious." He edged into the corner, though, intent on giving us a little privacy while we could have it.

Mason leaned back and cupped my face with both hands, staring deep into my eyes. "Carter said there was an incident in the holding cell, but he got you into solitary. Are you okay?"

I nodded, placing my hands over his. "I'm fine. Nothing happened. How are *you* doin'? You don't look so good." His face was pale and drawn, and there were dark circles under his eyes.

He laughed as tears filled his eyes. "Sweetheart, don't worry about me. I'm fine. You're all I'm worried about. I'm working to get you out of this." His voice broke. "I'm so sorry."

I grabbed his face. "This is not your fault. Carter's gonna get me out on bail, then we'll work on bringing J.R. down."

"Rose," he said, sounding desperate. "I'm not sure they're going to let you post bail."

I pressed my lips together and nodded. I needed to prepare myself for that possibility. "Then *you'll* have to bring him down."

He lowered his mouth to mine, kissing me with a mixture of longing and guilt.

I kissed him back, trying to commit his lips to memory since I had no idea if I'd ever be a free woman again.

Oh, God. What if I never got out?

I took a step back and tried to catch my breath. Claustrophobia had been a long-time friend since childhood. When I was a little girl, Momma used to lock me in a closet for having visions, but with my newfound independence I hadn't had an attack in months. However, the thought of being locked up for the rest of my life slammed into me hard, knocking the air from my lungs.

"Rose?" Mason asked, alarm in his eyes.

I held up my hands, gasping for breath, and backed up until my butt rested against the handrail.

Mason bent his knees so his face was level with mine. "Rose, it's going to be okay. I promise you. Do you trust me?"

Mason wouldn't rest until he made sure I was safe. I nodded, tears streaming down my face. I gulped in greedy amounts of air and felt myself calming down.

Deputy Miller looked at the control panel and grimaced. "I'm gonna have to press the floor button. They're waiting for us."

I nodded, then stood up straighter as Deputy Miller pressed the button for the third floor. Mason cautiously reached for me, and I fell into him, letting him wrap me up in his arms.

He kissed the top of my head. "I've failed you. I'm so sorry."

I shook my head, wishing I could stay here in this elevator with him forever. But I had to meet my fate, all while poor Mason racked himself with guilt for something over which he had no control.

How could one evil man destroy so many lives?

"This is *not* your fault, Mason. It's J.R. Simmons' fault." I looked up at him. "We have to stop him. You know I'm not the only person he's trying to destroy. He stole your job from you and he . . ." My voice trailed off as I realized I had almost told him I was sure J.R. had framed Skeeter.

The elevator saved me, the doors opening on the third floor.

Worry filled Mason's eyes. "I love you, Rose. I'm not giving up."

"I know. And I love you too." I gave him one last kiss before pulling loose and wiping my cheeks. Deputy Miller grabbed my arm, making a pretense of dragging me to the courtroom down the hall.

I wasn't prepared for the sight that greeted me—my friends were all gathered in the hall, waiting for me.

Neely Kate stood next to Mason's mother, Maeve, and my landscaping business partner, Bruce Wayne. The second my best friend caught sight of me, she ran toward me, nearly tackling me when she threw her arms around my back. "Rose. He won't get away with this."

I pulled back and looked her in the face. I had never told her about J.R.'s threats—how did she know?

Reading my confusion, she said, "Mason told me, Bruce Wayne, Jonah, and Maeve about J.R. Simmons, your birth mother's journal, and everything about Hattie," she whispered. Then, with narrowed eyes, she added, "We'll deal with *both* Simmons men."

I couldn't think about Joe and how he'd let Deputy Hoffstetter humiliate me, let alone the fact that he'd had me arrested in the first place. And stole the book of evidence my birth mother had died trying to bring to light—a book that would have helped implicate J.R. Simmons. He'd betrayed me in every way.

I wasn't sure I could ever forgive him for any of it. Not that Joe was asking for forgiveness.

I forced a smile. "They won't know what hit 'em when we get done with them."

"Yeah."

As I walked toward the small group, Bruce Wayne started to offer me his hand to shake, but I pulled him into a hug instead.

He patted my back awkwardly. "You did everything in your power to clear my name when I was accused of a murder I didn't commit, and I'm gonna do the same for you."

"Thanks, Bruce Wayne. But don't you be getting into trouble." Bruce Wayne had survived multiple scrapes with the law in the past. He was on the straight and narrow path now. I could never live with myself if he got himself back into the crime world because of me.

Maeve was next and she offered me a warm smile and a hug. "Don't you worry, Rose. I'm taking good care of Muffy."

"Muffy's with you?" I'd been worried about my little dog, but I'd presumed that Mason would take care of her since he lived with me out at my farm.

"Mason's been busy with his project. And I'm more worried than ever."

I sucked in a breath and searched her eyes. "The *feeling* you told me about?"

She nodded. "It's all happening soon."

The previous week she had confessed that she had strong feelings or premonitions that often came to pass. While she didn't know I was helping Skeeter as the Lady in Black, she *did* know I was up to something. She'd given me her blessing. Especially since she had a strong feeling that

Mason and someone else she didn't know were in danger. She wasn't sure how they were tied together, but she was convinced I was the only one who could save them.

That scared the bejiggers out of me. "I'm not sure if you've noticed, but I'm locked up."

She gave me a tight smile. "Hopefully you'll get out soon."

Lordy, I couldn't argue with that.

"Any feelings tell you that?" I asked wistfully.

"Just an old woman's fervent prayer."

More people waited behind her. Jonah Pruitt, my friend and the minister of the New Living Hope Revival Church, was there with his new girlfriend and church secretary, Jessica. My sister, Violet, waited behind them.

I quickly greeted Jonah and Jessica and moved on to Violet.

My older sister and I hadn't gotten along very well over the last several months, but we were sisters—whether we shared blood or not—and we stuck together in the tough times. I was relieved to see that she still believed that.

The look she gave me was so pathetic that I grabbed her hands in mine and gave them a little shake. "Don't you be worried, Violet. I'm gonna go into that courtroom and Carter Hale's gonna get me out on bail."

She nodded, her chin quivering. Her eyes were red and swollen.

Then a new thought hit me. "Has J.R. released information about you or Mike?"

She shook her head and pulled her hand from mine to wipe her tears. "It doesn't matter if he releases mine. Everyone already knows about me and Brody."

"And Mike?"

She tried to smile, but more tears leaked from her eyes. "He says he's at peace with whatever happens. Carter Hale said he'd take Mike's case if it came to that."

My eyes widened. "You've spoken to Carter?"

"He's been asking all kinds of questions about Momma's murder and who you knew then and know now."

"It's time to go in," Deputy Miller said, putting gentle pressure on my back. "I suspect they're ready for you."

I looked over my shoulder at him. "Okay. Thank you for this."

"I wanted you to know you have friends who support you and are trying to get you out of this. Myself included."

My mouth parted in surprise.

"Just be ready for it to get bad inside that courtroom. Rumor has it the DA is out for blood."

"Thanks for the warning, Deputy Miller."

He lowered his voice. "Call me Randy. What I'm doing makes us friends, don't ya think?"

My stomach tightened with worry. "Don't do anything to jeopardize your job."

His jaw set. "After what Chief Deputy Simmons pulled, I was planning to quit. But Mr. Deveraux convinced me to stay."

I shot him a look of surprise, wondering what that was about, but I didn't have time to give it much thought. He was already leading me through a door I recognized from my short stint as a juror on Bruce Wayne's murder trial.

My heart leapt into my throat as I entered the courtroom, and Randy tightened his grip on my arm to comfort me. We passed the empty jury box, and I saw Carter sitting at the defense table. He wore a serious expression, which looked out of place on him.

An elderly man sat at the opposite table, thumbing through pages of notes. He shot me a glare so filled with hate it took my breath away. It was the DA, Terry Snyder, Mason's old boss.

"Just ignore him," Deputy Miller said under his breath as we rounded the table, and he pulled out my chair.

As I sat down, I saw the back doors to the courtroom open. Mason, Violet, and my friends entered and found seats, but a new face in the back corner caught my eye.

Jed.

His arm was in a sling, and he looked just as bad as Mason. He'd been shot a few days before—because of me—and he probably had no business being up and about. Yet there he sat, doing the job that Skeeter had assigned to him months ago—the one he'd taken more personally than I ever would have expected. He was watching over me. He gave me a barely perceptible nod and a slight smile.

And that was my undoing.

My chin quivered and I fought to keep it together.

I'd gone from friendless and lonely to bursting at the seams with people who loved and cared about me. Here I was sitting at the defense table wearing an orange jumpsuit, but I was luckier than most people in the world.

Carter leaned close and whispered in my ear. "This will be surprisingly short. Now remember, you won't speak at all. I'll do all the talking."

I nodded and looked back at Mason, who gave me a tight smile of reassurance.

The bailiff stepped into the room. "All rise for the honorable Judge Berger."

Everyone stood, filling the room with a chorus of chairs scraping on the wood floor. The judge walked in with a no-nonsense look. He was younger than Judge McClary, probably in his late thirties. He sat down, and everyone else followed suit except for the attorneys and me.

The judge looked through some papers, and the DA responded to his questions in legalese and handed some papers to the bailiff. All I heard was "murder for hire" and "solicitation for murder" and "felony charges."

Then Carter answered with more legalese and paperwork, and then the judge asked for the prosecution's recommendation for bail.

The DA gave Mason a smug stare before turning back to face the judge. "We recommend that state hold the defendant without bail. She is a flight risk and a possible risk to society."

Carter listened to it all, not saying a word even though a full-fledged panic attack was brewing in my chest. The judge finally addressed him.

"Your Honor," Carter said in a slow drawl. "Rose Gardner is a respected member of the community. She's sunk money into not one but two profitable businesses. In addition, she's aided the Arkansas State Police, the Fenton

County Sheriff's Department, and the Henryetta Police Department in apprehending multiple criminals. To deny bail would be preposterous."

The judge looked me over, then said, "The prosecutor is concerned your client is a flight risk."

"Ms. Gardner has friends and family. She's a close friend of Jonah Pruitt, pastor of the New Living Hope Revival Church, and is in a relationship with Mason Deveraux, who was an assistant district attorney for the county until Friday evening. She has too much to lose if she flees."

The judge turned to the DA. "While I understand your concern, I'm going to post bail at one million dollars."

*One million dollars?*

I turned to Carter to protest. I didn't have one million dollars.

But Carter shot me a quick, silencing glare before returning his attention to the judge. "Your Honor," he said. "Ms. Gardner is woman of simple means. Posting one million will be prove difficult."

"Not my problem," he barked. "Now, on to the trial date. I've looked at the docket, and I'm setting the trial for three weeks from today."

"Three weeks?" Carter asked, sounding dismayed. "Your honor. I humbly request—"

"Denied." The judge banged his gavel. "Next case."

I turned to Carter. "*Three weeks.*"

The worried look on his face added to my panic. "I'll appeal. Right now I'm worried about bail."

Deputy Miller came forward and grabbed my arm to lead me out, but Carter held up his hand and turned to face Mason.

"Can you come up with the money?"

Mason looked grim. "I'll see what I can do. Don't take her back to the county jail. Hold her in the pens, and I'll try to get it together by the end of the day."

Carter nodded.

Mason turned his attention to me. "I'll come up with it, Rose."

The judge was getting irritated by our delay. Carter lowered his face to mine. "Just sit tight. We'll come up with the money."

"*One million dollars?*"

"Just sit tight." His answer was short. "I'll get it."

Carter Hale was going to get my bail money?

No. Skeeter.

Deputy Miller led me out the back entrance as another prisoner was brought into the courtroom—a man who looked like he'd done this a time or two. The deputy was quiet as he led me back to the elevator. We got off in the basement, and he guided me through a maze to a room that contained several jail cells.

Deputy Miller handed a paper to the guard on duty, and he looked it over, chuckling. "Whatcha doin' bringin' her here? She gonna come up with bail this high?"

Deputy Miller looked annoyed. "Her attorney says it's comin'. You just hold her here until it's posted."

"I'll give 'em until five o'clock, and if they ain't bailed her out, I expect you back here to haul her ass back to jail." He laughed. "Whadya do? Rob a bank?"

Deputy Miller glared at him. "Just do your job, Jim. Do you think you can handle that?"

Jim scowled, but he opened one of the empty pens and waved for me to enter. After I did, he shut the door behind me and grinned at Deputy Miller. "I would have thought she'd have cuffs with bail that high."

"She's not a threat to anyone. She couldn't hurt a fly."

If he weren't six feet under, Daniel Crocker might've had a thing or two to say about that, but now didn't seem like a good time to mention it.

Deputy Miller approached the bars. "It's probably gonna take them a while to come up with the money."

"Randy," I said firmly, my voice low. "I don't have that kind of money, and I know for a fact Mason doesn't have it either.

"He can post the title to your farm and also use your businesses as collateral. But it's gonna take him some time to pull it all together. He and I already discussed this possibility. Just sit tight."

I nodded. "Thank you."

"Someone should be back to get you out by the end of the day. Don't you worry."

"Okay." I looked up at the clock on the wall. 9:30 a.m.

It was gonna be a long wait.

# Chapter Three

By noon I'd gained and lost two fellow inmates—both had been released within an hour of their internment. Jim had brought me a tray with a bologna sandwich, and I half expected Mason to walk in and tease me about getting arrested just so I could eat the sandwiches. Of course, it was likely to be hours before anyone came to get me.

Much to my surprise, a sheriff's deputy walked in just as I put my tray on the floor. "Rose Gardner, your bail's been posted. You're free to go."

"Really?"

The deputy led me to a small changing room where I swapped out the orange jumpsuit for the clothes I'd been wearing when I was arrested, then on to a waiting room where I signed out and received my personal possessions. I looked around as I signed the form. "Where's Mason?"

"Who's that?" the receptionist asked.

"Mason Deveraux."

She squinted at me like I'd lost my mind. "Why would the assistant district attorney be down here? Besides, I hear he lost his job."

"Who posted my bail?"

"Darlin', I don't have that information, but your attorney should be able to find out for you."

"Thank you."

If Mason had posted my bail, then surely he'd be here waiting for me. Something told me it wasn't him.

So Carter really had come through. But did Skeeter Malcolm even *have* a million dollars?

I left the courthouse, figuring I'd head to my office since my truck was at home, along with my cell phone and wallet and anything else that would be of use. I wasn't prepared for the blast of cold air that hit me. The sheriff's department had shown up at my front door and dragged me away Friday night, so I didn't have a coat.

My landscaping office was across the street, but Carter Hale's office was on the way, albeit on the opposite side of the square. I decided to stop by and demand some answers.

Carter's receptionist looked up from her computer when I walked into the small waiting room. I'd been in this office only a few days ago, but at the time I'd been too preoccupied with watching Skeeter's goon, who had been loitering outside my office, to notice the decor. But today I took in the dingy lighting, the plastic office chairs, and the stained commercial carpet. I could only hope Carter was more skilled with the law than he was at decorating.

"Can I help you?" the woman asked, then her eyes widened. "Oh! You're her!"

I cringed. "You know me?"

"Of course. You and your friend sure stirred things up last week."

"Sorry."

"No! Don't be. It's usually dry as burnt toast around here. Carter was in a good mood for the rest of the day."

"You don't say?"

"But I also know who you are because Carter took your case."

"Yeah . . . and speaking of my case, can I talk to him?"

"I'll let him know you're here."

But just as she was getting out of her chair, a door at the end of a short hallway flung open and Carter came barreling down the hall.

"Greta! Did you get a call from the courthouse about—"

He took one look at me and stopped in his tracks. "You're here. You really are out."

"Yeah. I was hoping to talk to you about that."

He glanced at Greta and motioned to his office. "I think it's better if we have this discussion in private."

I nodded and followed him. He shut the door behind us and gestured to a chair in front of his desk.

"I need to call Mason," I said. "He said it was gonna take him all day to get the bail money, so I have a sneaking suspicion he didn't post it."

Carter sat in his office chair and leaned back. "He didn't. That's what I was on my way to see Greta about."

"Did Skeeter post it?" I wasn't sure being this direct was the best course of action, but I didn't have time to beat around the bush.

"No," he said with a frown. "Someone named Glenn Stout from Little Rock posted your bail. One million cash."

My mouth dropped open. "Who's Glenn Stout?"

"I don't know, but I intend to find out."

"You're sure it wasn't Skeeter using some kind of alias?"

He shook his head, looking even unhappier. "I know all his business names, and Glenn Stout isn't one of them." He leaned forward and handed me his cell phone. "Call your boyfriend. He's jumping through more hoops than you can imagine right now to get you loose. Tell him to come pick you up, and then you and I can have a discussion before he gets here."

I took his phone and called Mason. He answered in his no-nonsense voice, "Mason Deveraux."

"Mason, it's me. I'm in Carter's office."

"They let you go?" he asked in disbelief.

"Someone posted bail."

"Who?"

"I don't know and neither does Carter. Can you come pick me up?"

"I'll be there in ten minutes."

He hung up without saying goodbye, and I handed the phone back to Carter. "We have ten minutes, and I suspect we have a lot to talk about."

His mouth twisted into a half-smile. "I take it there are things you'd prefer to keep within our circle of attorney-client privilege."

"Yes. Like the fact that Skeeter Malcolm convinced you to take my case. How'd you explain it to Mason?"

His grin became more genuine. "You can thank your feisty friend for providing me with that plausible explanation. If Skeeter hadn't asked me to take it on, Neely Kate would have convinced me anyway."

I shot him a look of disbelief.

"God's honest truth. I swear. Like I told you, she can be very persuasive."

That part I knew to be true, but I didn't appreciate the gleam in his eyes as he said it. "Did Skeeter tell you why he hired me?"

"No, but I've strung a few theories together."

I had a pretty good idea of what he was getting at. Part of me wanted to put a pin in this, but I was protected by our attorney-client confidentiality. He couldn't tell anyone without my permission, and he was never going to get that.

"A few?" I asked.

He shifted in his seat, skewering me with his gaze. "You could be his secret girlfriend, although that's not likely. For one thing, Skeeter doesn't do girlfriends, and even if he did—" he gestured to my jeans and green sweater "—you're too prim and proper."

"And your other theories?"

"You have something he wants. The question is what? Does it have to do with Deveraux? Is he using your association with him for something? But Deveraux's out of a job, and everyone knows it." He shook his head and leaned forward. "You know, I asked him about the Lady in Black before. About a month ago. I'm a curious guy, and it's an intriguing mystery. But he refused to discuss it. In fact, he seemed flat-out irritated by my questions."

I remained silent.

"So his connection to the Lady in Black is both business *and* personal, and his concern for your safety is intriguing . . ."

"Just spit it out, Carter," I grumbled.

"The question is, how did Rose Gardner become the Lady in Black, and why would Skeeter use you? No one would ever suspect she was you, of course, your boyfriend included. He seems pretty intent on unmasking—or rather *unveiling*—her."

"He *still* is?" He hadn't mentioned it for weeks.

Carter grinned, waiting for me to continue.

I heaved out a sigh. "Surely you can figure out the why of it. Skeeter found out about my visions and decided to use them to his advantage."

"So he blackmailed you?"

I sighed again. "Not exactly. I helped him with the auction as a barter of sorts. Then he told me that Mason's life was in danger, so I joined forces with him to find out who was behind it." I paused for a beat. "They saved Mason's life. He was unconscious in Gems when the fire started, and Skeeter and Jed got him out of the place before it burned down."

"Skeeter saved the pain in the ass ADA?" Then he seemed to remember my personal connection with Mason. "No offense."

"I had to agree to continue to pose as the Lady in Black for six months. And I know what Mason does . . . or *did*. Helping Skeeter aside, I approve of Mason getting the horrible people who do horrible things off the street."

"But isn't that hypocritical? On the one hand, you support Deveraux's work, but on the other, you're helping the current king of the Fenton County underworld."

And that was the crux of it. My guilt spelled out in a simple statement. "I'm not proud of what I've done." I looked down at my lap, twisting my sweater between my finger and my thumb. Then I glanced up at him. "And I could have made a better choice when I first approached Skeeter in November, but I'm not sorry I made that agreement with him in the parking lot behind Gems. I'd do it again in a heartbeat. And the truth of the matter is, there are a lot worse things goin' on in this county than Skeeter's crime ring. J.R. Simmons is up to something bad, and by posing as the Lady in Black, I've been able to help ferret out who's involved and what they're doin'. I'm getting information Skeeter can't get on his own. J.R. Simmons is out to get Skeeter—even if I have no idea why—and he wants to bring Mason down with him. I'll do anything in my power to save Mason."

He watched me for a moment. "Seems to me you should put more energy into saving yourself."

"We're all tangled up in the same ball of yarn, Carter Hale. I save one of us, I save us all."

He laughed. "You really think you can save Skeeter Malcolm?"

"I already have, and I plan to again. I'm goin' to save both of them."

He turned grim after that. His phone rang, and he frowned as he picked it up. "Hold him off for a minute." He hung up and sighed. "Your boyfriend's already here and chomping at the bit to see you. Rest assured I'll keep your involvement with Skeeter to myself. And I'll let Jed know you're out and safe for the time being. I suspect he's goin' to want to talk to you to get your side of what happened." He winked. "Any favorable comments about my services would be greatly appreciated."

"Why Jed?"

"Skeeter's MIA."

My stomach plummeted to my toes. "*What?*"

"Darn near the whole sheriff's department showed up at his pool hall to arrest him for the murders of Scott Humphrey and Marcus Tilton, but Skeeter took off right before they got there."

Skeeter had left me to deal with this mess?

The door opened and Mason burst into the room, Greta fast on his heels. She wore an apologetic look.

"I'm sorry, Carter. He refused to wait."

Carter narrowed his eyes at my boyfriend. "And here I thought you were a rule-follower, Mason Deveraux."

But Mason's attention was focused on me. He was already pulling me to my feet and into a tight hug. "I've never been so happy to see someone in my entire life."

I held him close. "I'm okay. Really. Just glad to be out."

He released all but my hand, as if he couldn't bear to stop touching me, and when he sat down in one of the chairs in front of Carter's desk, I took a seat in the other. I distantly heard the door shut as Greta left the room.

"Who bailed her out?" Mason asked.

Carter made a face, picked up a paperclip off his desk, and leaned back in his chair. "*That* is the one million dollar question." He winked as he started twisting the clip with his fingers. "Does the name Glenn Stout ring any bells?"

Mason's hand tightened on mine. "Never heard of him."

"He posted bail this morning around 11:30 via a courier."

Mason shook his head. "Why would someone who doesn't even know her get a bail bond? They're going to lose one hundred thousand dollars."

My mouth dropped open. "What?"

"That's how this works," Carter said. "If you don't have enough cash, you gather up enough collateral to cover the bail should the defendant skip town and the trial. That's what your boyfriend was doing, gathering up collateral. But the fee for doing that is ten percent. One hundred thousand dollars. That's why the bail system is so effective. Most people don't have a million dollars lying around, and who can afford to forfeit one hundred thousand? I'm sure the judge knew you and Deveraux were too cash poor to pony up."

"Wait," I said, turning to Mason. "You were going to give up one hundred thousand dollars to get me out of jail?"

His eyes hardened. "I couldn't leave you in there."

"It was only for three weeks, Mason."

"Anything could have happened to you in three weeks. Carter wouldn't have been able to get you solitary indefinitely."

I shook my head. "Where were you getting the one hundred thousand cash?"

"My 401K." He gave me a wry smile. "Good thing I didn't cash it in to buy Joe out of the nursery, after all."

I hadn't even stopped to consider how all of this would affect the nursery I co-owed with my sister and Joe. I should have never offered him partnership after he sunk money into my business to save it. It was just one more hook he had in me.

"Isn't that sweet?" Carter groaned out, sitting upright in his chair. "Can we get back to the business at hand?"

Mason shot him a glare.

"This wasn't a bail bond. Glenn Stout posted one million cash."

Mason's hand tightened around mine again.

"And not only that," Carter continued, "Mr. Stout had one million in cash ready and available a mere two hours after her arraignment, even though he is supposedly from Little Rock, which is roughly two hours away."

Mason finally released his grip on me and leaned his forearms on the desk. "So this Mr. Stout was ready and waiting to post her bail."

"It appears that way."

"We need to find out anything and everything we can about this man," Mason said, casting a glance first at me and then at Carter. "Someone who forked over that much money wants something from her."

"Agreed. I plan to have Greta start looking into it as soon as we're done here."

"What's your plan for her defense?" Mason asked, switching gears.

Carter shook his head. "You and I both know there is no defense that's goin' to work in this case."

"That's the best you've got?" Mason demanded, his eyes blazing. "You always pull out every trick in the book against me, and not to boast, but I'm a far better prosecutor than my boss."

Carter smirked. "I've always hated pulling cases against you for that very reason. But you and I both know this case isn't goin' to hinge on the prosecution's argument. The judge is goin' to sway the jury to reach the verdict J.R. Simmons bought and paid for."

"Goddammit!" Mason shouted, climbing to his feet.

"We're goin' to have to fight this case out of the courtroom. Find out how the judge was bought. Find evidence linking Chief Deputy Simmons and the DA to abuse of power."

"You want to go after Joe?" I asked, my stomach tumbling like a washing machine.

"You bet your ass I do," Carter said, looking me square in the eye. "And the DA, and anyone else who's a part of this mess." He sat up. "I have some—ahem—contacts who might be able to help me gather some information."

Mason snorted. "I bet you do."

Carter gave him a pointed stare. "Isn't that why you came to me, Deveraux?"

Mason released a low growl and turned his back to us.

I stood up and put a hand on Mason's arm. I knew he was wrestling with his conscience. It had to kill him to be in this position, where our fates were riding on someone with ties to the criminal underworld.

If Carter Hale's connections upset him this much, how would he feel if he found out about my involvement with Skeeter? And how long could I keep it from him?

He turned to me and stared deep into my eyes. "Do it," he grunted. "I'll do whatever it takes."

"So that's my assignment," Carter said. "Yours is to attack the senior Simmons from another front."

"I'm already working on it."

"Any progress?"

His face darkened. "No."

Carter looked at me. "I have a few contacts who might be able to dig up a little dirt on the senior Simmons as well."

"Do I want to know who they are?" Mason asked.

A ghost of a smile lifted Carter's mouth. "I suspect not."

"Is there anything else?" Mason asked.

"No. As soon as I find out anything about Mr. Stout, I'll be sure to let you know."

Mason nodded and took my hand. "Come on, sweetheart. Let's get you home."

"Rose, you might want to stay at home and inside for a day or two," Carter said. "At least until we know more about your benefactor."

Mason nodded. "Agreed." Then he squeezed my hand and started to lead me out of the room.

I pulled him to a stop. "Carter. I know you and Mason don't see eye to eye, so thank you for taking my case anyway."

"Oh . . ." he drawled. "You can thank your friend Neely Kate for that. And be sure to tell her I'm still waiting for that cupcake she promised me."

I lifted my eyebrows. "Be careful what you ask for."

Mason didn't budge; he just looked Carter over, taking his measure. "Rose is right," he finally said. "Thank you for changing your mind about taking the case. You are the best attorney for the job."

Carter grinned from ear to ear. "Why, thank you, counselor. I'm sure it was difficult for you to spit that out."

"Maybe so, but it's true nonetheless."

"Not to worry, Deveraux. Between all of us, we'll save your girl . . . and you too, while we're at it."

I shot Carter a frown as I pushed Mason toward the door. "I'm eager to see Muffy. Let's get goin'."

Mason let me push him down the hall and out the front door. Once we were outside, we were hit again with a blast of cold air. He shrugged off his coat and wrapped it around my shoulders. "Are you hungry? Do you want to get a late lunch from Merilee's?"

The gun holster strapped to his chest caught my eye and sent a chill down my back that had nothing to do with the cold.

I glanced up at him, distraught by how exhausted he looked. "Does your momma have any of her delicious leftovers?"

A soft smile lit up his face. "She's been stress-cooking all weekend. You can have your pick of just about anything you like."

"Then let's go there."

He pulled out his phone and texted while we walked to his car, which he'd parked a few spots down from Carter's office. As he opened my car door, he slipped the phone back into his pants pocket. "Your sister's liable to take my head off. I just included her in a group text telling everyone you're out and safe."

"She'll get over it." She might not, but Violet was the least of my worries.

As Mason headed to his mother's, I asked, "Do you know where *my* phone is?" I worried what texts might be on it. If Skeeter really had left town, he might have texted or called to warn me.

"It's at home. Do you need it?"

I did, but it could wait. I was going to revel in being free for a few hours before I jumped back headlong into trouble.

# Chapter Four

Maeve greeted us at the front door with tears in her eyes. Muffy barked her fool head off until I scooped her up in my arms, and then she proceeded to smother my cheeks and nose with licks. Next came a plume of noxious fumes, but I'd missed her so much I didn't mind, even if my eyes watered a little.

Maeve heated up some meatloaf and mashed potatoes, and I ate half of the food on my plate before pushing it away, my stomach a basket of nerves. I might be out of jail, but I definitely wasn't free.

After we visited with Maeve for a little while longer, we took Muffy home to the farm. As soon as we were inside the front door, Mason ran into the kitchen to turn off the alarm. Muffy raced after him, probably assuming that he was in a hurry to fill her food bowl. I took a moment to look around the place I'd grown to love as home. My gaze landed on Mason as he returned to the front room. I was so lucky to have this man who would literally do anything in his power to protect me. I'd wasted twenty-four of my twenty-five years, but I had gained so much since last May. I couldn't help but think I was about to lose it all if we failed to best J.R. Simmons.

Noticing my subdued attitude, Mason took me into his arms and gave me a long, soulful kiss.

"What do you need, sweetheart?" he asked when he lifted his head. "What can I do for you?"

I was in such a pickle that I didn't even know where to start, but all I could think about was holding on to the man in front of me.

"I need *you*." I stood on my tiptoes and pressed my lips to his, threading my fingers through his hair.

He held me close, taking over the kiss, and then grabbed my hands and tugged me toward the steps. "Let's go upstairs. Our bed has been empty and lonely without you." His voice broke on the last words, making my heart swell even more.

I followed him into our room, and we came to a stop next to our bed.

Mason took off his holster and laid it on the dresser before turning back to me. He stroked my cheek with his thumb as I looked up into his sorrowful eyes.

"I failed you," he said again.

I put my finger over his lips. "Shh. I won't listen to another word of nonsense. Even if I spend the rest of my life in prison, you haven't failed me."

He looked devastated as he pulled my hand down. "How can you say that?"

"Do you have any idea how blessed I am?"

"Blessed? But you were arrested! I might not be able to stop J.R., Rose."

I shook my head. "You're doing everything you can. That's all I can ask of you. And you did everything in your power to get me out of there, including askin' for help from Carter Hale. That's not lost on me." I wrapped my hands around his neck and stood on my tiptoes, my lips inches from his. "Mason, people spend their entire lives lookin' for what we have." I gave him a soft kiss. "I'm so thankful I can truly count on you."

He kissed me back, his arm pulling me against his chest. Our mood became more desperate, and he pulled my sweater over my head and threw it on the floor. I unbuttoned his shirt, pausing only to run my hands over his bare chest before tossing the shirt into the growing pile of clothes.

He pushed me back onto the bed and unbuttoned my jeans and pulled them off. I was only wearing my bra and panties as I watched him unfasten his pants and drop them to the floor. He stood next to the edge of the bed for a moment, looking down at me.

"You're so beautiful, Rose. I don't think you know how beautiful you are."

I sat up and stripped off his briefs, leaving him completely naked. "You're beautiful yourself, Mason Deveraux. Every single woman in this county wants you, and you're mine."

I grabbed his hands and pulled him down next to me. We lay sideways on the bed, Mason naked and me in my underwear.

"You're definitely overdressed, Ms. Gardner," he murmured, reaching behind me to unhook my bra.

I quickly slipped it off and reached down to remove my underwear. Then I straddled his waist and leaned over him, my hair brushing the side of his face. "I love you, Mason."

As he reached up to fondle my breasts, he raised his gaze to meet mine. "I've missed you."

I laughed. "You missed my body?"

A grin lit up his eyes. "Yes. I think it's time I tell you the truth—I only love you for your body."

I slid my hands over his chest and down his firm abs, then lifted my eyebrows and gave him a sly grin. "That works out well, since I only love you for yours."

He rolled me onto my back and leaned over me, kissing me so thoroughly my toes curled.

"I want you," I whispered, wrapping my legs around his waist.

He plunged into me and I arched up to meet him, looking into his eyes. Our playfulness was gone now, and the gravity of our situation slipped back in. I reached my hand up to his cheek as we moved together. His face was blurry through my tears.

"I won't let you go to prison, Rose. I swear it." The intensity in his eyes scared me. I wondered what lengths he would go to in order to keep me safe.

I pulled his mouth to mine, my lips as demanding as the rest of my body. I came quickly with Mason close behind, and then he collapsed next to me and rolled me onto my side, our chests pressed together.

I closed my eyes and stroked his arm with my fingers.

"I can only stay a few more minutes before I need to get back to work," he said.

"What are you working on?"

He hesitated, and I knew he was deciding how much he should share.

"Mason, you can tell me everything now. You're not working for the county anymore. No more secrets." Guilt shot through me as I said the words. I suspected I had far more secrets than he did at this point.

He pulled my hand from his arm and gently held it. "J.R. Simmons is rumored to have influenced a judge in Lafayette County. But every time I think I have something substantial to tie him to it, the evidence slips through my fingers."

"That's all you have?" I tried to keep the disappointment from my voice. "I suppose it will establish a pattern if Carter manages to tie him to the Fenton County DA and the judge in my case." Still, as serious as the allegations were, I had doubts they were enough.

"That's the part that has me confused." He propped up on an elbow. "Carter Hale is trying to *prove* criminal behavior? That's a huge risk for him. Why would he do that?"

My heart beat hard against my chest. "He's just trying to give me the best representation possible."

"I don't know." He shook his head. "Something's not adding up here. Just like how he suddenly changed his mind about representing you. He hates my guts, and he took great glee in telling me no when I went to him on hands and knees. Less than an hour later, he took the case. When I asked him about paying the retainer, he told me it was covered. He claims he's doing it pro bono for the publicity, and because Neely Kate gave him a talking-to, but I'm not so sure."

I struggled to keep from jumping out of my skin. "What other reason could there be?"

"There's something I haven't told you about Hale, something that might make a difference . . ." He shifted to his back, pulling me with him so I rested on his chest. "Hale's good at representing the criminal element. He's outwitted me more times than I'd care to admit. But I'm pretty damn sure he has ties to Skeeter Malcolm."

I fought to take a breath. "Why do you say that?"

"He takes a high proportion of the cases that have ties to Malcolm." He was quiet for several seconds, and I could practically see the wheels spinning in his head. "When I went to Hale's office on Friday night, he told me that he'd seen one of Malcolm's men hanging around outside your office." I could feel his heartbeat quicken in his chest. "What if Malcolm convinced Hale to take your case?"

"Mason." I fought to keep my voice level. "What purpose would Skeeter Malcolm have for doing that?"

"To hurt me by using you? I don't know. I know it doesn't make sense, but something's not adding up here." He was getting agitated.

I stroked his face, searching his eyes. "I think you're reading too much into it."

"I'm not so sure," he said, pushing out a groan of frustration. "I think I should find you a new attorney."

I could only imagine what Skeeter would do if I fired Carter. But according to Carter, Skeeter had run off. He wasn't around to do much of anything.

But I couldn't ignore the fact that the two men who were in the thick of this with me—whether Mason realized it or not—had both turned to the same man. The coincidence was too great. "I think we stick with Carter."

"His ties to Malcolm are too strong. I don't trust him to do this for the right reasons."

I'd had an entire weekend to do nothing but think, and all that thinking had brought me to one conclusion. Mason, Skeeter, and I had to face this fight together. But for the life of me, I had no idea how to make that happen without telling Mason the whole, ugly truth.

Trying to sound steadier than I felt, I said, "I've been thinking about J.R.'s involvement in other things . . ."

"What do you mean?"

"I think Joe's father is up to something in Fenton County. If we can figure out what he's been doing here, it stands to reason that it would be easier for us to find proof of that than to investigate rumors of a case somewhere else."

I had his attention. He sat up and looked down at me. "What makes you think Simmons has other current ties to Fenton County?"

Something in his voice told me he knew something. "What do you know?"

His eyes darkened. "It's county business."

"And you're no longer a county employee."

"I'm curious about how you made the leap to a connection between Malcolm and J.R. Simmons."

Crappy doodles. What information did he have? And what was I gonna tell him? I looked out the windows overlooking the sun porch that had served as my nursery such a long, long time ago, and relief washed through me. Just like that, I knew what to say. "We know this isn't the first time he's fiddled around in Fenton County. He was here causing trouble twenty-five years ago. My birth mother had proof of it in that journal I found taped to the bottom of my crib. And we know it's important, because

right after Joe took it, he had you fired and me arrested."
Pain stabbed my heart at the reminder of his betrayal, but I
didn't have time to dwell on that. I sat up next to Mason,
starting to get excited. "We need to go back to the plant
and find the secret safe."

"Why? And I never got a good handle of what went
on there. All I had to go on was your short explanation,
and the sheriff's department won't tell me anything. Their
report is much too short. I went to the hospital to talk to
Hattie and get her take on things, but she'd already
checked out. And when I called her parents, they told me
she left town. That's all she said to them, though—they
have no idea where she went."

"She's gone?" I asked, although I wasn't sure why I
was so surprised. She knew about J.R.'s involvement in this
and was probably trying to get as far away from ground
zero as possible.

"Yeah. Why would she do that?"

"She's scared of J.R." I gave him a weak smile. "Hattie
told me to meet her there so she could provide me with
some kind of proof about my birth father."

His expression softened. "You really think Harrison
Gardner might not be your father?"

"I don't know," I said quietly. "Apparently my father
might be Paul Buchanan, the son of the owner of Atchison
Manufacturing. Hattie confirmed that Dora had an affair
with him right after her affair with Daddy. But Henry
Buchanan was about to give Paul everything. His daughter
Beverly didn't like it, so she tampered with Paul's car, and
he and his wife were killed in a car accident. Dora was
already pregnant with me, and Paul had told her that he

was going to leave his wife. He wanted to marry her and be my daddy."

"Oh, Rose. I'm so sorry."

I shook my head and gave him a tight smile. "I'm strangely okay with it. I just want the truth. But honestly, I'm still pretty certain Harrison Gardner was my birth father. Otherwise, how do I explain my visions? Daddy's momma had them too."

He tucked a stray hair behind my ear. "We can find out for certain. You can have a DNA test."

"I think I have bigger fish to fry right now. A whole school of them."

"Maybe, but you're still entitled to have feelings over this news. It's life-altering."

I shook my head. "It doesn't change a blessed thing. I still grew up with my hateful mother. I was still abused. Even if Hattie claims she and Daddy only left me at Momma's mercy to protect me."

"Why would she think that?"

"She said they were trying to hide me from Beverly. Henry Buchanan thought Dora was pregnant with his son's baby, and he changed his will to include me. Or at least some secret third beneficiary. Hattie's convinced that it's me. She thinks the documentation is in a secret safe in the old factory. And she's certain the combination is in the journal."

"You think proving your true parentage will help your case somehow?"

"No. But I figure if Dora kept evidence on J.R. in a secret journal, Henry Buchanan, the owner of the plant that was ultimately screwed over by Joe's father, would have kept his own evidence of how the man had wronged him."

Excitement filled his eyes. "Rose. You could be right. But we don't have the journal."

"Let's go see if there actually *is* a secret safe. Honestly, Hattie seemed a little crazy. She could have been completely wrong about the whole thing."

Mason climbed out of bed, grabbed his underwear off the floor, and stepped into them. "Make a map of the plant as you remember it."

"What are you talking about? Why would I make a map? I'll just show it to you."

"No." He walked over to the closet and opened the door. "You heard Hale. He thinks you should stay in the house and let things die down."

I got out of bed and followed him. "Just a minute ago you said you weren't so sure you trusted Carter. Why listen to him on this? I'm goin' with you."

He turned to me in exasperation. "Rose, it could be dangerous."

"Exactly. So why would I let you go alone?"

"I didn't just watch you get out of jail only to turn around and put you in a dangerous situation." His eyes widened. "In fact, we still need to investigate who this Glenn Stout person is."

"I thought Carter's receptionist was doin' that."

"Like I trust him to tell me the full truth." He snorted and pulled a pair of jeans from the closet. "I'll head out to the plant. You stay here and research the man who bailed you out."

"I have a better idea. We'll go out there together, and I can start lookin' him up on my smart phone while you drive."

He shot me a look of frustration.

"I'm goin' with you, Mason Deveraux, so do us both a favor and just accept it." When I noticed the worry in his eyes, I softened my tone and grabbed his hands. "You have to know by now you can't treat me like some china doll. You've trusted me to do some behind-the-scenes investigations before, and you yourself have said I'm good at it."

"But this is different. This is physically dangerous, Rose."

"So why should you take the risk alone? I know you want to protect me, but this involves me too much for me to hide from it. So please just accept that we're in this together and treat me as an equal."

His eyes widened. "Of course I see you as an equal. I'm just scared. If something were to happen to you . . ."

"You're in just as much danger as I am. Probably more so, since someone wants you dead. J.R. just wants me in prison. So no more bickering about it. From this moment forward, we're doin' this together."

He searched my eyes, then his gaze drifted down to my naked body. A grin lit up his face. "You know it's hard to argue with you when you're so damn sexy without clothes on."

"I'll be sure to remember that piece of information for future negotiations."

His smile turned slyer. "Why do I think I'll regret admitting to that?"

"Because you, Mason Deveraux, are a very intelligent man." I stood on my tiptoes and gave him a kiss.

"If you're going with me, you'd better get dressed. I'd prefer for you to use your naked wiles on me alone."

"Me too." I couldn't hide my smile. Mason wasn't going to fight me on being an active part of his investigation.

Too bad he had no idea how useful I could be.

# Chapter Five

Before we left, I grabbed my phone and hid in the bathroom. There were several missed calls from Violet and Bruce Wayne and—just as I'd expected—a message from Skeeter. Rather than leave me a possibly incriminating voice message, he had sent a vague text.

*Take care of yourself. Before everyone and everything else. Go to J if you need help. I'll be back as soon as I can.*

Was he hunting for a way to bring down J.R. or had he fled to save himself? The answer was most likely both. Still, he needed to tell me what he was up to instead of flying solo. We had a better shot of succeeding if all of us pooled our resources, but I suspected I'd have a hard time convincing him of that.

I needed to call Jed, but this was not the time for a long chat, particularly if I wanted it to be private, so I settled for sending him a quick text telling him I was fine and I'd call as soon as possible.

While we drove to the factory, Mason gave me more details about his meeting the previous Friday. He and Joe had come up with multiple pieces of evidence to bring charges against Mason's corrupt boss. The case had looked pretty solid, so Joe had convinced Mason to call in the special prosecutor. But as soon as the meeting had started, the investigator turned the tables and presented concocted evidence against Mason—all while Joe sat quietly and listened. When the investigator asked if Joe cared to refute the claims against Mason, he merely shook his head and said he had nothing to add.

It was compelling proof of something I still couldn't bear to believe: Joe had sided with his father. I was equally furious and heartbroken.

Mason finished just as he pulled into the parking lot of the plant, parking in almost the same spot my truck had occupied only days ago.

"Why in God's name did you agree to meet Hattie here?" Mason asked as he put the car into park. "This place is beyond creepy."

I had to agree. The building was blackened and partially caved in, the glass busted out in many of the windows.

"I thought she had answers. Besides, she seemed harmless enough. I had no idea Beverly Buchanan and Dirk Picklebie were followin' us." I patted his arm reassuringly. "Besides, I'm fine, thanks to that Taser you got me. It saved my life." I had it in my coat pocket now, mostly because of Mason's insistence that I continue to carry it, but also because it gave me a small sense of security.

He scowled slightly. "Joe's the one who got you the Taser."

"At your insistence." I'd had plenty of alone time to think about that as well. "I'm having a hard time understanding why Joe would follow through with arresting me, especially when only the day before he was thanking Neely Kate for watching out for me."

"There's no denying he loves you. Even if it's in his own selfish way," Mason said, looking out the windshield at the plant. "But he's a slave to his father's whims."

Which meant I couldn't trust Joe. Ever. "No more talk about Joe. If I ever see him again, it will be too soon. Right now we need to concentrate on his father."

"And we still need to figure out who's behind the alias Glenn Stout."

I'd spent the entire twenty-minute drive searching the Internet for any information about the man. The only real hit I'd found in the Little Rock area was a Glenn Stout who had been thirty-two years old in the 1940 census. It was a pretty safe bet that the guy had been dead for a few years.

"Do we have any way of knowing whether the person who created the alias actually lives near Little Rock or has ties to it?"

Mason shrugged and grabbed his backpack from the backseat. "Not really. But I plan to talk to the clerk at the courthouse to see what she remembers about the man who posted the bail."

"You think she'll remember?"

"Without a doubt. One-million-dollar bail bonds are pretty rare, let alone ones that are delivered in cash. She'll be talking about it for years." He paused and turned to me. "In fact, maybe we should ask Neely Kate to talk to her."

"Really?"

"Yeah. She's good at getting information, and besides, she probably already knows the clerk from working at the courthouse herself. Why don't you get her started on it before we go inside?"

Looking at him in disbelief, I picked up my phone.

"Don't look so surprised," he said. "You've heard of the phrase 'it takes a village.' Well, I'm beginning to suspect it's going to take a village to get you out of this mess."

"Us," I said, searching his face. "Someone is still after you, and I am *certain* J.R. is behind it. So it's get *us* out of this."

His gaze held mine and he nodded. "Okay. Us."

He was usually so quick to deny that Joe's father was as much a danger to him as he was to me. It felt like a huge step forward.

"Promise me you won't pull any more chauvinist crap," I said. "We're partners all the way in this."

His face softened. "Rose, I didn't mean to come off as chauvinistic. And as far as I'm concerned, we're already partners in this and everything else."

I leaned over and gave him a kiss. "I can't think of a single person I'd rather have as a partner."

"Me either." He gave me another kiss and then leaned back. "Now go ahead and call Neely Kate, then we'll go inside and find this safe."

I wasn't surprised that she was short with me when she answered the phone. "Well, imagine that," she grumbled. "You finally got around to calling me."

"I'm sorry, Neely Kate. I should have called you sooner. There's no excuse. I just wasn't thinkin' straight."

"Obviously." But the teasing tone in her voice let me know I was off the hook.

"I have a lot to tell you, but it will have to wait until later. Right now Mason and I have a request." I shot a glance at him, and he nodded. "We're trying to figure out who posted my bail. You would think a man who could post a million dollars would show up on an Internet search, but I can't find anything about Glenn Stout from Little Rock. Can you look into it?"

"Mason asked for my help too?"

"He knows you're good at this kind of thing. He's the one who suggested it."

"Oh, my stars and garters. Wonders never cease. Someone finally appreciates my skills. When this is all said and done, we really need to open our own detective agency."

"One thing at a time," I said with a grin. "Let's get Mason and me out of this predicament first."

"Fair enough. I'll let you know when I find something."

"Thanks, Neely Kate. For everything . . . including Carter Hale." Carter may have ultimately decided to take my case because of Skeeter, but I was pretty doggone sure Neely Kate's intervention hadn't hurt.

"What are best friends for? He has his shortcomings, but he came highly recommended."

She hung up before I had the chance to ask where she'd gotten her references. I stuffed my phone into my pocket as Mason and I climbed out of the car.

An eerie sense of déjà vu washed over me as we walked toward the warehouse.

Mason sensed a shift in my mood and reached for my hand. "Is it hard coming back here after what happened?"

I nodded. "Sorry. I'm trying not to be a baby."

"Rose." He held on tighter to my hand. "People died

in front of you in this place, and a crazy woman tried to strangle you. It's perfectly normal to be anxious. I sure as hell would be."

I led him past the front door covered with police tape and around the back. "I went through the front door last time, but it's dark and cluttered with metal junk. Since we're goin' to the back, we can walk around and climb through a busted out window close to the office area."

I couldn't tell him that Jed, who had been at the warehouse with me as my bodyguard, had climbed out that same window before the sheriff's deputies arrived. But thankfully, Mason didn't question how I knew to use that as an entrance.

He climbed through first and offered me his hand as I straddled the three-foot-high window frame. Once I was inside, I took a moment to look around. The office Hattie had taken me to was about thirty feet away, on the other side of a mess of metal desks, but directly in front of me was the open space where Beverly had shot Hattie, Dirk, and Jed. A wave of anxiety washed through my head, but I pushed it down.

I could do this. I *had* to do this.

"Are you all right?"

I gave Mason a tight smile. "I'm okay. Let's go find that safe."

He pulled a flashlight out of his bag and handed it to me. "Lead the way."

I avoided the open space, feeling sick to my stomach when I saw the blood staining the floor. Mason moved next to me, blocking my view. We exchanged a grim look.

"Let's find this thing and get the hell out of here," he said.

He didn't have to tell me twice.

I entered the small office Hattie had gone into, paying more attention this time. A desk and a couple of chairs were shoved against the wall. But Hattie had gone straight for the closet. Since she'd said the safe was still in the office, it seemed like the logical place to look.

Mason stopped behind me as I stood at the entrance to the walk-in closet and shined the flashlight around the space. The walls were lined with shelves, but any office supplies that might have filled them were long gone. A small square wood panel was on the left wall, about five feet off the ground, and a shelf was built in directly underneath it. It would have been an excellent hiding spot for a secret safe, perfectly hidden by stacked office supplies.

I pulled the panel open and found a gray metal safe with a numbered wheel. I tugged on it, not surprised to find it locked.

"Do you remember anything in the journal that looked like it could be a combination?" Mason asked.

"Honestly, I hardly looked at it at all. Besides, it was filled with numbers and shorthand. Even if we had it, it would probably take us days to find the code." I shook my head. "It took me long enough to find the secret message in the original journal."

Mason pressed his chest to my back, his breath gently blowing my hair over my ear. "I'm so sorry I didn't make time to listen to you."

"It didn't seem pressing. It was a twenty-five-year-old

case." I heaved a sigh. "Coming out here to see the safe was a total waste. I have no idea what I hoped to find."

Mason pulled his phone out of his coat pocket. "I wouldn't say that. Knowing the combination isn't the only way to get a safe open." He took several photos. "You just need the right tools."

"You mean a locksmith? Hattie said she couldn't get one out here because it's private property."

"She's right. But that doesn't mean we can't get someone else to do it."

I gasped in utter shock. "Are you proposing that we do something illegal?"

He grimaced. "One could argue that if the owners wanted the contents, they would have gotten them by now."

My eyes widened. "Mason Deveraux, I never expected to hear such a thing come out of your mouth." I leaned closer and whispered in a sultry voice, "Who knew you could be such a bad boy?"

"I can be very, very bad," he teased. "As bad as you want."

Before this was done, I had a feeling I was going to need to ask him to be a whole lot badder than he planned.

# Chapter Six

L et's get out of here." He turned around and headed toward the door.

"I want to look through the desk first." Its drawers were facing the wall it was shoved up against. I started to scoot it out, but Mason was there in seconds, pulling it out with me.

"You know there's little likelihood that anything useful is in there."

I glanced up at him. "I know, but we're already here, so why not look?"

After we got it situated, I held the flashlight while Mason started pulling out drawers and rummaging through the contents. All we found were pens, paperclips, and yellowed paper, but just when I was about to give up, I remembered how I'd found the journal. "Take out the drawers and turn them upside down," I said.

Mason shot me a look, but he pulled out the middle drawer and dumped the contents on the desk. I searched the bottom with the flashlight, finding nothing. Leaving the drawer where it was, he grabbed the next one and turned it over. This time my flashlight beam landed on something shiny.

"Well, I'll be damned," Mason muttered. "It's a key." He started to peel off the adhesive, but it was so old, the brittle tape broke into pieces. Mason cupped the key in his palm.

"What do you think it goes to?" I asked.

He turned it over in his hand. "It looks like an ordinary house key." He looked into my eyes. "It could be absolutely nothing, Rose. He might have kept it here as a spare because he continually locked himself out of the house."

"Taped under his drawer? Not likely."

"Bottom line is that we have no idea what it opens, so we'll just be on the lookout."

"Agreed. Now let's dump the other three."

He pulled them out in quick succession, but there was nothing else. "Let's get out of here."

We hurried out of the office. The sun had begun to set, so it was getting darker. As we headed for the window, Mason looked over his shoulder. "Wait a minute. I want to have a quick look at the crime scene."

I tried not to flinch. "Okay."

I handed him the flashlight and let him take point on this one since it was his idea.

He wandered around the area, then squatted down next to the bloodstains. "There's an extra one," he said, his gaze moving from stain to stain before returning to my face. "Do you feel up to walking me through what happened?"

Oh, crappy doodles. "Why don't you just read the report?"

"I told you. It wasn't exactly thorough. Besides, at this point, I don't trust the sheriff's department to do their job. I want to hear it directly from you."

"Okay," I said, trying not to sound breathless. I would just stick to the story I'd told Joe. "I met Hattie here with the secret journal, but I wasn't sure I trusted her, so I hid it in a desk drawer before I followed her into the office."

"Which desk?"

My blood ran cold. Mason was going to be very, very thorough. Ordinarily I'd applaud his attention to detail. Today, not so much.

"This one." I pointed to it.

"Can you literally walk me through it? Do you feel up to it?"

I would have loved to tell him no, but the last thing I wanted was for Mason to think I was fragile. "Yeah. Sure."

"Go ahead and start."

"After I shut the journal in the drawer, I walked to the office doorway." I imitated each step as I described it. "Then I got freaked out about being trapped inside with her, so I decided I needed to be out in the open."

"Okay," he said, deep in thought. "Then what happened?"

"So I walked out here." I made my way into the clear floor space, trying to avoid the bloodstains.

"What made you go with that choice?" he asked. "You usually have good instincts in these situations. It seems like you'd choose to stay between the desks . . . maybe use them for cover."

I held my breath. He was right. If I'd been alone, that's probably exactly what I would have done. The reason I'd stayed out in the open was to make it easier for Jed to serve as my backup, not that I could admit it to Mason. "I don't know," I finally said. "I just did."

"Then what happened?"

"Hattie and I were talking, and there was a gunshot."

"Someone got shot?"

My pulse throbbed against my temples. "Why do I feel like you're cross-examining me in the courtroom?"

That shook him up. "I'm sorry if I'm coming across that way, Rose. I'm just trying to piece it all together. Trying to see if there's anything there to help us."

"I know. I'm sorry." I ran my hand over my head. "Hattie. Hattie got shot."

"And then what?"

"Beverly Buchanan and Dirk Picklebie came out of the shadows. Beverly wanted the journal. I told her it was hidden and if she killed me, she'd never find it."

"That was good thinking," he said softly. "What happened next?"

"Uh . . ." I had to remember to keep all references to Jed out of my explanation, which got tricky since he'd been so much a part of what happened that day. "Hattie was still alive, so she threatened to shoot her again if I didn't give her the journal." That part wasn't true. Beverly had threatened to kill Jed. "Then Dirk got worried she'd kill him too, so he used me as a shield and told her he wanted a bigger split of the money J.R. had offered for the book. He wanted half. Fifty thousand dollars."

"J.R. Simmons was willing to pay one hundred thousand dollars for that book? What did Dora find out?" He grunted. "*Dammit.* We need that book."

"I know. I'm sorry I let Joe take it."

His expression softened, and he shook his head. "No, sweetheart. You had no say in the matter. Go on. What happened next?"

"Beverly promised to give him more money, so he dropped his hold on me, and Beverly shot him in the head." I shuddered as I remembered watching him fall to the ground.

A grim expression covered Mason's face. "Can you show me where Hattie and Dirk were situated at that point?"

I pointed to the spot where Dirk had held me, then to the one where Hattie had lain between two desks. "She threatened to kill Hattie, so I went to the desk drawer and pretended it was stuck. Beverly got frustrated and pushed me out of the way. She got out the journal herself, but when she spun around, I tased her. After she fell, I got the book out from underneath her, then went to check on Hattie."

"Where was Beverly at that point?"

"Here." I pointed to the space in front of the desk.

"So you went to Hattie, and then what?"

"I called 911, and then Beverly tackled me. I tried to get away, but she pulled me back down and began to strangle me. Then Joe showed up and shot her."

"And where did that happen?"

I pointed to the area, but I knew what he was going to ask next . . . and I had no idea how to answer it.

"So if this blood stain is from Beverly, how did this one get here?"

"I don't know." I turned away from him, the weight of my guilt making it difficult to breathe.

"You can tell me anything, Rose. You know that, right?"

Oh, God. He knew I was lying to him, which made it even worse. I wanted to tell him the truth, and he certainly deserved to know, but there was just no way my former assistant district attorney boyfriend would understand why I'd help Skeeter Malcolm. I didn't think he ever would.

"This place is gonna give me nightmares. Can we go now?"

"Yeah." The disappointment in his voice was like a knife to the gut, but I was keeping this secret to protect him just as much as myself.

I headed for the window, climbing out before him.

"What should we do now?" I asked. "What we really need is that journal. Where do you think Joe put it after he took it from me?"

"I know he didn't log it as evidence. Randy already checked on that."

"Deputy Miller did that? He told me that he believed I was innocent."

Mason nodded. "He's been keeping an eye on Joe for me." He took my hand, and we started walking around the building. "Apparently, Joe practically lived at the sheriff's office this weekend. He didn't go home at all on Friday night. Of course, he was busy trying to find Skeeter Malcolm and arrest him for that double murder south of town."

"Last week you told me that Joe thought Skeeter had done it, but what about you? Do you think so too?"

Mason squinted at me. "Why the sudden interest in Skeeter Malcolm?"

I shrugged. "It's just a feeling."

"You have visions, not feelings. Feelings are my mother's purview, and she seems to be having an awful lot of them lately."

"You should listen to your mother, Mason."

He smirked a little at that. "The world's going to hell in a handbasket. I'm counting on visions and feelings to guide my investigation. What would my law professors say?"

"I think you should use all the resources at your disposal. But you didn't answer my question. Do you think Skeeter Malcolm did it?"

He frowned. "No. He's not that stupid, yet Joe seems dead set on arresting him anyway."

"Could his father be behind that too?"

Mason stopped walking. I turned around to face him.

"Could he be?"

"It crossed my mind this weekend, but since I'm not the ADA anymore and I was so focused on getting you out of jail, I didn't give it much thought. But yeah, I think there's a good chance of that."

I tried to contain my excitement. I had managed to tie us all together without confessing my extracurricular activities. "Why does J.R. Simmons give a fig newton about Skeeter Malcolm?" I pressed.

Mason's mouth twisted—it was an expression I recognized all too well; he was trying to decide what to tell me. "I don't know for certain, but I don't think we're off in thinking there's a connection."

"What is it?" I genuinely had no idea why Joe's father cared about Skeeter. I was hoping maybe Mason would.

"Let's go home and discuss this on the way. I have some things to confess."

"About your investigation?"

"Yes."

"Okay," I said, suddenly nervous.

Mason had barely left the parking lot before he began. "You already know that I went to see Joe the night I found out he had paid off the loan for your nursery. You also know we got into a heated discussion and some punches were thrown. What I didn't tell you was that I asked Joe to help me protect you from his father."

My mouth dropped in shock.

"He told me no. It was his belief that trying to fight his father would be detrimental to you. But he called me the next day to say he'd changed his mind. He wanted to help, but only on the condition I didn't tell you."

"Why?"

"I don't know. I figured he had his reasons, and as long as he was helping, I didn't care. Still, he didn't have much information to offer until the day after Christmas."

"What happened?"

"He had me meet him in secret. I hated not telling you, especially since you were so upset I was keeping things from you, but I figured we could use all the help we could get."

That disagreement had been a bad one. "What did he say?"

"He said his father knew I'd been poking around in Little Rock. Joe was worried that my investigation would irritate his father enough to put you in danger." He paused. "But there was more."

"Okay."

"Joe's father wanted him to back off on finding Mick Gentry."

My blood ran cold. "Why?"

"His reasoning was that if Gentry was still on the loose, he would eliminate Malcolm."

My stomach clenched. "Why would he want that?"

"The hell if I know, and Joe wasn't in the mood to volunteer any ideas. The only theory I could come up with is that Simmons has some ongoing business here and Malcolm's in the way."

"What kind of business?"

"I have no idea, but there's more."

"*More?* Okay . . ."

"J.R. told Joe that I was pissing off the good citizens of Fenton County. Joe didn't get into specifics, but I always suspected that meant J.R. knew who was behind the attempt on my life."

"I'd bet money that person was Mick Gentry. Especially after the fire at Gems. We need to find Gentry to stop him from killing you both. And keep Skeeter from getting arrested for two murders he didn't commit."

Mason's eyes narrowed. "Why do you care about Skeeter Malcolm?"

Crap. "Because Joe's wanting to arrest him for something he didn't do. His situation is no different than mine."

He turned to me in disbelief. "His situation is *entirely* different than yours. Skeeter Malcolm has committed multiple crimes for which he's never been arrested, and if he didn't commit these murders, I'm sure he's guilty of others."

"Skeeter Malcolm is a person, criminal or not, and Mick Gentry is a despicable man."

"How do you know Skeeter Malcolm isn't an even *more* despicable man?"

Crap, oh crap, oh crap. "Look, all I know is that Skeeter took over Daniel Crocker's place in the crime world and Gentry wants it."

"How do you know that?" His words were more accusatory than his tone. If anything, he seemed genuinely curious. Besides, he was used to me knowing things, usually with the help of Neely Kate. "The part about Gentry wanting to take over has been purposely been kept out of the media."

What could I tell him? Then it hit me. "Jonah and all his ties to the criminal element." Jonah ran a support group for rehabilitating criminals at his church, which meant Jonah was more tapped into the criminal world than most people in town.

Mason was quiet for a long moment, and I had worked myself into a lather of worry by the time he spoke again. But he only said, "We need to figure out the significance of the key and get into that safe. They're our best leads."

I wasn't sure if the change of topic was a good thing or a bad one. But now I worried about the ramifications of Mason getting caught doing something illegal. "Mason, when we get this all sorted out, do you want your job back?"

He shot me a quizzical glance. "Rose, the last thing I'm worried about right now is my old job."

"Think about it, Mason. If you want your job back, you can't risk getting caught trespassing and breakin' into a safe. So do you?"

"Honestly, Rose, I'm not sure. For the most part I loved my job, but I love you a hell of a lot more. Now that I have you, I don't want to pour all of my time into some office. I've been thinking about pursuing real estate law."

I narrowed my eyes. "You've got to be kidding me."

He shrugged. "I would rarely have to go to court, and it's good money with more regular hours."

"And you'd be bored to tears in ten minutes, and only because you'd spend the first five getting a cup of coffee."

He didn't answer, so I leaned closer and rested my hand on his arm. "You love what you do, crappy hours or not. And our relationship is only going to work if you're happy with your career. I say we get this mess cleaned up, and then we work on getting your job back." I sat up straighter. "Which means little or no criminal activity for you."

"And no criminal activity for you, either. If you get caught doing something illegal, Joe won't waste a second before tossing you back in jail."

I purposely didn't agree. There was no way I was going back there, but I'd do whatever I had to do to fix this mess.

"I have another idea for how we can get the key figured out." He sounded hopeful.

"Oh?"

"I'll go talk to Henry's widow."

"I'm not sure she'll talk to you. She's a grumpy old woman who makes Miss Mildred look like Mother Teresa.

Besides, her daughter Beverly's funeral is tomorrow. You might want to wait."

"Dammit," he grumbled. "So we're back to square one."

"No. Just delayed a few days."

"We don't have time to waste," Mason said. I was surprised when he pulled up to the farmhouse—the drive had passed in a blur. "Your trial is in three weeks." He cursed under his breath, then said, "You think they'd make *some* attempt to make this case look like it hasn't been railroaded."

He was right. Three weeks hardly seemed like any time at all. The situation suddenly felt hopeless.

Mason turned the car off and started to get out, but I grabbed his arm and held him in place. "Mason. Wait."

He turned to me with an expectant look.

"I want to have a vision of you."

He looked surprised. "What brought this on?"

"I'm scared. I want to have a vision telling us that everything's gonna be okay."

He smiled softly. "That's actually a good idea."

"Okay." I grabbed his hand, lacing our fingers together and squeezing.

"Your hand is shaking."

I looked into his worried eyes. "I'm scared of what I'll see."

"You don't have to do this."

"But I do." I took a deep breath, then closed my eyes, thinking about where Mason would be in three weeks. A dark shadow swept in, and I saw . . . nothing. Icy blackness sunk its hooks deep into my head. The cold seeped into my veins, pulling me down into a pit of nothingness, and I started to panic.

*Calm down. You can get out of this.*

I needed to try thinking about something more generic. Like what Mason would be doing tonight. That would take me away from this black, blank space. Sure enough, the next moment I found myself in our home office, studying Mason's computer screen. The webpage for Crane Industries was on the screen.

"You're gonna investigate Crane Industries," I whispered, then slumped back against the seat, weak and lightheaded.

"Rose?" Mason asked, worry in his voice. "What happened? What did you see?"

My mind was sluggish, but I realized what I'd seen and started to cry.

"*Rose.*"

I needed to hold him. I needed to know he was here with me. Alive and okay. Gathering all of my strength, I sat up, threw my arms around his neck, and tried to slow my racing heart.

Mason grabbed my upper arms and pulled away a bit to study my face, his eyes full of fear. "Rose, you're scaring me. What did you see?"

I forced myself to calm down. "I had two visions."

"Two?"

"I've learned that if I try to force a vision of something that won't happen, I get stuck. When that happens, I have to redirect my mind somewhere else."

"What did you redirect it to?"

"The second vision was of what you'll be doing

tonight."

"And I was investigating Crane Industries?"

I nodded, my heart still racing. "You were in the office, working on your laptop."

"That was next on my research list. What did you try to see the first time?"

I started to shake, fear washing through me. "I wanted to see where you would be in three weeks."

He looked so solemn as he nodded. "And what did you see?"

"Nothing." I took a deep breath, trying not to cry. "I saw absolutely nothing. It was so cold and dark, and there was *nothing*."

He grabbed my face and gently wiped an escaped tear with his thumbs. "Calm down. We don't know what that means. Maybe the future's just too uncertain for you to get a clear picture."

I shook my head. "No. That's not it. If that were a possibility, I would have seen lots of empty visions after Momma died. Things were changing so much, my visions wouldn't have been able to keep up."

"Sweetheart, it's probably not what you're thinking."

"It's *exactly* what I'm thinking, and you know it." I looked into his eyes. "You were dead, Mason." More tears fell down my cheeks. "It was the scariest thing I've ever experienced. It wasn't just dark, it was *cold*. The cold sunk into my head and started spreading through my body."

"Your hand turned to ice while you were having your vision."

It was only further confirmation that I was right.

"I'm okay." He grinned. "I'm too stubborn to let something happen to me before I see this thing through." He gave me a kiss. "Let's go inside."

"We have to fight this thing, Mason. We have to stop it from happening."

"We will. We *are*. Let's go inside and let Muffy out. She's about to have a stroke from all that barking."

He got out of the car, and I opened my car door, but my knees buckled when I tried to stand. Mason was by my side in seconds, wrapping his arm around my waist and holding me up. "This has never happened to you with a vision before, has it?"

"No, but I haven't seen death very often, and I've never experienced it like that—like a blank slate."

He helped me up the porch steps. And when we reached the front door, we stood there for a moment, his arm wrapped around my back. I pulled free of his hold. "I think I'm okay now."

He studied me for a second. "I'm really worried about you. When you were having that vision, you turned ice cold and as white as a sheet. In fact, you're still pale. I think you should go inside and lie down for a bit."

"I'm feeling better. I'll take Muffy out, then I'll rest, okay?"

"Okay." He unlocked the door and pushed it open, heading straight to the kitchen to turn off the alarm, and I bent down and rubbed the top of Muffy's head. Her response was to make me wish I had a gas mask.

I frantically waved my hand in front of my face. "Let's go outside, girl." We went out onto the porch, and I shut the door behind me and sat on the steps as I watched my dog romp in the yard.

Seconds later, Mason came out and sat down next to me.

I grabbed his hand and held it tight. "Do you believe what I saw?"

"I'd prefer not to, but I trust your judgment."

"This changes everything."

He shook his head. "It doesn't change anything. You've had multiple visions of people dying that haven't come to pass—me. You. Even Joe. You changed it somehow. Besides, I've been at risk for months. And Joe's not going to give me protection now. He wouldn't have let the ADA get killed on his watch, but I'm not the ADA anymore." He paused. "Maybe that's why he let me get fired. To make things easier."

I wanted to argue that Joe wouldn't purposefully leave Mason unprotected, but I no longer knew what to believe about Joe. "Don't be so callous, Mason. We're not discussing the weather. Someone's trying to kill you. I don't think you should be out investigating *anything*."

"Rose," he sighed. "What are my choices? To either hide away until your trial or to try to stop J.R.? I think you know which one I'm going to pick."

"That doesn't seem like the prudent choice."

"I'm always aware of my surroundings. Even now." He pointed to the trees in front of the house. "In theory, someone could be out there, hiding in the trees with a long-range rifle."

I gasped and turned to face him. "Is that supposed to make me feel *better*?"

"*Yes.* Because no one's out there with a long-range rifle. Not in Fenton County, Arkansas. If someone wanted to kill me right now, they'd come down the driveway and do it. No hiding. But we have an advantage here at the house. We can hear any vehicle on our drive long before we see it, which gives us plenty of time to prepare."

"I can't believe I'm saying this, but I think you should have a gun with you at all times."

"I've been wearing this one since I was fired." He took my hand. "What I'm saying is that I'm always watching for potential danger. I'm being as careful as I can be."

"Okay."

He leaned over and gave me a kiss. "Come on inside. Apparently I need to start researching Crane Industries."

He had his task, and I had mine.

It was time to call Skeeter.

# Chapter Seven

Unfortunately, Skeeter Malcolm was a hard man to reach.

Mason headed for the office, and I told him I was going upstairs to take a bath. My physical reaction to my vision had really shaken him, so he looked relieved.

"Take your time, sweetheart. I'll check on you in a little while."

"I think I'll call Neely Kate and have a nice chat," I said as I started up the stairs.

"Good idea." He gave me a warm smile. "Let me know what she found out about Glenn Stout."

When I got to our room, I started the bathwater and then pressed Skeeter's speed dial, which sent me direct to voice mail.

"Skeeter, this is Rose," I said in a hushed tone as I wandered out to the sun room nursery, momentarily stunned by the state of it. I'd ransacked it while looking for the journal, but in the stress of everything that had happened since, I'd forgotten. "I'm out of jail, but we need to talk as soon as possible. Call me."

I hung up and called Jed.

"Rose, I got your message."

"Did Skeeter have something to do with getting me out?" Carter had denied it, but there was still a chance it was true.

"No. Skeeter was ready to do it, although one million would have been tough. We had the hundred K in cash, but we were trying to come up with the full cash amount so we could skip the bail bondsman. Hale was frazzled from trying to pull it all together, but he had strict instructions from Skeeter to get you out as soon as possible."

"So do you know anything about Glenn Stout from Little Rock?"

"No. But Hale is on it, and you can bet that Skeeter will track the guy down himself the minute he gets back."

"He's got other problems to fix." I bent down to pick up a drawer and put it back in the dresser. "I forced a vision of Mason three weeks from now to see if this thing went to trial, and Mason was dead."

"What?"

"Someone's definitely still out to kill him, and I have to stop it."

"That's secondary to what's goin' on."

"Like Hades it is. I started this whole association with Skeeter to save Mason's life."

"You started it to save your business. Now you're trying to save your own life. You won't last in prison, Rose. J.R. Simmons is countin' on it."

"I'm tougher than I look, Jed. You of all people should know that."

"You could be the toughest woman in the world, but you still wouldn't make it long. You'd be goin' to McPherson, and Deveraux sent quite a few women there during his time in Little Rock. Hard-ass women who would love to make him suffer the way he made them suffer."

"Well, crap."

"If this thing goes to trial, you have to run."

"I can't do that! Glenn Stout, whoever he is, will lose all his money."

"Then he shouldn't have posted your bail. I don't give a shit about the finances of some guy who doesn't exist. And you can bet your ass Skeeter won't care either."

I sat down in the rocking chair. "Hopefully, it won't come to that. Where is Skeeter anyway?"

Jed was quiet for several seconds. "He's taking care of some personal business."

"Does it have to do with J.R. Simmons? If so, he needs to pool his information with ours. We all need to team up."

"We *are* teaming up. What the hell do you think we've been doing?"

"No. With Mason."

"You think we're gonna work with the Fenton County ADA? Have you lost your mind?"

"Jed—"

"No."

I needed to choose my battles, and I had a bigger one to wage at the moment. "Fine. I can accept that. For now." I took a deep breath, ready for a fight. "I need to set up a meeting as the Lady in Black."

"Who with?"

Goodness, he was awfully grouchy. I was about to make him even more so. "Mick Gentry."

"*What the actual hell, Rose?*" His voice boomed out so loud I had to hold the phone a few inches from my ear.

"Now I know you've lost your mind. Get some sleep and call me tomorrow."

"*Jed*. Think this through. Mick Gentry had to be the one who set Skeeter up for those murders. Not to mention the fact that I *know* he wants to kill Mason."

"Which is why you can't meet with him! He's dangerous!"

"Jed! I've already set this up. I told Scott Humphrey that I wanted a face-to-face with Mick. And in my vision, Mick was open to meeting with me after Skeeter was out of the picture."

"What excuse could you possibly use to see him?"

"What if I play it like I want to be on the winning side? I'll meet him, show him I'm serious, and then insist on meeting J.R. What if I record J.R. saying he wants to kill Mason? And get him to admit to other criminal activity as well?"

"That's a whole lot of what-ifs. You have no idea if Simmons would agree to meet with you. Or if he's even directly involved."

"We both know he's involved. And who knows, maybe I'll get all the information I need from Mick Gentry." When he was silent, I knew I had him. "We just need to make sure it's admissible in court."

"You should ask your boyfriend," he said, his voice laced with sarcasm. "I'm sure he'll think it's a great idea."

"Or maybe we can ask Carter Hale," I added, trying to sound cheery.

"I already know the answer," he grumbled. "We would need a court order for it to be admissible, and seeing as how no judge in this county is going to issue one to the Lady in Black, it's a moot point."

I had worried that might be the case, but if I could actually get J.R. to meet with me as the Lady in Black, then I'd deal with the logistics later. "We can still use whatever we find out to save Skeeter and Mason. It's a good idea, and you know it."

"Skeeter will skin us both alive."

"Skeeter Malcolm's not here," I retorted, working myself into a snit. "He ran off to do God knows what. It's up to us, and *I* say we do this. You know it's a good idea."

He didn't argue.

"I gave Humphrey a fake number to call. Will that piss off Mick?"

"Maybe, maybe not. But not enough for him to refuse a meeting."

"So you think he'll want to?"

"I think he'd sell his grandmother to a traveling circus to meet the Lady in Black."

"Can you set it up? Do you guys have some sort of a bat signal to let each other know when you want to talk?"

He chuckled. "No. But we have other ways." There was a pause at the other end of the line, and when he spoke again, his tone was more serious. "I can't believe I'm asking, but when do you want to do this?"

"As soon as possible. I have no idea what I'll tell Mason, but I'll come up with something."

"Like you said, Mason is still on someone's hit list. You're both in plenty of danger."

I took a breath. "I know."

"I'm stayin' at our safe house. I'm sending Merv to bring you here too."

I snorted. "You know I'm not gonna do that. I have too much to do, and I'm not leaving Mason."

"If things keep heatin' up, you may not have a choice."

"I'll deal with that if the time comes."

"But in the meantime, pick up a burner phone tomorrow and send me the number. Skeeter should have gotten you one weeks ago."

"Okay." I waited a beat. "Jed, about the factory . . . I'm sorry you got hurt on account of me."

"I failed you, Rose. I was there to protect you, and I put you at risk. I should have just taken the bitch out without showing myself, but I knew you'd never approve of that."

I smiled. "Well, thank you for that. It means a lot to me, Jed."

"Don't be expecting it to happen again. Next time I'll just shoot first to avoid any unnecessary risks."

I hoped to God there wouldn't be a next time, but I was in so deep that it was probably a pipe dream.

"I'll put out feelers for Gentry," he said, sounding gruff. "I'll let you know when I hear anything."

"Thanks."

I hung up and realized the water was still running, so I went into the bathroom and turned it off. The steaming water was tempting. I'd told Mason I was going to talk with Neely Kate while taking a bath. No reason not to follow through on both. I stripped and climbed into the warm water. Resting my head against the high back of the tub, I grabbed my phone off the floor and called Neely Kate.

"Hey, Neely Kate. What did you find out?"

"Nita worked the desk today. She said a courier brought the paperwork and the check."

"Didn't the guy who paid it need to sign anything?"

"Technically, yes, but Nita was so overwhelmed from holding a cashier's check for a million dollars, she just pushed it on through. In fact, I had a hard time tracking her down because she got suspended for three days because of it. She was out at the Trading Post drowning her sorrows . . . although she didn't look too sorrowful. She just got three days off."

"Oh dear. Did she remember anything about the courier?"

"A young guy, maybe mid-twenties. He said he was from Little Rock, and he was dressed in jeans and a T-shirt. When she was going through the paperwork, he kept waving the check at her. Like he was trying to push the process along even though he knew he was missing some steps. She says he stayed there until she got it all uploaded to the system. The second she confirmed you were as good as free, he thanked her and took off."

"She broke the rules because she was distracted by a check?"

"Well, between you and me, I think she was distracted by some *cash*. There were several hundred-dollar bills in her wallet when she bought me a drink, and Nita is known for being cash-poor."

"That makes more sense."

"She got a photo of him on her camera phone. She refused to send it to me, but I got a good look at it."

"Could you pick the guy out of a lineup?"

"I'll say. And let's just say that the check and the cash probably weren't the only things distracting her."

"Maybe Randy can get some mugshots for you to look at."

"Who?"

"Deputy Miller. He's helpin' Mason and spying on Joe."

"You're kidding. Are you sure we can trust him?"

"He seems pretty doggone mad at Joe, so yeah. I think so."

I told her about our trip to the factory, the key we'd found there, and our need to get into the safe. Then my vision of Mason and my phone call with Jed.

"Oh, my stars and garters. You sure haven't let any grass grow under your feet."

"I can't afford to."

"What do you want me to do?"

"Are you sure you want to get mixed up in this?" It was a stupid question on my part, but I had to ask it anyway. "This isn't the same as you and me pokin' around about a factory fire."

"I'm *dying* to get mixed up in this. And besides, *everything* we've done has turned dangerous. This time at least we're goin' into it with our eyes wide open. Now what do you want me to do?"

"How about you take the safe job? See if Jonah or Bruce Wayne know someone who's willing to open it?"

"I don't even need to go that far. My cousin Witt should be able to get it open easy enough. He's an expert at gettin' into all kinds of things, from pickle jars to women's panties. Just tell me where it's at."

I wasn't sure that was the ideal résumé for breaking into a safe, but beggars can't be choosers, so I gave her directions on how to find the office and the safe. "Do you think you'll get to it tomorrow?"

"I don't see any reason to wait. I'll call Witt to see if he can do it tonight."

"Will Ronnie be okay with that?"

"Ronnie's not an issue."

Something in her voice caught my attention. "Is everything okay?"

"It will be eventually," she said, but her voice broke. "It just means I have more time to work on this little project."

Now I was really worried. "Do you want to talk about it?"

"Maybe tomorrow."

"How about we meet for lunch? I'll run by the nursery and check on Violet, then meet you at eleven-thirty at Merilee's?"

"Sure. I'll let you know what happens with the safe."

"Okay. I'll have Mason send you the photos he took so Witt knows what he's dealing with," I said, my stomach knotted with nerves. "Be careful, okay?"

"Don't you be worrying about me. I've got this covered."

"Uh, Neely Kate? One more thing. Did you get my message from Carter?"

"Yeah. I took care of it on Saturday when I brought Mason his dinner. I made him a tuna and peppermint creole casserole. The poor thing was so upset he couldn't even eat it, bless his heart. He took a few bites and headed straight for the bathroom. That's when I ran upstairs to get your things."

"I'm gonna need it back."

She was silent for a moment. I expected her to blast me, but she said, "Okay. Talk to you later."

As soon as we hung up, I texted Mason to let him know Neely Kate was using her own resources to open the safe. I asked if he could text the photos to her so her source knew to bring the right tools. To his credit, he didn't ask questions, simply texted: *Okay. Enjoy your bath. Muffy and I are out at the barn.*

What in tarnation was he doing out at the barn? Deciding to ask him later, I put my phone on the floor next to the tub and sank down into the water. My mind was like a whirligig, but for the moment, Neely Kate's marriage took top priority in my thoughts. I knew she and Ronnie had been going through a rough spot after her miscarriage, but it sounded like things had gotten a whole lot worse in the short time I was in county lock-up.

My mind spun around to Skeeter—where was he, and why was J.R. Simmons so determined to destroy him? J.R.'s motive for wanting Mason dead was a mystery too, though I understood why he'd arranged for him to lose his job.

I would do everything in my power to protect them both, even though I knew the price would be steep.

With any luck, J.R. Simmons would be the one to pay it.

# Chapter Eight

I ended up falling asleep in bed before Mason and Muffy came back inside, so it wasn't until the next morning, over breakfast, that I filled Mason in on what Neely Kate had discovered. "She says she'd recognize the courier again if she saw him. Do you think Randy could get some mugshots for her to look at?"

"I'll ask him. Now what's going on with the safe?"

"She thought her cousin would be able to open it last night, but I haven't heard from her. He might not have been available."

"Let me know as soon as you hear," he said. "And I think I'll text Neely Kate to see if she has Nita's phone number. I have a few follow-up questions. I was thinking I'd drive up to Little Rock to find out what happened before our meeting Friday night. I need to know how it got turned on its head. It must have taken quite a bit of finagling to get the meeting switched up like that, especially that quickly, so I'm hoping the speed of it led to sloppiness. Maybe there's something there that will help implicate J.R." He paused. "I'm also going to see if I can come up with anything about Glenn Stout. It's probably a wild goose chase, but I'll already be there."

I stood and took my plate to the sink. "Sounds like a good idea." I was worried about him being up there by himself. Little Rock was only two hours away, but two hours would seem pretty cotton-picking far if he found himself in mortal danger. Still, he had a shot at getting some helpful information, and we needed all the support we could get.

Mason grabbed his plate and followed me. "But I don't want to leave you."

"I'll be fine, Mason." I took his plate and turned on the water. "In fact, I'm meeting Neely Kate for lunch."

He took the plate from my hands and put it in the sink, then turned off the water and spun me around to face him, my bottom against the counter. "I'm not sure that's a good idea. Carter Hale himself said you should lie low. We have no idea why your bail was posted. You need to be careful until we find out."

"You both need to stop worryin'. If the person who did it wished me ill, they would have been waiting for me when I got out. They're gonna leave me alone."

His frown told me he wasn't so convinced. "What about J.R.? He could pull something else."

I reached up on my tiptoes and kissed him. "Neely Kate and I will be in public. I'll be perfectly safe."

He pursed his lips but remained silent.

I gave him a soft smile. "Do you have any idea how much I love you?"

His mouth tipped into a wicked smile. "Your demonstration this morning was a good indication."

"I felt bad about falling asleep before you came to bed last night. What were you and Muffy doin' out in the barn?"

"Just looking around."

"For hours?"

"I thought Dora might have hidden something out there." He released a huge sigh and ran a hand through his hair. "It was more than I was getting accomplished on my computer."

"No luck with Crane Industries?"

"No."

Muffy jumped up on my legs, and I picked her up and rubbed behind her ears, surprised she was gas-free. "Your daddy's headin' to Little Rock and leavin' us for the day. You gonna keep me company when I get back from lunch?"

Something flickered in Mason's eyes.

"What?"

"You just called me her daddy."

"Oh." I blinked. "Do you not like that?"

"I love it." He stroked Muffy's head. "It makes us a real family."

"We *are* a real family, aren't we?" As though to show her agreement, Muffy reached up and licked his hand. "See? She loves you."

Mason wrapped his arm around my back and held me close, Muffy pressed between us.

"Mason, if we don't . . . if I go to prison—"

"Rose. Stop."

I looked up at him. "Will you promise to take care of Muffy?"

"Of course. I love this little dog." His intense eyes bored into mine. "But you're not going to prison."

"I know I'm not," I said, mostly to appease him, "but it's like life insurance. You know, just in case." I set Muffy down, then reached up and pressed my palm to his cheek, soaking in the sight of him. "I want to have another vision of you."

Worry wavered in his eyes. "Do you think that's a good idea given how the last one turned out?"

"You're going two hours away from me. I need to make sure you're gonna be safe."

"Okay."

Keeping my hand on his cheek, I closed my eyes and thought about what he'd be doing tomorrow night. A restaurant appeared in my mind's eye. The vision was from Mason's perspective, and I was sitting across the table from my future self. The me in the vision was dressed fancy—my hair was up, and I had on a slinky wine-colored dress. Love and pure joy swelled through Mason, filling every part of me as I beamed at Vision Rose in the warm candlelit atmosphere. The vision quickly faded, and I said, "You're going out to dinner with me tomorrow."

I opened my eyes, and a smile slowly spread across his face. "That sounds perfect."

The emotions I felt from the vision lingered. "It wasn't a regular vision, Mason."

His concern was back. "Did something bad happen?"

I shook my head. "No. The opposite. Something good. I rarely have strong emotions in a vision—it's only happened a few times—but this one . . ." Tears filled my eyes.

"Rose?" His hand cupped my face as his eyes searched mine. "What happened?"

"Nothing happened, it's just . . . I could feel how much you love me."

His face lit up, and he gave me a soft kiss, his lips

lingering on mine for a long moment before he pulled away. "Then you know I'd do anything for you."

I nodded, still feeling emotional.

"I'm going to take off soon, but I hope to be back by eight or nine tonight. Check in with me today, okay?"

"I will. You too."

He kissed me again and smiled. "I love you, Rose."

His words seemed so small in comparison to the emotions that had rushed through me in the vision, as if they were the tiny tip of an enormous iceberg. "I love you too."

We left at the same time, and Muffy let us know her disapproval from the living room window. Before we got into our separate cars, Mason gave me a long, deep kiss.

When I got into town, my first task was picking up a burner phone at Walmart. I sat in my truck to set it up, then sent Jed a text. I also sent one to Skeeter.

*Call and text me at this number. LB*

I drove to the nursery next, steeling my back as I climbed out of my car. I had no idea what kind of reaction to expect from my sister. Lately, she was as mercurial as the Arkansas weather.

Anna, the new sales clerk, was watering houseplants. She gave me a blank stare when I walked into the nursery.

"Is Violet here?"

"No."

When she didn't volunteer more, I asked, "Do you know where she is or when she'll be back?"

"Yes."

"Okay . . ." I groaned. I could have forced the issue. I was her boss, after all, but I didn't feel like having a confrontation right now, particularly not with an almost-stranger. I pulled out my real cell phone and called my sister. When she answered, I said, "Vi, I'm at the shop. Where are you?"

"I'm out."

"I can see that. Will you be back soon?"

"Uh . . . not for a bit." She sounded distracted.

"Okay. I guess I'll see you later."

"Okay."

Violet was usually much coyer when she was hiding something, so I had to wonder what she was doing. Then it hit me. Hilary wanted Violet to decorate her baby's nursery. I wasn't sure why it bothered me so much. I'd given my sister my blessing. Maybe it was because the men who were colluding with Hilary had turned on me.

"I guess I'll be goin'," I said, heading for the door.

Anna didn't say anything, and I suddenly got irritated. Why was I being made to feel like an intruder in my own business? "You don't like me very much, do you?"

Her mouth dropped open, but she quickly recovered. "I'm not sure what you're talkin' about, Miss Rose."

I considered pressing the issue, but I didn't see much of a point. "Look, whatever you've heard about me is probably an exaggeration or an outright lie. I didn't steal my sister's inheritance and force her to work for me. And I'm not a badge bunny. Or whatever crazy rumor you've heard about me."

She lifted her eyebrows in surprise. "I hadn't heard any of those things, but I'll keep that in mind should I hear them in the future."

I left, wondering why it bothered me so much that

this one woman didn't like me. I was used to people treating me badly and thinking I was strange. Then again, maybe that was why it upset me. I didn't want to go back to the way things once were—to being a dumping ground for silent disapproval. The new me wouldn't take it. Still, I didn't need to settle things with Anna right now. There would be time to sort it out later.

My lunch date with Neely Kate wasn't for another hour, so I decided to drop by the landscaping office and check on Bruce Wayne. I parked my truck in front of our storefront. The front door opened just as I was walking toward it.

Kate Simmons walked out, and when she saw me, a sly grin spread across her face. "Just the person I was hoping to see." She was wearing a canvas jacket, a tight pair of jeans, and army boots. Her dark hair was cut into a bob that barely brushed her shoulders and her previous blue streaks were now purple. If she was going for a look that was the antithesis of the rich and socially elite Simmonses, she had definitely achieved it.

I resisted the urge to turn tail and hide. "What can I do for you, Kate?"

"I think it's the other way around, Rosie."

My eyes widened.

"What?" she asked, shifting her weight to the side and pulling on a strand of her violet-streaked hair. "You don't like the nickname?"

I crossed my arms. "What do you want?"

"What's with the hostility? I was just checking on you. Making sure you survived your time in the big house."

I shook my head. "You know, for someone who claims to want me to get back with her brother, you're awfully adversarial."

She gave me a coy grin. "Maybe it's because you insist on sleepin' with the wrong man."

"Even if I *were* interested in your brother, that's *never* gonna happen given the fact that he had me arrested."

She tsked and shook her head. "I told you to mind your P's and Q's."

"If that was your way of warning me I was about to be arrested, you suck at communicating."

Kate laughed. "I like you." She tilted her head and looked me up and down. "You're this perfect combination of the innocent girl next door and the girl who won't take shit. No wonder Joe likes you."

I groaned. "As you can see, I've survived, at least for the three weeks until my trial. After that, your daddy's puttin' me away, which is the sort of thing that puts a damper on a relationship. So, again, I can only tell you that it's never. Gonna. Happen. Now if you don't mind, I have work to do." I started to head for the office.

"Chin up, Rose Petal. One of the things you're seeking is closer than you think. Practically under your nose."

I spun around and put my hands on my hips. "Do you always talk in riddles? What in Sam Hill are you talkin' about?"

She laughed and took several steps backward. "Think bigger and wider than this backward county."

"If you think it's so backward, what are you still doin' here?"

She took another backward step and held out her hands. "What? You want me to miss the show that's about to unfold? Not a chance. It's a perfect storm that's been brewing for years, and it's all about to come to a head." Grinning from ear to ear, she shook her head. "No, I wouldn't miss this for the *world*." Then she turned around and walked toward the courthouse, whistling a happy tune.

"What was that all about?" Bruce Wayne asked in the now-open door to our office.

I kept my eye on her as she walked away. "I have no idea."

I didn't have time to mess with Joe's sister and her cryptic messages. I had bigger issues on my list.

"Welcome back."

I turned around to face him. "It's good to be back. Even if it's only for a short time."

His face fell. "Mason'll figure something out."

"And maybe Carter Hale," I added.

"Hale's only doin' this for Skeeter, but he's still pretty good. I feel better that he took your case."

"Strangely enough, so do I." I motioned for him to go back inside. "Let's get in out of the cold."

We headed into the cozy office, and I immediately felt less anxious. With our second-hand furniture and desks made out of doors, the office was far from fancy, but it was warm and welcoming. Other than the farm, it was my favorite place to be. "Have you seen Neely Kate since Friday?"

"Only at the courthouse yesterday. She said Ronnie took another day off yesterday and insisted she stay home with him."

I frowned. "That's weird. He's not usually demanding."

"Yeah. Something's not right there."

I shrugged off my coat and threw it on my desk before sitting in my chair. "Mason is going to Little Rock today to try and pin down how he got fired. We're hoping he can find a link to J.R. Simmons there because we keep running into dead ends here. Have you heard anything about J.R. taking part in the criminal world in Fenton County?"

"If someone like J.R. had an active role, don't you think people would be talkin'?"

"True." I leaned back in my chair. "Maybe he's getting Mick to do all the work for him. If he gets Mick to take over Skeeter's kingdom and kill Mason, he won't have to get his hands dirty."

"*Kill* Mason?"

I told him about my vision, and he looked pale. "So what's Mason gonna do?"

"Nothing." Fear rose up, trying to choke me again, but I smothered it back into submission. "He says he's bein' careful, but if they want him dead and he's not in hiding, things are gonna get ugly. At least he's wearin' a gun, although the thought of Mason being involved in a shootout scares the bejiggers out of me." I took a breath to try to calm my nerves. "I think he's safer in Little Rock today than he is here, where . . ." We both knew what could happen here. Still, I was proud of myself for not breaking down while I discussed the possibility of my boyfriend's murder. "The question is why would J.R. *want* criminal ties to Fenton County? Twenty-five years ago he invested in the Atchison plant, but was he already in at the time, or was it a new venture?"

"Beats me." He shrugged, worry lines creasing his forehead.

"He's obviously here now. So what's he got his thumb in? Other than the obvious?"

"Dunno. There's not much to be had here. Not anymore. The county had a lot more money twenty-five years ago. It would have made sense for him to get out after the factory burned down."

"The town thrived back when they were drillin' oil. Maybe he's got information that one of wells is profitable. Could be he wants to take it over."

Bruce Wayne shrugged again. "Doubtful. Only a few wells are producing anything to sneeze at, and that's not very much. Especially considerin' all the trouble he's goin' to."

"So this is mostly personal. But even so, he's the type who'd want some sort of financial gain out of it."

"I don't know, Rose. All that's here in Fenton County is moonshine, drugs, and a small amount of gun trafficking. Crocker was branching out with his stolen car parts ring. I can ask around, but everyone's all riled up over the charges against Skeeter. A good number of them want Gentry to move in as the crime boss."

"But that makes no sense. Gentry's facing charges of his own."

"Rumor has it that they're about to be dropped."

I leaned forward in my seat. "What?"

"Mason's not in the courthouse to put a stop to all the bribes and other nonsense."

"And apparently, the sheriff's department is part of it too."

"Yeah."

It made me sick. All the good Mason had done for our county had been wiped away in a matter of days. "So is Gentry still in hiding?"

"For the moment."

But if the charges were dropped, we both knew he wouldn't be in hiding for long. And all hell was gonna break loose when he resurfaced.

A thought occurred to me, and I started pacing as I chewed on it. "Relatively speaking, my arrest was probably easy for him to arrange, and J.R. had the right people in power in the right places to steal Mason's job out from under him. But that double homicide south of town . . . that was set up to look like Skeeter's work. That had to take some major planning, especially if Humphrey and his guy were working with Mick Gentry. Why would he go to that much trouble?"

Bruce Wayne gave me a blank look.

Then it hit me. "Oh, my word. Maybe J.R. plans to make it look like Skeeter killed Mason. That's why he planted Skeeter's knife in his desk drawer in our house."

"And you? Where do you fit in?"

"Me? I'm just a side dish for Joe."

The office door opened, and a blast of cold air rushed in as I heard a voice I recognized all too well. "Exactly. You are a side dish, Rose Gardner. You need to remember that and move on."

I spun around, preparing myself to face my third hostile woman of the day. I was really on a roll. "Hilary, what are you doin' here?"

Looking like he'd seen a ghost, Bruce Wayne took a step back. Smart guy.

She stood in the still-open door, wearing a pair of cream pants that showed her growing baby bump and a pale pink blouse topped with a stylish cream leather jacket. Her auburn hair was long and curled, and the cold wind had given her a rosy glow. There was no denying that Hilary Wilder was a beautiful woman. Unfortunately, her inside didn't match her outside. "I wanted to check on you. A sweet little girl like you in prison for two whole days and three whole nights. You were probably scarred for life."

"Well, sorry to disappoint, but I'm just fine, so don't let the door hit you in the butt on the way out."

She ignored me and shut the door, still on my side of it. Crinkling her nose as she looked around, she said, "A very quaint place you have here. You should let Violet decorate. She's really very good, you know."

I watched her as she made her approach, wary of her real purpose for being here. "So you told me when you said you wanted to hire her to decorate your nursery."

She glanced up at me, plastering on the brightest fake smile I'd ever seen. "We met yesterday, and she was bursting with ideas of how to decorate for a boy. We just need confirmation that I'm carrying little Joseph the third before we can get started. Joe needs a little boy, don't you think?"

Violet wasn't with Hilary this morning? Then where had she been? "What Joe does or doesn't need is none of my business. Not anymore."

She gave me a condescending grin. "You're not holding the fact that he had you arrested against him, are you?"

"Hilary, between you and Kate, I'm exhausted of the games. Just tell me what you want and go away."

That made her pause. "You talked to Kate recently?"

"Oh, yeah. We're besties now. In fact, you just missed her. She stopped by for a friendly chat. You two should pool your money on a 'welcome home from jail' basket. It would be more welcome."

"You do not want to be friends with that woman."

I cocked an eyebrow at her. "Because I'd rather be friends with you?"

She looked exasperated. "Believe it or not, I'm trying to help you by helping your family. I'm giving Violet a job, which will help support her children once you're in prison. In spite of everything you've done to me."

I gasped. "Everything I've done to *you?* How deluded are you?"

She moved closer, her smile disappearing. The mad look in her eyes scared me. "You were warned to back off, and now, Rose Gardner, you are going to pay the price."

My breath caught in my throat. "What does that mean?"

"J.R. Simmons doesn't believe in mercy."

*That* I had no problem believing. The question was why she'd felt the need to enlighten me.

A ghost of a smile lifted her lips. "Luckily for you, *I* do. It would be inhuman of me to watch you languish. You may find this hard to believe, but I do have a heart. I hate to see those less fortunate than myself suffer longer than necessary."

Crappy doodles. I knew I was desperate, but not enough to accept help from this woman. "Gee, thanks, Hilary. I appreciate that, but I'm goin' to pass." I grabbed my coat off my desk. "Now if you'll excuse me, I need to pay a visit to my attorney."

She moved in front of me, blocking my path. "Stay away from Joe."

"Here's an idea: Why don't *you* tell him to stay away from *me*? Because the next time I see him, I'm not going to be responsible for what I do to him."

A sad smile spread across her face. "Poor, poor, Rose. Caught up in a game you don't understand and aren't clever enough to figure out. Fate has a funny way of choosing our paths for us, don't you think?"

She didn't wait for an answer, not that I had one to give. She spun around and walked out the door, leaving me speechless.

"What just happened?" Bruce Wayne asked several seconds after she shut the door behind her.

"I'm not exactly sure."

"Do you really think she's gonna help you?"

"No. She just likes to hear herself talk. Plus, I suspect she's convinced herself that her vague warning was actually helpful."

"This town's got more than its fair share of nuts."

"You aren't kidding," I murmured, shaking my head. "We sure don't need any more imports like Hilary and Kate."

"You really going to see Carter?"

"Yeah, I'm gonna run my theory about J.R.'s end game by him. Maybe he'll see something we're missing."

But I knew it probably wouldn't be that easy. Nothing ever was.

# Chapter Nine

Y ou need to let sleepin' dogs lie," Carter said with a groan. "You've got no business diggin' around in Mick Gentry's business. Gentry is wild, uncivilized, and dangerous. You need to leave him to Skeeter while you and Deveraux focus on Simmons."

"Skeeter ran off. Mason's hit dead end after dead end. I have Joe's sister givin' me cryptic messages and his pregnant ex-girlfriend doing the same. I'm not just gonna wait around to let someone else figure this out. I'm doin' it. Besides, Simmons and Gentry are a package deal." I was pacing his office floor, too anxious to sit still. "What I need to know is if J.R. Simmons has any ties to Fenton County other than supporting Mick Gentry and backing that contract at Atchison Manufacturing twenty-five years ago—rumored or otherwise."

"Well, there are always rumors . . ."

"Spill it."

He sat up in his chair. "You do realize that I'm supposed to be interrogating you, not the other way around." He waved his hand back and forth between us. "That's how this attorney-client thing works."

"You're hidin' things from me."

"I'm telling you everything I know that will help your case." I glared at him, and he lifted his hands in self-defense. "God's honest truth."

I stopped and put my hands on my hips. "Don't you go trying to invoke the Lord's name in this, Carter Hale. I suspect it's been so long since you set foot in a church that a choir of angels would burst into a hallelujah chorus if you did."

He chuckled. "Be that as it may, I am a God-fearin' man, and if you're smart, the fear of meetin' your maker will keep you from embarking on this foolishness."

"You said there had been rumors of J.R. bein' here. What are they?"

"Simmons' name has never come up. *Not once.* But there have been rumors of a rich businessman who has been backing certain illegal activities."

"Such as?"

"Daniel Crocker's drug business."

I narrowed my eyes. "I saw the guys who were Crocker's business partners. J.R. Simmons definitely wasn't one of them."

He snorted. "You think J.R. Simmons is going to show up at a drug deal? He's too high class to get his hands dirty. J.R. would send one of his Twelve to do his work."

I shook my head. "Wait. One of his Twelve?"

He folded his arms in front of him. "Rumor has it that J.R. Simmons has twelve men spread across the state to do his bidding."

"His enforcers?"

"No. Not ordinary criminals. These guys are special. Kind of like his inner circle, his equals."

"J.R. Simmons has equals?"

"Okay." He shrugged and unfolded his arms. "Less

than equals, but still in high regard. They're powerful in their individual kingdoms. It's said that the state is sectioned off into twelve separate areas. Each of The Twelve has their own empire, but they all answer to J.R."

"Do you think Daniel Crocker was one of his Twelve? And that's how he got his money?"

"No. I think Crocker was just a pawn."

"So none of The Twelve is in this area?"

"On the contrary. I think *Skeeter* is one of The Twelve. Or used to be."

"*What?*" The blood rushed from my head, and I sat down in a chair in front of his desk. "*Skeeter?*"

"I don't know for certain, but I wouldn't be surprised. He left Henryetta when he was eighteen. He came back at twenty-five with enough money to open his pool hall."

"You think he was with J.R.?"

"Not that he'd tell anyone, and I mean *anyone*, even Jed, his best friend."

"Skeeter says he doesn't have friends."

"Skeeter can't see what's right in front of him." Carter kept his gaze on me. "If Skeeter has a critical flaw, it's that he looks too far into the future. He doesn't always give the immediate present the attention it deserves."

"That doesn't sound like Skeeter at all."

"I'm talkin' about people, not about situations."

I didn't like where this conversation was going. "If he left for seven years, where did he say he went?"

"Memphis. He said that's where he made his seed money. But I know for a fact he started that pool hall with cash. So I don't buy it."

"What did he say when you asked him about it?"

He snorted again. "I'm not stupid enough to ask."

*I* was definitely going to ask him the first chance I got. If Carter was right, it sure would explain why Skeeter had been so interested in my connection to J.R. Simmons. And also why J.R. wanted Skeeter dead. And maybe—just maybe—Skeeter had a shot at digging up the information that would bring J.R. down.

But I wasn't about to tell Carter Hale any of that.

"So the only thing you have that makes you presume Skeeter was part of J.R.'s secret circle is that he disappeared for seven years and came back with money? That seems like a stretch."

"No. That's not it. For the first few years after he came back, he'd run off for several days to a week at a time with no warning. And he never told anyone where he went. Not even Jed. Then about five years ago, it just stopped. No more trips."

"And you think he quit?"

"Yeah, although from what I can tell, that's damn near impossible. You don't retire from The Twelve. You are eliminated."

"So how is Skeeter still alive? Doesn't that fact negate your theory?"

Carter shrugged, but the answer had already come to me.

"J.R. Simmons waited until Skeeter had something worth taking."

Carter narrowed his eyes. "What are you talking about?"

"Skeeter just got his kingdom, right?"

"Yeah . . ."

112

"Mason said J.R. likes to make people suffer, and Joe didn't disagree. Wouldn't it be much worse for Skeeter to finally get control, only to see it stolen from him?" I'd told Skeeter the very same thing a few hours before my arrest. But now I was even more certain of it.

Carter pursed his lips, not looking happy. "If you're right, that's not the only thing Simmons will want to take from him."

The hair on the back of my neck stood on end. "The Lady in Black." But I knew that too. My plan to force J.R. to meet me was undoubtedly the most foolish thing I'd ever considered, but it might just work.

"You need to keep a low profile," Carter said, shifting behind his desk. "As both Rose *and* the Lady in Black."

"No," I said, already shaking my head. "I can't do that."

"Maybe you should trust Skeeter to take care of the situation."

That made my blood boil. "With all due respect, Mr. Hale, I have no earthly idea what Skeeter Malcolm is up to since he hasn't deemed it necessary to tell me. For all I know, he's holed up in a shack with blonde twins with big boobs, waiting for everything to die down."

Carter tried to hide the grin tugging at his mouth.

"Your reaction tells me it's not outside the realm of possibility."

He stood. "Rose, I can assure you that's not the case. Skeeter was genuinely upset when you were arrested. There's no way he's enjoying his time out of town with a couple of playmates while he thinks you might be going to jail."

"I would hope he's also trying to save himself."

He grinned. "I believe it was you who told me, 'Save one of us, you save us all.'"

"*I* was talking about *me*."

He laughed. "I had no idea you had such an ego, Rose Gardner. Skeeter's fascination with you becomes clearer and clearer every minute."

I was about to offer a retort, but my phone started to ring. It was Neely Kate's tone, and as I pulled it out, I realized I was late for my lunch. I turned off the ringer and glanced up at Carter. "I have to go, but before I do, I got a burner phone—at Jed's suggestion. I've texted Skeeter and Jed the new number. Do you need it?"

"No. I want to keep everything between us above board, but *theoretically* it's better to restrict any conversations that carry a hint of criminal intent or association to an untraceable phone."

I nodded and started for the door.

"Rose."

I stopped and turned to see what he wanted.

"You and I have discussed several topics that shouldn't be tied back to me."

"You mean your theory about Skeeter's past." I cocked my head. "You weren't even practicing law ten years ago. How do you know so much about Skeeter's behavior before he hired you?"

His expression hardened slightly, and his good old boy persona faded. I suspected this was the real Carter Hale, lurking under the surface. "I make it my business to know as much about my clients as humanly possible. And believe me, I'm good at my job."

With one hand on the doorknob, I narrowed my eyes at him. "If you're so stinkin' good, tell me what you found out about Glenn Stout."

His eyes clouded, and I snorted. "That's what I thought. Goodbye, Mr. Hale."

Greta shot me a questioning glance when I walked into the waiting area, and I waved goodbye as I walked through the door in turmoil. I was certain Carter was the best attorney to help me, but I couldn't rely on him to save me.

I was gonna have to save myself.

I was taking the lead on this, and for the first time in my life, I felt like I was totally in control. False murder charges and a possible incarceration aside.

Neely Kate was sitting at a table at Merilee's Café with a glass of tea in front of her and a glass of water in front of my seat. She lifted her eyebrows in reprimand. "You're late."

"I was talking to Carter Hale."

"Oh." She seemed contrite, which made me realize she had been genuinely upset with me. That was totally unlike her, so something was definitely going on.

"Bruce Wayne said Ronnie asked you to stay home with him yesterday."

She picked up her glass of tea. "Yep." The word, delivered as crisp and as sharp as a tack through a sheet of paper, told me a whole lot more than a lengthy explanation.

"He's just scared, Neely Kate. And worried about you."

"Last week I would have agreed with you. On Friday, he was smothering me, yet I knew he was only worried about how I was reacting to losing the babies. But yesterday . . . I have no idea what *that* was about."

"What are you talking about?"

"He was upset when I went to see Joe after I found out you were arrested because he was worried I'd get into trouble with the sheriff's department. But he seemed to deal with it, especially since we stayed home the whole weekend, other than me takin' Mason his casserole. Ronnie was acting weird, but I didn't take much notice. Then yesterday he said he was staying home again and insisted that I do the same. He blew a gasket when I told him I was goin' to see you at the courthouse for your arraignment." Her eyes bugged wide. "He actually *forbade* me to go! Can you imagine?"

I cringed. I preferred not to let my mind wander to how *that* had played out.

She whipped her hair over her shoulder, fire in her eyes. "I put that man in his place right then and there. No one forbids me to do *anything*."

"Did he say why?"

Anger filled her eyes. "Yes."

"So?" When she didn't say anything, I prodded. "Are you gonna tell me?"

"Wouldn't you rather hear about breakin' into the safe?"

I gasped. With everything that had happened this morning, it had slipped my mind. "Did you get it open?"

"No. My nitwit cousin didn't have the right tools. He says he can try again in about an hour. Which is why we need to hurry lunch along."

Mason and I had agreed to stay out of this part, but my meeting with Carter had left me unsettled. I needed to do something or I would burst. Besides, in the scheme of unlawful things to do, this was on the low end of trouble. Probably. "I'm goin' with you."

She gave me a pointed look. "You sure that's a good idea?"

"Is Witt gonna tell anyone I watched him commit an illegal activity? I don't think so. I'm goin'."

The waitress came to take our order, then left us in silence.

"Was it awful getting arrested and being in jail?"

"Yes. And no." I told her everything about the weekend, even about my near-miss with Janie. "I can't go to prison, Neely Kate. I just can't."

She patted my hand as our lunch showed up. "Don't worry. We're gonna make sure that doesn't happen." Then she gave me a grin. "Speakin' of getting out of jail, I have a surprise for you."

I gave her a leery glance. "What is it?"

She dug her phone out of her purse and opened an app before handing it to me. I looked down at a photo of a guy wearing a red ball cap, a T-shirt with a logo for a small brewery, and a pair of jeans with a ginormous belt buckle. He was standing on the opposite side of a counter, and even though he was looking to the side, it was easy to see he was a very good-looking man. I leaned closer and realized there was a light brown birthmark on his cheek.

I glanced up at her, lifting my eyebrows in question.

"It's the guy who posted your bail. I convinced Nita to send me the photo she took." Her grin spread. "So now we don't have to try and find a mugshot."

When we finished lunch, we got into my truck and headed toward the factory.

"Do you really think Paul Buchanan is your father?"

I shook my head. "I've had lots of time to think about it. Dora wasn't sure which of them was my father, although it sure sounded like she was hoping it was Paul. But how could Harrison Gardner not be my father? My daddy's mother had the same visions I do."

"I wonder what would have happened if Paul had left his wife and married your momma," Neely Kate said.

I stopped her musings. "It won't do any good to think about it. All it does is make me sad. What's done is done."

Neely Kate grabbed my hand resting on the seat and squeezed it. "You've got friends and family who love you now, Rose. I know you think all those years were wasted, but they helped make you who you are today."

Tears stung my eyes. "And I'm so grateful. But it doesn't take away the hurt of what Momma did to me. And what makes it worse is how many people just stood back and watched—Aunt Bessie and Uncle Earl, Daddy, and Hattie." I shook my head. "I just can't believe it."

"It's over now, and that hateful woman who called herself your momma is gone."

"But she's not," I said, casting a glance at my best friend. "She's haunting me now from the grave, threatening to destroy everything I've been blessed with since she died."

"You hush," Neely Kate scoffed, curling her upper

lip. "That hateful woman's not stealin' a thing. I made you a promise, and I mean to see it through. We'll get this sorted out."

Witt's beat-up red pickup was parked behind the factory. I pulled up next to him, and he hopped out of his truck, a toolbox in hand and a lopsided grin on his face.

"Hey, Rose," he said as we walked over to him. "How ya holdin' up?"

I cocked my head. "I'll be better if we find anything helpful in this safe."

"Well, let's get to it," he said, taking off behind the building. "I've gotta get back to the garage."

I gave Neely Kate a questioning look.

"Witt works with Ronnie at the mechanic's shop."

"How's Ronnie feeling?" he asked, traipsing through weeds. "He must have some kind of flu to be gone this long."

Neely Kate's mouth parted. "What are you talking about?"

Witt glanced back at her. "He's called in sick since last Friday."

She slowly shook her head. "He's not sick. He was taking time off to be with me."

Witt cringed. "Don't worry. I won't tell our boss. Besides, he'd never suspect Ronnie of lying."

"So he's not there today?" she asked in dismay.

Witt looked like he'd been caught with his hand in the cookie jar. "I think I need to stop talkin' now."

Worry furrowed Neely Kate's brow, but she didn't ask any more questions. We followed Witt until he stopped outside the window Mason and I had used to get in the day before. I helped Neely Kate through, worried about her overexerting herself after her surgery a few weeks earlier.

"This place is even creepier than when we were kids partying here," she said.

Witt laughed. "We were young and stupid. It's probably because of that Halloween party the Jorgensen twins hosted."

She shook her head. "Yeah. Maybe." Then she cast a glance at the bloodstained floor. "Or maybe it's knowing that two people died here a few days ago."

"Hey," Witt said, sucking in a breath and glancing around the space. "Do you think their ghosts are still here?"

"No," Neely Kate said matter-of-factly. "I'd know if they were."

I'd forgotten, but Neely Kate had decided that communicating with ghosts was her newest paranormal gift. I sure hoped she was right, because I had no desire to see Beverly Buchanan again, especially as a ghost.

When we got into the office, Witt put Neely Kate and me to work. Neely Kate held up an industrial-size flashlight and shined the beam on the safe while Witt put me in charge of handing him tools.

"I'm using this saw first," he said. "But I'm likely to go through a couple of blades and battery packs since this steel is pretty dang solid."

"Okay."

"Then I'll use the crowbar to pry it open."

"Sounds good."

He didn't waste any time getting to work. I could see where he'd tried to cut it open the night before. Several deep grooves were already gouged into the metal.

Witt seemed pleased to have made it through the partially cut side and a good ways into the next before the battery started slowing down. He pried off the battery pack and reached for another.

"This blade's working three times as fast as the one I used last night. We'll get it done in no time."

He got back to work, and I studied my best friend. She was holding the flashlight steady with one hand, but she kept staring longingly at the phone in her other.

"Neely Kate, go ahead," I said over the whine of the saw. "Go call him."

She handed me the light, flashed me a worried smile, and left the office.

Witt glanced over his shoulder as she left, then returned to his task. This time he made it through one and a half more cuts before the saw began to slow. I was already reaching for a new battery by the time he turned it off.

"What do you really think's goin' on with Ronnie?" I asked, wondering if I was overstepping my bounds, but too worried about Neely Kate to care.

"You want my honest opinion?"

"Yeah."

"Ronnie's a great guy, but some of the guys in his poker group are trouble."

"What does that mean?"

He grimaced and cast a look at the open door as he changed the saw blade. "Other than your weekend in the Fenton County Jail, I know you're pretty far removed from the crime world, breaking into safes aside." He grinned and winked. "There's big trouble on the horizon. Skeeter Malcolm's in charge, but some of the guys think Skeeter's a coward who ran off at the first sign of trouble. There's another guy who's telling everyone they need someone like him, someone who's strong enough to stand up to trouble."

My stomach cramped. "And what are the guys saying about that?"

"Skeeter's still pretty new, but they've known him for years. Besides, he didn't shake things up too much after taking over, and some of the Skeeter supporters think Gentry's a hothead who would do the exact opposite."

"Mick Gentry?" I asked, deciding that playing dumb would be the best way to get information. "He was a big animal vet before the police issued a warrant to arrest him for murdering the bank loan officer."

"Yep, that's him."

"Well, he ran off right quick. How's that any different from Skeeter running off because the sheriff wants to arrest him for the murders south of town?"

Witt narrowed his eyes.

I gave him a shrug. "I heard things in jail."

He pursed his lips and nodded.

"So what does all of this have to do with Ronnie?"

"The garage owner . . . let's say he's been known to pull a fast one or two from time to time. But he's a smart guy—he pledges his loyalty to the man in charge, who is currently Malcolm. But some of the guys from the shop— the ones in the poker game group—are siding with Gentry. I think Ronnie has gotten caught up in the middle of the mess."

"But Ronnie, he's not part of that world."

He gave me a sad smile. "Rose, everybody working at Ted's Garage in Pickle Junction is part of that world. Heck, it's part of the job. We all do odd jobs now and then, if you know what I mean."

Ronnie was mixed up in criminal activity? I felt like I was going to throw up. "Does Neely Kate know that?"

He caught his bottom lip between his teeth as he gave the drill more attention than necessary. "No. I don't think so."

"Witt, you have to tell her."

He shook his head. "No way. I'm not getting involved."

"She has a right to know."

"Well, I ain't gonna be the one to tell her. She's my favorite cousin, and I'm not screwing that up."

"Fine, I'll tell her myself."

He resumed his work and had made it to the fourth side of the safe before Neely Kate returned with red eyes. With any luck at all, Ronnie had confessed the truth of his situation, but I suspected it wouldn't be that easy.

She took back the flashlight, and within a couple more minutes, Witt had made all of his cuts and turned off the saw.

"Crowbar," he said, holding out his hand.

I took the saw and gave him the metal bar.

"It's like opening a can of sardines," Witt chuckled as he started to pry the safe open. "What are you hoping to find?"

"Papers about her birth father," Neely Kate grumbled. "Not that it's any of your damn business."

"Hey," Witt said, holding up his hands. "Don't shoot the messenger, cuz."

"It's probably just papers," I said, hoping to ease the tension between them. "But I'm hoping there's more."

Witt gave the crowbar a good yank, and a grin spread across his face as the metal curled back. "You said you were looking for more. You're about to get your wish."

# Chapter Ten

W ell?" Neely Kate demanded. "What did you find?"

He reached into the safe and pulled out a handgun.

"Oh, my stars and garters," Neely Kate gasped.

Witt handed it toward me, but I took a step back.

He tilted his head. "The way I hear it, you're after the contents of this safe and this was in it."

I hesitantly reached for it, surprised at how heavy it was. "What do I do with it?"

Neely Kate handed me the flashlight and carefully took it from me. She pressed a button and the clip popped out. "Yep. It's loaded."

I shivered.

Neely Kate looked up at me. "You should keep it, Rose. You need protection from everything that's goin' on."

"I can't right now. I have to think about it."

She searched my face, and the hardness in her eyes softened. "Okay. I'll hold onto it for now." She opened the purse she had looped over her shoulder and put the gun inside.

"Do you want to see what else is in here?" Witt asked impatiently.

"Yeah." But my mind was still reeling as to why Henry Buchanan had been hiding a loaded gun in his office. Then again, my mind didn't have to search very hard for the reason.

Witt took the flashlight from me and shined it inside the opening before he reached inside and pulled out a stack of money.

"Oh, my word," I said, looking over at Neely Kate. "I can't keep that."

"Of course you can."

"No. I can't! That money belongs to Henry Buchanan's family."

Her eyes widened. "Uh. Yeah. And Henry and Beverly were sure you were part of the Buchanan family."

I handed it to Neely Kate. "I'll sort this out later."

"Okay."

I steeled my back. "What else is in there?"

He pulled out a manila folder and handed it to me.

I opened the file, prepared to find just about anything. On top was a title to a 1980 Lincoln Continental. Underneath that was a copy of Henry's life insurance policy for $750,000, which had been paid to his trust. I flipped to the next page and found the document Hattie had been looking for, naming Rose Anne Gardner as his third beneficiary.

That was low on my priority list.

There was one more paper, and I flipped the legal document over to get a look at it, hoping it was something helpful.

It was a photocopy of a page from the journal Joe had taken from me.

I closed my eyes and pushed out a breath of relief.

"Rose?" Neely Kate asked. "What did you find?"

I turned to face her. "What I was looking for."

"Evidence to tie J.R. to something criminal?"

I nodded. "It's a photocopy of a page from the journal."

"Get out of town!" Her face bright with excitement, Neely Kate grabbed the edge of the folder and pulled it toward her, but her expression changed as she scanned the page. "It's in jibberish."

"It's shorthand. And the journal is full of it."

"So you have no idea what it says?"

"I just need to find someone who can read shorthand." Neely Kate started to speak, but I held up a finger. "Someone who can keep a secret."

Neely Kate rolled her eyes.

"I'm gonna give it to Mason when he gets back."

"But he won't be back for hours. And besides, why do you have to get his *permission?* Just get it translated on your own."

I gasped. "Neely Kate, what in the world has gotten into you? I never said I was asking his permission. I'm waiting to ask *my boyfriend*—the former assistant district attorney—his *legal advice* on how to handle this."

Tears filled her eyes. "You're right. I'm sorry."

She was in worse shape than I'd thought. "This place is unnerving." I reached for her hand and squeezed, then looked back at her cousin. "Is there anything else in there?"

"Just a key." He pulled it out and placed it in my open palm.

I wasn't all that surprised to see it was another house key. "Nothing else?" I asked. "Nothing to tell me what the key goes to?"

"Not unless it's in that folder."

"Not that I can see, but that's okay. Thanks for helping, Witt." I shifted my weight. "Do you want me to pay you?"

His eyes lit up, but Neely Kate shot him a glare.

He tried to hide a grin. "No, ma'am."

"Do you need us to stick around and help you pack everything?" I asked.

"I'm good." He looked at Neely Kate, then nodded. "It's gonna be okay, NK."

When she didn't answer him, I put my arm around Neely Kate's shoulders. "Then let's get out of here." I guided her out of the office, and we made our way out of the window and back to the truck.

The truck was cold, so I let the engine run for a minute while I pulled out my phone and texted Mason.

*Any luck in LR?*

He answered within seconds. *No*

I grinned, knowing my news would cheer him up. *We got what we needed from the box. One page copy from the book. Need translation.*

I sent the text, hoping he would understand my cryptic message.

*Great! I'll find a translator.*

"Well, there you have it," I said, backing out of the parking lot. "Mason said he'll find someone to translate."

Neely Kate made a face, then looked out the side window.

"Do you need to head home?" I asked as I pulled out of the parking lot.

She kept her eyes on the windshield. "No."

"What did he say, Neely Kate?"

"He told me he's at work."

"Did he leave this morning at the same time?"

"I dunno. He stayed at his friend's house last night."

"Why?"

She glanced at me like I was a fool. "I told you that he forbade me to go the courthouse. It came with an ultimatum. If I left, he wouldn't be there when I came home."

"Oh, Neely Kate."

She turned to look at me with hard eyes. "Don't you be feeling guilty. This has nothing to do with you."

"It has everything to do with me!"

Her eyes narrowed. "I had no idea you were such a narcissist, Rose Gardner."

I couldn't help laughing. "First Carter Hale accuses me of having a huge ego, then you call me a narcissist. Maybe it's time to reevaluate myself."

"Rose," she groaned, leaning her head against the back of the seat.

"Look, it's not hard to figure out. I was arrested, Neely Kate. I spent the weekend in jail. And not only that, I'm constantly getting into trouble. I can understand why he's worried."

A tear leaked out of the corner of her eye.

"Neely Kate." I tried to keep my voice strong. "I think you should go back home."

She sat up so fast it was as if she'd been struck by lightning. "Are you trying to get rid of me, Rose?"

Without a word, I pulled the truck to the side of the road and threw the gear shift into park before I turned to her. "Let me make this perfectly clear: You are like a sister to me. I am here for you no matter what. I will never, ever try to get rid of you. Do I make myself clear?"

"You just said you wanted to take me back home."

"Because I don't want to ever get in the way of you and Ronnie."

More tears fell down her cheeks. "I don't know if there's still a me and Ronnie."

"Don't be silly. We all say things in the heat of the moment that we don't mean. You wouldn't believe some of the arguments Mason and I have had."

"This is different, Rose. Mason never left you."

"Mason *almost* left me twice."

Her mouth dropped. "What?"

"Once after Joe kissed me and another time too. Mason knew J.R. was gonna have me arrested sooner rather than later, and he couldn't find anything big enough to stop him. He wanted to find dirt on Joe to use it as leverage—if J.R. used his fabricated evidence on me, Mason would release the information about Joe's past, including his DUIs and assault charges."

She turned to face me, a new look of purpose in her eyes. "So why doesn't he release all that now?"

"Because I stopped him. I wouldn't let him look. I said we'd be stooping to J.R.'s level if we did that."

Her eyes widened in horror. "Are you crazy? They are nothing alike. Joe actually committed those crimes. Yours are all made up."

I grabbed her hand, pleading with her. "But Joe was trying to change, and I just couldn't do that to him."

Fire seemed about ready to shoot out of her eyes. "Yeah, he's changed all right. He used to be a snake in the grass, and now he's slitherin' out in the open."

I sat back in the seat, feeling like a fool. "Was it all a lie, Neely Kate?" I asked, my voice softer. "Did he ever love me?"

"I don't know. I thought he did, but maybe he was like a kindergartner who wanted the new, bright and shiny toy so bad he'd do anything to get it, especially if someone else wanted it. Then when he realized he wasn't gonna get you back, he decided to go along with his father."

I shook my head. "That just doesn't sound like the man I know. He'd been changing. He was tryin' so hard."

"I don't know. I wish I had answers for you, honey. I don't even have 'em for myself."

I laughed even though tears stung my eyes. "Well, we're a fine lot, aren't we?"

"We're a mess."

Now that I'd expressed my dismay over Joe, my long-suppressed fear rose up and burst lose. "I'm gonna lose Mason."

"How can you say that? He was so upset this weekend, Rose. You have no idea. I made him take a short rest while I warmed up that casserole for him. He loves you so much."

My chin quivered. "He's puttin' it all together. He knows I'm not tellin' him everything. I'm not sure how much longer I can keep it from him."

"The Lady in Black?"

I nodded.

"Can't you just stop?"

"I can't." I wiped a tear off my cheek with the back of my hand. "J.R. Simmons is bent on ruining Mason and Skeeter through Mick Gentry, and I can't let him do it. I have to stop them."

"How do you propose to do that?"

"I asked Jed to set up a meeting between Lady and Mick. And when I meet him, I'll tell him I want to meet his big boss. If my theory is correct, J.R. will be tempted to take the meeting."

"And what's your theory?"

"That this is personal between Skeeter and J.R. Joe's father wants to steal away everything that matters to Skeeter."

"His business . . . and the Lady."

"Yeah."

"That's plum crazy, Rose. He's gonna kill you!"

"Not if I have help. Jed will go with me as protection."

"And so will I."

I sat up faster than a jack-in-the-box. "Now you're the crazy one. You're not goin' into a meeting with criminals!"

"Why not? You are."

I shook my head in frustration. "That's different!"

"How is it different? If anything, I'm safer than you are. I'll go as your assistant. Or your other bodyguard."

"What if someone recognizes you?"

"Who's gonna recognize me? I'll wear a wig. I got a whole closet full of 'em. And I've got my own gun. With the gun from the safe, now I have two of them."

"*Neely Kate.*"

"It's not *that* crazy. Not any crazier than you askin' Jed to set up the meeting. Besides, you'll feel better havin' extra protection, and you know it."

"I can't let you!"

She shuddered and jutted her head back. "You don't have a say in this. I'm goin'."

"What about Ronnie?"

"Ronnie can stick it up his backside."

"Neely Kate."

"Do you know when you're meetin' Mick?"

"No, but I told Jed the sooner the better. Tonight would be best because Mason won't be back from Little Rock until late. I won't have to explain my leaving. Just my comin' back."

She waved toward the road. "Well, then let's get goin'. We have to run by my house to get your Lady in Black clothes, if nothing else." She shot me a wicked grin, and she knew she had me. I needed my outfit to go to the meeting, but I still hoped to talk her out of coming.

Neely Kate was a bit bubblier during the drive, talking about what her persona should be. I kept quiet, foolishly thinking my silence would discourage her. She took my silence and ran with it.

My only hope was that the meeting would be set for another day. It didn't seem terribly likely I'd be able to ditch her if it ended up being tonight.

Since Ronnie wasn't at work, I wondered if he'd be home, and I spent a good portion of the drive planning what I'd say if I saw him. While I understood why he wanted to keep me away from his wife, I'd be lying if I said it didn't hurt. But the house was quiet and empty.

I followed Neely Kate toward her bedroom, but she stopped for a spell at the door to the second bedroom.

My stomach clenched as I realized what had caught her notice. "Oh, Neely Kate."

The room had a white crib, dresser, and rocking chair. The walls were painted a cheery yellow, and the bedding was a pale green and yellow sherbet color. The last time I'd seen this room was a week before she lost the babies. Back then, it had still been a guest room.

"I didn't think you'd decorated yet. I thought Ronnie was makin' you wait."

Her voice was tight. "He was. But I did it anyway."

"I'm so sorry." I wrapped an arm around her waist and buried my cheek into her shoulder.

"He's not comin' home tonight. I don't think I can stay here alone."

I spun her around to face me. "Then you won't. Pack a bag for a couple of days until Ronnie Colson comes to his senses." I pursed my lips and shook my head. "What in tarnation is goin' on with the men in this county? First Joe. Then Ronnie. It's like there's something in the water."

"If only that were the explanation."

The look in her eyes was so pathetic that I pulled her away from the doorway and shut the door. "Come on. I have a craving for ice cream."

"But it's freezin' outside."

"So what? You know I never do things like everyone else. Let's get you packed, grab my clothes, and get out of here. Deal?"

She threw her arms around my shoulders and pulled me close. "Deal."

"I love you, Neely Kate. We're gonna get through this. The both of us."

She nodded, her tear-streaked cheek brushing against my neck. "Yeah."

When she let me go, I grabbed her face between my hands. "You can stay with me as long as you'd like, okay?"

Her bottom lip trembled. "Thank you."

"Now let's get packin'."

Apparently Neely Kate had a different idea of what "packing" entailed. She headed straight for her room and pulled a shoebox off the top shelf in her closet. After setting it on the bed, she took off the lid and pulled out a revolver. She flipped out the barrel bullet chamber, and then flipped it back closed.

"I'm not sure that's necessary."

Her gaze jerked up to mine. "It's completely necessary. And I have a concealed carry permit, so don't you be worryin' about that part."

"Neely Kate."

Her eyebrows rose so high she looked like she'd gotten a facelift. "You're in a dangerous situation, and you need someone to protect you. Trust me. I know what I'm doin'."

She seemed so adamant, I found myself nodding my head.

"In fact," she said, laying the gun on her nightstand, then grabbing a duffel bag out of the closet, "I think you need to learn to fire a gun yourself."

"I already fired a gun. I shot Daniel Crocker twice."

She stopped and put her hand on her hip. "And did it feel natural to you?"

"No, of course not."

A smirk lit up her eyes. "Then we still have work to do."

I considered fighting her on it, but the more I thought about it, the more I thought learning to shoot was a good idea. "Okay," I said with a shrug. "We'll do it."

Her face lit up like a Christmas tree. If I'd realized how happy this would make her, I would have suggested it weeks ago.

She quickly finished stuffing her bag full of clothes and toiletries, then reached into the back of her closet and pulled out a pink backpack with white polka dots and handed it to me.

My glance bounced back and forth between the bag and her face.

"You'll be needing that later." Then she retrieved another small bag and stuffed it with a black wig, a pair of black boots, and several items of clothing—all black.

"Other than the black dress you loaned me on Thanksgiving Day, I didn't know you owned anything black." Neely Kate was known for her colorful—and often bejeweled—wardrobe.

"You have your secrets. I have my own." She hefted the bags onto her shoulders and walked out of the room with more confidence and purpose than she'd exuded in weeks.

What secrets was she talking about?

We hefted the bags onto the back seat of my truck and headed back to town. Midway through the drive, I cast a glance at her. "So have you decided who you'll be if you come with the Lady in Black?"

She turned to me in genuine surprise. "You've finally agreed to the idea?"

"No, but I confess you've piqued my curiosity."

A sly grin spread across her face. "No one needs to know what role I have. Only that I'm there." She turned to face the road. "Where do you want to go for ice cream?"

*That* was a very good question. Owing to Hilary's antics, we'd been banned from the Emporium, a business that consistently changed its purpose but was currently a coffee shop and ice cream store.

"I guess we can't go the Emporium, but Burger Shack seems like a bad idea."

"Because of what happened to Eric."

The assistant manager, Eric Davidson, had been found dead in his garage with his car running, so the police had deemed it a suicide. On the surface, it sounded plausible. Eric had thought he was about to be arrested for trying to run Mason off the road with the intent to kill him. The whole thing stank like week-old fish, but true to Henryetta P.D. style, they'd picked the path of least resistance. Eric was dead, so no one was fighting their explanation of events.

I suspected Eric had been murdered to keep him quiet. The real question was who had done it.

"On second thought," I said, an idea hitting me, "Burger Shack is exactly where we need to go."

# Chapter Eleven

I thought this place gave you the creeps after they found Eric smoking his last bong before he found his big one in sky," Neely Kate said.

"Neely Kate." I shot her a dirty look. "It still does, but I never bought Detective Taylor's explanation about Eric's death. Maybe we could ask a few questions."

Neely Kate turned to me in surprise. "You want to ask questions a month after the incident?"

"Yeah, it can't hurt, right?"

"Sounds good to me, but what are you hoping to find?"

"A clue to help us figure out who killed him."

"I know we're good and all, but how many mysteries do you expect us to solve at one time?"

"They're all connected, Neely Kate. I just know it."

"Okay," she drawled. "Since you feel so strongly about this one, I'll let you take the lead."

"Good," I said, flashing a smile. A couple of months ago, I would have shied away from this. Now I was eager to find answers. "But I need to check in with Mason."

I pulled my phone out of my purse to text him again, but the burner phone caught my eye first. I frowned when I saw I had missed a text from Jed.

*We're on. Tonight. Our usual spot. Eight-thirty.*

"It's tonight," I said, sounding breathless. "We're gonna meet Jed at eight-thirty."

"You're lettin' me come?" Excitement filled her voice.

"What? No!"

"You just said *we're* gonna meet Jed. Not *I'm*. You want me to come. Just admit it."

I snuck a glance at her, worrying my bottom lip. "It's selfish and wrong of me to bring you."

Her smile fell, and she grew serious. "No. We're partners. And we're good at this. You need me now more than ever. Who else will have your back?"

"*Jed* will have my back. He was there with me when I met Hattie on Friday."

Her mouth made a perfect O. "Why would Jed be there? Were you meeting her as Lady?"

"No," I scowled. "Skeeter convinced me to call Jed if I thought I needed backup . . . even in my personal life. Hattie was desperate for me to meet her there with the coded journal, but she just seemed kind of crazy. It seemed equally crazy to agree, but I wanted answers. So I called Jed and asked him to stay in the shadows as backup."

"He didn't do a very good job," she grumbled.

"He saved my life and got shot in the process."

"What?"

"He tried to tackle me to keep Beverly from shooting me. Every time I'm the Lady in Black, Jed is always there, watchin' over me. Protectin' me . . . even from Skeeter." I paused, holding her gaze. "I trust him with my life." I didn't tell her that Skeeter had effectively made him my bodyguard by instructing him to protect my life above all others—even Skeeter's. I wasn't sure how she'd react to that. *I* still wasn't sure how to react to that.

She stuck out her bottom lip. "Well, I still want to come."

I took a deep breath. Bringing her seemed so wrong, yet something deep inside told me I needed her. Maeve had told me to trust my instincts, so I was doing just that. "Okay. I suspect if I tell you no, you'll do something crazy and get hurt trying to sneak up on us." I narrowed my eyes. "Jed won't be happy."

"Too bad."

"Nevertheless, he's in charge of watchin' my back. You'll do as he says."

A smug grin lit up her eyes with mischief.

I pointed my finger at her nose. "I know that look. This is non-negotiable, Neely Kate. Jed has experience with these guys, and I suspect they'll find you expendable." I shivered at the thought. "Jed will tell you what to do to help keep both of us safe."

She scowled. "Fine."

"Promise me!"

She rolled her eyes and held up her pinky finger. After I locked mine with hers, she lifted her eyebrows and said with plenty of sass, "Pinky promise. Happy?"

"No," I said, dropping my hand. "But it'll have to do. Now let's go look for answers about Eric."

We walked inside and headed to the counter. I was happy to see there were only two other people in the restaurant, an older couple reading a newspaper together while they nursed their soft drinks.

I hadn't been in since Eric's death, and it felt strange

not to see him there. While I knew he'd robbed several places trying to get money to outbid Skeeter, he'd never struck me as a murderer. Maybe I could help clear his name if he were truly innocent.

An older teen stood in front of a register. His nametag read Eugene. "Welcome to Burger Shack. May I take your order, please?" He couldn't have sounded more bored if he had been reading the ingredients off a cereal box.

"I'll take a hot fudge sundae," I said, then glanced back at Neely Kate.

"Vanilla ice cream mixed with Oreo cookies, then drizzled with chocolate syrup, but not too much. Three cherries on top. Not one. Not two. Not even four. Three." She leaned forward. "It better be exactly as I ordered it, Eugene. If you get any of it wrong, you'll have to start all over again."

The guy gave her a dumbfounded stare. "Wow. You sure do take your ice cream seriously."

She put her hand on her hip and cocked her head. "You have no idea."

He rang us up, casting worried glances at Neely Kate. She gave me a wink when he was counting the change, which was when I realized what she'd done. She'd just bought me more time to question him.

She was right. We really did make a great team.

I leaned my hip into the counter as the kid started to make my sundae. "Say . . . I haven't seen Eric in ages. Where's he been?"

His eyes flew open. "Oh. You mean Eric Davidson?"

I shrugged. "I guess. I didn't know his last name. Just that he was an assistant manager. I love a man with power

141

and authority, you know?" I gave him a knowing grin. "It doesn't hurt that he's also cute . . . mmm. Do you know if he has a girlfriend?" I tried not to flinch as I posed the question. It felt all kinds of wrong lying about a dead man.

"I bet he ain't lookin' so cute now," the guy said with a scowl.

"Why the heck not?" Neely Kate asked.

"He's six feet under."

I pressed my hand to my chest in feigned surprise. "What? What happened?"

"He killed himself." He shook his head. "Went into his garage and smoked his last reefer, if you know what I mean."

Neely Kate gave me a smug grin.

"That doesn't seem like the guy I knew," I said thoughtfully. "He told me he had some big plan in the works. It was gonna make him a ton of money."

He laughed, but it was short. "Yeah, he always had some big plan in the works. Right before Thanksgiving, he said he was about to hit it big. He thought it was gonna be his last week to work. He was so certain he wouldn't be comin' back, he put in his notice, but he was beggin' for his job on Monday morning, sure as shoot."

That backed up my theory that Eric hadn't been all that bright. "Did he say what he was countin' on?"

He set my ice cream on the counter, then grabbed a cup for Neely Kate's. "Nope, but he had a new plan a few weeks later. He told me the last guys were losers. He was sure these new guys were gonna help him make it big."

I tried to contain my confusion over his statement. Mick Gentry had been the ringleader of the group responsible for the robberies, and their aim had been to win the Fenton County underworld out from under Skeeter. I'd assumed Eric had stayed in allegiance with Mick, but now I wasn't so sure. Did this mean someone else was involved in the plan against Mason and Skeeter?

"So what happened?" Neely Kate asked after I'd been silent for a beat too long.

"It must have all fallen through. He didn't want to look like a loser, so he killed himself."

I jumped in with a question. "Do you have any idea what the second thing was about? He told me he was working for some really powerful guy."

He laughed again and turned his back to us as he started to fill the cup with ice cream. "Yeah, he told me the same thing."

"Only fill it halfway," Neely Kate told him in a bossy tone. "Then put in the crushed cookies . . . they are crushed, aren't they?"

He gave her a look that told us his true thoughts regarding her request, but said in a polite tone, "Yes, ma'am."

"Ma'am?" Neely Kate screeched. "Did you just call me *ma'am*? Do I look like an old woman to you?"

"No, ma'am." Panic filled his eyes, and his hands began to shake. "I mean miss."

"How old do you think I am?"

His panic increased, and it was obvious he was in fight or flight mode—leaning heavily toward flight. There was no right answer to that question. "Uh . . . twenty?"

"That's pretty doggone close, so does that sound like a *ma'am* to you?" She spat out *ma'am* as though it was synonymous with slug.

He shook his head violently. "No, miss."

She pointed her finger at him. "That's right. I'm a *miss*, and don't you forget it."

"Yes, ma'am . . . I mean miss," he added hastily as he turned his attention to the cookies he was adding to her ice cream.

Neely Kate turned to me, her eyebrows high and her eyes darting toward her victim.

Crappy doodles, she was good.

"Do you remember anyone talking to him here at the restaurant?" I asked in a breezy tone, as though nothing had just happened.

"Uh . . . yeah." He sounded flustered. "Not when he was workin' on the first plan, but someone was here a few days before he died."

"Do you remember what he looked like? Since Eric isn't available, maybe I'll look him up. I *do* love me a powerful man."

"I don't remember."

The kid added more ice cream, then glanced at Neely Kate. She nodded her head. "Now you be sure to mix that up real good, you hear?" Her tone had more bite than I was used to hearing from her, and I had to admit I'd be nervous in our server's shoes.

"Yes, ma'am." He cringed and turned red. "Miss! I mean miss!"

She scowled, looking like she was about to give him another tongue-lashing, but he turned on the mixer, which made it too loud for me to ask him more questions. Neely Kate leaned into my ear. "I think he knows more. I'll keep shaking him up, and you keep peppering him with questions."

"You are truly evil," I said with a grin.

Her eyes twinkled. "And you love me that way."

"As long as I'm on your good side."

I took a step away, and the machine stopped a few seconds later.

"You let me see that cup before you do another thing to it," Neely Kate demanded.

He brought the cup over to her, and she shook her head and tsked. "You call that sorry mess good? It's not nearly mixed enough."

He took a step toward the machine.

"*What on earth do you think you're doin'?* Stir it by hand, or you're gonna crush all the cookies!"

His eyes widened in dismay, and she gave him a shooing motion. "Well, go on. What're you waiting for? Jesus to come back in all His shining glory to do it for ya? He'll have better things to do than your job, don't ya think?"

He looked around for something to stir the ice cream with, his hands shaking.

I continued with my line of questioning. "If you remember the guy comin' in and talkin' to Eric, you must remember what they did."

The kid finally found a spoon and started stirring. "They just sat at a table in the dining room and talked for a few minutes."

"And you said it was a few days before he died?"

"Um . . ." He was starting to recover. "Yeah."

I really needed to know more about this guy. On cue, Neely Kate slammed her palms on the counter. "Are you kidding me? You're stirring too slow!" she shouted. "Speed it up!"

Flustered, he started stirring faster.

"You said he had blond hair?" I asked.

"No, he had dark hair."

I wanted to break out into a grin. "What was he wearing?"

"How the heck would I know?"

"Jeans? Dress pants?"

"Uh . . ."

Neely Kate groaned. "Oh, my word! If you stir that ice cream any slower, the spoon's gonna freeze up in there! I'm about to make you start all over again!"

His eyes widened in panic, and his arm started spinning the spoon like a whirligig.

"Did he have on nice clothes or jeans and a T-shirt?" I pressed.

"Uh . . . jeans and a T-shirt . . . The shirt had a beer logo. One of them fancy breweries."

The courier who posted my bail wore one too. I snuck a glance at Neely Kate and decided to take a shot at this even if it was a bust. "Did you notice a birthmark on his cheek. A faint brown spot?"

He curled his nose. "How would I know? I wasn't checking him out. I'm into girls."

Neely Kate put her hand on her hip. "What in the cotton-pickin' hell are you doin' to my ice cream? Now you're stirring it too fast! Slow down, or you're gonna smother those cookie pieces. Now you take a good look and see how big those pieces are."

He looked down, and Neely Kate handed me her phone. The photo of the courier was already queued up.

"Bring that cup over here," she said in an exasperated tone. "I wanna see it for myself."

He walked over to her, fear in his eyes, and held the cup out at full arm's length.

She rolled her eyes. "You've crushed them too small, but I don't have time to wait."

He looked thoroughly confused, and I decided to strike while he was still racked with indecision. I held up Neely Kate's phone. "Is this the guy?"

"What?" He shook his head as if trying to clear it.

"The guy who came to see Eric. Is this him?"

I held it closer, and he cast a glance at Neely Kate.

"Answer the woman."

"Uh . . . yeah," he said, standing back up. "I think so."

"I think so isn't good enough," Neely Kate said through clenched teeth. "Take another look and be more sure."

His nostrils flared, but he glanced at the phone in my hand. "Yeah. That's him."

"You're sure?" I asked.

"Yeah. I recognize that belt buckle." He pointed to the screen. "It's a winner's buckle from the Fenton County Fair Rodeo."

"Which year?" Neely Kate asked.

His brow lowered. "I dunno."

She grabbed the phone from my hand and zoomed in on the buckle, then held it out to him. "Try. Again."

Crap. If I hadn't known she was on my side, I would've been scared spitless.

"Last summer. It has a star on it."

She shoved the phone in her pocket. "Thank you, Eugene. Now where's my ice cream?"

Poor Eugene couldn't keep his hands steady, so he ended up drizzling chocolate on the side of the cup before he added the three cherries to the top, counting them out loud for Neely Kate's benefit. He set it on the counter and cautiously slid it toward her.

She picked it up and gave him a hundred-megawatt smile. "Thank you," she said in her sweetest voice. "You have a nice day now, ya hear?"

He looked like he'd just witnessed the detonation of an atom bomb. I supposed he had.

She spun around, still grinning. "Let's go."

I picked up my sundae and followed her out the door and into the truck, trying to process everything we'd just figured out. But first I had to address Neely Kate's performance.

"You were . . . That was . . ."

Her eyes twinkled. "Amazing? Awesome? Awe-inspiring?"

"All of the above."

"Any more doubts about bringing me along tonight?"

"No."

She took a big bite of her ice cream and made a sound of pure contentment. "This is really pretty good. I should get my ice cream made this way every time."

I laughed. "You mean with fear and terror mixed in?"

A smug grin spread across her face, and she gave me a

half-shrug, then took another bite and said, "Okay, let's focus on what we learned."

"First we have to address the fact that the guy who hired Eric to run Mason off the road is the same guy who posted my bail."

She frowned. "Yeah. That is, if the guy he met actually hired him to do it."

"The timing is pretty coincidental, but I agree. We can't jump to conclusions. But we do know it wasn't Mick. Eric said his new plan was with someone else, someone more powerful."

"I can't see J.R. Simmons workin' with someone as dumb as a stick." She cringed. "No offense to the dead."

"Yeah, I agree. But this guy he met had to be some kind of middleman. Someone who could show his face in public. It's obvious he's not the power guy because otherwise he wouldn't have shown up at the courthouse. They have cameras there."

"They do, although not too many. Whoever this guy is probably turned his face away from the cameras . . . well, except for Nita's. But I think you're right. This isn't the guy who's behind it all. We still need to find him, though. Let's head to your house and see what we can find out about last summer's rodeo winners. *The Henryetta Gazette* will have a photo with names."

I pulled out of the parking lot and pointed the truck toward home, feeling more hopeful than I'd felt in ages.

# Chapter Twelve

After we got home, I texted Mason to let him know we had some helpful information. He responded: *In a meeting. Will call you later.*

I let Muffy out and told Neely Kate she could pick out whichever room she wanted upstairs. I hurried Muffy along, which made me feel bad, but we had work to do. And in the scheme of things, I figured she could deal with a shorter romp now if it meant she'd get to spend the rest of her life with me and Mason.

After a few minutes, I headed upstairs with my backpack full of Lady in Black clothes. I found Neely Kate in the front bedroom, sitting on the end of the bed and staring out the window toward the road.

"It's a pretty view, huh?" I asked, sitting next to her.

"Yeah. I like it here. It's peaceful."

It had its moments of chaos and danger, but I wasn't going to ruin the illusion for her. "I meant what I said, Neely Kate. You're welcome to stay here as long as you want to stay, although for your sake, I hope it's not too long."

She kept her gaze focused out the window but gave me a lopsided grin. "What's Mason gonna say about that?"

"You seriously have to ask that? You know what he's gonna say. He's your friend too."

Tears filled her eyes, hanging on her lower lashes, but they didn't spill out.

"Do you want to take a rest? We've had a busy afternoon, and we have an even busier night ahead. You're still recovering from your surgery."

"Yeah. That might be a good idea." She turned to look at me. "But we need to look up that rodeo guy."

"Send me his photo, and I'll see what I can find while you nap."

She pulled her phone out of her pocket and sent me the photo in a text.

"Now you get comfortable," I said, pulling an afghan off a chair in the corner.

She kicked off her boots and scooted back on the bed. She lay on her side, her long blond hair spilling over her shoulder and onto the pillow, and I tucked the afghan around her. She glanced up at me, looking sadder and lonelier than I'd ever seen her. "Do you know how long it's been since someone took care of me like this?"

My head jutted back in surprise. "What about Ronnie?"

"He sits with me and holds my hand, but . . . this is a different kind of affection. You know?"

I sat on the bed next to her. "No, I don't know."

She took a deep breath. I worried she was going to brush me off, but instead she stared at a spot on the wall and said, "Ronnie *does* take care of me, but it's because it's his job as my husband."

"I'm sure that's not true, Neely Kate. You're just confused after all the turmoil and pain of losing your babies. He loves you. I saw it with my own eyes when you were in the hospital."

"I know he loves me. That's not it . . ." I could see she was getting frustrated. Her head turned slightly, and her blue eyes locked onto mine. "He does things for me because he loves me as my husband. It's like a contract or agreement between us. He takes care of me, and I take care of him."

I wasn't sure I agreed with her assessment, but I decided to keep that to myself for now.

She looked away again, her cheeks turning pink. "My momma didn't do a good job raisin' me. And while I love my granny, she's not a soft woman. That's part of the reason I love Maeve so much. She's everything my momma wasn't."

I picked up her hand and held it in mine. "I know exactly what you mean. I worry I'll lose her too if Mason finds out the truth about the Lady in Black and leaves me."

Neely Kate's gaze found mine again. "No. She loves you for you, Mason aside. I can see it. You'd still have her."

I gave her a tight smile. I sure hoped she was right.

"But Rose, what you just did . . . what you've been doin' . . . I've never had anyone do things for me without expectin' something for it. You, though, you take care of me just because."

"Not just because," I said with a lump in my throat. "I love you. I've told you a dozen times this side of Sunday. We're closer than friends. It's like we've got this invisible thread tying us together. And you're right; it's different than what we have with Ronnie and Mason or what I had with Joe. What you and I have is unconditional. I can't think of a single thing that would make me turn from you. I might get angry enough to spit, or you might disappoint the bejiggers out of me, but I'm not going anywhere. I'm here for you no matter what. I've told you that before, but *you* have to believe it."

A tear slid out of the corner of her eye and rolled over the bridge of her nose before sinking into the pillow. "I asked you if you knew how long it's been since someone had taken care of me like this, but it was a trick question." She closed her eyes. "The answer is never. No one has *ever* taken care of me like this."

I had a million and one questions about Neely Kate's life. I had always known her to live her life loud and large, which she did, but she also hid pieces of herself from the people around her—even me. She'd confessed that her mother had abandoned her, leaving her with her grandmother, who had reluctantly given her a home and raised her. But I knew little about her teen years and even less about her life with her mother. She was sitting on a powder keg of pain, and when this mess was done, I was going to make her share it with me.

I leaned over and smoothed her hair off her cheek. "Well, I hope you get used to being spoiled, Neely Kate Colson, 'cause I'm only just gettin' started." Then I stood and moved to the door. "You rest and I'll have some soup ready when you get up."

"Thank you, Rose."

"You're welcome."

I closed the door behind me, my heart heavy with Neely Kate's pain. First her babies, and now Ronnie. I wasn't sure how much more she could take.

My phone started vibrating in my pocket when I reached the bottom of the stairs. I pulled it out and was relieved to see it was Mason.

"I have so much to tell you," I gushed.

"Me too," he answered in excitement. "You go first."

I headed into the kitchen and grabbed a bag of potatoes out of the pantry and began to chop them for a pot of potato soup. As I worked, I told him about Witt opening the safe and finding the folder, the key, and the cash.

"How much money was in there?" he asked, sounding worried.

"I don't know. I'm guessing several thousand dollars. What should I do with it?"

"Put it in the desk drawer in the office for now. I'll give it some thought."

"Any ideas about finding a translator for the page from the journal?"

"I was thinking Mom might be able to do it. She was a secretary when she met Dad. I remember her saying she knew shorthand. Why don't you ask her?"

"That's a great idea. I found out something that might be even more helpful." I told him about our visit to Burger Shack and Eric's tie to the guy who'd posted my bail.

"I fought like hell to get them to do a more thorough investigation of his death," Mason said. "I knew there was more to it. Let me know if you manage to figure out the guy's name. I'll have Randy run a background check on him."

"Okay."

"But promise me you and Neely Kate won't go looking for him on your own. He could be the guy who killed Eric Davidson, which means he's dangerous."

"Okay." I shuddered. "But why would someone who tried to have you killed want me out of jail?"

"I don't know," he said, his voice fading as he tried to puzzle it out. "I still wonder if it's safe for you to be out and about."

"It's safer for me than for you. Now tell me your news."

"I met an assistant in the secretary of state's office that sent the investigator to hear my evidence against my boss last Friday. According to her, the investigator received a mysterious phone call right before he left for Henryetta."

"Mysterious. How?"

"She stayed on the line after she patched the call through."

"So she overheard the call? Can you trust the testimony of an employee who snoops on her boss?"

"Ordinarily I wouldn't, but she's questioned his integrity for the past few months. She started taking notes on what might be construed as inappropriate activity on his part."

"Can she do that? Is it admissible in court?"

"It is if it's sanctioned by his boss."

"What?"

"Rose, she took her preliminary suspicions to her boss's boss, and he told her to start logging anything suspicious for them to investigate."

"And this is one of those suspicious things?"

"Yes. The call was from a blocked number, which is why she stayed on the line. The man told Ted—the investigator—to proceed with the plan or else."

"Or else what?"

"It sounded like he was being blackmailed. That's probably why he agreed to come in the first place. The person insisted Ted see to it that I was removed from office before he left Fenton County."

"So this came from J.R.?"

"Most likely. But even better, Betty—that's the assistant's name—thinks she's seen the guy who threatened Ted. He showed up at the office a few times without an appointment, and even though her boss never seemed happy to see the guy, he'd always change his schedule to accommodate him. He stopped coming after a while, but that's when the blocked calls started. The great thing is that Betty swears she remembers what he looks like. So I talked to a detective in the state police department, and he's agreed to have Betty meet with a sketch artist today. With any luck, we can identify the guy. The detective and I are going to take Betty's evidence and the sketch to someone higher up in the secretary of state's office. We have an appointment at nine tomorrow morning."

"Wow," I murmured, stunned. "That's good news, right?"

"It's great news."

"Can you trust the state police detective? What if he's friends with Joe?"

"He can't stand Joe. He was more than happy to jump on board when he heard about Joe's role in getting me fired and arresting you on trumped-up charges. He's determined to take out Joe, J.R., *and* my boss."

"Mason. This is too good to be true."

"I know, and I confess, it almost seems too easy."

Threads of anxiety wrapped tight around my chest. He was right. He'd searched for months for evidence to use against J.R. without finding anything, and this was happening so fast. It almost seemed too perfect. "Do you think it's a trap?"

"No . . ." He sighed. "I don't know. I don't see how it could be a trap, but I'm more worried it's a distraction. Like what I'm looking for is so close they're throwing me this bone to get me off the right track."

"So what's the right track?"

"Damned if I know." He groaned. "I'm probably just being paranoid."

"I don't think so. You have great instincts, Mason. I think you should listen to them." Even when they told him I was keeping things from him. "Do you think you're safe up there?"

"I can't stop looking, Rose. All I can do is be careful, and I promise you that I will be."

"I'm just scared." My voice broke. "I don't want to lose you."

"And I'm not going anywhere, okay?"

"Okay."

"But that being said, I need to stay up here in Little Rock tonight. I have that meeting in the morning, and I need to spend the night gathering my thoughts into a convincing argument. I'd feel a whole lot better about leaving you alone if you and Muffy would go stay with my mom."

I took a breath. "Actually, there's something else I need to talk to you about."

"Okay," he said in a gentle tone, obviously noticing my hesitation. "What is it?"

"It's about Neely Kate. She and Ronnie are still havin' a rough patch, and it's worse than ever."

"What's goin' on?"

I glanced toward the door, then moved closer to the sink. "I need you to promise that you won't take what I tell you and use it to press any kind of charges."

That perked up his attention. "Is Neely Kate in some kind of trouble?"

"More like Ronnie."

"*Ronnie?*"

"Yes. I need your word."

"In case you hadn't noticed, I'm currently out of a job."

"And the key word there is currently."

"Rose, Neely Kate's cousin just broke into a safe on private property at my suggestion. I think I can overlook some minor infraction by our friend."

"That's just it. I'm not sure it's minor. Well, I'm not sure he's done anything at *all*, but Witt insinuated that he's involved in something shady."

"Maybe you better start from the beginning."

I told him what Witt had said about Ronnie's poker buddies shifting their loyalty from Skeeter to Mick Gentry.

Mason heaved a sigh. "It kills me that you're being forced into this world. Last July you didn't even know who

Skeeter Malcolm was. Now you've been forced to listen to me talk about all kinds of criminal turf wars, and you know a whole lot more than most law-abiding citizens. I just hate that you're exposed to all of this."

I felt guilty about hiding things from Mason, but as soon as he, Skeeter, and I were safe, the Lady in Black could become a distant memory. Maybe I would finally confess as we bounced our great-grandkids on our knees.

"I'm a big girl, Mason. And I'm more worried about Ronnie. Witt said he's getting all kinds of pressure from his buddies to do something illegal, and they're takin' Mick Gentry's side. That's gonna be nothin' but trouble." Then I told him about his strange behavior with Neely Kate—how he'd forbidden her to go to the courthouse, how he'd left her alone in the house, and how he kept calling in sick.

"You don't know that you're the real excuse for his behavior," Mason said. "If his men are loyal to Gentry, then they might have it out for me. And if Ronnie knows that, it would be natural for him to want to protect his wife."

"He didn't have any problem with her comin' out to the farm to see you on Saturday. And if he's really that worried, why on earth would he leave her? You'd think he'd want to stay to protect her."

"I don't know. That part is worrisome."

"Neely Kate isn't handling it very well, Mason. In fact, she's staying here tonight and possibly indefinitely. She can't stay in that house, not when Ronnie's gone and the nursery is still decorated for her lost babies."

"She can stay as long as she likes," he said softly. "You know you don't need my permission. It's your house, sweetheart."

"I may own it, but it's *ours.* And I knew you would say yes, but in hindsight, perhaps I should have cleared it with you first."

"No. It sounds like a spur of the moment situation. I'm glad she has you."

"Me too."

"I still don't feel right leaving you alone tonight, but I'm glad you'll have Neely Kate with you."

"I'm worried about you too, but we both have our jobs to do tonight."

"What job do you have to do?"

Oh crap. "Look up the courier, of course. And call your mother."

"It shouldn't take too long for you to identify him now that you have the belt lead. Maybe you and Neely Kate can have a girl's night at home and watch some sappy rom-com."

We were definitely having a girl's night, but it wouldn't be much like the one he was envisioning. "Yeah, we'll figure something out."

"I love you, Rose. I wouldn't leave you alone overnight if I didn't think this was important."

"I know. And I love you too. Come back to me safe."

"I should be home by tomorrow afternoon. I'll let you know how the meeting goes."

"Okay. Good luck." After I hung up, I finished some more preparations for the soup and headed to the office.

I pulled up *The Henryetta Gazette* on my laptop, then

searched for last summer's Fenton County Rodeo. It took about three seconds to find photos of the winners. Sure enough, I found the guy in the pic Neely Kate had sent me: Sam Teagen, calf-roping champion. He stood in front of the camera, holding up his belt buckle with a cocky grin that told the world he was used to getting his way.

I plugged his name into Facebook next. His profile came up right away, and to my relief, his page seemed to be set to public. There were only a few photos of his friends, but there were plenty of pictures of his rodeo events. Surely that would be helpful. I copied down the links to the rodeo article and the guy's Facebook profile and texted them to Mason.

All within ten minutes.

Mason was right. My task, like his, had been almost too easy.

I got up and checked on the potatoes. The water hadn't even begun to boil yet, which meant I probably had a good half hour before it would be ready. The sun was close to setting, and my little dog had been sorely neglected, so I decided I'd take Muffy for a quick walk.

"Muffy, wanna go for a walk?"

She'd been asleep in her dog bed, but she perked up at the sound of her name and began to dance around my feet. I wrote a quick note for Neely Kate, grabbed my coat, patting the pocket to make sure I still had my Taser, and headed out the front door.

I loved my house at this time of day, when the land seemed to hover between day and night. My farm was far enough from town that the night sky lit up with millions of stars, but the daylight was always bound and determined to hang on as long as it could. I couldn't see the horizon because of all the trees lining the highway, but parts of the red and golden glow made their way through the cracks in the foliage, making the bare trees look magical.

At times like these, I couldn't help but wonder what it would have been like to grow up here—in a warm, cozy house with a loving mother. But Beverly Buchanan had taken that away from me. Her and J.R. Simmons.

How much would that man take from me?

Because I knew he wasn't done. He still wanted more.

Something dark and fierce rose up inside me, a need to protect the people I loved—Mason, Neely Kate, even Violet—no matter what. While I hoped to God Mason was successful in Little Rock, I had a feeling that our success or failure would come down to the Lady in Black. I had the power to bring J.R. Simmons to his knees.

But I was going for his head.

Muffy bounded down the steps and started running circles in the front yard and sniffing the bushes in front of the porch. There was still enough daylight left for us to walk into the fields or the edge of the woods behind the barn. It was close to six o'clock, which meant we still had time to eat dinner, get ready, and meet Jed at the Sinclair station.

"Come on, girl. Let's explore."

Muffy understood the word *explore* as her cue to have free rein on the farm. She took off and ran straight for the barn. I followed along behind her, letting my mind mull over everything we'd learned today. I was still worried about Mason. The threat to his life was real, and if he'd found out something juicy enough to put J.R. away, the elder Simmons was bound to do something about it.

Would it be a job for one of his Twelve?

I still had a hard time believing that Skeeter had ever worked for such a despicable man, although I wasn't sure why. Skeeter had made no secret of what he was—a criminal. And he didn't apologize for it either, a trait I found equally disconcerting and enviable. He was a man following a dangerous path, yet he didn't give two figs what anyone thought about him. How different would my life have been if I'd adopted that same attitude early in life? Of course, I was no Skeeter Malcolm.

Yet I couldn't deny that we were alike in some ways. He'd told me once that I was more like him than like Mason or Joe. While they saw the world in black and white, we saw it in shades of gray. At the moment I thought we might have something else in common too— my thirst for vengeance was growing. I wanted to make J.R. Simmons pay for all the pain he'd caused the people I loved.

I was determined not only to make him pay, but to make him suffer.

And that part scared me more than a little.

Muffy sniffed around outside of the barn, then ducked into a hole by the double doors. I lifted the metal bar that held the doors closed and swung one of the sides open. As I followed my dog into the barn, I remembered how long Mason had spent in there searching for clues. No wonder it had taken him hours. Between the hayloft, the tack area, and the remains of a storage area, there were plenty of hiding places.

Muffy was rustling around in a pile of leftover hay in the back corner, probably ferreting out a mouse. She'd found a few in the house, and there were plenty out here for her to chase.

"Muffy, come back here," I called out into the darkness. "Leave that poor creature alone." Too lazy to walk over to the tack area to flip on the overhead light, I pulled out my phone and turned on the flashlight. Muffy didn't heed me, so I stepped around the old pickup truck that had likely belonged to Dora's grandfather to get closer to her. It was then I noticed that the back door facing the woods was standing wide open.

There was no way Mason would have left it that way.

My blood pressure elevated, and my blood whooshed in my ears, making me read every creak and groan as a possible disaster.

"Muffy," I said in a low, direct tone. "Come."

Her rustling stopped, and she trotted toward me as I gripped the handle of the Taser in my pocket. She stopped at my feet, then hunkered down and growled at something behind me.

Oh, crappy doodles.

I considered bolting out the back door, even though I had no idea what was behind me. But part of me was tired of running. I was tired of letting people use fear to push me around. And this was my home—my safe place. A deep anger rose up as I prepared to turn around and face whatever monster stood behind me.

So it seemed more than fitting that the man I saw when I spun around was the one who'd helped shape this mess I was in.

I narrowed my eyes and pointed my Taser right at Joe Simmons.

# Chapter Thirteen

He held up his hands. "Whoa! Don't shoot."

Muffy still stayed at my feet, releasing a low warning. I was following my dog's instincts on this one. She usually ran to Joe, tail wagging, and covered him in licks. The fact that she was on edge wasn't lost on me.

I held my Taser up in a defensive stance. "I just caught you trespassing on my property, so give me one good reason why I shouldn't."

"I'm here protecting you," he said in exasperation. He was wearing jeans and his familiar winter coat.

But Muffy was still growling, so I kept my hand up. "That's the biggest crock of bullshit I've heard all day, and I've heard quite a bit, so try again. I'm giving you to the count of three to tell me, and then I'm pulling the trigger."

I could barely see his face. I still had my cell phone clutched in my left hand, but the flashlight was pointing down at the floor, casting long shadows on his face.

"Rose, I'm the damned chief deputy sheriff."

The ire in his voice only pissed me off more. "Do you have a warrant to be in my barn?"

"No, but—"

"*One.*"

"I swear to God, Rose. I was walking the back end of your property and I heard noises in your barn, so I came to investigate. Just like when I found you in your shed last June, remember?"

There was a wistfulness in his voice that plucked at one of my heart strings, making me soften. Then I remembered the rest.

"Yeah," I said, my voice hard and tight. "You started to lock me in there—"

"I thought you were a trespasser!"

"—and then you hid a gun in there to make me look like a murder suspect."

"I was trying to protect you from Daniel Crocker!"

"You had me arrested last Friday, Joe!" I spat out. "You stood in front of my house and let that evil woman arrest me!"

"I did it to protect you." His voice broke.

I shook my head violently. "Don't you *dare* tell me that!" I shouted, keeping my Taser aimed as I took a step toward him. "Don't you pull that patronizing *bullshit* on me!"

Surprise flickered in his eyes, and he took a step backward. "My father . . . he forced me into it."

"That's right. Your daddy told you to jump, and you asked how freaking high. But I guess I'm expendable."

"No. *You're wrong.*" Anger permeated his words. "I was *protecting* you. I still am."

"Are you kidding me? When you go to bed at night, does that explanation make it easier for you to sleep? Or do you not even spare a thought for me?"

167

"Don't you dare try to trivialize my feelings for you." His voice shook with his fury.

"I am not a child, Joe Simmons, so don't you treat me like one. I almost got beat up in the county jail before Carter Hale had me moved to solitary confinement! How is that protecting me?"

He ran a hand over his head, his eyes darting from me to the old truck next to us. "I was scrambling . . . I hadn't thought about you dating Mason—"

"It wasn't Mason who got me into trouble. It was killing Daniel Crocker. Guess what? The county jail is full of people who loved that man. Thank God Carter showed up when he did!"

"Why in God's name did you hire Carter Hale?" he demanded, his anger returning. "Why didn't you hire Deanna Crawfield?"

"The attorney I had when I was accused the first time?" I asked, incredulous. "Why do you even care?"

"Do you have any idea about Hale's reputation?"

"You mean that he's *good*? That he has a shot in hell at helping me stay out of jail?"

"Rose! It will never come to that. Do you really think I'd let you go to prison for something you didn't do?"

I took two steps toward him. "I don't know, Joe," I said, my tone cold and hard. "I never thought you'd just stand aside and let me get arrested."

He stood in place, his hands raised up to his shoulders. "I'm sorry about that. You have to believe me."

I held the Taser to his chest and stared up into his eyes. Anger billowed up inside me like an atomic mushroom cloud. "That is where you are wrong. You swore to me you would never let this happen. You swore to me that you loved me, that you would protect me. But you have broken that promise at every turn, Joe Simmons. I loved you. Even after we parted, a small part of me still loved the old you—Joe McAllister—who stood for justice and doing what was right. But that man isn't real." A lump burned in my throat. "He never was. It was all a lie."

He shook his head. "No, Rose. That's not true. You made me want to be Joe McAllister."

"You liar," I choked out, fighting back tears, angry with myself for letting him hurt me all over again. "Mason says you've gotten away with despicable things your entire life."

"I told you that myself," he said, sounding broken. "When I told you about Savannah. But I've changed. I swear. You *know* that."

"Where's my journal?"

His eyes became guarded. "What?"

"My journal. The one you stole right out of my hands. Where is it?"

He closed his eyes for a couple of seconds before opening them again. "He was going to kill you for it."

"So you were protecting me. Again?"

He released a sigh of frustration. "Believe it or not, yes."

"Well, guess what? I *don't* believe it." I shook my head in disgust. "The one thing that could have saved all of us, and you handed it right over to him."

"I mean it, Rose. I'm sure he told Beverly Buchanan to kill you once she had it in her possession. My father isn't one to leave unfinished ends."

"If he had the journal, why arrest me?"

"I was trying to buy us more time."

"More time for what?"

"To figure out how to keep you protected. If I didn't do it, he would have had you killed that very night."

"Let me get this straight. You had Mason fired. You stole the journal containing evidence that would have toppled your father, and you had me arrested, all in the name of protecting me. Forgive me if I'm not that blind and stupid girl you kissed on my front porch last summer."

Fear filled his eyes, and he reached a hand out toward me, but I took a step back. "When you put it that way, I know it sounds bad, but I have a plan."

"Why didn't you just warn me? I could have gone into hiding."

His jaw tensed. "He would have found you."

"And now? Is he trying to kill me now?"

"No. He's waiting for the court to seek its justice."

I released a short laugh. "Aww . . . justice, J.R. style. Forgive me if I don't wait for *that* to be meted out."

"Rose, listen to me. I mean it. I have a plan. Just let it all play out."

"Fine. I'd love to hear your plan. What is it?"

He swallowed, and I could see he was mulling it over, but then he said, "I can't tell you."

"So I'm supposed to trust you when you say you'll make sure I don't go to prison for the rest of my life? After everything you've done?"

"I know it's a lot to ask . . ."

"You're damn *right* it's a lot to ask." Bitterness drenched my words.

His eyes narrowed. "You've changed."

"*Are you serious?*"

He stared at me, dumbfounded.

"I don't need you to save me, Joe Simmons. I'm not some helpless princess waiting for some man to come along!"

His shoulders stiffened. "Then what the hell is Deveraux doin'? *He's* trying to save you."

"We're trying to save *each other*, you imbecile!"

His mouth parted.

"You just don't get it! I'm not a *child*. I'm not some precious doll you can set on a shelf for protection, then take out and play with whenever you feel like it. I'm a grown woman, and I have a brain in my head. A pretty stinkin' good one. Mason sees that. He encourages me to think for myself. To make my own decisions. I don't need someone to take care of me. I need a *partner*." I took a deep breath and lowered my voice. "And you and me, we were never partners. Not really. You were always big strong Joe who knew what was right for poor hopeless, stupid Rose."

"I never thought you were stupid."

"But you thought I was incapable of managing the world on my own."

"You *were* incapable! You'd been sheltered for so long you were clueless about how the world worked. You kept stumbling from one pile of trouble to the next."

I shook my head, suddenly exhausted. "I'm not that girl anymore, Joe. I haven't been that girl for a long time."

"That's not true!"

"Part of me will always be the woman you met. But I'm not that naïve anymore. I've seen too much—a whole lot more than you even know—and I've grown up. I don't need someone to pull me out of the holes I fall into. I need someone to crawl out of them with me."

He didn't respond.

"*You* need someone you can control, and *I* am uncontrollable."

"That's not true."

A wry smile lifted my lips. "Which part?"

He started to answer and then closed his mouth.

"You say you hate your father, but you're more like him than you know." I took a step back. "Now what are you doing here? Looking for more evidence to use against me? You're not wearing your uniform, but I guess that doesn't matter. You wouldn't officially report it, anyway. You'd give it to your daddy."

Anger burned in his eyes, and he took a step toward me. "You are being incredibly stupid right now, Rose. Whether you believe it or not, I *am* trying to help you. This is the only way I know how to keep you safe until I can do what needs to be done."

"Fine," I said, waving my left arm in an arc. "Why don't you enlighten me, Joe. Tell me what I'm supposed to do right now." I moved closer until just a few inches separated us. "If you were the puppet master, what would you have me do?" I lifted my eyebrows. "The sky's the limit."

"Look, I know you find it hard to trust me right now—"

"What do you want from me?" My voice came out

softer and more pathetic than I'd intended.

He started to speak, but then stopped, his eyes full of pain. "You know what I want, but I want you to want it too. And you damn near hate my guts, so that's not a possibility right now. But maybe you'll give me another chance when this is over . . . when I've had the chance to prove to you that I'll do anything to protect you."

"Hell would have to freeze over first."

"So you'd rather play house with that uptight prick?"

I held the Taser up again and shoved it into his chest. "You're the one who showed me how to use this, so you know I can do it. Now get the hell off my property."

Joe shook his head in disgust. "You couldn't have me, so you ran to him. You don't love him. You just found a place-filler until you could have me back."

"Get the hell off my property!"

"You can dish it out, Rose, but you sure as hell can't take it."

"You expect me to stand here in *my own* barn and let you insult Mason? Would you have liked it if I'd let him insult you when you and I were together?"

"I'm pretty damn sure he did. He shoved a wedge between us. And I'd be lying if I said I wasn't looking forward to seeing him suffer like I have."

"*You* shoved a wedge between us, Joe." Then a new thought hit me like a lightning bolt. "Oh, my word. You're doing this for revenge."

Confusion flickered in his eyes.

I gasped as the idea sunk its teeth into me. "If you can't have me, then no one can. Maybe you'd rather see me rot in jail than spend the rest of my life with Mason."

"*No!* How can you think that?"

It didn't seem like the man I'd loved, but I wasn't sure what to believe of him anymore, and I was tired of trying to figure it out. All I knew was that Mason and I were in danger, and all roads led to J.R. Simmons. And by letting his daddy's conspiracy unfold, Joe had chosen his side. "If Mason dies because of you—" I waved my hand between us "—because of this, I will never forgive you. Do you hear me? Not only will you not have me, but you will have an enemy for life."

"I can't be held responsible for what happens to him. I'm doin' the best I can to keep *you* safe."

"And what exactly are you doin'?"

"I can't tell you. But your arrest . . . Mason's dismissal from his job . . . all of it and more are part of my plan. You just have to trust me."

"Same damn song, thirty-second verse. How am I supposed to trust you when you won't even trust me with the truth?" I asked in disgust, shoving the Taser at him again. "Now get the hell off my land."

"I'm still going to protect you, Rose."

"*Protect me?*" I laughed bitterly and held out my hands. "Do your worst, Joe."

He wisely kept quiet and walked out the back door, heading in the direction of his house.

A war raged inside me. The woman who would always love the Joe I'd met that hot Saturday on Memorial Day weekend wanted to believe he was telling me the truth. But the woman I'd become, the jaded and rough-around-the-edges woman, didn't trust a word that had come out of his mouth.

I suspected the answer was somewhere in the middle. Only I didn't have time to puzzle it out.

# Chapter Fourteen

I was putting the finishing touches on the soup when Neely Kate came into the kitchen. She still looked groggy as she sat down at the table.

"Maybe you should stay home tonight," I suggested.

"Not a chance. I just need to wake up is all."

I ladled her a bowl of soup and set it in front of her. "I saw Joe."

Her gaze jerked up to mine. "What?"

"I took Muffy outside and she headed into the barn. The next thing I knew, he was inside there with me."

"What in tarnation was he doin' there? Spyin' on you?"

"I never got a satisfactory answer. He said he was checkin' on me. That he's tryin' to keep me safe."

"Keep you safe? Did you confront him about arresting you?"

"Oh, you bet I did. He said he did it to protect me from J.R. And he claims that's why he took the journal too."

"That makes no sense whatsoever."

"I know." Yet in his own twisted logic, perhaps it did. Still, if Joe really was trying to protect me, he sure was going at it the wrong way. "We got into a huge fight—

nothing unusual there—and I threatened to tase him if he didn't leave."

"The nerve of that man!"

"I know." I scooped myself a bowl of soup too, grabbed some leftover homemade bread from Maeve, and sat down at the table. "Mason is spending the night in Little Rock, so I won't have to worry about explaining our absence to him." I filled her in on what he'd discovered, and we sat in silence for a moment.

"I have to admit," she said, sinking her spoon into her bowl, "it sounds like it might be scary for him to be up there."

"Agreed. The sooner he gets home, the more relieved I'll be. I also figured out the identity of the guy with the belt buckle."

She gave me a smug grin. "I told you it would be easy. We can check him out later. We just won't tell Mason."

I pointed my spoon at her. "No. We're not confronting him or following him, or whatever you want to call it. I already sent the name to Mason, and he's going to have Deputy Miller look into it."

Neely Kate made a face, but she didn't say anything.

"Besides," I said, "this meeting with Mick Gentry is enough for us to worry about." I grabbed a piece of bread and began to slather it with butter, then put it back down. My stomach felt like a bag of popcorn popping in the microwave. "I'm not telling Jed you'll be there until we drive up, but he's gonna pitch a fit. So be prepared."

Her eyebrows rose. "I can handle Jed."

"No. You let *me* handle Jed. If you go shootin' off, he's gonna think you're a loose cannon." And I had to wonder whether there was something to that. I half considered sneaking off without her, but I knew I'd royally pay for it later if I tried. "Jed is in charge. Say it."

Her mouth puckered around her spoon.

"Neely Kate. This isn't some game. In fact, this is probably the most dangerous thing I've ever done."

"Yet you're still doin' it."

"I don't trust what's goin' on in Little Rock. If I were sure something would come of Mason's meeting tomorrow, I'd call this off in a heartbeat. I would postpone, but Mick Gentry isn't the kind of guy to take being blown off lightly. If I ever want a shot at talking to him—and J.R.—I have to follow through with this. But you—" I pointed my spoon at her "—*you* don't have to go at all. So I strongly suggest you reconsider."

She studied me for several seconds. To my relief, I could see she was giving it serious consideration. Finally she spoke, all sass gone. "We're a team. We stick together."

"Neely Kate." My voice broke. "I don't know if I could live with myself if something happened to you because of me."

"You'd live with yourself just fine. Do you know why? This is my choice. My decision. For all my life, I've tried to make myself into someone other people want me to be. I did it all through high school—why do you think I was popular? I even do it with Ronnie. But I'm tired of trying to follow everyone else's rules. I want to follow my own. And I'm goin' with you. My choice. My decision. If something happens, you'll know I died doin' exactly what I wanted to do."

I swallowed, the soup in my stomach now a lump

weighing me down. "Nobody's dyin' tonight. You hear me?"

She gave me a soft smile. "Yes, ma'am."

I grinned. "Did you just call me ma'am? *Just how old do you think I am?*"

She laughed. "Sorry, miss." She stood and picked up her bowl. "Now let's get ready to go."

It didn't take us long. All I had to do was put up my hair and put on some bright red lipstick and pack my bag of clothes. Neely Kate had been known to spend over an hour getting ready, but tonight she appeared in my bedroom doorway within fifteen minutes. She had pinned up her long blond and highlighted hair and pulled on a sleek black wig. It gave her full bangs that brushed over her mascara-darkened eyebrows, and the length hit just below her chin. Her eyes were dark and smoky, and her lip color was a pale pink. She wore black pants, a long-sleeve black silky shirt—buttoned just at her cleavage—and black boots.

"Well? What do you think?" She stood in front of me, her face expressionless.

I shook my head in amazement. "If I didn't know better, I never would have guessed it was you. Not in a million years. You look like one of those butt-kickin' women in the movies."

She grinned. "See? No one's gonna mess with me."

On the contrary, Mick Gentry's men might want to mess with her, but not in the way she was suggesting. She looked super sexy. In fact, I suspected most of the men would be watching her instead of me.

Maybe that was a good thing.

"I wish I could find some way of concealing my appearance without this hat." I picked it up off the bed. "It's so cumbersome."

"What about a mask?"

"That seems too superhero-y, don't you think?" I tossed the hat on the bed next to my black dress. "Besides, I've told them all I wear the veil because I have a scar. I can't very well start parading around without it."

"True . . ." She jutted out her hip and studied my face. "Let me give it some thought. Maybe we can come up with something different for next time."

With any luck, we'd be meeting with J.R. next time, and I suspected I'd want the veil to hide from him. A wig and some makeup wouldn't fool J.R. Simmons.

She looked me up and down, taking in my jeans and sweater. "Aren't you gonna get dressed?"

"No. I wouldn't put it past Joe to pull me over. If he or some other deputy does, it would be easy for them to put this all together. I'll change behind the Sinclair station."

Her eyes widened.

"But you'll be fine. You can just wear a hat and your coat, and no one will think a thing about it."

She nodded. "Yeah, that's smart."

I shrugged, trying to act nonchalant even though I was practically buzzing with nervous energy. "I've done this a time or two. You ready?"

"Almost." I followed her down the hall to the front bedroom. She slipped through the open door and strapped on a gun holster over her shoulder, then put on her regular coat and slung a sleek black leather coat over her forearm.

"Where'd you get that?"

"This coat?" She shrugged as she stooped over her purse and pulled out the gun from her closet, which she put into her holster. "I bought it online."

"I was talkin' about the holster, but now that you mention it, none of these clothes seem like *you*."

She grinned and grabbed another gun from her bag— this one the older weapon from the safe. "I bought them last week."

"Is this the new you? Are you reinventing yourself?"

"No." She slipped the second gun into the waistline of her pants at the small of her back and turned to look at me, cold fury in her eyes. "This is me waiting for you to let me help the Lady in Black."

"You've been planning this?"

She snorted. "*Please*. I'm insulted you would think I *wouldn't*. I wouldn't have done anything dangerous while I was pregnant, but now I can take all kinds of risks." She brushed past me and headed down the stairs.

I followed behind, wondering if that was what this was really about. Was she taking unnecessary risks because she'd lost her babies and had been told there was no hope of her carrying any more?

But there wasn't time to think about it. I grabbed my truck keys, and we took off toward the Sinclair station, both of us unusually quiet.

Jed was waiting for us when I pulled up, sitting in the driver's seat of his car with a deep scowl on his face. He was out of the car before I pulled to a full stop. He yanked my door open with his uninjured arm.

"What the hell, Rose? You think I'm not enough backup? You went and hired someone else?"

I glanced back at Neely Kate. She had already shed her hat and replaced her coat with the leather one. A huge grin spread across her face as she climbed out the passenger door.

"Jed, it's Neely Kate," I said as I slid out of the truck. Without waiting to gauge his reaction, I opened the back door and dug into the bag holding my Lady in Black clothes.

She walked around the front of the truck, stopped next to me, and struck a saucy pose. "Hey, Jed."

"*What?*" His voice was loud enough to wake the dead, and I thanked my lucky stars we were out in the middle of nowhere. "Why in the hell would you bring her?"

"Look, I tried to get her to stay behind, but she wouldn't take no for an answer." I pulled my sweater over my head and tossed it onto the seat.

A moment of panic filled Jed's eyes as he took in my nearly naked torso, but he switched his gaze to her, his face hard. "Then let *me* say it: No."

Neely Kate cocked her head. "I'm goin', Jed. And you can't stop me."

"The hell I can't!"

"I'll just follow you," she said in a smug tone. "Rose knows I'm dead serious."

I sighed, stepping out of my jeans and into my dress. "I tried my best to talk her out of it, Jed. She's bound and determined to go."

Jed glared at my best friend. "No. I'm scared enough putting Rose at risk."

"I know how to shoot better than most of my cousins, and I know how to fight." She turned to me and made a face. "And that fight with Tabitha doesn't count. She's a girl." She put her hand on her hip. "I broke my cousin Witt's nose and Alan Jackson's collar bone."

Jed's mouth dropped. "You met Alan Jackson?"

I rolled my eyes. Several of Neely Kate's cousins were named after country music singers. I zipped up my dress and stepped into my heels. "Not the one you're thinkin' about, but he's a big beefy guy. Neely Kate's scrappy."

"I'm goin'," she said, then walked around to the passenger side of Jed's car and tugged on the handle. "Open up."

Jed shot me a look.

I lowered my voice. "Look, I'm nervous about her comin' too, but something about it feels right, as crazy as it seems."

"Crazy is right, Rose. We're goin' to see Mick Gentry himself. He's gonna have his best and his brightest guys there, and they'll be expectin' trouble."

"I told her you're in control and she's to follow your orders."

"Then I order her to stay here."

I grabbed my hat out of the bag and shut the truck door. "You're wastin' your breath. Maybe we can have her wait in the car."

He snorted. "You really believe that?"

"No, but it's worth a shot."

He shook his head and opened the back door of the car. I started to get in, but he blocked my path. "Wait. I want you to carry some protection."

"I was gonna bring my Taser, but I don't know where I'd carry it." I didn't typically bring a purse when I posed as the Lady, and now didn't seem like a good time to start. Mick's guys would probably be worried about what was inside.

"I want you to wear this." He pulled out a black elastic circular strap and stretched it open with both hands, grimacing from the effort. "Step your left leg into this."

"What is it?"

"Just do it," he barked in frustration.

I could have protested, but I figured I'd given him enough grief. I needed all of us to be on our A-game. I stepped out of my black heel and put my foot through the elastic. He pushed it up past the hem of my dress, continuing until it was high up on my thigh.

"Sorry," he murmured. My skirt was still splayed up, but he was trying to glance down. "Does that feel snug?"

"Yeah. What is it?" Were we recording the meeting? It wasn't a bad idea, so long as we didn't get caught.

He ignored my question and pulled on the elastic. "It's good that it's snug. The weight will pull it down."

"The weight of what?"

He reached into his pocket and pulled out a small handgun.

My eyes flew open. "No."

His eyes found mine, his jaw tight. "Yes. Either you wear this gun or we don't go at all."

"But you have yours, and Neely Kate has hers. Why in the world do I need one?"

"Because they might take ours, but I doubt they'll ask to frisk the Lady in Black. You might be the one to save all three of us. Do you know how to use it?"

"No."

His gaze found mine again. "Yes, you do. You shot Daniel Crocker in the heart."

"How did you know that?"

He groaned. "*Everyone* knows that."

"That doesn't mean I know how to use it. I was plumb lucky."

"Then let's hope you have more plumb luck tonight if this thing falls apart." He handed the gun to me and stood. "Get a feel for it. It's small enough for you to comfortably hold, but accurate enough for you to get the job done."

My hand shook as I thought about what *getting the job done* might entail. I pointed the gun out into the field behind the building. "I wouldn't even know when to use it."

"You'll know. You said your gut told you to bring Neely Kate. Listen to your instincts—they'll tell you if you need it."

I took a deep breath and blew it out. "Okay."

"Now tuck it into the holster."

I lifted my dress and looked down at the strap.

"Slide it into the sleeve on your inner thigh."

I did as he asked, but the foreign feeling of the cold lump of metal against my thigh sent a jolt of uneasiness through my body.

"You're gonna have to walk like you don't have anything there, but it has to be facing your inner thigh or else they'll be able to see it."

I slid my shoe back on. "Is the safety on?"

"No. You won't have time to switch it off if you need it."

"What's to keep me from shooting my leg off?"

185

"The trigger is behind the elastic. You'll be safe."

I looked up at him and searched his face.

"I don't like it any better than you do," he said. "But if we succeed in getting a meeting set up with the senior Simmons, it'll be even more dangerous than this one. You'll need to practice drawin' it out quickly."

I swallowed.

"We'll practice," Neely Kate piped up, now standing behind Jed. "In the field behind the farmhouse. And with any luck at all, Joe Simmons will be snoopin' around again, givin' me just cause to shoot him."

Jed gave me a questioning look, but I just shook my head. "Never mind. Let's go." I slid to the center of the backseat, my stomach in knots.

Neely Kate started around the front of the car, but Jed called out her name. She spun to face him, her eyes blazing. She was ready for a fight.

"If you're goin', then you can drive," Jed said. "I outrank you."

A grin spread across her face, and she looked up at him and winked. "For now you do." Then she slid behind the wheel. "Nice car."

Jed groaned as he shut both of our car doors and walked around to the passenger side.

"Where to?" Neely Kate asked.

"We're heading west. Out to Westminster, but don't leave yet." He pulled his phone out his pocket.

"Westminster?" Neely Kate asked. "That's neutral territory, right? No one's staked a claim there."

Jed jutted his head back in surprise. "How'd you know that?"

Neely Kate rolled her eyes. "Please."

I placed my hand on the front seat and leaned forward. "She knows things, Jed. Don't question it."

He looked at his phone screen, then shifted his gaze to me. "She has the gift of sight?"

"No. She knows them the good ol'-fashioned way. Snoopin'."

I sat back as Neely Kate gave him a smug grin.

Jed shifted in his seat to face Neely Kate. "Gentry's laid claim to it, but there's an undercurrent of anger in the community. Quite a few people don't like him there. We might be able to use it to our advantage."

"Where are we meeting him?" I asked, feeling the gun between my legs. The weight of it made me even more nervous about this meeting.

"You got any other guys comin'?" Neely Kate asked. "As backup?"

"Yeah. But I don't want Gentry knowin' that. That's why we're holding up a minute." He turned to me. "Before I tell you where, I want you to have a vision."

"What?"

"Force a vision and see how this all plays out."

That was actually a great idea. "Okay, but I have to touch one of you."

"Me," Jed said. "If one of our guys turns traitor, he'll definitely go after me. And if Gentry double-crosses us, he'll take me out first too."

"So either way, you're a goner?" Neely Kate asked dryly.

"Neely Kate!" I shouted.

"What?" she looked at me in the mirror. "It's true."

"Jed's not goin' to be a goner. I'll put a stop to it." There was no way I was going to let anything happen to him. I literally owed him my life.

I put my hand on his shoulder and closed my eyes, thinking about what was going to happen when we showed up for the meeting.

Darkness filled my vision, and for a few terrifying moments, I thought I was seeing Jed's death, but it quickly gave way to a neighborhood road.

In the vision, I was sitting in the passenger seat of the car as Neely Kate pulled up to the curb in front of a small white clapboard house that had seen better days. A faint glow lit up the curtain-covered windows. I looked around, but I didn't see anything worrisome, so I said, "Okay, let's do this."

As soon as I opened the door and stood, I heard a gunshot and ducked behind the door.

"Lady. Get down!" I growled as I spotted the shooter. He was in the window of the neighboring house, his shotgun pointed out the second story window. The cocky bastard hadn't thought I'd seen him. It was Bert Winnowman, one of Skeeter's men. I took him out easily with one shot, even though I wished I could have played it out to make him suffer.

Another shot rang out, but I expected this one. If Bert was part of this, his buddy Gil was a player too.

Gil was on the other side of the street with his gun aimed right at us, which made it awkward for me to get a shot at him. Several more shots rang out, one coming through the middle of the windshield. Then Gil fell flat on his face. Neely Kate was turned in her seat, her arm sticking out the window, her gun pointed across the street.

"Rose?" I called out in panic.

"I'm okay," I heard myself say.

"Any more?" Neely Kate asked.

I scanned the street. "No. Let's go. The police will be on their way any minute."

The vision faded, and I blurted out, "Bert Winnowman is a traitor. He and his friend Gil tried to kill us when we pulled up to the house."

Jed's shoulder tensed under my hand. "I suspected as much."

"And you asked him to guard us anyway?" I asked in disbelief.

"No, that's why I asked you to have a vision first."

"So what are we gonna do?" I demanded, pulling back my hand.

"I'm gonna tell Merv to take out the trash," he said, sending a text. "Where were they?"

"Bert was in the house to the left, up in a second story window. Gil was across the street hiding in a bush."

He nodded and sent another text.

"So we're not meeting Gentry after all?" I asked.

"We'll still meet him, but I'll suggest we meet at the old fertilizer plant instead." Jed glanced back at me. "Can you have a vision of that?"

"Yeah." I returned my hand to his shoulder. I started to look for what would happen if we met Gentry at the fertilizer plant, but at the last moment, I made it more generic—what would happen when we met Gentry.

The vision filled my head in seconds. We walked into a warehouse. I set the pace, while Vision Rose and Neely

Kate filed in behind me. Mick was waiting for us at a table, and Bull, the former manager of Mick's strip club, sat beside him. They stayed seated, and I moved to one side, letting Vision Rose stand next to me at the head of the table.

"The infamous Lady in Black," Gentry said in an amused voice. "I'm honored to be in your presence."

"Did you try to have us killed?" Vision Rose asked in her Lady voice, a sultry mixture of culture and confidence.

Gentry sat back, a huge grin spreading across his face. "Your own men were more than willing to take care of that for me."

"Not *my* men," she said with an air of disgust. "You can see why I'm here."

Gentry's eyes twinkled as he waved to a chair. "*Now* we have something to talk about. Let's get down to business."

The vision faded, and I said, "Gentry thinks I'm working with him because Skeeter's men have turned against me."

Jed pushed out a sigh of relief. "Then it worked."

Neely Kate turned to him. "You *planned* that?"

"It took care of two things at once. We got rid of two guys I suspected had turned, and Gentry's suspicions about the Lady have been smoothed over."

"What reason did you give Gentry for the meeting?" I asked.

"That Skeeter's men had turned on you and you were looking for a new alliance."

Something slimy coursed through my veins. "I feel like I'm betraying Skeeter."

"That's how we have to play it." He checked his phone and sent another text.

"That's pretty smart," Neely Kate grudgingly admitted.

A slow smile spread across Jed's face. "Merv says it's done. Part two should kick in soon enough."

"Done?" I asked. "What does that mean?"

"I sent Merv and another guy over there in a car similar to mine." He looked over his shoulder at me. "They were where you said they'd be, which made it easier."

"They're dead?"

He shrugged. "Their choice. And don't you feel an ounce of guilt over it. They would have killed you, no hesitation."

In theory, I knew he was right, but it didn't make it any easier to accept.

"Do we head to the fertilizer plant now?" Neely Kate asked while I wrestled with my conscience.

"No," he told her. "Now we wait. Ten to one, Gentry wasn't even at the original meeting place. A stupid man would have figured there wouldn't be a meeting at all— we'd show up and be eliminated, end of story. But Gentry's not stupid, so he probably guessed we'd escape the trap. Once he gets the all-clear that we survived, he'll let us know where to meet." He looked down at his hand. "And there it is." He studied his screen.

"Well?" Neely Kate sounded short. "Don't keep us in suspense. What'd he say?"

"He wants to meet at a warehouse up in Columbia County."

My heart seized in my chest. "I can't leave the county."

Jed glanced back at me. "If you get picked up by the police, you'll have bigger problems than breaking your bail terms."

That made my anxiety even worse. "Will Glenn Stout lose all his money?"

His eyes narrowed. "Like I said, I don't give a shit about Stout's money. Not that Glenn Stout is even his name."

I considered sharing the information we'd found out about the courier but decided to let Mason deal with that one.

"What do you want to do?" Jed asked, fully turned to study me.

"My vision was in a warehouse," I mused, staring out the windshield. "And Mick Gentry seemed happy to see me. I say we go."

"Okay." Jed turned around. "Let's do it."

I wondered if I was making the worst mistake of my life.

# Chapter Fifteen

Between giving Neely Kate directions, Jed lectured her on how to behave and what to expect.

"I still think you should stay in the car," he said.

"No," I interrupted. "She took out one of the guys in my first vision. You got Bert, but Neely Kate took care of Gil. No hesitation." That part worried me a bit. That she'd reacted so quickly. But in a situation this dangerous, that could only be a good thing.

"Well . . ." Jed drawled. "Okay, but you'll need a name."

"I've been thinkin' about that." She grinned. "I like Black Orchid."

"This isn't a superhero show, Neely Kate," I groaned.

"Well, your name is odd."

"And given some time to think, I would have chosen something more normal. Besides, I didn't even choose it at all." I would have done a lot of things differently, but given everything I knew now, I was pretty sure I would have still gone through with meeting Skeeter on that cold November day. I still saw the Lady in Black as our best—and maybe only—chance to save all of us.

"How about Lily?" I asked. "You can be Black Lily in your head, but we'll drop the black."

She pursed her lips and glanced into the rearview mirror. "It sounds exotic. I like it."

Jed shook his head. "You two are gonna be the death of me."

I sure as hell hoped not.

The warehouse was a good fifteen minutes over the county line. It was out in the middle of nowhere, which was probably a good idea given the potential for collateral damage.

Jed told Neely Kate to pull around to the west side of the building. There were three other parked vehicles there, one of them a pickup truck. Neely Kate had lost her bubbly smile and was now silent and stoic.

"Rose, do you want to have another vision?" Jed asked quietly.

He was nervous. I'd never once seen him nervous—cautious, yes, but not nervous—and it spooked me.

"Yeah." I put my hand on his shoulder one more time and thought about what would happen at the meeting.

The vision started as soon as I closed my eyes. We were in the car, pulling away from the warehouse.

"That went better than I expected," I said in Jed's deep voice.

"You're kidding me," Neely Kate said in disbelief.

I turned to her, finally letting myself relax as we drove away. "At least we got what we wanted."

The vision ended, and I said, "We got what we wanted." I took a deep breath and repeated what I had seen.

"Okay," Jed said, his hand on the door handle. "It sounds like it might not go smoothly, but we'll get what we're after in the end. Stay on your toes."

"Deal."

Jed and Neely Kate both got out of the car, and Jed opened my door, offering me his hand. Neely Kate stood next to the front of the car, her gaze fixed on the doors of the warehouse. She looked more serious and focused than I had ever seen her.

I grabbed Jed's hand and climbed out, the gun between my thighs making me feel awkward and a little off balance. Jed grabbed a small bag off the floor of the backseat. He handed it to Neely Kate, and she hung the long strap on her shoulder without question.

What did Jed have in that bag?

My stomach was tied up in a heavy ball that slowed my steps. Jed was leading the way, and Neely Kate was following behind me.

A kid met us at the entrance. He was dressed in jeans and a T-shirt, and he looked to be in his late teens. He was medium height and lanky, so his shirt swam on him. His eyes were wide with fear.

"Carlisle?" the kid asked.

It took me a second to realize he was talking to Jed.

"Yeah." Jed's answer was gruff, and he pushed back his jacket to show the kid the gun in his holster. "Where's Gentry?"

The boy swallowed. "I'll take you to him."

Jed slowed until I was about a foot behind him, and Neely Kate moved closer to my back. My skin was prickly, and I was beginning to have major second thoughts about this whole scheme.

The boy led us through a maze of shelves stacked with boxes toward a door with a glowing rectangular window. Neely Kate's and my heels clicked against the concrete floor, echoing in the large space, and I wondered if I should get quieter shoes. But my Lady in Black persona was all smoke and mirrors, and it needed to stay that way to distract the dangerous people I was meeting from the fact that I was nobody Rose Anne Gardner, not some rich and powerful woman from Louisiana. Rose wore boots to dig in the dirt. Lady wore fancy high heels to poke out someone's eye should it come to that.

The heels would remain.

The kid opened the door, and Jed stopped in the doorway, his broad chest blocking my view.

"Carlisle," a familiar voice called out. "I see you made it. Did you bring the guest of honor?"

Jed stepped to one side, and I walked through the doorway, surveying the room. It was a lot like my vision. Mick sat at the head of the table while two men sat on either side of him. One of them was Bull.

I'd stood in front of both of these men once before, only they'd been in total control last time, and I'd been desperate to save Mason's life. While my motivations were not so different this evening, neither man knew it. A feeling of hopelessness washed through me, but I shoved it down. This man thought I had something he wanted. I would do well to act that way.

He stood and his eyes lit up, though with evil, not with glee. "The infamous Lady in Black. I'm honored to be in your presence." He made a slight bow.

His condescension pissed me off. "Did you try to

have us killed?"

I felt ridiculous repeating what I'd seen in my vision, but altering anything could change the vision of us driving away safely. Vision Neely Kate had already suggested things would get a little hairy.

Mick sat down and leaned back in his seat. "Your own men were more than willing to take care of that one for me."

"Not *my* men," I spat out. "But you can see why I'm here."

Gentry's eyes twinkled as he waved to a chair. "*Now* we have something to talk about. Let's get down to business."

Jed pulled out a chair for me, and I sat directly across from Gentry. Jed and Neely Kate took the chairs on either side of me.

Gentry turned his attention to Neely Kate, his gaze immediately dropping to her cleavage. A slow grin spread across his face as his eyes rose to meet hers. "Who do we have here?"

"None of your business," I said in a harsh tone. "She's with me."

He smirked, then slowly shifted his attention to Jed. "And you? You turned on your man?"

Jed's steely gaze bored into the other man. "Let's just say a man needs to serve his own interests."

"I never saw you as a turncoat."

To his credit, Jed didn't flinch. "Malcolm took off, and I'm not about to lose everything."

"And her?" He pointed toward me.

"She's an investor with a sharp business sense. I see no reason to let her loose, even if Malcolm's no longer in the picture. I've pledged my loyalty to her."

Mick tilted his head, staring at Jed. "Why should I trust you? How do I know she's not his whore?"

Jed nodded to Neely, who put the bag on the table and slid it toward Gentry.

"Proof we're serious."

Mick opened the bag and pulled out a stack of money. He released a low whistle. "There must be fifty thousand in here."

"One hundred," Jed said, his voice firm.

Crappy doodles. That was more money than I'd ever seen at one time. Where had Jed gotten that much cash?

"You makin' a deposit?" Mick asked, flipping through the bills.

"No," I said, interrupting Jed. I was supposed to be the money person. "It's a show of good faith. Jed is my associate, but I'm the money source. Just like you have a money source."

Mick's eyes narrowed. "I have my own damn money."

I sat up tall. "Let's get one thing straight, Mr. Gentry. I can cut through bullshit like a knife through butter. I consider you barely one step above Skeeter Malcolm right now. Jed claims you are a sound investment, but I'm skeptical. Like Mr. Malcolm, you're hiding from the law. That makes you unstable and unreliable."

He clenched his fist. "If that's your opinion, why are you here?"

"*Opinion?*" I asked. "What properties do you own in Fenton County? Your strip club burned to the ground.

What else do you have?"

"I have a distribution ring in Big Thief Hollow."

"Which was busted by the sheriff weeks ago and hasn't regained its footing since. Frankly, I think I'm backing the wrong horse."

Mick scooted his chair back and banged his palm on the table with a loud thud. I was proud of myself for not flinching. "Your man here said you wanted to discuss a partnership. All I hear is you insulting me."

My hands were in my lap under the table, but I lifted the hem of my dress slightly, my trembling right hand just below the band on my leg. "Mr. Gentry," I said with forced patience, "you are not your own man. You have been bought and paid for. I would love to continue my presence in Fenton County, but you're not even there. We're currently in Columbia County. I want to either meet your backer and hear his long-term goals, or I'll find a surer bet for my investment." I shot him a dismissive sneer as my fingers grabbed the handle of my gun. "I don't deal with middlemen."

Mick's face reddened and he released a loud growl as he stood, flinging his chair behind him. He turned his attention to me, looking about ready to lunge across the less than three-foot-wide table to throttle me.

Jed tensed, but I had already pulled out my gun.

"Go ahead, Mr. Gentry," I said, pointing the weapon at Mick's forehead. "Make another brash move, and I'll eliminate the middleman all together."

Bull made a move for his weapon, but Jed already had a gun trained on him.

Mick cursed a blue streak, teaching me a few phrases I'd never heard, but I just stared at him with feigned patience, trying to hide my fear and keep the gun steady. My heart was pounding so hard and fast in my chest, I struggled to catch my breath.

Mick's eyes narrowed. "I'm going to kill you. I'll wrap my hands around your neck and squeeze the life out of you."

My heart skipped a beat, but it was galloping so fast I barely noticed. "I'm sure your benefactor doesn't want that. Otherwise you wouldn't be here talking with me now. Am I right?"

He didn't say anything.

"*Sit down*, Mr. Gentry."

If looks could kill, I would've splattered around the room in a million small pieces. But Mick retrieved his chair and sat, looking like he was about to have a stroke.

"Are you ready to have a civilized discussion?" When he didn't respond, I continued. "Here's what is going to happen. You are going to call your benefactor and tell him that I'm giving him forty-eight hours to contact me to set up a meeting. If I don't hear from him within that time, I'll set up my own operation in Fenton County. Mr. Malcolm's run off, and Jed's pledged his loyalty to me, so I'll have him take over." I pushed out a breath. "But frankly, I like to have equal partners, not just underlings. So tell your benefactor that I have a plan for Fenton County that will increase his investment tenfold within a few short years. But I need to meet him face to face, and he'll need to tell me his own plans for the county."

"He's never gonna meet with you," Mick spat out.

"I think he will," I said with more confidence than I felt. "Forty-eight hours." I stood, still pointing my gun at him. "Jed will send you my number. You will call or text me. *I* am in charge now."

If I'd just pissed off Jed, he hid it well.

"Now slide that money back over, please," I added sweetly. "That isn't for you."

Gentry gave the bag of money a forceful shove. Neely Kate zipped it closed and slung it over her shoulder.

"And be sure to tell your benefactor that I refuse to meet in backwoods hovels. I'll name the place, and it will be civilized." I lifted my chin. "We're leaving now, and if you try to touch one hair on any of our heads, you will regret it until your dying day, which will be much, much sooner than you'd like."

Neely Kate headed for the door first, and I backed up until I reached the doorway. Jed was close behind, still facing the two men, his gun trained on them until he left the room. Then he gave his attention to the door.

Neely Kate made a beeline for the exit, but I whispered, "Slow down." She set a slower, more purposeful path. I wasn't about to let those guys think I was intimidated by them, even if I was.

We exited the building and quickly climbed into the car. Neely Kate started it up and drove across the parking lot toward the road.

Jed looked over his shoulder, his gun still out. "What the hell was *that?*"

"That was me taking charge."

"He would have killed you, Rose." He was furious.

"No, he wouldn't have. Besides, I put him in his place." I still had the gun in my hand, so I set it down on the seat next to me.

Neely Kate turned toward Fenton County, and Jed continued to look out the window. "It looks like they're not gonna follow us."

"Even if they did, they wouldn't do anything," I said.

Jed still didn't look happy. "We may have gotten what we wanted, but we royally pissed him off."

"He was too full of himself," I said. "He was gonna try to broker a deal on his own. We need J.R."

"You should have let me handle it!" Jed shouted.

"But the Lady in Black is supposed to be in charge!"

"I was negotiating!"

"And I was *right there*. And now I look a helluva lot stronger."

"I'll say you looked strong," Neely Kate finally said, awe in her voice. "Are you like that every time?"

"Yeah," Jed mumbled, obviously still unhappy. "And she's gotten bossier every time."

I shot him a dirty look.

Neely Kate shook her head. "I didn't even recognize you in there."

"I'm glad you didn't, because I'm scared to death J.R.'s gonna figure out who I am."

"We'll cross that bridge when we come to it," Jed said. "But we're gonna have to do damage control. Skeeter's bound to find out we've turned on him."

"We haven't turned on him. We're just makin' Mick Gentry think we have."

"Word's gonna get out. Gentry will do everything he

can to weaken Skeeter's position." Jed was silent for several seconds. "Where are you plannin' on meetin' the big guy?"

"I don't know yet."

"He might not even call." Jed sounded a little more hopeful than I would have liked.

"He's gonna call," Neely Kate said. "They're intrigued by her. Sure, they're infuriated, but they're intrigued too."

Jed made Neely Kate drive around county back roads for an extra half hour before he decided we hadn't been followed. Neely Kate pulled to a stop behind the Sinclair station, and I started to get out of the car.

"Rose." Jed sounded hesitant.

I turned to look at my friend, because after everything we'd been through together, we *were* friends. "Jed, I'm sorry if I stepped on your toes."

"No." His jaw was tense, but his eyes were filled with worry. "Your instincts are good. Almost too good."

I scowled. "I can't say that doesn't worry me."

"Go with it for now, since this will likely save your hide."

"And Mason's and Skeeter's."

He nodded. "But don't get too caught up in it. You can't keep up with this double life, no matter what Skeeter thinks."

I wanted to remind him that just last week he'd been upset that I was about to quit my role as the Lady in Black. But this was different. I'd crossed a whole new line tonight, and we both knew it.

I started to get out, then turned back around. "Where'd you get the money?"

A ghost of a smile appeared on his face. "It was your bail bond money."

"He was really gonna pay it?"

"Yeah. But someone else beat Hale to it."

"But he was gonna lose it, right? He'd never let me go to prison."

Jed didn't answer, which was answer enough.

I climbed out of the car and quickly changed, then got behind the wheel of my truck. Neely Kate got into the passenger side without speaking. Jed waited for us to drive off first, so I pulled out of the lot and started back toward the farmhouse. The silence in the truck gave me time to brood. When I performed my role as the Lady in Black, there was always a separation between the Lady in Black and Rose. But tonight, the line I usually skirted had not only blurred but faded altogether.

I couldn't help wondering which part of me would be strongest when this was all said and done.

# Chapter Sixteen

It was after ten o'clock when we got back to the farm, but Neely Kate and I were too wound up to go to bed. I took Muffy outside, then Neely Kate and I changed into pajamas and the three of us snuggled up on the sofa with pillows and afghans to watch Netflix.

Around eleven, Mason sent me a text.

*Are you awake?*

Neely Kate was dozing on the opposite end of the sofa, so I hopped up and padded into the kitchen, where our conversation wouldn't disturb her.

He answered right away, his voice as comforting as a warm blanket. Suddenly it all seemed to make sense. Mason was why I was taking these crazy chances. He was the reward at the end of this insanity.

"How's Neely Kate?" he asked. "Did you girls have a good night?"

"I made potato soup, and we snuggled up and watched Netflix." Okay, so I had left out a considerable chunk of the middle of our night. Feeling guilty about holding so much back, I added, "And I saw Joe." I'd considered keeping it from him—at least until he got home—but maybe it would distract him from all my other secrets.

"What? *Where?*" he barked, although I knew his anger wasn't directed at me.

"Out in the barn."

"What was he doing in the barn?" He took a deep breath. "Please tell me you didn't talk to him. He can take anything you say and use it against you."

"Oh, Lordy." Mason was right. Why hadn't I remembered that before I'd spouted off at him? Had I said anything incriminating? "I did."

"It's okay," he said, although he didn't sound convincing. "Just tell me what happened."

My back tensed. "I took Muffy outside to wander around, and she headed right for the barn. I figured she'd sniffed out some mice the other night and remembered. Anyway, when we got inside I noticed the back door was standing wide open."

"That door was closed when I left the barn, Rose." His voice was tight with worry. "You need to stay away from the barn. In fact, maybe you girls should go stay with Mom after all."

"I think we're fine. I'm sure it was Joe. He said he was checking the property for trouble, and he came to investigate when he heard noises in the barn. I accused him of snooping around to look for evidence to use against me, but he swore he's tryin' to protect me. He says he has a plan."

"Hmm . . ."

"Wait. *You* think he might have been telling the truth?" Given time to think about it, I was beginning to think he had been too, even if I didn't appreciate the way he was pulling it off. But after my arrest, I was surprised Mason believed it.

"In hindsight, the way he was behaving after your arrest leads me to believe he *might* not be on his father's side, but damned if I know what he's doing. Not that I trust him. I take it he didn't share his plan with you?"

"Of course not. He gave me his usual bullcrap answer of he knows what's best and I should blindly follow. He said J.R. was fixing to kill me, so arresting me was the only way he could protect me. He might have a plan, but I'm sure as Hades not waiting for him to work on his plan to save me. If anything, I'm worried he'll end up doing more harm than good."

"I plan to talk to him tomorrow when I get back," Mason said, his tone angry again. "He has no business being on your property without a warrant."

"No, don't confront him." The thought of the two of them *chatting* made me anxious. "Just leave him be. Hopefully, your meeting tomorrow will be the first step in getting us out of this mess. How'd it go with the sketch artist?"

"They have a good sketch, but now the state police detective is working on identifying the man. I've come up with a pretty solid argument for why the secretary of state's office should formally investigate the guy who helped get me removed from office. The state detective is coming with me to corroborate my request."

"Why don't you sound more excited?"

"I still have that feeling that it's too easy. I guess we'll find out tomorrow."

"When do you think you'll be home?"

"I can't imagine the meeting will run more than a few hours, but I suspect there will be some loose ends to tie up. I'm hoping to be back by late afternoon." His voice lowered. "I've been thinking about your vision, and I'd like to take you out for dinner tomorrow night. How about I make a reservation at Jaspers?"

"A date?"

"We need more of those, don't you think?"

"Yeah. I'd like that." The timing seemed wrong, in spite of my vision, but for all we knew, I might only have less than three weeks of freedom left. We needed to make the most of our time together. "Any news on the guy who posted my bail?"

"No. Randy hasn't gotten back with me with anything on Sam Teagen. But in the meantime, stay inside tonight, okay?"

I had no desire to see what was lurking in the darkness. It would be coming for me soon enough. "Yeah."

"If you feel threatened in any way, call Randy and he'll come straight away. I'm going to bed, sweetheart. I'll call you after I finish the meeting."

"Good luck. I love you."

"I love you too." He paused. "We're going to get out of this, Rose. I promise."

I only hoped it was true.

\*\*\*

The next morning, I slept later than usual and woke up to the smell of coffee wafting up the stairs. For a split second I thought Mason had woken up before me and started a pot brewing. Then I remembered that Mason was in Little Rock and Neely Kate had spent the night.

I found her in the kitchen, wearing a pair of yoga pants and a long-sleeved T-shirt and standing in front of the stove. Her face was free of makeup, and her hair was pulled back in a ponytail.

She turned to look at me as I walked in, a smile wavering on her face. "Good morning."

"Something smells good." My stomach growled, but then I remembered that she'd spent the past several weeks concocting bizarre recipes inspired by the cooking show where the contestants were given random combinations of ingredients. "What is it?"

"Pancakes. I was gonna make some bacon, but your refrigerator is freakishly empty."

"I'm still banned from the Piggly Wiggly, although this time it's because Mason's insisted that we ban them."

"Well, *I'm* not banned, so I'll pick up a few things when I'm in town today."

I grinned, but then remembered why she was here. "Have you talked to Ronnie?"

"No." That one word was delivered in such an emphatic tone, I decided to leave that subject alone.

After pouring myself a cup of coffee, I set the table and took the syrup out of the cabinet.

"I figured we'd need a hearty breakfast to get us through this morning." Her words had an ominous sound.

My hand froze as I lifted my coffee cup to my mouth. "Why am I suddenly afraid you're gonna take me out into the woods and re-enact *Naked and Afraid?*"

She gave me a look that suggested my statement was as ludicrous as if I'd announced I no longer knew my own name. "Don't be so dramatic. We're gonna have target practice. I figure it's gonna take a while since you're so inexperienced."

"Oh. I almost forgot." I took a sip of coffee as she brought a plate of pancakes to the table and sat down. "I left the gun Jed gave me in his car." We could have used one of Mason's guns, but I didn't feel like volunteering that information. This had seemed like a good idea last night, but now I was having second thoughts.

"Lucky for you, I grabbed it while you were changing. It's already in my purse."

"The only bullets I have are in the gun."

She groaned in exasperation. "I'll go buy some. I already checked Mason's stash in the basement, and you need a different caliber. You're not gettin' out of this. If you're gonna start pullin' a gun on someone like Mick Gentry, you need to practice. You need to get used to the feel of the weapon you're carrying and how it fires."

In the light of day, what I'd done the previous night seemed incredibly stupid. I was lucky that none of us had gotten killed. "I think I screwed up last night."

Neely Kate shook her head. "No. I think you did the right thing. You had to shake that guy up to get him to take you seriously. But—" she stabbed a pancake and put it on her plate "—if you're gonna use a gun, you need to know how to use it."

What we were doing was crazy. This was a Bonnie and Clyde, Thelma and Louise level of insanity. I had to let Neely Kate know what a predicament we were in. "Neely

Kate, you killed a man in my vision last night. Doesn't that freak you out? It sure scares the heck out of me."

She stopped slathering her pancake with butter and looked me in the eye. "Was one of the guys trying to kill you?"

"Kill *us*. And yes, but you just whipped out your gun and shot him. No hesitation. You weren't even freaked out!"

She gave a quick nod and then returned to her task.

"Neely Kate. Could you really do such a thing?"

"Didn't *you*?"

"What are you talkin' about?"

"You killed Daniel Crocker in November."

"He was gonna kill Mason and Joe!"

"And the man in your vision was going to kill you. And me and Jed. How is that any different?"

"But the *you* from last night—both in my vision and in the warehouse—was so different. Where did that come from?"

She was quiet for a moment, and when her eyes met mine, they were dead serious. "Don't ask questions you don't want answered."

What in the world did that mean? But she was right. I wasn't sure I wanted to know all of her deep dark secrets. At least not right now. I had more than I could handle at the moment. But as soon as this mess was sorted out, I was digging in with a backhoe.

When we finished breakfast, I gave Neely Kate the keys to my truck. I tried to give her money, but she waved it off and ran out the door to pick up more food and ammunition. I grabbed my phone and called Mason's mother while I cleaned up the kitchen.

"Good morning, Rose." Maeve's greeting was so warm I felt the comfort all the way down to my toes. But then she continued in a hushed, conspiratorial voice. "Have you made any progress?"

"Actually, yes, on several fronts. In fact, I have a question for you about one of them. I need your help."

"You know I'd be more than happy to help in any way I can, whether it involves Mason or not. What do you need?"

"Mason said you might know how to read shorthand."

"Oh, my. I used to back in the Stone Age." She chuckled. "What makes you ask?"

"I have a photocopy of a page covered in shorthand. I need it translated. I have no idea what it says, but I can't take it to just anyone. It might contain sensitive information."

She hesitated. "I see."

"Do you think you can look at it and try to read it?"

"Of course, but can it wait until after lunch? I'm helping Violet with the shop. She has an appointment this morning, so she asked me to help cover the store."

That surprised me. She'd been gone the day before too. "Yeah, sure. I wonder why didn't she ask me?"

"She probably doesn't want to bother you. We all know you have more pressing issues to deal with at the moment."

I wasn't so sure, but then Maeve was always looking for the good in people. When had I stopped?

"In any case," she said. "I'd love to look at it after

lunch. Why don't you come by the house around one?"

"Thank you, Maeve."

I felt better that Maeve was going to take a stab at deciphering the page, but we still were no closer to figuring out the significance of the key. With any luck at all, the page would tell us.

I called Bruce Wayne next. While our landscaping business was as dead as the majority of the plants in the ground since it was early February, I still felt guilty about heaping so much of the responsibility on my business partner's shoulders. I needed to at least check in to see if anything needed my attention.

"Hey, Bruce Wayne," I said after he answered. "How's everything with the business?"

"You've got great timing. We got another landscaping bid request. It's out in your sister's old neighborhood, so it might not be that big of a job." He sounded reserved, like he was miffed. Was he upset that we were so short on work? That I'd been gone so much?

"That's a good sign, right? That we're still gettin' work even though I was arrested? It doesn't matter how big or small it is. Right now we need every job we can get. Maybe I can get to it tomorrow."

"Okay." He sounded dubious. "But you've got a lot goin' on. Maybe Neely Kate can handle it."

"She's only been on two jobs with me, and even then, she only came along because I dragged her out of the house. She's nowhere near ready. It'll have to be me." I sighed. "I have some things I need to take care of with my case, but I'll try to come in later today."

"I might not be here. Violet and Anna need me at the nursery this afternoon."

"Anna will be there?" While I was excited that Bruce Wayne had a crush on someone, I tried to overlook the fact that she had so much animosity toward me.

"Don't you be startin' somethin'."

"I'm not. I'm just askin' what you're doin' and who's gonna be there. It's a perfectly innocent question."

"I'm moving bags of mulch. Don't be makin' more of it than that." He paused. "If you really want to get in each other's business, how about we talk about the fact that Lady made a special appearance last night?"

My blood ran cold. There it was. The reason he was mad at me. I tried to sound noncommittal. "What did you hear?"

"That she and Jed turned on Skeeter."

Oh crap. "That's out already?" It was one thing for us to deceive Mick, but I'd hoped we would manage to put this put to bed before the rumors started flying. But this was huge news. It was going to spread like wildfire.

"So it's *true?*" he asked in disbelief.

What should I tell him? The fewer people who knew my plan, the better. Even my partner. "It's nothing to worry about, Bruce Wayne."

"What the Sam Hill are you doin', Rose?" He sounded angrier than I'd ever heard him.

"I have a plan. Leave it be."

"Like hell I'm leavin' it be! You're playing with fire, and you're about to get burned to a crisp."

That was exactly what I was worried about, but I couldn't let him know that. "I'll keep your concerns in mind."

He was silent for several seconds, but his voice was cold when he responded. "So you're just blowin' me off?"

I tried to keep my voice steady and sure. "No. But I know what I'm doin'. You have to trust me."

"*No. I don't.*" He sounded hurt and angry. "I think you've crossed a line this time. You need to stop this *right now.*"

"I can't."

"You mean you *won't.*"

"*Bruce Wayne.*"

"You won't listen to me because you think I'm feeble-minded and stupid."

"What? *No!*"

"I expected better of you, Rose Gardner. I thought you were different than everyone else."

"I swear to you that's not it. How can you believe I'd think such a vile thing?"

But he didn't respond because he'd already hung up.

I sat down at the kitchen table, feeling sick to my stomach. My heart was bursting with the pain and guilt of hurting him, but I had no idea how to fix this. I considered calling him back and telling him everything, but he'd insist on helping, and this was just too dangerous for him. He'd finally gotten his life together. I couldn't let him throw that away. Especially not for me. Even if I broke his heart.

Neely Kate found me still at the table, alone in my despair. She set down the shopping bags of food and listened as I told her about my conversation with Bruce Wayne. "If it makes you feel any better," she said with a tight smile, "I think you did the right thing."

"He's certain that I think he's stupid," I said in defeat. "He's spent his whole life hearing that very thing from people, and he was just finally starting to crawl out of the hole of believing it. What am I gonna do?"

She patted my free hand. "You can tell him everything after this is all said and done. I know it sucks, but if you tell him now, he's gonna wanna be in the thick of it, especially since he got you into this in the first place. But his loyalty to you is gonna get him arrested or worse. Keepin' him safe is more important than protectin' his feelings right now."

While what she said made sense, hurting him didn't settle well on my soul. "But that makes me no better than Joe. *He* says he's keepin' everything to himself to protect me. How is this any different?"

It gave me a whole new appreciation for Joe's reaction to my anger toward him.

She cringed. "Oh, honey. When you put it that way, it does sound the same, doesn't it? But what else can you do?"

My heart ached so bad I could hardly breathe. The only thing I knew to do was go with my gut, and it told me to keep Bruce Wayne as far away from this situation as possible.

But I wondered how much I was going to lose to take down J.R. What would be the ultimate price for my lies and deceptions? Would the outcome be worth the risk?

It was far too late to ponder that now.

I sucked in a deep breath and stood. "We have work to do, so let's get to it."

After we put away the groceries, we stepped out into

the crisp cool morning. It was Muffy's perfect kind of day, so she protested vehemently when I made her stay inside. But I worried that the noise from gunshots would spook her enough that she'd run off.

In addition to picking up food for us to eat, Neely Kate had bought some cheap canned vegetables to use for targets. We carried them out behind the house, and she set four of them up on the wooden fence posts lining the pasture on the right side of the barn. In days past, I was certain it used to contain Dora's horses, but now the field was overgrown and full of weeds.

Neely Kate paced us about fifty feet back, then explained that my gun was a semi-automatic and hers was a revolver. Mine held more ammunition than hers, but she said it didn't matter to her.

"It's important to be comfortable with your weapon. This was my grandfather's gun, and I learned to shoot with it. I'm a pretty accurate shot, so I make each one count. But you definitely need the practice."

She showed me how to line up the gun with the target, then gave me tips on how to try to make my shots more accurate, since Mick Gentry's men weren't going to stand still and let me get them lined up before I fired on them.

"You killed Daniel Crocker with a pretty accurate shot. How'd you do it?"

"He was lunging at me. He was close, and I pulled the trigger in self-defense."

Her lips pressed together as she gave it some thought. "If it makes you feel any better, if you end up shooting anyone, it will probably be up close. Jed and I will take care of anyone who threatens you from a distance."

The gun shook in my hands. "How can you say that so casually?"

"What do you want me to do? Whine and cry about it? I put myself in this position, and I know what I'm doing."

"But how? *How* do you know what you're doin'? You would have killed that man last night if I hadn't forced a vision."

"There are things about me you don't know."

"Obviously."

She stared at me for a moment. "I lived a hard life. Before and after I went to live with my granny. I've seen things. I've done things. I've had things happen to me." She lifted her chin. "We'll just leave it at that."

She had hinted that life with her mother had been awful, but I'd never known *how* awful it had been. I reached out and put a hand on her arm. "*Neely Kate.*"

Determination filled her eyes. "My cousins taught me how to defend myself. I can bring a grown man to his knees and then shoot his acorns off without even aiming." She took a step away. "But *you* need practice. So let's get to it."

Turning into a no-nonsense drill sergeant, she taught me how to load the chambers of both of the guns. Then, without any warning at all, she lifted her gun and shot the can of green beans clean off the fence post. She turned to me with a grin. "Your turn."

I moved to the next fence post and lifted my gun, aiming for a can of corn. I fired off several shots, but the can was still in pristine condition. Well, as pristine as a can of corn could be.

"Hmm . . ." she murmured, glancing from me to the post. "Maybe you should move closer. Especially since we've already established that if you shoot someone, you'll be within a short distance."

"I don't want to shoot anyone at all."

"And I don't want to take Granny to Bingo next Tuesday night, but we all have our crosses to bear. So be that as it may, you need to be prepared in case you do."

I let her drag me closer. "After I get J.R. to confess, I'm going to leave my short foray into a life of crime behind."

"That's probably for the best, but we still gotta survive this adventure. So shoot that can of corn."

"I'd rather shoot the lima beans. I hate lima beans."

"Fine," she huffed, moving us over to the post that held the hated vegetable. "Now show me how much you hate these suckers."

She moved back behind me, and I lifted my gun, standing about twenty feet from the target. I fired five shots before I nicked the side of the can.

"Okay . . ." she drawled. "So you need a little work . . ."

I put my hand on my hip. "You *think?*"

She laughed and picked up another can from the bag she'd set in the middle of the backyard. She set the sauerkraut on the empty fence post where the green beans had been, then started stomping toward me. "Come on. I'll show you how it's done."

I stood behind her as she lifted her gun and shot all four cans off their posts—one right after the other, all in a matter of seconds.

219

"Oh, my word," I murmured in amazement. "Why did you never tell me you were like Annie Oakley?"

"Because I don't want Ronnie to know."

Given Neely Kate's family history, it wasn't all that odd that she knew how to shoot a gun. And being a great shot didn't seem like any cause for shame. So why was she keeping it from Ronnie? I started to ask her, but my heartbeat kick-started into a gallop when I heard a siren approaching from a distance.

Neely Kate gave me a perplexed look, and we both turned to face my driveway as a sheriff's car came barreling toward us, shooting gravel and dust out behind it.

What were they here to arrest me for this time?

"Oh, my stars and garters," Neely Kate sighed. "It never occurred to me. Give me your gun."

"What?" I asked, watching in disbelief as the sheriff's car ignored the end of my driveway and continued to tear through the yard toward us.

"Joe's farm is close enough to hear the gunshots." She took a step toward me and grabbed the gun I still held at my side, then took a couple of steps away from me. She looked wild and untamed, both guns at her sides, her long blond and pink and purple streaked hair blowing slightly in the wind. There was an edge in her eyes I wasn't used to seeing, and I had to admit she was a bit scary.

The car stopped about twenty feet in front of us, and Joe climbed out, wearing a look of frustration along with his uniform and coat. "*What the hell are you doin'?* You scared the ever-lovin' shit out of me!"

"Why do you even care, Joe-traitor-Simmons?" Neely Kate shouted. "It looks to me like you're trespassing. Now go the hell away!"

"Trespassing?" he shouted back. "I damn near got in a wreck trying to get here in time to save you!"

"Save us or arrest us?" she asked, taking several steps toward him, the guns pointed toward the ground.

He glanced down at her hands, then up at her face. "I hope you have permits for those weapons, Neely Kate."

"You think I'm fool enough to be shootin' without them?" she fibbed. The ownership of the smaller gun was questionable at best.

He pursed his lips and shook his head, his chest heaving as he tried to catch his breath. "What the hell are you doin'?"

"Target practice." She waved toward the exploded cans on the ground behind the fence. "What's it look like?" Her face scrunched in disgust. "No wonder you arrested Rose on the lamest charges ever thought up. You're just as inept as Officer Ernie."

His jaw clenched. "Why the hell are you doing target practice here?"

She tilted her head and sneered. "The last time I checked, the Second Amendment was still in place and *this* is private property. But if you must know, I'm practicing to protect my best friend, thank you very much."

"That's why I got you Tasers! Why have you resorted to guns?"

She gave him a condescending glare. "I don't have to answer that."

He turned to me, anger flashing in his eyes. "Why's Neely Kate doin' all the talking? Don't you have anything to say?"

I put my hands on my hips. "My attorney has advised me not to speak to you outside of his presence."

His eyebrows rose. "So, you've already talked to Carter Hale this mornin', have you?"

I'd meant Mason, but I saw no sense in correcting him.

He looked across the field toward his house before returning his gaze to me. "I realize this is your property, and Neely Kate certainly has the right to hold target practice on your land, but I formally request that you let me know if you do this again in the future. I think I just aged ten years. I thought you were being attacked."

Something in me softened, although I wasn't sure why. If I left my future in his hands, I had little doubt I'd be shipped off to McPherson in a few weeks.

He took a step toward me and stopped. "Rose. Can I speak to you for a moment?"

"Didn't you hear what she said?" Neely Kate sounded incredulous. "She can't talk to you without her attorney!"

Joe grunted and opened his jacket, jerking his badge off his uniform and tossing it onto his front seat through the open car door. "*Will you talk to me now?*"

Tears filled my eyes. My anger from the previous night had faded . . . all that was left was a sense of betrayal. "Why?"

"Rose." The pleading in his voice was nearly my undoing, but why? Why did this man still pull at my heart after everything he'd done?

"Don't do it, Rose," Neely Kate warned.

"*Please*," he begged.

I was such a fool, but I heard myself say, "Okay."

"Rose!"

My chest heaved for several breaths as I fought tears. "I need your promise you won't use this against me somehow," I said to him, ignoring Neely Kate.

He looked more serious than I'd ever seen him. "I swear it."

Neely Kate stomped toward us, her eyes wide in disbelief. "What are you doin'? You can't trust a word that man says, Rose! He stood in your landscaping office and asked me to watch out for you. And less than forty-eight hours later he turned around and had you arrested for the most asinine charges in the world."

But I walked away from her, passing him as I walked toward the tail end of his car. I stopped there and crossed my arms. "What do you want?"

He followed and came to a stop a few feet in front of me. "I think we both said things we regret last night."

"Speak for yourself." That caught him off guard, although I wasn't sure if he was reacting to my words or the tears in my voice. "You can spin it any way you want, Joe, but the bottom line is that you betrayed me," I said without malice. "As long as I live, I'll never be able to forget the look on your face as that awful woman manhandled me and shoved me into the back of her patrol car."

"Rose, I'm sorry."

"Yet it doesn't change a thing." I looked toward the house, wishing things were different. But I'd been wishing that same thing my entire life, and never once had it ever done me any good. "I'm so tired, Joe. I'm so tired of fighting with you. I can't do this anymore."

He moved closer to me, standing at my side. "This isn't what I wanted."

"Me neither, and yet this is how it is." He didn't say anything for several seconds, so I turned a little to look at him. "I think you should go."

"If I hear gunshots again, I'll be back to check on you."

I looked away. I knew I should have thanked him, yet I couldn't bring myself to do it. Because despite his intentions, he'd hurt me. "You do what you need to do . . . and so will I."

"Joe," Neely Kate said. I hadn't realized she'd walked up behind me. "You need to go."

Joe started to get into his car and stopped. "Neely Kate, I'm serious. If you're gonna start shooting guns, let me know unless you want me to come back again."

"Fine." But the word lacked any bite.

As he drove off, Neely Kate put her arm around my shoulders. "You okay?"

"I don't know."

"Fair enough."

I sucked in a deep breath and pushed it out. I didn't have time for this. I had to save everyone. God knew, I'd probably end up having to save Joe too. "We need to get back to practicing."

Her forehead wrinkled with worry. "Maybe we should take a break."

I shook my head. "Nope. We need to do this before Mason gets home." I suspected he wouldn't disapprove, but I wasn't sure he'd be thrilled either. Besides, the less I called attention to my alternate life, the better.

224

# Chapter Seventeen

A half hour later, I'd improved, but that wasn't saying much. I still couldn't adequately protect myself from someone at any distance. Crappy doodles, I only had a one in five chance of saving myself from a can of lima beans. Hopefully, it wouldn't be an issue.

Neely Kate and I ate a quick lunch and then headed into town to talk to Maeve. We brought Muffy since she was ticked off about being left inside all morning. She curled up at Neely Kate's feet, facing away from me, as we drove. Neely Kate was unusually quiet too, and I felt liable to choke on the tension in the truck cab. I figured it was as good a time as any to add more.

"Have you heard from Ronnie?" I asked, trying to keep my tone light and breezy.

"No."

"Are you goin' to call him?"

She turned to look at me, her eyebrows arched. "And why would I call him? He's the one who left me!"

"I know, Neely Kate, but I think Ronnie's in some kind of trouble and needs our help."

She shook her head and turned away. "He doesn't want my help. I know all about his boys in his poker group, but when I tried to talk to him about it, he told me to mind my own business."

"Why didn't you tell me that?"

"You don't need to know everything."

I pinched my lips together as I tried to figure out what to do next. Neely Kate might be hurt enough to let it go, but I wasn't. When we pulled up in front of Maeve's, I grabbed my phone and texted Bruce Wayne.

*I know you're upset with me right now and you have every right. I'm not insulting you, BW, I'm protecting you even if you don't see it that way. But you and me aside, I'm worried about Ronnie. He left NK and supposedly he's thick as thieves with a group of guys at his garage in Pickle Junction who are loyal to Mick Gentry. Can you do some digging?*

I was starting to put my phone back into my pocket when it vibrated.

*Are you sure I can handle it?*

I was tired and cranky enough to consider sending a retort. Instead I sent: *Of course.*

After several seconds, he sent: *Okay. I'll do it for NK.*

"Who are you texting?" There was a suspicious look on her face.

"Bruce Wayne. He's working at the nursery today. With Anna," I added brightly, hoping she'd want to talk about the possibility of their relationship. Neely Kate normally thrived on gossip.

Instead, she opened her truck door and climbed out.

Sighing, I grabbed my purse and Muffy and followed her out of the truck. I set my little dog down in the yard to sniff around and do her business, but Neely Kate had already knocked on the door. Moments later, Maeve appeared in the open doorway, holding her worn bulky cardigan across her chest.

"It's my three favorite girls. Come in! I just pulled a coffee cake out the oven."

Muffy heard her voice and made a beeline for the front door, jumping up on Maeve's legs in excitement.

Maeve laughed and scooped her up, leaving the door open for Neely Kate and me to follow.

"It sure smells good in here," I said, my stomach suddenly growling, even though we'd just had leftover soup and bread.

"How do you not weigh five hundred pounds?" Neely Kate asked as we followed her into the kitchen. "You've always got so much good food."

Maeve laughed. "I have plenty of people stopping by to eat it." A smile lit up her face, but I saw the worry lurking in her eyes. "Moving to Henryetta was the best decision I ever made, save for marrying Mason's father, of course." She winked. "I've made more friends here than I ever could have imagined."

"How could you not?" Neely Kate asked, smiling as she leaned over to look at the still-steaming coffee cake. "You're the sweetest person I know, and you feed everyone you meet."

"Well, thank you, Neely Kate." Maeve patted her arm. "You know you are always welcome here." Something in her voice let me know that she knew things weren't right with my friend.

Neely Kate pulled her into a hug, not saying a word, and Maeve rubbed her back in small circles. After a moment, she pulled back and cupped Neely Kate's cheek.

They stared wordlessly into each other's eyes for a long moment, some secret and meaningful exchange passing between them, and then Maeve dropped her hand.

"Would you girls like some coffee cake?"

"That's got to be the silliest question I ever heard," Neely Kate said.

"Well, then I'm putting you to work." Maeve handed her a bowl of icing and a spatula. "You take care of that, and I'll start the coffee."

I sat at the table, basking in the warmth and love and acceptance I always felt when I walked into this house. It was the same way I always felt when I was with Mason.

Thinking about Mason made my stomach cramp with anxiety, and I was overcome with the familiar fear that I was going to lose him. One way or the other.

Maeve put a hand on my shoulder. "Rose, are you okay?"

I looked up at her, my mouth flapping like a fish out of water.

"Neely Kate, could you keep icing the cake while I show Rose a photo album I found the other day?" Maeve asked.

Neely Kate glanced over her shoulder. "Are there photos of Mason as a little kid? Bring them out. I want to see them too."

"We'll bring it right out. I just need some help getting it down from the shelf."

I followed Maeve into her bedroom, and she shut the door behind her, the smile sliding off her face. "Have you had a vision?"

I pulled her over to the bed, and we both sat down. "I

did, but I'm doing everything in my power to change it."

The color fled from her face. "You saw him die?"

I grabbed her hand and squeezed. "No. When I got out of jail, I forced a vision of Mason three weeks into the future, hoping to see there was no trial. Instead, I saw absolutely nothin' and this icy darkness started to spread through my body. Mason tried to blow it off, but I told him I knew he was dead."

"What's he doing to prevent it from happening?" she asked, her voice shaking.

"Nothing," I said, guilt seeping through my blood. "He says he refuses to hide away and do nothing when there's a chance I might be locked away for good. He's in Little Rock right now at the secretary of state's office, trying to get them involved. But I'm scared." I squeezed her hand harder. "I want him to be more careful, but he won't listen to me."

She gave me a weak smile and cupped my cheek, just like she'd done minutes before with Neely Kate. "I know you do, sweet girl. He loves you. He'd move heaven and hell to save you. He wouldn't dream of doing it any other way. And it would be wrong to force him to do otherwise."

"I can't let him get killed because of me."

She shook her head. "No. I don't think it's because of you . . ." She looked down. "Do you know who the other person tied into this is?"

She was referring to the premonition she had told me about last week—how Mason and another man were in mortal danger.

"Yes."

She nodded. "It's dangerous."

"Very."

She looked up at me, unshed tears in her eyes. "It feels wrong to ask you to keep doing whatever you're doing."

"You haven't asked me to do a thing I hadn't already decided to do. If anything, your feeling has given me the confirmation I need to move forward, even if it feels a little nuts." I struggled to catch my breath. "But I'm gonna lose him, Maeve. Either way, I'm gonna lose him."

"Mason?" she asked in disbelief.

"Have you had a feeling about what will happen after I save him?"

She shook her head. "No, I'm sorry."

I nodded. "Promise me something."

She swept a few stray hairs away from my face. "Of course."

Tears stung my eyes. "When he hates me, please tell him I did it all to save him. I've dug myself deeper and deeper into this hole to save him." A tear rolled down my cheek, and I brushed it away with my fingertip. "When it's over, please make sure he knows that."

Confusion swept over her face. "Rose. Why would Mason hate you? What are you doing?"

I stood. "I'm sacrificing everything."

I started for the door, but she stood and grabbed my hand, pulling me back. "Rose?"

I leaned over and kissed her cheek. "I'm gonna try really hard to keep it from him, but he's a smart man. He's gonna piece it all together. He's already started. Just promise me you'll tell him." I started crying harder. I didn't want to think about life without Mason.

"Okay. Okay." She pulled me into a hug. "This is my fault. I've pushed you into something because I confided my premonition."

I pulled back and wiped my face. "No. I was on this course months before you told me about that." I opened the door. "I need to get back into the kitchen. Neely Kate's gonna ask questions."

I headed back to the kitchen to join my friend before Maeve could respond. She followed seconds behind me, carrying a photo album. "You girls can look this over while I scan that paper you brought me."

"Oh. Yeah." I had forgotten all about the photo album. I sat down at the table, hoping it wasn't too obvious I'd been crying. Neely Kate gave me a weird look, but then turned back to the cake. She had finished icing it and was now slicing off three pieces. She set the plates on the table as I pulled the paper out of my purse and handed it to Maeve.

Maeve headed for the coffee maker, but I motioned for her to sit down. "I'll do it."

Once she was settled, she leaned over the paper and heaved out a sigh. "Rose, there's a small notebook and a pen in that drawer by the refrigerator. Can you hand it to me?"

"Of course."

I gave her what she needed and then poured three cups of the coffee.

When I sat back down, Maeve groaned and looked up at me. "I've forgotten quite a bit."

"You can't read it?" Neely Kate asked.

Maeve made a face. "I'm getting bits and pieces. It's just been so long."

"Do you have a shorthand dictionary or something?" I asked.

She shook her head. "I can try to order a book, but it will probably take a couple of days to get here."

A couple of days? I knew I was being impatient, but we were so close . . .

"Rose, I'm so sorry." Maeve must have seen the dismay on my face.

I forced a smile. "What's a couple of days? I've got plenty to do to keep me occupied in the meantime. Can you make out *any* of it?"

"There's something about a bank account. It looks like it says $35,000. But I can't tell where the account is or why it's important."

I nodded. "Okay. Anything else?"

"It looks like there are a few times listed. I think they might be appointments, but I have no idea who they were with or where or *anything*." She sounded frustrated.

"It's okay, Maeve. It was a shot in the dark." But I was sure it had to be important. J.R. had gone to great lengths to ensure no one saw that diary. "Do you see anything about a key?"

"A *key?*"

"Yeah, like a house key?"

Her lips pressed into a thin line of frustration as she scanned the paper. "No, but I've forgotten the mark for key. I'm sorry." She sounded close to tears. "Can you take it to someone else?"

"We'd rather give it to someone we know we can

trust. Can you think of anyone?"

She shook her head. "No. Shorthand is a lost language."

I hated putting this pressure on her, so I turned to Neely Kate and lifted my eyebrows. She grimaced and shook her head. "I only know a few people who'd be able to do it, and they'd blab about it everywhere."

I released a huge sigh. "Okay. It's only a couple of days. It can wait." But that meant I'd still have to go through with my meeting with J.R. If he called. It had been nearly eighteen hours.

What if he didn't call? What if J.R. Simmons wasn't even Mick Gentry's backer?

My phone vibrated in my pocket, making me jump. For one brief moment, I thought I'd conjured a call from the devil himself, but it was the wrong phone. I pulled my cell out of my pocket and checked the screen before answering. "Mason! How did it go?"

"Well . . . good and bad. They're going to look into a possible misuse of office by the investigator, but there's no obvious tie to J.R. At least not yet. The state police detective ID'd the guy in the sketch, the one who kept coming to see the investigator. His name is Pete Mooney. He has a checkered past. He's had a few charges brought against him, but he's always managed to get off. He's from the Pine Bluff area, so they're gonna send someone to pick him up and ask a few questions."

"But none of that really helps me, does it?"

He was silent for a moment. "No, sweetheart, but we'll figure something out."

I chose to ignore the fact that he sounded desperate.

"I'm sorry it took so long to call. I've been in meetings all morning."

"That's okay. I knew you'd call when you could."

"Have you had an eventful day?"

"Oh, I'll tell you about my morning later. Right now Neely Kate and I are with your momma, eating her delicious coffee cake." I gave Maeve a warm smile.

"So no luck?" he asked, sounding more defeated than I'd ever heard him.

"She's gonna order a book to brush up on her shorthand, but there's a few things that sound promising. I can tell you about it later. When do you think you'll be home?"

"I'm about to leave now. I should be there a little after four. I made an early reservation for Jaspers. Does that still sound good?"

"It sounds perfect." For some reason tears sprang to my eyes. Then I realized what was bothering me. This could be one of my last dates with him. "I'll see you when you get home."

Both women were watching me as I hung up the phone. I forced another smile. I seemed to be doing that a lot today. "Mason's on his way home, and he's taking me out to dinner. Isn't that wonderful?" My voice broke and I pushed away from the table, the chair scraping the floor, and stood. I couldn't pretend anymore. I needed to do something productive—*now*—and this was currently a dead end.

"That sounds lovely," Maeve said, looking distraught herself.

"I think I'm gonna go see Carter Hale."

Maeve and Neely Kate both eyed me as if I were about to sprout horns.

"That's a good idea," Neely Kate finally said, standing and picking up her plate. "I'd like to drop in on Carter Hale myself." Her next words caught me off guard. "Would you be willing to teach me how to make your famous white bread?" she asked, looking at Maeve. "Tonight?"

Maeve's despair seemed to lift a little. "Of course. Why don't you come over for dinner? We can make it a girls' night."

Neely Kate smiled. "Sounds fun."

I headed for the door, and Maeve called out, "Why don't you leave Muffy here while you run your errands? She can keep me company."

"Thanks. Carter might not appreciate having her in his office. I can take her to mine, but I'm not sure if Bruce Wayne is back yet." Not to mention he probably wasn't too eager to see me. "Say, do you know where Violet was this morning?"

Maeve shook her head. "No, she didn't mention it, and neither did Anna." Her eyes lit up. "Anna's such a sweet girl. I'm glad your sister hired her. She's had a hard life."

"Really?" I asked. "She barely talks to me." Maybe because she was always too busy glaring at me.

"If you'd like, you can leave Muffy here while you and Mason go on your date. She can either spend the night, or you can pick her up before you go home. I can make a fresh batch of Muffy's biscuits."

"Okay . . ." I looked down at Muffy, who almost looked like she was grinning in anticipation. Maeve had recently begun baking her doggie treats that seemed to make her existing gas problem even worse. But since Maeve loved to make them and Muffy loved eating them, I didn't have the heart to tell either of them no. I bent down and rubbed her head. "I'm gonna leave you with Maeve tonight, but I'll come get you tomorrow."

She jumped up and licked my cheek in response.

Neely Kate and I said our goodbyes and headed out to my truck. Letting it run for a moment, I grabbed my burner phone from my purse. Still nothing. Maybe Jed had sent them the wrong number. I texted him my concern, and he answered back within seconds.

*I know how to text a damn phone number.*

Somebody was crabby today.

"Why are you frowning?" Neely Kate asked.

"I still haven't heard from J.R."

"It's J.R. You know he's gonna string you along and make you suffer."

"Yeah, I suppose you're right."

"Besides, you don't want it to happen tonight, do you? Not if you and Mason are goin' out."

"True." But the sooner this meeting happened, the better.

"Where's Mason taking you?"

"Jaspers."

She smiled, but it looked wobbly. "The last time I was there I barfed all over Samantha Jo Wheaten's ex-husband."

"That's a sight I'm not likely to forget anytime soon."

It was also the night Mason had punched Joe. Maybe going there wasn't such a good idea.

"My life was so different then." Her voice was so quiet it could have floated away on a cloud.

"Neely Kate. Call Ronnie. Please. You miss him something fierce, and I know he's missin' you."

She sucked in her bottom lip. "I was thinkin' about seein' if I could stay with Maeve tonight." She gave me a wink. "Give you and Mason some privacy."

"You don't have to do that."

Her eyes glistened with held-back tears, but she forced a grin. "I know. But I really do want to learn how to make Maeve's bread."

"I thought your granny made white bread."

"She does, but Maeve's is different." There was a hint of desperation in her words, and I sensed she needed to soak up some of Maeve's nurturing.

"You know, now that I think on it, it's a great idea for you to stay at Maeve's. Then Mason and I can have sex on the kitchen table again."

She scrunched her eyes closed. "I can live without that visual."

"Ha!" I shot her an ornery look. "If you really do make bread, be sure to give me one of those loaves."

"Deal, but if you eat too much of it, the table's liable to collapse from all the weight."

"Neely Kate!"

We drove downtown, and I parked outside of my office, but the closed sign was in the window. Given where I stood with Bruce Wayne right now, I wasn't sure whether to be disappointed or relieved. I got out of the truck, and someone with black hair and purple streaks caught my eye down the street.

It was Kate. She was walking toward the dry cleaners—wearing a dress and nice boots, no less. Why was she wearing something nicer than usual, and where was she headed on foot?

"Why do I keep seein' Kate downtown?" I said absently.

"Because she's renting an apartment over the antique shop."

I spun to face my friend. "You're kidding."

"No. I thought you knew."

"No." But I could only handle one thing at a time. "We'll deal with her next. First let's pay a visit to my second favorite attorney."

"Carter Hale is your second favorite?" Neely Kate murmured. "You've reached a new level of desperate."

That was putting it mildly.

# Chapter Eighteen

When we walked into the law office of Carter Hale, the proprietor himself stood at the corner of his assistant's desk. He grimaced when his gaze landed on me, but his demeanor changed the moment his eyes shifted to Neely Kate.

"Ms. Gardner," he drawled. "Did we have an appointment? I *do* have other clients that require my attention, you know."

"I want to know what you've dug up since I saw you last."

"Not nearly as much as you have, apparently." He winked. "The crime world's all abuzz."

Greta glanced up at him with a look of confusion.

The blood rushed from my head. "I have no earthly idea what you're talkin' about."

"I'm sure you don't," he teased. "Why don't you girls come back to my office?"

His assistant stayed at her desk, though she looked mighty curious now, and Neely Kate and I followed him down the hall. He shut the door behind us, then headed behind his desk while we took the chairs in front of him.

"So the Lady in Black is back." He kicked back in his seat. "And without Skeeter Malcolm this time. I thought I told you to keep a low profile."

"Really?" Neely Kate cooed. "You don't say."

"And she had a new handler with her." His eyes bored into hers. "A woman."

Neely Kate leaned to the side and crossed her legs, still holding Carter's gaze. "That's *amazin'*. I had no idea the Fenton County crime world was so forward-thinking."

"I know, imagine that," Carter said with a sly grin. "We're so cosmopolitan now."

I groaned. "Cut to the chase, Carter Hale. What's goin' on in the rumor mill?"

"Well . . . first of all, criminals don't admit they listen to rumors."

Neely Kate pursed her lips and nodded her head, both in an exaggerated fashion. "Criminals pretend they don't gossip. Got it."

He chuckled.

"Can we get back to my case?" I asked, getting irritated.

Carter kept his gaze pinned on my friend. "Is she always this narcissistic?"

"Her life *is* hanging in the balance," she retorted.

"What have you found out about Glenn Stout?" I asked.

When Carter didn't answer, Neely Kate said, "That's a trick question to test your investigatin' skills."

His playfulness fell away. "I don't know squat about Glenn Stout, but I take it from Neely Kate's smug response that *you* do."

"Not enough," I said. "We only know that the courier who deposited the money at the courthouse met Eric Davidson a few days before his death. And that he won first place in the calf-roping competition at the Fenton

County Rodeo last year. Oh, yeah, and his name is Sam Teagen."

A grin spread across his face as he studied us. "You ladies are in the wrong profession. Your skills are wasted in landscaping."

Neely Kate whacked my arm. "That's what *I* keep saying."

"Ouch." I rubbed my sore bicep. "We were just lucky."

"You get lucky a lot," Carter said.

"Mason gave the name to a source we have in the sheriff's department, but I haven't heard anything yet. Now tell me what you know."

He frowned. "I know my appeal to postpone your trial has been rejected."

"Of course it has been." I'd expected as much, but it was still disappointing.

"Simmons has it out for you."

"Lucky me. Good thing I'm taking things into my own hands."

"And this has something to do with the infamous Lady?"

"The less said, the better."

"And what does Skeeter think of this?"

"Skeeter's not here."

"Yet Lady's still takin' meetings?"

"Mr. Hale. What exactly are you doin' to save me? Because from where I'm sitting, it looks like I'm doin' all the work."

He laughed, but it was a short, abrupt sound. "I'm doing what little I can. Skeeter has assured me he's on this."

"Forgive me, but Mason and I seem to be the only ones makin' any progress."

He didn't respond.

"What information have you dug up from all those leads you were bragging about? Finding out who bribed the judge and the DA?"

He made a face, and if I hadn't known any better, I would have suspected he'd made the mistake of eating the jumbo wing special at Big Bill's and was now desperate for the restroom. "My usual sources are keepin' mum about the instigator of the bribes."

"So you've got a big fat nothin'."

"Everybody's runnin' scared right now. This potential war between Gentry and Skeeter . . . there's a general feeling of overall impending doom. Everyone's takin' cover."

This was a waste of my time.

"If you've got absolutely nothing to report to me, I might as well be goin'."

He sighed in exasperation and held his hand out at his side. "I'm not the one who suggested you drop by."

"I have to do *something*, Carter! I feel like I'm stuck on the tracks, just waiting for a runaway freight train to slam into me. I have to stop this!"

His expression softened. "I know. And for what it's worth, you've already accomplished quite a bit."

Neely Kate jumped out of her seat and pointed her finger in his face. "That's not acceptable, Carter Hale! You get off your lazy ass and *do* something, or I'm gonna cut off all your toes and feed them to the squirrels that live under the park bench across the street."

He lifted his hands as if in surrender, but a grin tugged at his lips. "Better my toes than another appendage I'm quite fond of."

"*Get busy.*" She spun around and stomped out of the office, leaving me to trail behind her like a baby duck.

She didn't stop until she was on the sidewalk, and I didn't try to stop her because I'd taken to storming out of places too.

A mischievous grin slid across her face. "Do you want to spy on Kate?"

I blinked and shook my head. "You're gonna give me whiplash, Neely Kate. I'm still reeling from your mutilation threat."

She put her hands on her hips. "Well, do you or don't you?"

It was definitely tempting. "What exactly do you have in mind?"

She pursed her lips and lifted her shoulder into a half-shrug. "I figured we could make it up as we go along."

"Code for you have no idea what you're doin'."

"Hey." She cocked her head. "Do *you* have a plan? No? I didn't think so. Besides, I *do* have a little bit of a plan. Come on."

I walked beside her as she headed toward the antique store. "So what are we doin'?"

"I'm thinkin' this through. She moved into her apartment a couple of weeks ago. But why would she want to live here on the square? There are plenty of places to live in Henryetta. Rumor has it the apartment over the antique store is nasty."

I shrugged. "Well, there's no denying she's the polar opposite of Hilary, who rented the absolute nicest house in town. That place wasn't even for rent."

She stopped in front of the antique store and looked up at the windows above the storefront. After shifting her gaze to survey the area around us, she peered back up at the apartment windows. "Hmm. Maybe the location of her apartment has *everything* to do with what she's doin' here in Henryetta. She rarely sees Joe."

I turned to look at her and lifted my eyebrows.

"What?" she asked, sounding defensive. "Deputy Miller tells me things."

"Maybe she happens to like living on the town square. Maybe she's into quaint towns. Or maybe she wants to be close enough to my office to spy on me."

She released an exaggerated sigh, then waved her hand toward the center of the square. "She's spyin' all right, but I don't think it's just on you. She's directly across the street from the courthouse."

"Why would she be spyin' on the courthouse?"

Neely Kate pointed to the apartment windows and then trailed her finger through the air and pointed at the old stone building. "Those windows. Whose are they?"

"Mason's." A cold sweat broke out on the back of my neck. "The district attorney's office takes up that block of windows, and Mason's old office is directly across from her apartment."

"What if Kate is the person trying to kill Mason?"

My head felt fuzzy, and I lifted my hand to my temple.

"That's plum crazy, Neely Kate."

"Is it? She's made no effort to hide the fact that she wants you and Joe back together."

"Wanting us back together and trying to kill the assistant district attorney are two *very* different things. Besides, she's J.R. Simmons' daughter. She has people she can call to take care of that for her."

"Exactly. She's J.R. Simmons' daughter. Why's she here all of a sudden? Seems like awfully convenient timing."

"She told me just yesterday that all of this trouble has been brewing for some time and she came here to watch it go down."

"Even if she's not the one tryin' to kill Mason, maybe she was spying on him to get information for that meeting that ended with him gettin' fired. Maybe she and Joe aren't seeing each other in public to throw everyone off the fact that they're working together. Shoot, for that matter, maybe she's doin' the same thing with Hilary."

I felt like I was about to be sick. "Their hatred for each other seems pretty genuine."

"You know what they say—conspirators make strange bedfellows."

I shook my head. "I have never once heard that, but you could be right. They might have agreed to join forces for the greater good."

"But what exactly is the greater good?" Neely Kate asked, staring up at the windows. "There's a few big pieces missing from this puzzle."

"Kate said she's here as an observer, but she has at least some knowledge about what's going on. She called me a few hours before my arrest—right after Joe took the journal—and told me to mind my P's and Q's. I confronted her about it yesterday, and she pretty much admitted she was trying to warn me about the arrest."

"Hmm. I'm not sure that works with my theory that she might be here to kill Mason or set him up."

A vein in my temple began to throb. "I don't know. Maybe she's into games. She *is* a Simmons."

"True." She gave me a long look and then walked into the store directly below Kate's apartment without another word.

"Neely Kate!" I murmured, but she was already inside the Henryetta Found Treasures Antique Emporium.

Calling Henryetta Found Treasures an antique emporium was like calling a rusted 1972 Cadillac a luxury car. And that was being generous. The entire store was basically a thrift store. The items were supposed to be antiques, but the majority of the merchandise only looked old.

Neely Kate made a play of browsing. When I moved up behind her, she picked up a chipped blue pottery bowl and held it out toward me. "Didn't you say you were lookin' for one of these?"

I tilted my head to the side. "Hmm . . . I think I need one in tangerine."

A woman stood behind a small counter, watching our every move as though she suspected Neely Kate might stick the bowl in her purse and run out the door.

Neely Kate turned to her and smiled. "Do you have this in tangerine?"

She shook her head, her mouth puckered in

disapproval. "All we have is what you see. And if you drop that bowl and break it, you buy it."

Neely Kate turned her back on the sour woman and put the bowl down, then glanced at me and rolled her eyes. I had no idea what she was scheming.

I followed her as she made her way to the back, past a wooden high chair with three legs, an old-fashioned phonograph like my grandma used to have in her parlor, and a whole host of junk. Neely Kate stopped in front of a velvet-covered chair with dark wooden arms and legs.

"Is this Victorian?" She turned to me. "This looks Victorian."

I wouldn't know Victorian if Queen Victoria rose up from the dead and hovered in front of me. "Maybe . . . ?"

"Is this Victorian?" Neely Kate called over to the woman.

"Yeah . . . sure it is."

Neely Kate looked at the price tag. "Two hundred? Would you take one-fifty for it?"

My eyes bugged out. Surely she wasn't really gonna buy that rickety chair for that much money. The thing would collapse if Muffy sat on it, let alone her.

"I don't know . . ." the woman hedged. "It's pretty valuable. It came over on the *Mayflower*." She circled the corner and limped toward us, moving as stiffly as if *she* had come over on the *Mayflower*.

Neely Kate's eyelashes fluttered, and she touched a hand to her chest. "Oh, my stars and garters. You don't say?"

I turned my back to the saleswoman and mouthed to Neely Kate, "The *Mayflower?*" I wasn't a history buff, but I was fairly certain the *Mayflower* predated the Victorian era by a couple hundred years.

But Neely Kate ignored me. "Wow. Here in Henryetta, Arkansas? I think I'm gonna have to have it."

The saleswoman laughed, but it sounded more like an evil cackle. "Will you be taking it with you?"

Neely Kate's smile faded. "Can you hold onto it? I'm lookin' for a place first." She lowered her voice. "I'm leavin' my husband, and I haven't gotten everything arranged just yet."

A burst of shock jolted through my body. I knew she was play-acting, but something told me there was a truth embedded within the lie.

First Violet and her husband Mike had split up, and now Neely Kate and Ronnie seemed like they were on the verge of a divorce too. Two marriages I'd previously thought were perfect had been shot to heck. In hindsight, I had to admit I'd seen the cracks in my sister's marriage, but this trouble between Neely Kate and Ronnie had blindsided me. Would I feel the same way when Mason left me?

I fought the rising panic, shoving it back down into my chest of locked up feelings. Mason loved me. We were gonna be fine. Mason would never know about my deception. I'd pull off my last performance as the Lady in Black, and then I'd burn all my hats in a roaring bonfire.

While I was all wrapped up in panic and self-doubt, Neely Kate had moved on with her story. "It's hard for a single gal, you know? Rent's pretty doggone expensive. But it's just me—not even any pets—so I don't need anything too big." Her face lit up. "Say! Henryetta Found Treasures!

Don't you have an apartment over your store?" She leaned closer and lowered her voice. "I work down the street at the landscaping office, so I'd love to live close to work, you know?" Then she winked. "I'd be willing to pay a little extra on the deposit."

The woman shook her head. "Yer two weeks too late. I done rented that apartment to someone else."

Neely Kate waggled her eyebrows. "Is it a single guy? Is he cute?"

"Nah. It's a woman. Kind of surly. But she's only staying for two months. If you can hang on for another month, it's yours."

"You don't say?" Neely Kate said. "Any chance I can see it today? If I like it, I'll leave a deposit."

"Well, I'm not supposed to let you in on account of that other woman's things."

"Oh, come on," Neely Kate egged her on. "I bet you have a key. I'll just pop in to take a peek and then pop right back out. I'll only be a few seconds."

"I don't know . . ."

"Is there a light bulb that needs changing or something?" Neely Kate gave her a big smile. "I can do it for you, and then we'll kill two birds with one stone. You can tell her I'm your maintenance woman if she asks questions."

"Do you know how to use a wrench?" the woman asked. "Miss Prissy Pants keeps griping about a leaky faucet in her bathroom."

Neely Kate shook her head, then waved her thumb toward me. "Not me, but my friend here is a wiz at it.

She's got one of those old farmhouses that's always needing work done. She can fix it for you."

Oh mercy. I barely knew which end of a wrench was the one you used, let alone how to fix a leaky faucet, but Neely Kate's plan was pure genius.

The woman looked us over, then gave a quick nod. "Okay, but you better make it quick. And don't touch nothin' and definitely don't steal nothin'."

"Deal."

Neely Kate and I followed her to the counter, where she opened the cash register and pulled out a silver house key. She started to hand it to Neely Kate, but pulled it back at the last minute. "You have ten minutes."

Neely Kate leaned over and snatched the key. "Then we better get goin'." She bolted for the door, leaving me to follow.

"Aren't you forgetting something?"

Neely Kate stopped in her tracks and turned around.

The woman held out a wrench. "Yer gonna be needin' this."

I laughed, hoping it didn't sound as forced as it felt. "Silly me. I thought maybe it was already up there."

I walked back and grabbed the outstretched tool, but the woman held on tight.

"Why do I smell some funny business here?"

I tried to look confused instead of nervous. "I don't know what you're talkin' about."

She gave me a long look.

I lowered my voice. "I'm just here to support my friend. That's all. This apartment, the *Mayflower* chair. It might be exactly what she needs to move on with her life."

I was laying it on a bit thick, but the woman let go. Forcing what I hoped was a friendly smile, I hurried out the front door after Neely Kate.

"What was that all about?" she asked, stopping at a door a few feet away from the antique store entrance, then inserting the key into the doorknob.

"She's suspicious, so we need to hurry."

Neely Kate grinned. "We don't need much time for what I have in mind."

Oh, crappy doodles.

# Chapter Nineteen

As Neely Kate and I headed up the stairs, it occurred to me that Kate might have come home while we were visiting Carter. I was about to warn Neely Kate, but she already had the key in the lock.

I cringed as I followed her into the apartment, debating whether to call out Kate's name as warning, but once I saw the space, I realized it wouldn't be necessary.

Neely Kate hadn't been exaggerating about the apartment being in bad shape. It was a loft—if you could call it that. The far wall was the brick exterior of the building, and windows lined the walls facing the street and the alley. The wall attached to the connecting building was a bare lathe wall—minus most of the plaster—and the floor was of unfinished wood.

"What the Jiminy Cricket?" Neely Kate gasped when we walked in and saw the bathroom that was tucked in behind the door. Multiple shower curtains were suspended from a rod attached to the ceiling. The curtains currently hung open, revealing a grody toilet, a cheap oak cabinet and sink topped with an oval mirror that hung from the lathe slates over it, and a clawfoot tub.

"Where's the kitchen?" I whispered.

"Over here?" But it was more of a question. She was pointing to a six-foot-long run of cabinets equipped with a sink and a two-burner hot plate. A half-sized fridge stood at the end, and a tiny microwave was on top.

The room was mostly devoid of furniture. A mattress lay on the floor, and a big kitchen table with two mismatched chairs on either side sat in the middle of the space. The table was strewn with papers. The mattress was covered with sheets and a blanket and a couple of pillows. A duffel bag and a pile of clothes lay next to it.

"Well . . ." Neely Kate sighed. "This explains why she looks like a homeless person most days."

I thought "homeless person" was an exaggeration, but not by much. I set the wrench on the kitchen counter. "Let's see what those papers are about and get out of here."

We reached the table at the same time. I couldn't make heads or tails of the mess. Multiple slips of paper—each the width of a normal sheet of paper, but only about two inches high—were marked with dates, times, and one-line sentences.

*M seen in black sedan with mark*

*Ten minute phone call, subject unknown.*

*Fire destroyed evidence.*

The papers were rumpled, as if they had been folded over and over and stuffed into something.

"What are these?" Neely Kate asked in dismay.

"I don't know."

Neely Kate walked over to the window and let out a low whistle. "She's definitely spying on the DA's offices. You can see Mason's desk from here. The DA's too."

I looked up at her, cold dread settling at the base of my neck. "That could be a coincidence."

She squatted and held up a pair of binoculars. "And I'm sure these are for star-gazing in Henryetta Square."

I looked down at the table again, and this time I saw something under one of the papers. Trying not to disturb anything, I lifted it and pulled out a cell phone. I touched the power button, and the blood rushed from my head the moment the screen came to life.

"This is Mason's phone. The one that was stolen from his car when he was run off the road."

"What?" Neely Kate ran over and took it from my shaking hands. "Are you sure?"

"That's his start-up screen." I pointed to it. "It's a photo of the Arkansas University logo."

"But plenty of people around here are Razorback fans."

I took it back from her and entered his passcode. All his apps filled the screen. I opened the photos and pulled one up. "But how many people have a photo of me and Muffy?"

"Oh, my stars and garters," she whispered, examining the photo. "You were *not* having a good hair day."

"*Neely Kate!*"

"Okay, sorry." She looked shaken. "What do we do?"

"I don't know. Keep looking and take pictures of everything."

Neely Kate picked up one of the slips. "*M.* M is for Mason. He also drives a dark sedan and was there for the fire at Gems. She's been following him."

I shook my head, fear washing over me in hot, sticky waves. "Why? Why would she do that?"

"You said so yourself. She wants you with Joe."

I shook my head again. "But that's just plum crazy. Why steal his phone? It has to be more than that. Was she the one who hired Eric? Did she hire Sam Teagen?" I started getting light-headed. "Was she the one who posted my bail?"

Neely Kate stepped in front of me and grabbed my hands. "I don't know. But we need to keep lookin' so we can get this figured out. She could come back at any minute. Why don't you go over to the windows and keep watch while I search, okay?"

"But I should be the one lookin'."

"You're shakier than tassels on a belly dancer, and besides, one of us needs to look out. She's obviously dangerous, so she can't find us here. I'll tell you what I see, okay?"

I nodded. "Yeah. Okay."

She looked deep into my eyes. "We're gonna figure this out. We're gonna stop her."

I nodded again, feeling dangerously close to losing it. I had had no idea what we'd find in Kate's apartment, but it didn't even come close to this. "We have to."

"Then go watch the window, and I'll keep looking and take some photos." She released my hands and turned back to the table, leaving me to make my way to the windows. I picked up the binoculars and looked over at the courthouse. I could see Mason's office in amazing detail, including his desk and the bookcases behind it. If she'd been watching for a couple of weeks, I had to wonder what she'd seen.

Neely Kate started flipping through another stack of documents. "These are court cases. And police reports."

"What?" I asked, my voice shaking as I set the binoculars down.

"From Little Rock. They're cases Mason prosecuted."

"Why would she have those?"

"I don't know, but she's awfully interested in this one from five years ago. She's got multiple highlights on the thing."

"What is it?"

"It looks like a hit-and-run case. But it didn't go to trial. The witness died."

"Who was the witness?"

"A little boy."

I gasped. "How did he die?"

"He drowned in a pond by his house." She looked up. "It was an accident, but it happened a few days before the trial."

"Why would she have that?" I shook my head. "It doesn't make sense."

She started taking photos. "We'll show it all to Mason and see what he says." She uncovered a large envelope and looked inside. "Hello, stalker."

"What?"

"This is stuffed full of photos of Mason." She scattered them across the table and quickly sorted through them. "And this one was definitely taken last summer," she said, lifting it up. "Your hair was shorter."

She turned it around to show me. It was a photo of me, Mason, and Joe on the courthouse steps. And the only time we'd ever been together there was right after Jimmy DeWade was arrested for the murder of which Bruce Wayne had been accused.

My blood ran cold. "Keep lookin'."

I turned back to the window and scanned the square. There was no sign of Kate, but there was a duffel bag on the ground, so I knelt beside it, opened it wide, and started to riffle through the contents. It was full of clothes, but at the bottom my hand touched metal and plastic.

"She has a gun."

"What kind?" Neely Kate's voice was cold.

"I don't know." I pulled it out and held it up.

"Sweet baby Jesus. Where'd she get a Sig? She's serious."

She sounded equally impressed and horrified.

"Put it back and try to make it look like you weren't in there."

"I don't remember how it was."

"It's fine," Neely Kate murmured, taking more pictures. "Everything's such a mess, I doubt she'll notice."

I put the gun back and replaced the clothing. As soon as I stood up, I noticed a figure hurrying across the street. "Oh crap."

"What?"

"She's coming back! And she's in a hurry."

I looked around to see if the apartment looked like it had obviously been disturbed, but Neely Kate was right. It all looked like a tornado had been through it. I had more immediate concerns. "We're trapped. She's almost to the door downstairs."

Neely Kate took one last photo, then started stuffing the pictures back into the envelope. "Lock the front door."

I rushed over it and threw the deadbolt as she adjusted a few papers. "Okay, let's go."

"Go? *Where?*"

"Out the window."

"What?" But she was already moving toward a back window. It was then I noticed the fire escape.

She grabbed the window and tried to lift it. "Karma Chameleon!" she cursed. "It's painted shut!"

I tried to tug it open with her, but it refused to budge. "Try the one next to it, and we'll climb over."

She moved on to the next window without questioning me. This one was stuck too, but she gave it one last tug and it scooted up, sending Neely Kate flying backward onto her backside.

I gasped in alarm. "Are you okay?" She was still supposed to be taking it easy after her surgery. So much for that.

Her face contorted in pain, but she grabbed my outstretched hand. "I'll whine about it later. We have to go."

I climbed out the window first. It was a couple of feet away from the fire escape, the top railing of which was a little higher than the bottom of the window. I leaned out the window and reached for the railing, resting my knees on the windowsill. When I had a good grip, I climbed to my feet and swung first one leg over and then the other, landing with a thud.

"Shh!" Neely Kate was already climbing out behind me, but she was moving with more grace. She landed on the fire escape floor with barely a thud. "You have longer arms. You shut the window, and I'll lower the ladder."

I leaned over and grabbed the side of the window, precariously unbalanced as I leaned my body over the open space, trying to push it shut. "It's stuck again! I need to get more in the center of it," I whispered in a panicked voice. I heard the soft moan of metal from the fire escape ladder.

"Push harder!"

I leaned over more and pushed all my weight into the bottom of the window. The window gave way and jerked down with a soft thud just as the apartment door opened. The panel hid the tenant from me. Or, more aptly in this case, me from her. But I had a millisecond to register this as my body's downward momentum started to pull me over the railing.

Neely Kate grabbed my jacket and pulled me up and back, then immediately guided me down to the grate floor. I stared up into her terrified face.

"You're stronger than you look," I whispered, trying to catch my breath and recover from my near-death experience.

"They say adrenaline does funny things."

I heard the click of heels on the wood floor inside. "What are we gonna do?" Both of us were crouching now, but if Kate happened to look out one of the windows near us, she would probably see us.

"Let's wait a minute to see if we can hear anything," she whispered. "If not, we'll slide over to the steps and carefully make our way down."

"Okay." But I really didn't want to stick around. I felt liable to jump out of my skin. But staying was a good idea, my feelings aside. We might hear something useful.

After about thirty seconds, it was apparent we weren't going to hear anything helpful—Kate wasn't rushing to call anyone, and she didn't seem to have a habit of talking to herself—so Neely Kate started scooting toward the ladder.

If anyone had been watching from below, we would have looked a sight, but the alley was blessedly empty. When we reached the bottom, Neely Kate frowned. "We need to get the ladder back up, but it's gonna creak."

"Maybe we can create a diversion out front."

Her face lit up. "Good idea. You wait here, and when you hear a commotion, push the stairs up. Then head to the landscaping office, and I'll meet you there."

"Okay." The antique store was the next to last store on the street, so Neely Kate walked down the alley and around the corner. About thirty seconds later, I heard yelling and banging.

"I'm gonna sue!" Neely Kate hollered. "How can they just put a trash can there!"

I pushed the ladder up as carefully as I could, cringing when I heard a soft clanging noise. Then I took off for the landscaping office like Miss Mildred after a door-to-door salesman.

As soon as I unlocked the back door and stumbled inside, someone bumped into me. I screamed, imagining the worst.

"Rose!" Bruce Wayne shouted. "It's me. What on earth is goin' on?"

I took a deep breath and braced my hands on my thighs, trying to catch my breath. "Neely Kate's coming. I'll tell you everything when she gets here."

My legs were shaky as I made my way to my office chair. Neely Kate burst through the front door seconds later, a blast of cold air coming in with her.

"Did you get the ladder up?" she asked as she shut the door behind her.

"Yeah."

"Good, because Kate was watching me make a spectacle of myself."

I cringed. "That can't be good."

"No. If she figures out someone was in her apartment, she's gonna tie it back to us." She shook her head and held her lower abdomen, looking pale as she took a seat in her own chair. "Not my finest moment."

"Are you okay?"

"I will be. I just need to rest a minute."

"You've had an eventful couple of days."

"I'll say," Bruce Wayne said dryly as he stared out the window and down the street. "What with the two of you becoming criminal masterminds and causing public disturbances left and right."

"Listen to you," Neely Kate said, sounding snippy. "Gettin' all sassy."

He glared at her. "I'm not the one makin' deals with criminals."

"Both of y'all stop." I rubbed my forehead, feeling a headache brewing. "We need to focus on what we just discovered. Neely Kate, will you send me the photos?"

She stuck out her tongue at Bruce Wayne, then pulled out her phone. "Sure."

I shook my head. My heart rate was returning to normal, and I felt like I was thinking more clearly. "We need to figure out why Kate was so interested in Mason's Little Rock cases and the police reports from Little Rock."

"What in Pete's sake are you talkin' about?" Bruce Wayne asked.

"Did you know that Joe's sister Kate is living in the apartment over the antique store?" Neely Kate asked.

"No."

Neely Kate gave him a smug grin. "Well, I figured out that it's directly across from the DA's offices. So I convinced the store owner to let me look at the apartment. When we got up there, we found binoculars by the window and all kinds of papers proving Kate's been spyin' on Mason. She's got a stack of papers about his court cases from when he was a prosecutor in Little Rock. One case in particular seemed to catch her attention—something from five years ago. She'd highlighted it like crazy. In fact, she'd highlighted it so much I couldn't read the defendant's name because it was covered in blue. He was charged with a hit and run for plowing into some guy crossing the street. An eight-year-old boy was the only witness, but he drowned before the trial. They ended up dismissing the case."

Bruce Wayne's forehead furrowed. "Why would Kate be interested in a five-year-old hit-and-run case?"

"Why is she obsessed with Mason at all? She's got tons of photos of him too," I said, feeling a goose walk over my grave. "I'm not buying that it's because she wants me to get back together with Joe. This goes a lot deeper."

Neely Kate leaned to the side in her chair. "She knew about what Mason was doin' in Little Rock a year ago. She was the one who told you that he and Hilary had history."

"Yeah, but she blew it out of proportion." I stood, wringing my hands. "Besides, she couldn't have been in

Little Rock at the time. She moved to California two years ago. How'd she know what Mason was doin'? How did he even fall into her radar?"

"I don't know," Neely Kate murmured.

Figuring I could at least share *this* with Bruce Wayne, I explained about the slips of paper and what they said. "What's weird is they were all folded up. Like someone was passing her notes."

"That is strange," Bruce Wayne said.

Neely Kate picked up a pen from her desk. "Obviously Kate thinks Mason is doing something wrong. She stole his phone. She's spying on his office. She's going through his files. The question is why would she think that?"

"It sounds likes she believes Mason was taking bribes from Mick Gentry," Bruce Wayne said. "His phone disappeared before the fire. Maybe she was trying to get information about Gentry and Gems from the phone. That would explain the note about the fire too—maybe she thinks the information linking him to the whole debacle burned up in the fire."

"But *why* does she think that? Sure, Mason and Joe were doing that sting operation on Gems, but how would she know?"

We were silent for a moment, then Neely Kate said in a quiet voice, "She's looking at his old files too. She must think he was taking bribes in Little Rock first."

I shook my head. "There is no way on God's green earth Mason would take a bribe."

"Maybe not, but Kate thinks so," Neely Kate said.

"Why does she even care?" I asked, my anger growing. "It's none of her business."

Bruce Wayne sat on the edge of his desk. "Maybe she's doin' it for her daddy."

I shook my head. "She hates her daddy."

"So she says," Neely Kate said. "What if she's lying to cover her tail?"

"No," I protested. "Even Joe says she hates him."

"Joe had you arrested. On his daddy's orders," Bruce Wayne said. "Do you really think you can trust him?"

I looked him in the eye. "Maybe not. But this still doesn't make sense. Surely she knows she's not gonna find any dirt on Mason."

Neely Kate's eyes grew wide. "Oh, my stars and garters. She's not lookin' for evidence. She's plantin' it."

"What?" I asked.

"Think about it. J.R. planted evidence that you paid Daniel Crocker to kill your mother."

"But she's been here for weeks. What's takin' her so long?"

"She told you herself she wants to see the show," Bruce Wayne said. "Maybe she's gettin' everything in place so she can watch it all unfold."

"It's all a game to her," I said, starting to pace again. "She called and left me that cryptic message before I was arrested. Then she gloated about how she tried to warn me." I stopped and spun around to face them. "She gave me another message. She said something I'm looking for is under my nose."

"What's that mean?" Neely Kate asked.

"Beats me. I ran her off and told her to keep her

worthless messages to herself. I can't very well go ask her to give me a better explanation. Especially after we were in her apartment." Then a fresh wave of horror washed over me. "Oh! Neely Kate! The wrench!"

"What about—" Her eyes turned into silver dollars. "Oh, my word. We forgot it. I didn't give the owner a chance to ask for it. I just slapped the key on the counter and told her I wasn't interested in the apartment."

"What are you all talkin' about?" Bruce Wayne asked.

Neely Kate told him about how we'd schemed our way into the apartment and then left the wrench on the kitchen counter.

"I didn't fix the faucet," I said, getting scared. "She's gonna ask her landlord why the wrench is there, and that woman's gonna describe us down to a T, especially since she was so suspicious. And if Kate has any doubts, she'll remember seeing you out front. What are we gonna do?"

Bruce Wayne looked worried. "I'd suggest going to the police and tellin' them what you found, but who are you gonna tell? The Henryetta police are gonna bungle it, and they hate you to boot. They're more likely to arrest you for breakin' and enterin' than they are to help."

"And the sheriff's out," Neely Kate said. "For obvious reasons. Maybe we should tell Carter."

I shook my head. "No. I'll tell Mason and let him decide what to do. He's workin' with a state police detective. Maybe he can get them to look into it."

"Good idea," Neely Kate said.

"I'm glad you're plannin' to stay in with Maeve tonight. No one will look for you there."

Bruce Wayne's face puckered with confusion. "Why're ya stayin' with Maeve?"

Neely Kate sighed. "It's a long story."

I gave Bruce Wayne a look that said we'd fill him in when there was time.

"The next question is what is Kate capable of? If she hired Sam Teagen as the middleman to hire Eric to run Mason off the road and steal his phone, did she also have him killed? I found a gun in her bag."

Neely Kate gave Bruce Wayne a pointed look. "And not just any gun. A Sig Sauer."

Bruce Wayne whistled. "She ain't playin'."

"We know she's dangerous, but what's she going to do to us?" I gasped as a new thought occurred to me. "Did she leave those notes on my car? The ones that warned me to stay out of other people's business? Did she have someone run *me* off the road?"

Fear filled Neely Kate's eyes. "I don't think it's safe for you to be alone."

"If she really posted my bail, she's not gonna kill me. She could have left me in jail."

Neely Kate didn't look any more relieved about that.

"I need to get home. Mason's gonna beat me there at this rate."

Neely Kate stood. "My car's still over at Merilee's from yesterday. I can drive myself to Maeve's."

"But your stuff's still at my house."

She shrugged. "I'll figure it out."

"Call me when you get to Maeve's, okay? I'm worried about you."

"You're in more danger, Rose. You call me too."

Bruce Wayne grabbed his coat. "I'm following you home, Rose."

I almost told him it wasn't necessary, but two things stopped me. One, I'd hurt his feelings earlier. I wanted him to feel needed and trusted. And two, I really *was* worried about being out by myself.

I wrapped my arms around him. "Thank you. I'm sorry I hurt you this morning. You have to know I don't think those hurtful things. I never have."

He patted my back, then pulled loose, keeping his eyes on the floor. "I do. But I was hurt. And I still think you and Neely Kate are playing with fire, but I also think you might be able to accomplish something meetin' with those guys."

"Thanks, Bruce Wayne. That means a lot to me."

We all walked out the front door together, and Bruce Wayne locked up behind us. I looked around to see if anyone suspicious was lingering nearby, but it was a bare early February afternoon in Henryetta. Hardly anyone was out and about, so anyone watching us would have stuck out like a sore thumb. But as I made my way to my truck, I couldn't help but look up at Kate's apartment windows. She stood in front of the glass, looking down at me.

She lifted her hand and waggled her fingers, a huge smile spreading across her face.

# *Chapter Twenty*

The house was empty when I got home. Bruce Wayne followed me all the way to my front door and then insisted on checking the house before he left me there. He gave me a confrontational look, but I didn't say a word. I just turned off the alarm and followed him around like a lost puppy. When he declared it safe, he looked around. "Where's Muffy?"

"Mason's takin' me out to dinner tonight, so I left her at Maeve's for the night." I pulled my phone out. "And Neely Kate's there too." I sent her a quick text to let her know I was home, then looked up at him. "Everyone's safe and sound."

"Well, I better be goin'. Be careful, and let me know if you need anything."

"Okay. Thanks."

I watched him leave, then locked the door and turned the dreaded alarm back on. Then I dug in my purse and pulled out my burner phone.

Nothing.

Worried, I texted Jed.

*No word yet. You?*

*No. From either player.*

He was talking about Skeeter. I considered texting him again, but I knew he'd reach out when he was good and ready. Though I hadn't heard squat from him, I could only hope he was working on his own plan to take down J.R. I was dying to know what he'd discovered, if anything. But then, he was probably dying to know what Jed and I were up to . . . Rumors had a way of spreading, so I was sure I'd hear from him soon.

The news about Kate was bound to put a damper on my date with Mason, but I was bound and determined that we would have one anyway, even if we stayed at home. I was going to make the most of my time with Mason.

I went upstairs and took a shower and spent more time than usual putting on makeup and fixing my hair. I finished in the bathroom and stood in front of my closet, looking over my dress selection. Then I remembered the dress I'd been wearing in my vision. We'd both been so happy, and we needed all the happiness we could scrabble together. I started to reach for it when I heard Mason's voice.

"Rose?"

"Upstairs!"

His footsteps sounded on the stairs, and I turned to watch as he came through the doorway, his overnight bag slung over his shoulder.

His eyes lit up at the sight of me. "You're beautiful."

I glanced down at my bathrobe. "I'm not dressed."

He tossed his bag on the bed and moved toward me. "You're still beautiful." Then he pulled me into his arms and gave me a soft, lingering kiss. "I missed you more than I would have thought possible."

I couldn't help wondering if he was thinking of my imminent incarceration. I sure was. "I missed you too."

"I made a reservation for six." He pulled my robe open. His hands skimmed across my stomach, sending shivers through my body, before they came to rest on my naked hips. "We have a little time before we go."

His mouth covered mine, and his hands began to wander, but I groaned and leaned back. "As much as I want this too, I have to tell you about my day." Well, part of it.

Worry filled his eyes. "Should I be concerned?"

I grimaced. "Maybe."

"Is it an emergency?"

"Well, no . . . I think it can wait a bit."

"Let me grab a five-minute shower, and you can tell me while I get ready."

"Okay."

"Where's Muffy?"

"At your mom's."

"And Neely Kate?"

"The same."

He gave me another kiss. "I can't believe I'm saying this, but would you please get dressed before I get out of the shower? I'm afraid I'll be too busy trying to seduce you to listen."

I chuckled. "I'll see what I can do."

I put on the wine-colored dress with a deeper V-neck than I usually wore, my Lady in Black clothes aside. I'd just picked out a pair of black high heels when Mason emerged from the bathroom with a towel wrapped around his waist and water droplets clinging to his skin.

I couldn't help gawking at him. He truly was a gorgeous man.

He noticed me staring and grinned. "I'm not sure that dress is going to be any better for my attention span."

I laughed. "Do I have to put on my winter coat and zip it all the way to the top?"

"You very well might. How about you tell me your news while I shave?" He turned his attention to the mirror and slathered his face with shaving cream.

I leaned into the doorframe. "How was the rest of *your* day?"

He picked up his razor and began to shave. "They located Pete Mooney."

"That's good, right?"

"It would be better if he wasn't dead."

"What?" The news ran a chill down my spine. "What happened?"

He rinsed his razor in the running water and resumed his task. "They found him in an alley in Little Rock over the weekend. He'd been beaten to death."

I shuddered. "Someone tried to keep him quiet?"

"The official police report says he was mugged. But Terry—the state police detective—is going to question the Little Rock police about their investigation."

"Well, that's good."

He rinsed his razor again. "I'm trying to see this as a good sign."

"How can you say that?"

"It's like I said on the phone. I'm getting the sense that we're making someone nervous. We're close to something." He washed his face and patted it dry. "Now tell me about your day."

"Just like the news about Pete Mooney, I'm choosing to see what we found as a good sign." I took a deep breath as he pulled out a shirt and a pair of pants, then tossed them on the bed and moved on to the dresser.

"That *definitely* sounds ominous." He pulled out a pair of underwear and put them on.

I sat on the edge of the bed. "When we were in town, Neely Kate told me that Kate Simmons is renting the apartment over the antique store, which explains why I keep running into her on the square. Then Neely Kate realized the apartment is directly across from the courthouse, and more specifically, directly across from the DA's offices."

He paused and looked at me. "That could be a coincidence."

"While it could be, we're pretty sure it's not. Especially after what we saw." I watched him step into his pants. "Neely Kate told the store owner she was interested in renting the apartment after Kate moves. She tried to convince her to let us take a look at it, and the woman finally agreed when Neely Kate told her we could fix the leaky faucet. That way she could explain to Kate that we were maintenance workers."

He shook his head. "And Kate just let you in?"

"No, Kate wasn't there. But the owner gave us a key."

His eyes narrowed. "You used a key to get into Kate's apartment, and then proceeded to fix her leaky sink?"

"The key part is correct, so we were there with permission."

He grimaced. "I'm not so sure that would hold up in court."

"We almost got caught, but we made it out. And the important part is what we found in the loft. It made us forget all about the sink."

He pulled on his shirt and started to work on the buttons. I hopped off the bed and brushed his hands away, taking over the task.

"Have you noticed that when it comes to clothing, I'm always trying to get yours off and you're always putting mine *on?*" His eyebrow rose playfully, but his tone was subdued. He was just as nervous to hear what I had to tell him as I was to tell it.

"Everything has a time and a place, Mason," I said, trying not to sound so serious. In reality, I felt like I was standing on the edge of a precipice, waiting for someone to topple me over.

He put his fingers under my chin and gently lifted my face. "What did you find out?"

"She's investigating you."

He searched my eyes, giving away nothing.

"The windows in the front of the apartment give her a perfect view of the DA's offices, and she can see into your old office and your boss's. She even has a pair of binoculars by the window."

"I can't think of a single thing she'd see in my office that she could construe as either good or bad. What happens in my office is as dry as burnt toast."

"Except when I visit sometimes."

His hand slid up to cup my cheek. "I've always closed the blinds. There's no way she saw us in there."

"There was more. A *lot* more." I looked down as I worked on his last button. "She has a table full of papers

273

about you. And she has your old phone. The one that was stolen when you were run off the road."

That got a reaction. "She has my *phone?*"

"I turned it on, and sure enough, it was yours. I couldn't believe it still had power. That was over a month ago."

"It means she's trying to get into it. Or already has."

"But does that mean she hired Sam Teagen to arrange for someone to run you off the road? And if she did, was she also the one who posted my bail?"

His eyes clouded. "That means she might have also had something to do with Eric Davidson's death."

"She had a bunch of papers and police reports associated with some of your cases in Little Rock. There were a bunch of highlighted sections on one in particular. It was from five years ago. A hit-and-run case with an eight-year-old boy as the only witness."

He grimaced. "That was one of my first cases. I wasn't looking forward to putting the kid on the stand, but he was smart. About a week before the trial, I met with him to go over his testimony. I was worried about how he'd handle everything, so I met him and his mother at an ice cream shop to put him at ease. He was sharp, though, and not too frightened. He would have done a good job. But he drowned before we could go to trial. I was pretty shook up when I heard about it."

I smoothed my hand over his chest. It was obvious the boy's death still bothered him. "Why would Kate be interested in the case?"

"I have no idea." He wore a troubled look, but I could see he was putting something together. "Unless."

"What?"

"This is a total long shot, but it's worth pursuing." He took a breath. "One of Mooney's charges was a hit-and-run case."

"You think it's the same one? Neely Kate said the defendant's name was too heavily highlighted for her to read it. But wouldn't you remember?"

He shook his head. "I literally saw hundreds of cases, and it was one of my first. That one only stands out to me because what happened to that boy haunted me for some time. I'll text the detective and ask him to look into it. Kate Simmons seems like an immediate concern."

"She's been following you too. Or more likely someone else has been. She has photos of you that date back to last July. There's a photo of you, me, and Joe on the courthouse steps after Jimmy DeWade was arrested. Kate was supposed to be in California back then."

"I suspect you're right about someone else taking the photos."

"Why would Kate be so interested in you and what you were doin'?"

He shook his head. "I have no idea."

"There were also little slips of paper that had short sentences with times and dates on them. They look like they've been folded and stuffed into something. They all seemed to pertain to you, although they were very vague."

"I have no idea what she's doin' or why." Yet he didn't seem all that surprised. I supposed nothing about the Simmons family would surprise him now.

"We think she's either trying to find evidence that you've misused your power in the DA's office or she's trying plant it. But if she's planting evidence, she's certainly playing a long game. I doubt she'd spend so much time doin' it."

"I agree."

I hesitated. "Mason, she also has a gun."

He pursed his lips. "I'm not surprised. I'm sure she's doing her father's handiwork. Just like her brother. And now they've trapped you here in this town." Fear filled his eyes before the shutters to his emotions could snap shut. "I'm going to do everything in my power to stop them."

"Is there anyone we can turn to for help? I know the Henryetta police and the sheriff's office are out. But what about that state police detective you're working with? Can he do something to help?"

"I don't know. I'll definitely tell him when I asked him about the hit-and-run case." He searched my eyes. "But I'll be vague about how I found out. I don't want to bring you into it."

"That's just gonna make it harder to get him to do something, right?"

"I can't risk you getting in trouble for breaking your bail agreement. Your explanation for why you were in that apartment is sketchy at best."

"Mason, we have to do *something*. She's investigating you."

He gave me a soft kiss. "I know. And we'll get that sorted out too."

"What if she's the one who kills you?"

He studied me for a moment. "Maybe knowing she's involved will change things."

"I should have another vision." But the other vision

I'd had—the dark, cold one—had freaked me out more than I cared to admit.

Mason sensed my hesitation. "Only if you want to."

I nodded. "I do. I want to see if we've made any progress in changing things."

He took my hand and led me to the bed. "Let's sit down, okay? You nearly passed out last time."

"Okay," I said, sitting on the edge.

He sat next to me, his right hand holding my left, his other arm wrapped around my back. "Ready?"

"Yeah." I closed my eyes and started to think about where Mason would be in three weeks, but then I switched the time frame, focusing instead on what we'd be doing over the weekend. The same inky darkness swirled in my head, an icy sharpness following close behind. Panicking again, I thought about dinner. The scene popped into my head immediately. We were in Jaspers, the same as what I'd seen the previous day.

"We're gonna eat dinner at Jaspers."

My eyes flew open. Mason had pulled me closer to his side, and his hand held mine in a tight grip.

"You saw it again?" he asked softly. "My death?"

I nodded, tears welling in my eyes. "But not in three weeks." I looked up to meet his worried gaze. "By this weekend." I paused. "I want to see who's trying to kill you."

His eyebrows rose, and he studied me for several seconds. "You can make it that specific?"

"I can try."

He nodded. "Okay." His thumb rubbed over the back of my hand. We were discussing his upcoming murder, and *he* was the one offering *me* comfort.

I closed my eyes again and focused on his death, preparing myself for the worst. I found myself plunged into the scene. I was in Mason's car, parked in front of his mother's house. The hands that opened the door were his. As I climbed out, a wave of overwhelming grief hit me. Before I could focus on that, another vehicle pulled up beside me. I heard several pops, and then I was plunged into darkness.

When I roused from the vision, I was back in Mason's arms.

My eyes flew open. "You're murdered outside your mother's house."

His hold on me tightened. "What did you see?"

I shook my head, trying to catch my breath. I'd just experienced Mason's death. Tears bubbled up, but I stuffed them back down. I couldn't afford to let myself cry. I needed to focus on saving him.

I parted my lips, about to tell him what I'd seen, but something tripped me up. What had upset Mason in the vision? Could he have just found out about my role in the crime world? If I told Mason about the weird wave of grief, he'd probably figure it involved me. Then he'd focus on keeping me safe rather than protecting himself. "Umm . . . it was a very short vision. It was night and you were in your car outside your momma's house. You'd just gotten out, and a car drove past. I heard several popping sounds, and then there was nothing."

"So I was shot."

I looked in his face, horror washing over me. "How can you say that so matter-of-factly?"

He gave me a weak smile. "I'm not going to lie to you. Hearing about my death freaks me out. But we need to focus on averting it, right?"

I nodded, trying to get a grip on my emotions. "Yeah. Obviously you should stay away from your mother's house at night, but how else do we stop them?"

He was still for a moment. "I don't know."

"You should run away, Mason. Go somewhere far away, where you're safe from all of this."

"And leave you here to face this alone?" he asked, sounding incredulous and hurt. "Do you really think I'd do such a thing?"

"No," I said softly, reaching my free hand out to touch his cheek. His warm skin was a sharp contrast to my cold hand. "But I had to try. I don't know what I'll do if . . ."

He gave me a tight smile. "We'll stop it, okay? Trust me, I don't have a death wish. I want to grow old and gray with you." His smile became more genuine. "I have plans for us."

I reached up and kissed him, our emotions pouring into our kiss, then I leaned back and stared into his eyes. "I think we should stay home. We can stay dressed up, but I can cook, and we can just have our date here."

He shook his head. "No. I really want to take you out, and besides, we'll be in a public place. In fact, we might be safer at Jaspers than we are here at the farm."

"That's a comforting thought."

"The truth of the matter is, if someone wants to kill me, they're going to try, as evidenced by your vision. Short of going into witness protection, there's not much I can do beyond being as careful—and as prepared—as possible."

"Maybe we should hire a bodyguard for you."

"That sort of thing is expensive. But if we don't make more progress in the next day or so, I think I'll hire someone to at least watch us at night while we sleep." He held me close. "If it makes you feel better, maybe I'll see if Randy is willing to come and act as my bodyguard tonight." He grinned. "I'll pay for his dinner. I bet he won't turn me down."

"Will he sit with us?" I teased.

"No." He looked mischievous. "Most definitely not." When I hesitated, he added, "But if you would rather stay here, I understand. I want you to be comfortable."

"Let's go. I hate that other people have so much control over our lives. This can be us saying we're gonna live our lives no matter who's threatening us."

He stood and pulled me to my feet. "Good. I feel the same way. I'll go call Randy to make sure he's up for it. Then place a call to the detective."

"Okay."

He leaned over and gave me a lingering kiss that had the potential to lead to more. But he lifted his head and smiled softly. "We'll save that for later. I have plans for you first."

# Chapter Twenty-One

Jaspers wasn't very crowded on a Wednesday night, so Mason had no problem getting a table for Randy, who had jumped at the chance to play bodyguard. He'd even offered to do it without having his dinner comped.

He met us in the lobby, wearing dress pants and a shirt and tie. I smiled and tilted my head. "Why, Randy Miller, you clean up quite nicely. Still no girlfriend?"

His face turned pink. "No, ma'am."

"We'll have to work on that. Maybe you should go hang out in the bar later. As handsome as you look, I'm sure you'll catch some lovely woman's attention."

He turned even redder.

"Rose," Mason said with a laugh. "The goal is for Randy to be looking for danger, not his next date."

I feigned a haughty look. "Haven't you ever heard of killin' two birds with one stone? If he's lookin' around the place anyway, he might as well be checkin' out the single women too."

Randy seemed to have recovered. "Mr. Deveraux, I wouldn't compromise your safety by checkin' out women."

"I know you wouldn't, Randy," Mason said. "But Rose does have a point. If I anticipated any serious trouble, we wouldn't be here. You're just a precaution."

The hostess called our names and led all three of us back into the dining room. She sat Mason and me in a dark corner table lit by candlelight, and placed Randy several tables away. His back was to the wall, and he could see the entrance as well as the hall that led to the kitchen, bathrooms, and bar. It was perfect.

Randy took his seat, ignoring us, while Mason helped me remove my coat and then pulled out my chair. It amazed me how we were still able to find these pockets of peace and joy amidst the misery and chaos that had swirled around us for months.

The waitress came over and introduced herself while pouring our water. Mason ordered a bottle of wine before she walked away.

He reached across the table and curled his fingers over mine. "Tonight, let's not talk about Kate, Joe, J.R. Simmons, or me losing my job."

"Or my arrest or my business. Not even my sister or Neely Kate." Even though I was worried about her something fierce. "Tonight it's only you and me."

He lifted his water glass and held it up. "To you and me."

I picked up my water and clicked it against his, my heart bursting with joy. We spent the next hour and a half enjoying a leisurely meal. We were just Mason and Rose, two people in love who wanted to spend our lives together, not Mason Deveraux, the former Fenton County ADA whose life was in danger, and Rose Gardner, who had been wrongly charged with orchestrating her mother's murder. Or even the Lady in Black. Part of me had worried that when the craziness finally faded away, we'd be left with nothing. My experience with Joe and his secrets had scarred me. But tonight, as the rest of the world fell away, it was nice to feel this confirmation that we had a solid foundation and that the connection we shared was deep and strong.

After our dinner plates were cleared away, Mason insisted we order dessert, even though I protested I was too full. There was a strange look in the waitress's eyes—almost like excitement. Were the desserts here really that good? "The special, Mr. Deveraux?"

He studied me for a second, then turned back to her. "Yes, please."

While we waited, he glanced around the hall, an anxious look on his face.

I turned around to see what he was looking at, but there was nothing in particular there. "Are you okay?" I asked. "You seem on edge."

His eyes widened slightly. "No." He grabbed my hand and smiled. "I'm sorry. It's nothing."

But I could tell there was something amiss.

A minute later, the waitress returned with a bottle of champagne I hadn't remembered Mason ordering and a tiny cake I knew Jaspers didn't offer on the menu. The round cake was about six inches wide with white, sparkly frosting and tiny pink roses around the base. But it was what was in the center that took my breath away. More tiny pink roses surrounded a white gold engagement ring with a round diamond in the center and smaller diamonds on either side of the band.

Mason got out of his seat and knelt on one knee beside me. "Rose, I know this is terrible timing. I wanted to do this in the spring, at my uncle's cabin when the dogwood and redbud trees are in bloom, but I didn't want to wait."

Tears shimmered in my eyes as I stared down at this man who would literally do anything for me.

"I love you, Rose. I know without a doubt that I want to spend the rest of my life with you. When this mess is all sorted out, we can get married with all our family and friends. I don't care about my job or where we live. As long as I'm with you, I'll have everything I need."

Then he took my hand. "Rose Anne Gardner, will you marry me?"

I nodded, my tears finally escaping. "Yes. Yes."

He reached over to the cake and lifted the ring, staring at the frosting on the band like he wasn't quite sure what to do. Laughing, I handed him my cloth napkin, and he wiped off the sugary mess. He picked up my left hand and slid the ring onto my finger. The fit was perfect.

I stared at the sparkles on my hand, barely able to make out the design of the ring through my happy tears. "It's beautiful."

Then he pulled me to my feet and wrapped his arm around my back, beaming. "You've just made me the happiest man in the world."

I grabbed the back of his neck and pulled his mouth to mine. His hold on me tightened, and it was only when he lifted his head that I realized the people in the restaurant were applauding and cheering and offering their congratulations.

Randy sat at his table, grinning ear to ear, and I could tell he'd been in on it.

"When's the wedding, Mr. Deveraux?" a woman called out from across the restaurant.

He kept an arm wrapped tight around my waist, as though he was worried I might change my mind and take off. He looked down at me, his gaze full of adoration. "We're not sure yet."

"In the spring," I said, staring up at him, knowing I would normally feel embarrassed about all the attention. For once I didn't care. I wanted the world to see how happy I was. "When the dogwoods and the redbud trees are blooming. We can have it at the farm."

I knew there were plenty of obstacles to that plan, but I chose to believe we would overcome every single one of them. Mason and I could overcome anything if we continued working together and fighting for each other.

The waitress popped the cork on the bottle of champagne and filled our glasses. After holding out my chair out for me, Mason took his own seat.

Once we were both settled, he handed me a glass and lifted his. "To forever."

I clinked my glass against his and took a sip, then glanced down at my ring. "It's gorgeous, Mason. It's the most beautiful ring I've ever seen."

He reached for my hand and touched the band. "Does it fit right? I guessed on the size, but they said they can resize if need be." He paused. "I had it specially made, but if you would rather have another ring, you—"

My mouth dropped open. "You had it specially made?"

"Yeah, in Little Rock. When I had your Christmas present made, I talked to the jeweler about making you an engagement ring. They came up with the design and emailed it to me a week later. I told them to make it, and they've been holding it for me for a little while now."

"Mason."

He looked apologetic. "I knew you wanted to wait, and if you feel pressured, we can make this a longer engagement. I know it's kind of silly to want to be engaged. We're living together already. I just wanted . . ."

I squeezed his hand. "No. I understand, and I don't want to wait. I know what I want, and it's you."

"I had the cake made at Dena's. I called her on the way back from Little Rock this afternoon. I wasn't sure she'd be able to fit it in, but she was thrilled to help. She even ran it over here."

"It's beautiful, and this is so wonderful." I shook my head. "I can't believe you did this." I cocked my head. "Why did you look so nervous while you were waiting for the waitress to bring out the cake?"

He chuckled. "I was worried you'd say no. A few months ago, we decided to wait."

"And that was a few months ago. Besides, things have changed."

He took my hand. "I still want to wait to have kids," he said, looking sheepish. "But when things settle down, I want to just relax with you and catch our breath."

"You know I want kids, but I agree. We should wait."

He looked relieved. "Good."

I stared at my ring again. "Do you mind if I call Neely Kate? She'll be so excited."

"That's a great idea. She's with Mom, so we can tell them together." Mason dug out his phone, scooted his chair next to mine, and then video called his mother.

She gave him a disapproving look, but we could see the twinkle in her eyes. "Mason, you're supposed to be on a date. What are you doing calling?"

Mason's smile lit up his face as he held up the phone between us. "Rose and I have something to tell you. Is Neely Kate there?"

Neely Kate appeared next to Maeve, streaks of flour on her face and in her hair. "I'm here. Did y'all have Kate arrested?"

"No," I said, sneaking a glance at Mason before glancing back to the screen. I held up my hand, showing off the ring. "We're getting married!"

The squeals of excitement made my heart burst even more, and I reached up and gave Mason another kiss.

"When?" Neely Kate asked, bouncing with excitement. "When's the big day?"

"This spring," I said. "Out at the farm with everyone. It'll be a party."

"It will be a celebration," Maeve said, sounding subdued. "A celebration of overcoming the insurmountable."

Mason grabbed my hand and squeezed tight. "As always, my wise mother is right."

"You two go enjoy your night," Maeve said, making a shooing motion. "Muffy is fine, and Neely Kate and I are making bread, although she's taken to wearing it as well. We'll have a loaf waiting for you tomorrow."

"Goodnight, Mom," Mason said. "We just couldn't wait to share the good news with the two of you."

"Congratulations!" Neely Kate shouted as Mason hung up and put the phone into his pocket.

He looked down at me with the type of hunger that food wouldn't satisfy. "I know we've barely had our champagne, but let's box up the cake, pay the bill, and go home."

My skin flushed. "Yes."

He flagged the waitress down and asked for the check while I spun the band around on my finger. Some of the frosting was still on the band, making my skin sticky.

"While you pay, I'm going to go to the restroom."

"Okay. I'm going to ask Randy if he'll follow us home. Just to be on the safe side."

"Oh, good idea."

Both of us stood, and Mason took me into his arms and gave me a soft kiss. "Thank you for agreeing to be my wife."

"I can't wait to become Rose Deveraux."

A huge grin spread across his face, and I kissed him again, grabbed my purse, and headed down the hall. As I passed the entrance to the bar, I saw someone I thought I recognized in my peripheral vision, but when I backtracked a few steps to look in the bar area, whoever it was had already left. I shook off the sensation that something wasn't right and headed to the bathroom. The one-person restroom was empty, so I used the toilet and then washed my hands, rubbing on the back of my band to get the rest of the frosting off. I didn't dare take it off, worried it would fall down the drain.

After I dried it off, I lifted my hand, examining the design of the ring. It was much more detailed than I'd realized. The larger center diamond was probably about one third of a carat, with two smaller diamonds on either side. But carved into the metal were tiny swirling roses. It was so beautiful and thoughtful. The fact that he'd had it made for me made me love it and him even more. But now that the joy and excitement of the moment had dissipated a little, a cloud of guilt hung over my head.

I stared at my reflection in the mirror. All I could see was the face of a liar. I couldn't help thinking that I wasn't the woman he thought he was marrying. He considered me sweet and fairly innocent, untouched by the criminal world. But even without Skeeter, it had left its mark. My stint as the Lady in Black had changed me more than I'd ever anticipated.

As I stared at the frightened woman in the mirror, I struggled with what to do. Part of me insisted it wouldn't be fair to marry him without telling him my secret. I couldn't bear for him to be blindsided by the truth if it ever came from someone else. He deserved to hear it from me. And besides, he would get his old job back, whether here in Fenton County or somewhere else. He needed to know.

I'd tell him. But not tonight. Tonight I was going to go home with the man who adored me, make love to him in our bed in the farmhouse—the most loving home I'd ever known—and bask in my happiness, however fleeting it might be.

I took a deep breath and assured myself this would all work out. I just had to believe it.

I picked up my purse off the counter and pulled out the burner phone. I nearly dropped it when I saw a text from an unknown number.

*I will meet you tomorrow night. 10 pm. Name the place.*

It was on.

This was good news. Despite my fear, I was hopeful. My vision indicated that Mason would die before the weekend. I hoped to God this meeting would save him.

Feeling better about the whole thing, I opened the door and headed into the hall, ready to go home with Mason. But as soon as I left the bathroom, I noticed the hallway was much darker than it had been before. A moment of confusion made me stumble, and it was exactly then that someone grabbed me from behind, pulled me against his chest, and put a rag over my face.

My adrenaline kicked in, and I fought like a banshee and screamed into the rag as he dragged me backward down the dark hall. I scratched at his arms, but he had on a black leather coat. He was taller than me, and he was pretty solid too. But I only had a few seconds to register that because a sweet, chemical smell filled my nose, and as my lungs begged for a breath, I sucked in a lung-full of something cold. My arms and legs began to go numb, and every one of my senses was fading. In a last-ditch effort to save myself, I reached back and sunk my nails into his cheek, digging deep.

He cursed under his breath, and that was the last thing I remembered before my legs collapsed and everything faded to black.

# Chapter Twenty-Two

I woke up with a massive headache and my face pressed to a leather seat. My hands were secured behind my back, a cloth was tied over my mouth, and I was in the backseat of a moving car. A heavy blanket covered my body.

Panic made me lightheaded, and I resisted the urge to scream. It would be better if my captor thought I was still passed out. I was lying on my stomach, and from the way I was positioned, my face was tilted in the direction of the backseat. Somewhere along the way, I'd lost my shoes.

I remained still, hoping my captor or captors would speak so I could figure out who they were and what they wanted. But the driver remained annoyingly quiet, not even bothering to put on any music. I listened to the road instead, trying to figure out where they were taking me. Because I had to escape. Mason was waiting for me.

Mason. What would he do when I didn't come back? How long would he wait before he went back there to check on me? I'd been in the bathroom a long time, after all. Maybe he and Randy were already coming after me.

Panic raised its ugly head again, roaring for attention, but I beat it back into submission. I didn't have time to panic. I had to think this through.

We drove on asphalt for what seemed like an eternity, but was probably only fifteen minutes, making several turns—a right, then a left, then a right again. It was another asphalt road, only this one was rougher, more likely a county road.

Finally, I heard a man's voice say, "Turn here."

So there were at least two of them.

We drove for a short time before we turned right onto a gravel road. Several minutes later, we came to a stop.

My captors still hadn't said anything else.

Terror washed through me. I had no idea what they had planned. My hands were tied, but my legs were free. I hoped the blanket would fall off my head as they pulled me out of the car, and if it did, I could try to take off running.

Except we were on a gravel drive, and I was now barefoot.

It was a moot point. One of my captors opened the back door and half-dragged me out of the backseat. He threw me over his shoulder, the blanket still over my head. I considered kicking him in the stomach, but it would serve no purpose other than to make him mad. If I couldn't run, pretending to be agreeable was probably my best course of action. Unless he had nefarious plans for me. I considered forcing a vision, but I wasn't sure what I'd do if I saw something awful.

The cold air hit my legs, and his hand grabbed my bare thigh, but thankfully he didn't attempt to move it up any further. In a few short strides, we were inside, the wood floor creaking under his weight. After several more steps, he stopped and lowered me onto a chair. He left the blanket over my head and untied my hands, giving me a momentary burst of hope, but then his friend tied my left arm and leg to the chair while he worked on the right side of my body.

The blanket was pulled off my head, and I found myself in a bedroom with cedar-paneled walls and a full-sized bed. A small lamp on a nightstand next to the bed gave the room a warm glow. The wall to my left was solid, but there was a window covered by a heavy blanket on the right. But my kidnappers stood behind me. One of them untied the cloth over my mouth, and I started to cough.

I expected one of them to explain what they wanted, but they both stood behind me, not saying a word. I considered staying equally mute, but I hated not knowing what was going on.

"Do you want money? My boyfriend doesn't have much, but he'll try to come up with whatever you want." There was a slim chance this was about money, but at least whoever was in charge hadn't killed me yet.

Neither of them answered. Instead, I heard their boots thud away from me, followed by the sound of the door creaking shut. I closed my eyes, tears stinging behind my eyelids, but I refused to cry. Crying wouldn't get me out of this. I had to figure out why I'd been abducted.

The possibilities were endless.

The murmur of voices on the other side of the door was too low to hear, so I squeezed my eyelids tighter, straining to listen. I couldn't make out enough words to learn anything about their plan.

I sat in the chair long enough for my fear to become a dull roar, and I even started to doze off. But I awakened with a start, my heart kicking into an immediate gallop, when I heard noises outside the door. Shouts and then a gunshot.

A door banged open in another room, followed by yet more yelling. Then the bedroom door was flung open, and a bearded man I didn't recognize dragged a chair into the room and placed it next to mine. I *did* recognize the man who was brought into the room a moment later, one of my kidnappers restraining him on either side.

Jed.

His left eye was red and partially swollen. He took one look at me and rage exploded from him like a match tossed into gasoline.

Jed gave them a good fight, even with his arm in a sling. He tore loose of the guy who was restraining his good arm, then head-butted him in the nose. The man grunted as blood spurted from his nostrils and stumbled backward.

The guy standing behind Jed was wearing a baseball cap. He wrenched Jed's injured arm backward and out of the sling. Jed growled in pain, but he spun around and punched Baseball Cap in the face, getting in two quick hits before the man with the busted nose and the man with a beard grabbed Jed and dragged him back. Baseball Cap punched Jed in the gut and the face a couple of times before they pushed him down into the chair. He bucked and fought, delivering the bearded guy a good kick in the ribs before they tied his bad arm to the chair.

A new surge of energy burst through Jed, and he bolted out of the chair and to his feet, bringing the chair with him. He swung it around and slammed it into the head of Baseball Cap, knocking him to the floor. The chair shattered into pieces and fell away from him, leaving him unencumbered.

Bearded Guy and Busted Nose stood on opposite sides of Jed, and Bearded Guy started to circle by me as though looking for an opening to pounce. My calf was tied to the chair leg, but there was nothing securing my foot. His attention was on Jed, so he tripped on my extended foot and fell onto his side. After squawking out a surprised shout, he started to reach for me. Jed was there in an instant, stomping on the guy's back as he shoved my chair across the floor toward the wall. He barely made eye contact with me before returning to his task.

He stomped on the guy's back again and got in two more good kicks before Busted Nose made a run for him. Or at least I thought so—he lunged straight past Jed, heading toward me. A look of pure evil filled his eyes as he reached for me, but Jed grabbed him by the shoulder and swung him around, smashing his already injured nose several times with his fist. The guy crumpled to the floor with a whimper next to his cohort, who had now pulled out a gun.

Bearded Guy trained his weapon on Jed. "Go ahead, Carlisle. Make me shoot you."

Jed's shoulders relaxed, and he held his hands in the air in surrender.

Bearded Guy climbed to his feet, none too gracefully, and moved slowly toward Jed. "Turn around and put your hands behind your back."

Jed started to turn, but when the guy was within a three-foot radius of him, Jed spun and gave him a sideways kick in the stomach. The second he doubled over, Jed grabbed his gun and shoved him backward. He stumbled over Busted Nose on the floor and hit his head on the wall, then slumped to the floor, unconscious.

"Drop it, Carlisle," Baseball Cap growled from the floor. "Or I'll shoot her."

I turned my attention to him, horror washing from my head to my toes when I saw his gun was pointed straight at me.

A gunshot rang out, and I was surprised I didn't feel any pain until the guy slumped to the floor, blood trickling out of the hole in his forehead, his eyes wide and vacant.

I stared at Jed, wide-eyed with shock and horror.

He quickly turned his gun toward the two guys piled on top of each other. Busted Nose was reaching for his gun, but Jed's deadly calm voice stopped him.

"I'd love to blow your hand off, so keep reaching."

The man wisely stopped, putting his hand palm down on the floor.

Jed moved closer and pulled the gun out of the back of his pants, then rose and backed up toward me, keeping an eye on the men. "Are you hurt?"

"No," I croaked.

He set one of the guns on the floor, then pulled a small knife out of his boot and set to work, slicing through the rope around my right arm. Once it was free, he handed me the knife, picked up the second gun, and aimed both weapons at the men.

Bearded Guy began to come around, his eyes blinking open, and he started to scramble to his feet.

"Keep your ass on the floor, or you'll get a gut full of lead. I hear it's a painful way to die."

With a shaky hand, I cut the rope off my left hand. The sparkle of my engagement ring caught me by surprise. How much time had passed? An hour? Two?

But I didn't have time to dwell on how ecstatically happy I had been. As soon as my left hand was free, I leaned over and sawed through the ropes restraining my legs. The need to hurry wasn't lost on me, but fear made me sloppy. *Calm down, Rose. Just cut through the rope, then get out of here and find Mason.*

Surprisingly, my simple plan helped me focus. Once I was free, I stood up from the chair, wondering what to do next.

Jed handed me the spare gun. "If one of them even looks like he's about to get up, shoot him."

I aimed my weapon at them as Jed reached under the dead guy across the room and pulled out his gun.

"Back out of the room, Rose."

*He used my real name.*

New fear washed through me. If they had kidnapped me as Rose, they would have to wonder why Jed was so concerned about saving me as well as himself. And if they'd wanted the Lady in Black, the fact that I had been snatched without my veil, mere minutes after my boyfriend proposed to me in a public place was a very, very bad sign.

Either way, this was disastrous.

But I didn't have time to dwell on that. I did as Jed instructed, backing out of the room while holding the gun aimed at my would-be captors, moving into a sparsely furnished living room and dining room, the walls covered in more cedar paneling.

"You'll never get away with this Carlisle," Busted Nose grunted, still lying on the floor.

Jed didn't respond. He simply backed out of the room. Then he tossed the gun into his left hand behind him to pull the door shut and started to turn the key in the lock.

A gunshot rang out as a hole appeared in the wooden door, close to the doorknob. "Shoot!" Jed shouted as he backed up and shot his own gun too.

I shrieked, but I took a step back and pulled the trigger. Several bullets went through the door, and whoever had been shooting inside stopped.

"Did I kill him?" I whispered, shaking again.

"I don't know. But he deserved it if you did. Now we need to get out of here before *he* shows up." Putting himself between me and the door, he led me to the ajar front door, the cold wind gusting inside through the cracked opening.

I was about to ask who he was talking about, but the door flung open. Nothing could have prepared me for the angry man filling the doorway.

Skeeter Malcolm.

# Chapter Twenty-Three

Was Skeeter the one we were running from? He sure looked murderous, and I took an unintentional step backward, bumping into Jed. "Where are they?" he asked through clenched teeth.

Jed's voice was cold. "The bedroom."

"Did you find out anything?"

"Nothing other than what I already told you. I just got her free. I thought I took all their weapons, but they got off a shot after I locked the door. Rose and I fired a few times, and it's been quiet since. I suspect there's at least one alive, maybe two."

Skeeter nodded, his attention on the door. He didn't even look at us. "I have a car out front. Take her to the safe house. I'll find your car down the road and meet you there."

My gaze pivoted between them. "What on earth is goin' on?"

Skeeter's eyes darkened. *"Get her out of here."*

I started to protest, but Jed didn't give me the chance. He stuffed his gun into the back waistband of his pants, grabbed my gun, and put it into his jeans pocket, then squatted and threw me over his shoulder. It was just like how I'd come in, only this time I could see my surroundings.

The cabin was surrounded by trees, and two cars and an SUV were parked haphazardly in the yard. It was a secluded location. Definitely the perfect place to hide a kidnap victim.

Jed strode toward the SUV, opened the back door, and set me down inside.

Once I was settled, I turned my attention to the cabin. "What's he doin' in there?"

"Getting answers."

Fear pumped through my veins. I knew this side of Skeeter existed, yet it was easier to pretend it didn't. But this was a reminder that a darkness lurked inside him—one he hid well from me—yet it resided there, nevertheless. I'd do well to remember that.

Jed shut the door and climbed behind the steering wheel.

"Jed, do they know I'm Lady?"

He shook his head and turned the key, bringing the engine to life. "No. I suspect they work for Gentry and they took you to use against Deveraux, even though he's not the ADA anymore. Which means this is personal."

"Then why did they kidnap *you?*"

"They didn't. I was outside of the restaurant. I saw them take you out the back door, then I followed them here. They found me lurking outside the house, and one of them jumped me." He looked over his shoulder and backed up the SUV, the bumper nearly touching the trees.

The fact that Jed had been watching me that closely caught me by surprise, but the fact that Skeeter had shown up grabbed my attention more.

"How did Skeeter get here? I thought he was off

running his 'errands.'"

"I called him."

Jed started to turn down the drive. Then something hit me like a bag of mulch. "My purse! Do you know if they got my purse?"

Jed gave me a look that implied I'd lost my mind.

"My phones are in there! I'd just gotten a text from an unknown number saying he wants to meet tomorrow night at 10:00 p.m. We need my phone to answer him. Is it in the car they used to kidnap me?

Shaking his head and groaning, Jed threw the car into park and hopped out. He climbed into the back of one of the cars, then climbed out seconds later, my small bag in his hand. But instead of getting back into the SUV, he turned to face the house, his back stiffening.

Skeeter was headed straight for him, and it would be an understatement to say he didn't look happy.

They exchanged words for a half-minute, then Jed handed Skeeter my purse and headed back into the cabin. After pausing to give my bag a disdainful glare, Skeeter stomped toward the SUV. He got into the driver's side of the car, opened my purse, and pulled out the burner phone. His eyes shifted to meet mine after he read the message on the home screen. It was like looking into two twin flames of rage.

I really was in a world full of crap . . . and not just from my enemies.

I threw open the back door and made a run for it, the gravel and pine needles poking my bare feet and slowing me down. Though I knew I didn't have a prayer of getting away, my fight or flight response had kicked in and there was no way I could fight him.

But Skeeter caught up to me in seconds, his arm reaching around my waist and hauling me hard against his chest.

"Let go of me, Skeeter Malcolm!" I kicked his legs and tried to pry his arm loose, but he held me in a tight grip and lifted me effortlessly off the ground, then turned around and stomped to the SUV, not saying a word.

It was his silence that scared me the most. Was he like this because he knew what I had done?

Jed stood on the front porch, watching us. The light from inside made his face unreadable.

"I gave you a job," Skeeter said, his voice hard. "Now get in there and *do it.*"

Skeeter tossed me none too gently onto the backseat and slammed the door shut. I landed awkwardly, and by the time I righted myself, he was already tearing down the drive.

Then a new horror hit me.

Mason.

In my vision of his murder, Mason had been overcome with grief. It wasn't from finding out my secret. It was because I'd been kidnapped. I *had* to warn him.

I leaned over the seat and snatched my purse, trying to get to my phone.

But Skeeter pulled the truck over to the side of the drive, screeching to a halt and slamming me against the back of the front seat. He practically dove over the seat to snag my phone out of my hands.

"Give me my phone!"

He tossed it onto the floorboard of the front passenger seat and snarled, "Who in the hell do you think you're gonna call?"

"Mason!"

"There's *no way in hell* you're callin' him. Not until we get this sorted out."

"The only thing we need to sort out at this moment is for you to *give me my phone!*"

To my extreme aggravation, he ignored me and continued to drive.

"*Skeeter!*"

"Give it up." His voice was cold. "I wouldn't let you have that phone if it was to call God Almighty Himself."

A lump filled my throat. "I have to call him, Skeeter," I choked out. "I saw a vision of his murder. I think it happens tonight. I have to let him know I'm okay."

"No."

I started to cry, fear and shock twining with my worry over Mason. "I have to call him! *Please!*"

He gave me the silent treatment, and no matter how much I begged, pleaded, and cried, he wasn't swayed.

After about ten minutes, Skeeter pulled to a stop in front of another cabin tucked into the woods. He opened his door and got out, leaving my phone on the passenger floorboard.

I sucked in a breath as I came up with a quick plan.

The moment he shut the driver's door, I pounced on the automatic lock and swung my leg over onto the front seat.

"*Goddammit, Rose!*"

I ignored him and slid the rest of the way over, diving for the floorboard and feeling under the seat for my phone.

A loud gunshot filled my ears. I flinched out of reflex as the window of the back passenger door shattered onto the backseat.

Panicked, I snagged the phone, then reached for the passenger door handle with my left, but my hand slipped off.

That was all the time Skeeter needed to get the back door unlocked and jerk the front door open. He grabbed my legs and pulled me across the seat. He leaned over me and snatched the phone from my hand, tossing it back into the truck, then jerked me out of the cab. I almost fell to the ground, but he hoisted me up and over his shoulder and strode toward the dark cabin.

"Let go of me!" I beat on his back and shoved my knee hard into his abdomen. He grunted, but he held my legs tight as he walked into the dark house.

As soon as he entered the house, it hit me. I'd been here before. A couple of months ago, Jed had driven me here blindfolded so I could force a vision of a mostly unconscious guy.

"Who else is here?" I asked, my voice shaking.

"Not a goddamned soul."

"I want to go home."

"No." He dropped me onto my side on the dilapidated, dirty sofa, then switched on a lamp.

Blinking as my eyes adjusted to the light, I sat up.

Skeeter dragged a chair in front of me and straddled the seat, resting his forearms on the back. His face gave nothing away.

Fury pushed away my fear. "You may own the Lady in Black, Skeeter Malcolm, but you don't own *me*."

He remained silent, his face a blank slate.

"What do you want?"

He shifted slightly. "We'll wait for Jed. This seems like a conversation I should have with the two of you."

So he *was* ticked about us meeting Mick Gentry. I wasn't about to apologize.

He lifted his index finger toward my hand. "I see you have a new piece of jewelry."

I looked down at my hand, then glared at him. I didn't like his tone. "Mason proposed tonight." I lifted my chin. "And I said yes."

His eyebrows rose slightly. "Seems to me that you've been too busy to spend much time thinkin' about your love life." His head tilted to the side. "What with you gallivantin' around the county lettin' everyone know you think *I'm a goddamned coward*!"

"I never once said you were a coward!"

He stood, his eyes blazing. "Well, you sure as hell left that impression!"

"Well, I had to give Mick Gentry a good reason to agree to see me."

"Why in God's name would you want to see Mick Gentry?"

His voice was so loud I cringed. "If you'd just calm down, I would be happy to explain."

He burst out of his chair and towered over me, his hands clenched at his sides. "After everything that's happened, how the hell am I supposed to calm down?"

"Skeeter." Jed stood in the open doorway. "I'm the one to blame."

He turned to look at Jed, his eyes wide. He started to advance toward him, but I jumped up and grabbed his arm.

"Skeeter, we managed to set up a meeting."

He swung his head down to look at me and said, "Oh, don't worry. I heard *all* about your meetin'!"

"Not that one. With J.R. Simmons."

His eyes widened and his arm tensed. "What the hell are you talkin' about?"

Jed entered the room and shut the door behind him. "We're pretty sure Simmons is backin' Gentry, right?"

"It's why we went to see him," I said. "I wanted to set up a meeting with J.R."

His eyes narrowed to slits. "You're not goin' anywhere *near* J.R. Simmons."

"I haven't gone to this much trouble for nothin'!"

A war waged in his eyes, and he shook me off. "We have more immediate issues at hand." He turned to Jed. "Did you take care of it?"

"It was up in flames when I left."

I gasped. "What was? The cabin?"

Skeeter looked at me like I was crazy. "No, the bonfire we're gonna go sing Kumbaya around before we make s'mores. *Of course, the cabin!*"

"But those men were inside!" I turned to Jed. "You set it on fire with them still in there?"

"Rose, they were dead."

"What?"

Skeeter released a low growl. "You're focusing on the

wrong thing. They kidnapped you in a very public place. You need to be askin' why."

"I don't know." I shook my head. "They didn't say anything."

"It was a rhetorical question. I *know* why."

"What? How?"

"I asked them."

The blood rushed to my feet. I knew what he'd done, yet knowing it and having the reality of it in front of me were two different things. But he must have seen my shock.

"If you're gonna play with the big dogs, Lady, you're gonna have to roll around in shit." His face was hard enough to match his words.

"Skeeter," Jed cautioned.

"What? She jumped feet first into this mess. She's gonna have to accept the consequences."

I swallowed the bile in my throat. "Did they know I was Lady?" I hoped to God Jed was right—otherwise there was no way my plan with J.R. would pan out.

"No." Skeeter walked toward the grungy kitchen. "They only knew they'd kidnapped Rose Gardner, the girlfriend of Mason Deveraux."

That calmed me down a bit, but it reminded me of my need to warn Mason. "I have to call him and tell him that I think he's going to be killed tonight. I have to tell him I'm okay. He's bound to be sick with worry."

Skeeter pulled his flask out of his coat pocket and took a swig. "No."

"*Why not?*"

"We need to let this play out. Jed got their phones, and we'll wait until they get the call to carry out their order."

"And what was that?"

He took another swig, then said matter-of-factly, "To kill you."

"*What?*"

"They were gonna video it and send it to your boyfriend in a text." He walked closer and handed me the flask. "No one says shit to anyone until I know who gave this order."

My legs started to buckle, so I sat in the kitchen chair Skeeter had vacated and took a big swig from the flask. I promptly began to choke as the liquor burned a path to my belly. It wasn't Skeeter's good stuff that usually went down as smooth as honey.

"There wasn't anyone left to tell you who's behind it?" Jed asked.

"No. There was only one, and he was already close to meetin' his maker. My attempts at persuasion only helped him get there sooner."

"I knew one of them," Jed said. "Cody Channing. Last I heard he was working for Crocker. He never pledged his loyalty to you. Maybe he sided with Gentry."

Skeeter grunted in response.

"Their plan doesn't make sense," Jed countered. "What could they possibly stand to gain by killing her?"

"It could only be to make Mason suffer," I said, then took another drink, prepared for the burn this time. "I can't even imagine how he'd react if he saw that."

"Sounds like J.R. Simmons, all right," Jed murmured.

Skeeter pulled another kitchen chair into the living room and sat in front of me, gently taking the flask from my shaking hand. "I need you tell me everything you remember. Start with how you got to the restaurant."

I looked up at Jed, then back at Skeeter. "Mason took me out to dinner, and he asked Deputy Miller to come with us."

Skeeter gave me a wicked look. "I had no idea you and the former county prosecutor were into threesomes. Otherwise, I might have requested an invitation."

A blush rose to my face. "You know good and well that's not why we asked him. Mason thought it would be prudent to have a bodyguard given the fact that everything's so unsettled."

"You mean dangerous."

"So Randy sat a couple of tables away while we ate. We were there a long time, almost two hours by the time Mason proposed and we called his mother and Neely Kate."

Jed's mouth opened in surprise.

"That's right, Jed," Skeeter said dryly. "Congratulations are in order."

"I don't know what business it is of yours," I retorted.

Skeeter was out of his chair in a flash, leaning over me with so much rage I shrank back from him. "The very fact we're in this goddamned safe house right now is proof enough that it's my goddamned business!"

"Skeeter." Jed's calm voice of reason interrupted.

Skeeter threw the chair across the room and stalked out the front door.

I sat there in shock, wondering what I'd done wrong. He was used to me back-talking him, so that couldn't have set him off.

"He knows how close they came to killing you," Jed said softly, perching on the edge of the nasty sofa. "When I got there, they were discussing how they were gonna do it."

"What were they gonna do?" I asked, unsure whether I really wanted to know.

"Let's just say it tracks with your theory about someone wanting to make Deveraux suffer."

It was surreal to talk about my attempted murder. While this wasn't the first time I had found myself in this type of situation, I sure hoped it would be the last.

"I almost missed it, Rose. They dragged you out the back while I was checking out the front of the restaurant, watching Deveraux's car. If I hadn't turned back at the last second . . ." He took a deep breath. "I still wasn't sure it was you, but I knew it was sketchy as hell for a guy to toss a woman wrapped in a blanket into the backseat of a car. I called Merv to come take over for me and followed."

I grabbed his good hand and squeezed it, swallowing my fear. "Thank you. You saved me. I couldn't believe what you did when they brought you into that room."

"There was no way in hell I was lettin' them hurt you." He glanced back at the door, then lowered his voice. "There's a reason Skeeter assigned me to watch over you, you know."

"Why?"

"I had a little sister, and our momma always put me in charge of watching over her. She was a lot younger than me, but she was the sweetest little thing, and everybody loved her. She often tagged along with me and my friends, Skeeter included, but none of them minded."

"Skeeter?"

He nodded. "We grew up together."

That explained so much.

"One day we decided to go fishing, and Daisy begged to come. She was learning how to bait a hook with the earthworms from the backyard. I got her set up, and then Skeeter's brother, Scooter, caught a huge catfish that damn near broke his rod. All four of us boys—our friend Pete was there too—we all fought that fish, trying to get it ashore, and I never once looked back at Daisy."

My stomach cramped.

"When I finally did, she wasn't on the bank." He paused. "I found her floating in the water. I have no idea how long she'd been in there. Not long, but long enough. Skeeter helped me drag her out onto the bank. We tried CPR, and after a couple of minutes, Skeeter—who was older than me and bigger—picked her up and hauled ass for his house. But it was too late."

"I'm so sorry." When he didn't volunteer any more information, I asked, "I still don't understand why he asked you to protect me."

"He knows you remind me of Daisy."

I sucked in a breath. "Oh, Jed."

"He knows how much I regret my mistake, so he's given me a second chance. But tonight . . ."

"It's not your job to protect me. I'm *not* your sister."

"I know. But you're more important to Skeeter than you know. I don't know what he would have done if they'd killed you." He lowered his head until we were eye to eye. "You think Crocker went batshit crazy? That was nothing compared to the vengeance Skeeter would have meted out."

I shivered. "Well, I'm safe, but I really need to call Mason. Just let me borrow your cell phone, and I won't tell Skeeter about it."

"Skeeter's right. We don't know who's behind this, and they think the evil deed is still waiting to be done. He's hoping to flush them out with this call."

"But what does that have to do with me calling Mason?"

The front door opened, revealing Skeeter in the doorway. "Because whoever did this is watching him like a hawk. I can guaran-damn-tee you that they'll want to see his reaction when he watches that video. That's why they haven't called in the order to kill you. They're plannin' on time-stamping the damn thing and sending it moments after it happens."

"*Skeeter!* I can't let him think I'm dead!"

"If we don't follow through, they're liable to kill him and be done with it. Whoever orchestrated this is a sick son-of-a-bitch, J.R. Simmons or not."

Jed pulled out his phone and grimaced. "Merv texted. He just heard from our contact at the sheriff's department. Apparently, Deveraux just arrived. Simmons Jr. is talking with him in his office now." He looked up, his face grim. "We should be hearing any time now."

"What?" I asked. "Why would you expect to hear *now?* Do they have someone in the sheriff's office?"

Both men gave me a sorrowful look, then as if on cue,

a cell phone rang. Skeeter picked it up off the kitchen table and nodded to Jed.

Jed sent a text while Skeeter answered in a gruff voice that didn't sound like his own. "Yeah?" He was silent for several seconds. "Got it." He tapped the screen, then put the phone on the table. "They're waiting for the video."

Jed looked at me. "We need to sniff out who's behind this, particularly if it's not one of the known players."

"We have to send Deveraux a video that convinces him you're dead," Skeeter added.

My breath came in quick pants. "I'm not doing it."

Skeeter moved across the room and knelt in front of me. The softness I saw there surprised me. "You know, we don't *have* to do this. The fact that we got the call minutes after your boyfriend walked into Simmons' office wasn't for nothin'. I'll have my men take care of him, and we don't have to send a thing to Deveraux."

It dawned on me what he was insinuating.

"No! Joe would *never* do this!"

Skeeter's face hardened, the softness slipping off like melted wax. "The evidence is stacked against him. He had you arrested."

I violently shook my head. "No. He still loves me. He would sooner die himself than order my murder."

"Rose," Jed said softly. "You know he's following his father's orders."

"*No!*" I stood. "He didn't do this. Maybe if you two pulled your heads out of your behinds, you'd see that whoever is doing this wants to hurt him too!"

A stunned look crossed both of their faces.

"Yeah, that's right. Joe taught me that the obvious answer isn't always the right one." I pointed my finger at Jed. "You text Merv right now and tell him to find out who else is in the sheriff's office." When he hesitated, I raised my voice. "*Right now!*"

"Do it," Skeeter barked.

Jed started texting, and Skeeter stood and began to pace. "We have to send a video, Rose, especially if there's any doubt about who did it."

"No. I'll send Mason a text from my phone telling him that I've escaped and I'm okay, but he's in grave danger. I can tell him to act horrified. Joe too."

"Whoever is watching will expect to hear the sounds of your murder," Skeeter said bluntly.

I felt like I was going to throw up.

"We have to stage your murder and make it convincing enough for Deveraux and Simmons to believe it."

"No, we *don't*. I'll still send the warning text, and then we can follow up with a short video of my 'death.'"

Skeeter shook his head. "There are so many things wrong with this plan."

"He can do this. I saw him perform impromptu at Gems when the guard found me listening and threw me into their meeting. Trust me, he'll follow along."

Skeeter looked grim.

Jed glanced up. "Merv says there are six deputies in the office—including the off-duty deputy who was at the restaurant, a receptionist, and Simmons' sister."

I gasped. "Kate is there?"

Skeeter's eyebrows rose. "Does that mean anything?"

"Yes! She has a table full of crap in her apartment—photos, court cases, police reports, and surveillance—all of it about or related to Mason."

Skeeter's eyes widened. "You think she set this up?"

I shuddered. "I don't know, but there's evidence she may have hired the guy who ran Mason off the road in December and stole his phone. The phone was on her table."

"Shit." He turned to Jed. "Where in the station is she?"

Jed sent a text and waited. "She's sitting by Simmons' office. She's filling out a police report."

"What for?" My breath stuck in my throat. "Oh, my word. I did this."

"Did what?"

"Neely Kate and I were in her apartment today. I think she figured it out. Maybe that's why she orchestrated this. To keep me quiet about what I found out while hurting Mason in the process."

"*If* she did this," Jed amended.

Even *I* had a hard time believing it. Still, I couldn't think of a single soul capable of such a thing, other than Mick Gentry and J.R. Simmons.

"Rose." Skeeter sounded anxious. "We have to send him something."

I reached out my hand toward my phone. "Trust me. Give me my phone. *Please.*"

He looked me in the eye for several seconds, then stood and went outside.

"Are you sure there isn't anyone else in there?" I asked.

Jed nodded.

Skeeter was back in seconds, my phone in his hand. He approached and held it out to me. "Let's get the video ready first."

A sudden thought occurred to me as I opened the camera app. "Do we need the sound of a gunshot in the video?"

Jed stiffened. "No. They were gonna slit your throat."

I sucked in a breath at that cheery thought. "Well, okay then."

"Remember, you've gotta make it convincing," Skeeter said in a gruff tone.

I nodded and prepared myself, wondering if I should do a dry run first. Especially since my limited theater experience consisted of my non-speaking role as a dog in my second grade class play. But rehearsing would feel ridiculous and wrong, and I plain didn't have time.

Jed took the phone and held it in front of me. "Whenever you're ready."

I nodded, trying to control my anxiety, but I was dangerously close to losing it. "Okay."

I looked into the phone. "Mason, I love you. This isn't your fault." My voice was shaky with nerves, which I supposed would make it authentic to whoever might be listening in the station. But what if Mason didn't believe the text? What if he trusted the video instead?

I closed my eyes and went along with the plan. "What are you doin'?" I called out, choking back real tears. Everything about this scared me to death. So much could go wrong. "No!" I released a short scream, then stopped as if it had been cut off.

Jed nodded and lowered the phone. "That was good."

Skeeter snatched the phone from him and turned his back to us. I heard my shaky voice, followed by the scream. He pushed out a long breath. "This might actually work if your boyfriend goes along with the plan and the spy isn't watching the screen."

"That's a lot of ifs," Jed added.

"We still have to send it," I said.

I took the phone from Skeeter, pulled up Mason's name, and started typing.

"Shit," Skeeter said after a moment. "Deveraux might be able to pull this off, but if your theory is correct, they'll expect a reaction from Simmons too. How are you gonna manage that?"

I stopped typing. "I'll tell Mason. He'll have to pretend he believes the video is real, but if the two of them are alone in that office together, he'll find a way to get the message to Joe."

Skeeter swiped the phone out of my hand. "No. Simmons can't know the truth."

"I can't do this to him either!"

His eyes darkened. "I trust Deveraux to keep this quiet to protect you, but I don't trust Simmons one iota. Despite your protests to the contrary, I'm still not convinced he's uninvolved."

"Skeeter! He's gonna think I've been murdered!"

"Good. That's what I want him to believe." He held up the phone, his fingers suspended over the keys. "Now what do you want to say?"

"I can type my own stinkin' text!"

"Not this time. You want to send him a text, I'll type it. Your choice. I'm good with just sending the video."

Tears burned my eyes. "This is wrong." I wasn't sure if I could live with myself for doing this to Joe, but I couldn't let Mason die either.

"Joe Simmons chose his side just like I chose mine. Now we both have to live with the consequences. You have three seconds to start talking, or I'm pressing send."

I was terrified this would backfire on me, but it was better than sending only the video. I told him what to type:

*Mason, it's me. I escaped, but the person who's behind this doesn't know. The men who took me were supposed to video my murder and send it to you. I know you're in Joe's office and they want the video sent now. They can't know that I got away, so your reaction is key. So is Joe's. He has to believe it's true. Otherwise both of your lives are in danger. I'm going to send you a video of me, but be prepared to hear me scream like someone's hurting me. When you see it, you have to act distraught and immediately delete this text and the video. I'll be in touch.*

Skeeter read it back, and I said, "Let me send it."

His gaze narrowed, and it was obvious he thought I was up to something.

"I'm not going to add to the text. I promise." Not that I was happy with this decision, but I needed to take ownership of it. "I need to be the one to send it."

He studied me for a moment, then handed me the phone. "Jed, tell Merv she's sending it now."

My heart was beating so furiously it felt like it was trying to escape from my chest. I paused to ask myself if this was the right thing to do, and then I said a quick prayer and pressed send.

# Chapter Twenty-Four

As soon as it had been sent, I again felt like I was going to throw up. What if I'd just signed Mason's death warrant? What if I'd just pushed Joe over the edge?

"If Simmons or one of his minions sent that text to your burner, they'll have expected a response by now," Skeeter said.

I just shook my head, unable to think about that right now. "Jed? Any news?"

"No."

I wrung my hands. "What's goin' on over there at the station?"

"Merv will text us when he knows something."

I stood and began to pace.

"Rose." Skeeter's voice was stern. "I need you to focus."

I flung my hands out in exasperation. "How can I focus when I have no idea if Mason pulled this off or even went along with it!"

"Because you started this thing, and you need to follow it through. If Mason did what you asked, he needs you more than ever."

That stopped me in my tracks. "You're gonna let me meet J.R.?"

Skeeter's jaw tightened. "I haven't decided yet, but we might as well string him along."

"If he's behind my kidnapping, won't it look a bit odd if Lady answers him around the same time Mason got the supposed video?"

Skeeter stared at the wall for several seconds, but then his eyes lit up. "No. It's perfect. You ask him if he's behind the ADA's girlfriend's murder, and say that if so, you're impressed. It shows you've got your fingertip on the pulse of the county."

"That I'm a real player."

"Exactly."

"I just got a text," Jed murmured, reading his screen. "Deveraux played his part. Simmons lost his shit and stormed out of the building."

"And Kate?" I asked.

"She ran out after her brother."

I wasn't sure what to make of that. I was devastated that Joe thought I'd been murdered, but deep down I knew Skeeter was right. After Joe stole the journal and had me arrested, I couldn't trust him with my secrets, especially not if Kate was spending time around him.

"What is Mason doing now?" I asked.

"Forget about Deveraux," Skeeter said. "Is anyone else acting strange?"

Jed looked exasperated. "I'm getting this second hand, so it's slow going."

"Then text the real source!" I protested. "Cut out the middleman."

He shook his head. "No dice. The source only talks to Merv."

I wanted to ask more questions, but another part of me didn't. Someone working in the sheriff's department was sharing official information with criminals. That person may very well have saved Mason's life, but what if he or she had previously been loyal to Daniel Crocker?

I shook my head. That was an ethical dilemma for another day.

"Deputy Miller is shaken. The other deputies are worried about Simmons. Deveraux went to the bathroom. No one seems to be acting suspiciously."

Skeeter picked up the burner phone off the kitchen table. "I'm gonna send them a message."

I marched over and snatched it from him. "This was my idea, and I set it up. If anyone's sending a text, it's me, especially since you wouldn't let me type the last one."

He glared at me for several seconds, but I didn't miss the hint of amusement in his eyes. Finally, he handed me the phone. "Go ahead, but I want to read it first."

"Fine."

I pulled up the previous text and started typing, surprised to realize how much better it made me feel to do something productive.

*I've just been informed about the ADA's girlfriend's untimely demise. I can only presume you were behind it. Impressive. We're on. Location TBA.*

I showed it to Skeeter. "Perfect."

After I pressed send, he took the phone back and set it on the table. "We need to discuss how this will go down."

I nodded, but then I heard something that made me freeze in place—my ringtone for Mason.

I sucked in a breath.

"It's Deveraux," Jed said, looking at the screen of my personal phone.

Skeeter pointed his finger in my face. "Do *not* answer that. He's still at the damned sheriff station."

"Skeeter! Jed said he was in the bathroom. No one will know!"

His jaw tightened. "Why is he calling? We told the fool you'd get in touch with him later."

"Would *you* be content with that order?"

He waved his hand at Jed. "Give her the damned phone." He narrowed his eyes at me. "Text only. And do *not* tell him where you are or who you are with."

"I'm not stupid." I grabbed the phone from Jed.

Skeeter shot me a look, but I didn't plan on fooling him. I declined the call and composed a text.

*You can't talk to me now. Someone on your end is watching. I'm safe. I promise.*

*Where are you?*

"Do *not* answer that," Skeeter said from behind me.

He'd been spying on the screen over my shoulder, but I wasn't exactly mad. He was in this too. In a way, he had a right to know.

"I'm not," I said, weariness suddenly washing over me.

*I'll tell you when I can. Do not go to your momma's house. My vision's coming true and you're not safe. PLEASE be careful.*

I pressed send and closed my eyes. "They'll go after him next."

"Not in the sheriff's station," Skeeter said. "They'll wait. Probably until he gets home. If it were me, I'd attack in the dead of night. But I suspect they don't just want to kill him—this plan is proof enough of that. They want him to suffer. They'll probably hold him hostage for a bit and torture him before they off him."

I spun around, light-headed with terror. "Is that supposed to make me feel better?"

"Fuck, no. But it's the goddamned truth."

Jed cleared his throat. "Skeeter."

He shook his head. "This isn't some spat at recess, Rose. This is deadly serious. And if you're making deals with the devil, then you need to know all the facts, ugly or not. You can handle this." He leaned closer. "You are not some hothouse rose, painstakingly nurtured and trimmed in a carefully controlled environment. You are a rose bush left out in the wild, scraping for survival. You have fought for everything you have, and you thrive on the struggle. You're called to it. The harder things are, the better you get."

I stared up at him in disbelief.

"So no more coddling. No more babying. I want nothing more than to protect you and tell you can't take part in this game. But the truth is, half the time *you're* the protector." He glanced at Jed. "So she needs to know the facts—as ugly as they might be—and she needs to help us make informed decisions."

Jed gave a quick nod, although he didn't look happy about it.

I stood there in stunned silence, surprised by how empowered I felt. Before, I'd believed I had a chance of seeing this J.R. Simmons mission through, but now I was certain I could make it work.

"I need to protect Mason." I lifted my chin. "It's a deal-breaker. We have to take him somewhere safe."

Skeeter glanced at Jed, who released a long sigh. "Do you have any idea how impossible that is? Where are we gonna take him? Like he's even gonna go."

My head swam with fear, but I was tired of living half of my life in fear and the other half in deceit. It was time to face the consequences of my decisions, no matter how much I stood to lose.

"Here." I looked Skeeter in the eye. "We need to bring him here."

# Chapter Twenty-Five

That went over like a lead balloon.

Both men started shouting, but after watching them bluster for several seconds, I shook my head. "Someone has to go pick him up. I'll tell him to park behind the Sinclair station. Whoever gets him can blindfold him to keep from compromising your safe house."

"No damn way," Skeeter growled.

Jed eyed me like I'd lost my mind. "Mason's never gonna agree to it."

"He will," I said. "If he thinks he's coming to me." I choked on the lump in my throat. "Who do you trust to get him?"

Skeeter looked stunned, but he gave me an answer nonetheless. "Merv."

"Skeeter!" Jed protested.

"Look." I put my hand on his good arm. "He's smart, and he can help us. He wants the same thing we do."

Skeeter gave me a sardonic grin. "I suspect we have very different ways of going about it."

I dropped my hand and turned away, my impending loss sinking into my skin. "Not in this instance. We need to have someone around who knows the law if we have any hope of getting our charges dropped." I took a deep breath and turned around to face them, feeling even surer of my decision. "We need him, don't you see? We're all in the thick of this together, like it or not."

Neither one of them said anything for several heartbeats, and then Skeeter finally turned to look at me. "Think this through, Rose," he said softly. "It's all gonna fall apart if you do this."

I looked down at my ring, my heart grieving. "It was already unraveling. He was puttin' things together." I looked up at him, his face blurry through my tears. "See? I told you." My voice cracked. "He's a smart man."

"You're certain?"

"Yes."

He nodded. "Call Merv. Make the arrangements."

Jed looked furious, but he dug out his phone.

I turned and walked into the kitchen, getting a glass out of a cabinet so I could pour myself some water. The clock on the microwave read 12:20.

Skeeter walked up behind me. "Merv will pick him up. Tell Deveraux to be behind the station at one a.m. He'll have to wear a blindfold, and if he even hints that he's takin' it off, Merv will dump him onto the street."

I nodded.

He leaned his mouth close to my ear. "Rose, you better be damn sure you want to do this. You *have* to know the outcome."

I bit my bottom lip and racked my brain for some other solution. The bottom line was that he deserved to know the truth. Even if it killed him metaphorically, at least he wouldn't be literally murdered. Besides, I'd sensed all along that we needed to be working together and pooling all of our resources.

"Yes." I turned around to look at him. "Does he know who Merv is? That he works for you?"

Skeeter sighed. "Most people know Jed works for me, but Merv tends to keep a low profile, and both of them are careful enough they don't get charged with anything. There's a chance he won't put it together."

I nodded. "Good. I want to be the one to tell him."

"I figured as much. I'd send someone else, but this is dangerous enough without adding any more unknowns. If Deveraux's in the back of a car blindfolded, he's a sittin' duck. Merv's bound to protect him, which means his ass is on the line."

I hadn't thought of that.

Skeeter must have sensed my guilt. "That's his job, so don't worry about him. He does what I say. Even this."

"Okay."

He turned to Jed. "Where's Deveraux now?"

Jed checked his phone. "He left the sheriff's office a few minutes ago."

"Then we're good to contact him." His gaze turned to me. "You ready?"

I nodded, then sucked in a deep breath and pushed it out before I called Mason. He answered on the first ring.

"Rose?" He sounded so desperate, I started to cry.

"It's me. I'm fine, really."

"Oh, my God. I was so scared." His voice broke, and he took a moment before he spoke again. "Where are you? How'd you get away?"

"I'll tell you all about it, but I need you to come here."

"Of course. Just tell me where you are."

I fought back a sob. Would he be so eager to see me after he found out my secret? "Mason, you have to listen to me—you're in danger and I need to protect you, but you have to do as I say."

He hesitated. "What are you talking about?"

"I need you to come to me, but you can't know where I am. Someone I trust is coming to get you."

"Who?" I could hear the suspicion in his voice now.

"Someone who's helping me. Helping us."

"Rose?" He sounded worried again. "Are you in trouble?"

More trouble than he could even guess. But I couldn't tell him that. "I'm safe for now—that's what matters. Just get here, and I'll explain it all. Okay?"

"Okay." But I heard the hesitation in his voice.

"I need you to go to the Sinclair station, the one I saw you at last week. Be there in forty minutes. Park behind the building, and the guy who comes to pick you up will bring you to me . . . but here's the unusual part. You have to wear a blindfold. That's the only way they'll bring you here. But make sure you're not followed. "

"Who, Rose? Who has you?"

I fought another sob.

"Sweetheart, can you tell me where you are? I'll come get you."

"I can't," I said through my tears. "I'm so scared for you, Mason. They were going to make you watch me get murdered, then I'm sure their plan is to kill you next. Whoever hired them thinks they took care of the first part—now they'll move on to the second. Just like in my vision. The only way I know how to protect you is to bring you here. Will you come? Please?"

"Sweetheart, I know you can't talk because of whoever is there. But I'll come for you, and then we'll figure out how to get out of this together." He released a short chuckle, but it was a strained sound. "We're partners, remember?"

"I love you so much," I choked out.

"I love you too. I'll be there soon. We'll get out of this. I promise."

For the next hour, I was a mess. Skeeter wanted to talk more about the plan to meet J.R., but I refused to discuss any of it until Mason showed up. He wanted to know more about what I'd found in Kate's apartment, but I put him off on that too. Part of me worried Mason would find out the truth, then turn around and walk away from me forever. But the rest of me knew he wouldn't. He'd told me that he'd do anything to bring J.R. Simmons down, and though I knew that was, in large part, for me, it wasn't only about me. J.R. Simmons stood for everything Mason had fought against for his entire career.

Still, I was pushing his promise to the limit.

A little after one, Merv texted Jed that he had the package.

I pounced on him like a cat on catnip. "Did Mason give him any trouble? Was he followed? Was Merv nice to him?"

Skeeter shot me a look of disgust, but Jed tried to be more patient. "He didn't give me details, Rose. He literally texted: *I've picked up the package.*"

I stood and wrung my hands. I wasn't sure if it were possible for someone to die of nerves, but if so, I was a goner. "How long will it take them to get here?"

"Merv's gonna drive him around a bit to throw him off and make sure they aren't tailed, so maybe twenty-five minutes . . . a half hour?"

I nodded, trying to catch my breath.

"Rose." Jed stood and gently cupped my elbow. "Why don't you lie down and try to get some rest? It's after one in the morning, and you've had a traumatic evening."

I shook my head. "I'm not laying on any nasty surface in this house."

"Where the hell do you think you're gonna sleep?" Skeeter barked.

My mouth dropped open. Stupid me hadn't even thought that far ahead.

Skeeter got to his feet and rubbed the back of his neck. "We should never have gotten him tonight. We should have picked him up tomorrow morning after getting a good night's sleep."

I put my hand on my hip. "It was tonight or not at all. Sure as shoot that they were going to kill him tonight. And besides, you yourself said you thought they'd kill him in the middle of the night!"

He groaned and stomped outside.

Jed sighed as he watched Skeeter walk off, then moved his injured arm and released a low moan.

It was then I remembered he'd lost his sling in the fight, and when I looked more closely, I could see a dark spot on his black long-sleeve T-shirt.

"Jed, you're bleeding. Let me look at that."

He sat at the kitchen table and took off his shirt. The sight of his rippling muscles caught me off guard, like suddenly finding out your geeky cousin has become hot. I made myself focus on the white gauze tied around his bicep and the dark spot of blood.

"I expected you to put up some macho fuss."

He leaned his head back, looking exhausted. "I'm too tired, and I can't change it myself. I figure I might as well get your help before all hell breaks loose."

I cringed, but I suspected his assessment of our situation was right.

"There are fresh bandages in the hall closet. Clean sheets too. You'll sleep in the bedroom at the end of the hall. And Deveraux too . . . if he wants to sleep with you."

I sighed. "I know you think this is a mistake."

"I *know* it is." He sounded so sure of himself it almost gave me second thoughts. "People like Deveraux don't hop over the line of legality so easily. He's got a very clear picture of right and wrong. Have you considered what's gonna happen if he gets here and decides he wants to wash his hands of the whole thing? Even worse, what if he demands to leave and tell the whole world about you and your secret identity? Or what if he decides to use this against Skeeter, me, or Merv and run to the sheriff? Do you really think Skeeter's gonna let that happen?"

I gasped.

He gave me a sympathetic look. "Didn't think about that part, did you?"

I didn't say anything. The answer was obvious.

Skeeter walked in as I finished tying the gauze over Jed's wound. There was a no-nonsense look on his face, which I'd learned to mean he was about to issue an order. "When he gets here, we're gonna deposit him in the living room without taking his blindfold off. He can remove it after we go outside. You have until tomorrow morning to sway him to our side. If he says no, we'll take him back to town, blindfold on, but tied up this time. And if he threatens to turn any of us in, he will be dealt with." His eyes found mine. "That is non-negotiable."

I nodded.

After I cleaned up the dirty bandages and put away the supplies, I found the clean sheets Jed had mentioned and decided to make the bed. The light in the room didn't turn on with the switch, and there weren't any lamps to be found. In fact, I realized there wasn't anything in the room except for the bed. I used the light in the hall to put on the linens, and I was in the process of smoothing a fresh blanket over them when I heard a scuffle in the living room.

"Rose?" Mason's voice called out. "*Where the hell is she?*"

Merv's voice followed. "Just stay where you are, and she'll be out in a minute. But keep that blindfold on until she takes it off."

I'd already hurried out of the bedroom and was standing at the entrance to the hall, my heart in my throat.

Mason's hands clenched at his sides. "If you hurt her—"

"Mason," I said, taking the few steps toward him. It felt like I was dragging a fifty-pound weight with each step. "I'm here."

He reached for his blindfold, but I stopped him,

waiting until all three men had left and shut the door behind them.

His hands covered mine as I lifted the handkerchief off his head, and the tenderness of the gesture almost brought me to tears.

Relief washed over his face, and he pulled me into a tight embrace and buried his face into my hair. He broke down. "I thought I'd lost you."

"I'm fine. I promise."

He leaned back and searched my face, worry filling his eyes. "How'd you get away?"

"Someone rescued me."

"The people who brought me here?"

I nodded.

"They want something from you? Or from me?"

"Let's just say we have a common agenda." I pulled on his arm, leading him toward the two kitchen chairs in the middle of the room. "Sit down, and I'll tell you everything."

He resisted. "No, let's try to get out of here. Based on the sounds I heard when I was walking into the cabin, I think we're close to woods. If we can make it into the trees, we can lose them in the dark."

I gave him a sad smile. "They're watching closely. We can't leave." That was the truth. Even if I walked out that front door and told Skeeter I was finished, he'd never let me leave. Not until this was all said and done.

Mason let me lead him to the chairs, and we sat there together, his hand holding mine in a tight grip. "What happened, Rose?"

I told him about being kidnapped outside the bathroom in Jaspers, regaining consciousness in the back of the car, and being carried into the cabin and tied to a chair.

"Did they say anything?" he asked gently, but the fire in his eyes told me just how much this was affecting him.

"No. I told them you'd pay to have me released, but they didn't answer. They left me in the bedroom, and about an hour or so later, I heard a commotion outside. They were dragging a man into the house. They brought him into the room where I was being held and tried to tie him to a chair too, but he wasn't havin' any part of that. He put up a huge fight."

"Who was he?"

I decided to ease my way into this. "They found him in the woods, spying on the cabin. But like I said, when they started to tie him down, he lost it. He slammed the chair into one guy's head and then tackled the other two. He wrestled a gun from one of the kidnappers, and when one of them pointed his gun at me, this man shot him. He saved my life."

Mason's hold on me tightened.

"He helped me get loose, and then they brought me here."

"They? The guy who drove me here?"

"He's one of them."

"Who are they?"

My blood rushed through my head, giving me a dull headache. "Like I said, they want the same thing we do. To bring J.R. Simmons to his knees. And we have the perfect plan to do it, but we need your help."

He stiffened. "*We?*"

I took a shallow breath. I had to be strong. I had to get him to go along with this. "I've agreed to help them."

He stood, his mouth gaping open in disbelief. "Why would you do such a thing?"

I struggled to hold back my tears. "Because I'm the one who's going to do it. I'm the one who's going to get J.R. to confess."

He shook his head and leaned forward. "Rose, sweetheart. I don't know what they've told you to convince you of this, but there's no way in hell it will work. J.R. Simmons is a dangerous man." He stood upright. "I'd be shocked if he wasn't behind your kidnapping tonight." He pointed to the door, his voice rising. "How do you know these guys aren't Part B of his scheme?"

"Because it's *my* plan. My idea. I know it will work."

Mason ran his hand over his face, looking like he was about to fall over from exhaustion. Skeeter was right. It might have been better to wait until the morning. I should have let Mason get a little sleep. But the risk would have been too great.

He took a breath and seemed to ponder something before he sat down next to me and took both of my hands in his, staring at me in earnest. "Listen, I don't know what you've gotten mixed up in, but we can get out of this. Both of us. Just tell me exactly how they got you to agree to help them, and we'll get this worked out, okay?" He gave me a soft smile, so full of hope that everything was going to be okay.

He was breaking my heart, and he hadn't even left me yet.

I got to my feet and began to pace. "I'm sure J.R. is the moneyman backing Mick Gentry's bid for Fenton County. There's no way Gentry has the cash to do it on his own. He and his buddies robbed multiple places to get the money to make a bid at the auction on Thanksgiving Day, but he lost it all in the end. His strip club burned down. His drug operation in Big Thief Hollow has been knocked to the ground, and it'll be a long time before it's operational again. But Mick's not the kind of man who believes in working his way up the ranks. He wants an instant power grab, so he found someone with deep pockets to help finance and support him."

Mason gaped at me like I'd broken out in fluent Russian. "How do you know all that? I've been careful to keep as much of that mess as possible at the office."

I ignored his question. "Who's big enough to help and not afraid to get his hands dirty so long as he keeps lookin' and smellin' clean? J.R. Simmons has kept his hands out of the Fenton County pie, so there would be no reason for anyone to suspect him. But then I found out he hasn't . . ." I swallowed my fear and continued. "He was in Fenton County twenty-five years ago. With the Atchison Manufacturing contract. So we know he's been here before. He's been looking for that journal, so he still has an interest in Fenton County. But even before I dug up this whole mess with Dora, J.R. had a master plan. One he'd been waiting to pull the trigger on for a while."

Mason's jaw was slack with shock.

"Your momma came to me last week and told me she had a feeling that you were in danger and that your life was tied to someone else's. At first I thought it might be Joe, but then I realized I needed to think bigger. J.R. Simmons is out to destroy someone else in this town too. Your fate is tied to his."

His eyes widened. "Skeeter Malcolm?" He jumped to his feet. "Oh, Rose. *What did you do?*" He was in a panic now. "Oh, God." He scrubbed his hands over his face, then dropped them and grabbed my shoulders. "It's okay." He nodded slowly as if trying to convince himself too. "We'll figure a way out of this. Malcolm's in enough trouble that he doesn't have time to mess with small fish like us." He forced a smile. "He's got to be more worried about his murder charges and the Lady in Black's attempts to take over his territory."

How had he heard that part?

He saw my confusion. "You and I put it together that Simmons is after Malcolm, so I called Randy on the drive home from Little Rock. He has a source who keeps him updated on all the rumors in the crime world. I figured if I could keep tabs on Malcolm, it might lead me to Simmons."

I took a shallow breath. "Mason, the Lady in Black will lead you to J.R."

He shook his head. "Finding her is like finding a needle in a haystack. She's like a ghost. She doesn't exist. She shows up at these meetings, and then she just disappears. No one knows where she lives. Rumor has it she's from Louisiana, but there's no evidence to suggest that's true."

"The Lady in Black has already set up a meeting with Mick Gentry's backer. Tomorrow night at ten p.m."

His eyes narrowed. "Did Malcolm tell you that?" He shook his head. "Why does he need you or me, anyway? What's he getting out of this? And that story about my mother saying our fates are tied together is not an answer."

I rubbed my forehead. "You asked me who saved me tonight." I held his gaze with mine. "It was one of Skeeter's men. He was watching the restaurant when he saw the guy carry me out of the back. He followed them to the cabin, and he called Skeeter on the way. They discovered Jed and dragged him into the room where I was being kept, but his orders were to protect me. So he beat the crap out of them, and they brought me here."

"Malcolm's men have been following you?" The terror in his eyes was nearly my undoing, but I had to keep going.

"I told you the truth in the text I sent you. Jed heard them plotting to kill me. They were supposed to video it with a time stamp and send it to you while you were in the sheriff's office. They wanted you to watch me be murdered. Skeeter refused to let me go home after that. He's worried they'll kill me. So he brought me here to protect me."

Confusion washed over his face like he'd been given a bag of spare parts and told to build a toaster. "Was he the one who posted your bail?"

"No, but he wants to know who did." I licked my bottom lip. "He *was* the one who convinced Carter Hale to represent me."

Anger burst on his face. "We'll be finding you new representation in the morning."

I didn't respond. We had bigger things to worry about.

"Okay." He took a deep breath and softened his

expression, as though he worried his emotional pendulum would scare me. "It's okay. We just need to figure out why Skeeter Malcolm is interested in you."

I forged on, wondering whether all this buildup would help, or if it would be better to just rip off the Band-Aid. "Remember the extra blood stain on the factory floor? The one you asked me about? That was from one of his men."

"They were at the factory to hurt you?" he asked in dismay. "Are they aligned with Joe?"

"No. They can't stand Joe. They think he's in allegiance with his father. Jed was there to protect me."

"*Last week?*"

"And the fire at Gems . . . Skeeter knew I was there. When he realized I was in trouble, he sent his men in to get me. He and Jed were the ones who dragged you out of the burning building."

"*What?*" He grabbed the sides of his head and gave it a couple of shakes, then dropped his hands. "How long has he had you under his thumb? Why didn't you tell me? I would have figured out a way to help you!"

I fought the tears burning my eyes. I had to keep it together. "I'm the one who went to him."

He grabbed my shoulders, fear washing over his face. "Why would you do that, Rose? What did you hope to gain from him?"

"Information. I wanted to trade information with him."

He dropped his hold and took a step back, panic filling his eyes. "County secrets? You were feeding him inside information?"

"*No!*" I shook my head. "I swear to you, I never told him anything that was a county secret." But then I realized that wasn't entirely true. I'd told him about the knife in Mason's drawer. I'd told him that Joe was fixing to pin the double murders on him.

"Then what? What could you possibly have that he wanted?"

I broke down, hiccupping on a sob. "Information about the robbers."

He shuddered as it hit him. "*The bank robbers?* That was back in November!"

I gave him a pleading look. "I needed to get my money back. I found out the men who'd stolen it were going around the county, stealing more money to make a bid at the auction for Crocker's business."

He took a step backward, horror washing over his face.

"It was supposed to be a simple trade. I would tell him what I knew, and then he would find them. It was in his best interest to find them. Once he did, he'd get my money back for me, and the deal would be done. But Skeeter's a smart man." I shook my head in a slow swing. "He wanted to know how I got my information. So when he threatened me, Bruce Wayne told him about my visions."

He squeezed his eyes shut, and then opened them as he gasped for breath. "Bruce Wayne?"

"I convinced him to set up the meeting. He's regretted it ever since. But Skeeter found out about my visions. And he figured he could use my ability to his advantage. He forced me to have a vision in his office, and I saw his death at the auction."

Realization flooded Mason's face, and he shook his head. "No."

I forced myself to continue. "I didn't want to do it, but he intimidated me into agreeing. My job was simple. Keep him alive so the vision didn't come true. If I did as he asked, I'd get my money back and everything would be fine."

"No."

"But then he called me a few weeks later, knowing exactly what carrot to dangle. He'd caught word that your life was in danger."

"How altruistic of him," he spat in disgust.

"He was worried you'd be murdered and it would be pinned on him. My job was to figure out who was behind it. That's what I've been doing."

Mason looked totally shell-shocked, but I continued. "I found his turncoats. Skeeter was sure they were the same ones after you—" I took a breath, "—but obviously he was wrong."

Mason just watched me in horrified silence.

"After that, I told him I was done. He couldn't make me do it anymore. But you were in Gems." I started to cry. "Skeeter was behind the building, and he found Rich Lowry dragging me out back. Lowry figured it out because of how pissed off Skeeter looked. He was about to break my neck to goad him, but Skeeter shot him instead. You were still inside, so I begged him to go back in and save you. He refused to do it, and he made sure I couldn't run in there myself. So I made a bargain. Six months of service for your life."

His eyes filled with tears, and I could feel tears coursing down my own cheeks. "Rose."

"I didn't want to do it, Mason, but I'm damned good at it. Last week I met with Scott Humphrey. I had a vision of him meeting Mick Gentry. They talked about their list. They were waiting for the order to off Skeeter and then they were gonna move on to the next name on the list. I was sure it was you."

He stared at me, emotionless.

"I needed to know who was behind that list. Before I had the vision, I told Humphrey I wanted to meet Mick Gentry. I said I had Skeeter's permission to negotiate a truce. But in the vision Gentry said he wouldn't meet with me until Skeeter was out of the way. So after I got out of jail and found out that Skeeter was missing, I told Jed to set up a meeting. I knew it was dangerous, but your leads weren't panning out quickly enough. I couldn't sit back and let you be killed when I knew I had at least a small chance of saving both of us. After the vision I had of you dead, I knew time was running out. And I *know* J.R. Simmons is the mastermind. The only way I could think to stop him was to meet with him as his equal and take him down with his own arrogance."

His eyes glistened with unshed tears, and he looked dangerously close to breaking down.

"So tomorrow night at ten o'clock, I'm meeting with Mick Gentry's backer. I need your help to figure out if we can use what he says against him legally. I need you to help me figure out what questions to ask. How to bait him and get him to confess."

His mouth dropped open in shock.

"I know you probably hate me right now, and I understand. *I do.* But just know that in almost every single instance, I did this to save your life. And I'd do it again in an instant." A fierceness radiated through me. "Because it was the only way to save you."

His face softened. "Rose."

I choked on a sob. "I hoped to God you'd never find out. I hated lying to you. I hated the secrets. I hated that I was jeopardizing your job. But the bottom line was that I was saving your life. You told me you'd do anything to save me, and this is proof that I'd do anything to save you."

When he didn't say anything, I started crying harder.

"But the sad truth is Rose Anne Gardner couldn't do it, no matter how much she wanted to help. There was only one person who could save you. And you know who it is. I think part of you has known for weeks. You just didn't want to believe it."

I lifted my chin. "Mason, *I* am the Lady in Black."

# Chapter Twenty-Six

He blinked as if he'd just awakened from a nightmare. He cleared his throat. "This started the week of Thanksgiving?"

I nodded. "Yes."

"And you met Mick Gentry last night while I was in Little Rock?"

"Yes."

"You're meeting Gentry's backer tomorrow night? What solid evidence do you have that it's J.R. Simmons?"

"Only my instincts and a lot of circumstantial hints."

"So Malcolm's making you do this? He's got you tucked away here until you do his dirty work?"

I shook my head, tears still streaming down my cheeks. "No, I told you. This part was my idea. I decided to use my role to save all of us."

"But Rose," he pleaded with me. "You still don't know for sure J.R. is Gentry's backer, so you're planning on risking your life for possibly nothing."

"No! Even if the backer doesn't turn out to be J.R., which seems really unlikely given everything we know, he's still supporting a terrible person and ordering terrible things. *I* can put a stop to that."

"What if he doesn't even show? What if he sends his men to kill you and be done with it?"

"The Lady in Black is bigger than me. Those men respect her. She has power. J.R. *will* be there. He's beyond curious to meet her."

"And you think you can keep your identity from him with a *hat?*"

"It's worked up until now."

He was quiet for several seconds, but then his shoulders stiffened. When he looked at me again, he was all business. "Simmons wants Malcolm dead, and I think your theory that he's going to make it look like Malcolm murdered me makes sense. But why does he want to meet with the Lady . . . you?"

"Just like you, Skeeter was raising money and property to get me out of jail. But Sam Teagen bailed me out before he could get everything together. Jed had put together one hundred thousand cash, and he showed it to Mick Gentry. I told him it was just the beginning of what I planned to invest in Fenton County, but I didn't deal with middlemen. I needed to meet with his backer. If nothing else, J.R. is going to want to meet with the potential competition and size me up."

He wore the distant look he got when he was working out a problem. "You must be on to something. It looks like it worked."

"I told Gentry that I would share my own plans for the county, but I knew his backer had plans as well and he had to share them with me. I said I didn't want to run Fenton County on my own and I was looking for a business partner. I gave him forty-eight hours to let me know. He texted late last night, a little over twenty-four hours later. I told him I'd set the location, so now we need to figure out where would work best."

He sat down on the kitchen chair, still all business. "So your plan is to meet him and get him to incriminate himself?"

I sat next to him. "And record it, but it has to be admissible in court. Which means we need a court order, right? Do you think you can get one?"

His eyebrows lifted. "On what grounds?"

And that was the first big clue that Mason wasn't taking this as well as he appeared to be.

"That he's backing a known criminal who has murder charges against him."

"First of all, the DA dropped all of Gentry's charges yesterday afternoon. Second, he's never been convicted or even charged with any other crime. Yes, he owned Gems, but there was nothing illegal about it."

"Mason! You were investigating Mick Gentry yourself! You were trying to catch him bribing you."

"But I didn't, did I?"

"But Joe was working with you!"

"And Joe turned against me in the meeting with the state investigator."

"Are you really telling me that I can meet with J.R. Simmons and there's nothing we can do to make sure what he says can be used against him?"

"Let's back up a few steps and focus on why Skeeter Malcolm is so interested in you."

My breath stuck in my chest. "I told you."

"Okay, then let's discuss what role the Lady in Black actually plays."

I nodded, biting my lip. "I go to business meetings with Skeeter and interview some of the attendees."

"And what does that entail?"

"I meet with them and ask them a few questions. Then I force a vision."

"And you blurt it out in front of them?"

"Well, yeah. But I always play it off somehow. And Jed is there to intervene."

"Oh, Jed." He nodded, and it was impossible to miss the disgusted look on his face. "I want to know more about Jed in a minute, but first I want to know what questions you ask."

"To focus the visions?"

"Both. Interviews and visions."

I took a breath, trying to concentrate. "It depends on the situation. I'd start off by asking what they did for Skeeter to kind of warm them up and get a feel for them. The first time I did it, I followed up with two questions. One was if they knew anything about the attempts on your life."

"And the other?"

"If they had turned on Skeeter."

"So you were helping him."

"He wasn't going to let me sniff out your murderer if he didn't get something out of it." I sounded more indignant than I'd intended.

"Well, I guess I wouldn't expect anything less from a known criminal and thug," he said.

I sighed and rubbed my forehead. "No. I suppose not."

"Have you ever done anything illegal?"

"Questioning them probably isn't illegal."

"I would venture not, but have you done anything else?"

"I carried a gun on Tuesday night. And I pulled it on Mick Gentry. Oh, and I left the county to meet him."

He jumped to his feet. "You did what?"

"I know all of those things violated the terms of my release."

"I don't give a shit about violating your release right now!" he shouted. "*You pulled a gun on a known murderer? You barely know how to use one!*"

"I had to," I said quietly. "He was out of control."

"*That's because he's a goddamned psychopath!*" His voice was so loud it shook the pictures on the walls.

The front door flew open, and Skeeter stood in the opening. His expression was guarded, but his hands were clenched at his sides. "Good evening, Mr. Prosecutor."

Rage filled Mason's eyes. "It's no longer evening, and I'm no longer the prosecutor. But I guess that's all part of your repertoire, isn't it? Spinning things to your advantage."

Skeeter ignored him and turned his attention to me. "Is everything okay in here, Rose?"

Rage exploded from Mason's body, and he pushed me behind him. "How dare you insinuate that she's unsafe with me? I'm not the one who put her alone in a room with dangerous criminals."

Skeeter shrugged, his face empty of emotion. "When I need a job done, I hire the right person. Rose is definitely the right person."

Mason looked like he was about to launch toward him, so I grabbed his arm and held him back. "Mason. I was never alone. I had Jed."

Skeeter's eyes twinkled. "Until you took matters into your own hands with Humphrey. You locked Jed out and spent a good five minutes or so alone with that psychopath."

I gasped, my fingers digging deeper into Mason's arm to hold him back. "What on earth are you doin', Skeeter Malcolm? That's not helping!"

Mason pulled loose from my grasp. "What is this really about, Malcolm? It must have been quite a feather in your cap to get the ADA's girlfriend to work for you."

Skeeter grinned. "You have no idea. Too bad I couldn't tell a soul."

Mason's body tensed again, and my own anger rose up. "Skeeter!" I shouted. "*Stop.*"

Surprisingly, he did.

I turned to Mason, pleading with him. "It may have started off that way, but by the end, he had my safety in mind at all times. In fact, at the meeting last week he told his men that my protection was more important than his own."

"Why?" Mason asked suspiciously, his gaze moving from me to Skeeter and back.

"Because she's a very valuable asset," Skeeter said. "I take care of the things that matter to me."

Mason's hands clenched at his sides. "What the hell are you insinuating?"

"I'm not insinuating a damned thing, but you sure feel guilty as hell about something, don't you? Maybe because she was snatched out from under your nose and I was the one to save her."

"Skeeter! Stop it!" I grabbed Mason's arm, my temper rising. "Mason has done everything in his power to help me."

A sardonic grin lifted Skeeter's lips. "But it's not enough, is it?"

"What the Sam Hill are you doin'? You're supposed to be gettin' him to help, not turning him away. And if you're gonna berate him for letting me get kidnapped, you didn't put a stop to it either! *So stuff it!*"

He clamped his mouth shut, and Mason's eyes widened in surprise.

I sighed. "We're all too tired to have a productive conversation. Maybe we should get some sleep and discuss this in the morning."

"Good idea," Mason said, grabbing my hand. "Rose and I will be leaving now. We'll be sure to contact you in the morning."

Skeeter stepped in front of the doorway, his eyes cold. "Ahh . . . that's not gonna happen, Mr. *Former* Prosecutor. Rose isn't going anywhere. Like I already told you, I protect my property."

"I am not your property, Skeeter Malcolm!" I shouted. "So you get off your high horse!"

He leveled a cold hard gaze on me, and if I hadn't known he truly had my best interests in mind, I would have been terrified. "You most certainly *are* my property. You made a deal, and you gave me your word. We are still well within your six-month term."

"What on earth are you doin'?" He had already freed me from that agreement, but something clicked and I realized what he was up to.

"This is called kidnapping, Malcolm," Mason said, wrapping an arm around my waist. "And I think my fiancée has been through enough."

Skeeter snorted. "I'd rather subject her to my insufferable personality than a bullet to the head. Someone wanted her dead, and your measly bodyguard didn't even realize she'd been snatched until the kidnappers were long gone. So no, Deveraux, *she's not leaving my custody!*"

"Mason, it's okay."

He turned to me, his eyes blazing. "There is nothing okay about this entire situation."

"I know, but you have to admit we're safer here."

"With Skeeter Malcolm's men watching us?" he asked, incredulous.

"They saved me tonight, Mason. Jed almost died trying to save me. Skeeter would skin alive anyone who let anything happen to me."

"You might as well accept it, Deveraux," Skeeter said with a grin. "You are both my guests until the meeting tomorrow night. We'll discuss the logistics in the morning, but until then, I suggest you retire for the night."

I tugged on Mason's arm, and he swung his gaze to me. I nodded slightly. "We'll figure this out."

There was still fire in his eyes, but he snugged me tight against his side, which told me my situation wasn't totally hopeless. "Rose stays with me."

Skeeter laughed. "You are *not* in a position to negotiate."

"Skeeter!"

He waved a hand in dismissal and looked away. "Go. Rose knows which room to use. I'll give you five minutes to use the restroom, and then I expect you to be in that room with the door closed behind you." He started to open the front door, but turned back to deliver a final warning. "And don't even think of trying to leave. We're watching, and a couple of my men are trigger-happy." Then he walked out, leaving me alone with Mason and all my biggest fears.

Mason pulled me into a hug, crushing me to his chest. "We'll get out of this."

"I know." But I was certain we were referring to two different things.

We went to the restroom, and Mason insisted on standing outside the door while I was inside, acting like he was afraid to let me out of his sight. I couldn't say I blamed him since I was feeling the same way. After we finished, we headed to the bedroom. Mason stopped short of entering the room.

"There's a lock on the outside of this door."

My heart raced, although I wasn't sure why. I hadn't noticed the lock before, but it stood to reason they'd lock Mason up so he couldn't run away and spill what he knew. And truth be told, I wasn't altogether surprised Skeeter wanted to lock me up too. I *had* tried to escape tonight. Twice. But my sense of betrayal came from the fact that Jed had been the one to steer me toward this room.

Mason hesitated, but though it clearly killed him to do it, he ushered me into the dark bedroom and shut the door behind us.

My voice broke. "Mason, I'm so sorry."

I barely finished my sentence before his mouth found mine. He pulled me tight against him, as if he couldn't get me close enough, and buried his other hand in my hair. His mouth ravaged mine, and I could barely keep up.

I clung to him, crying again. I couldn't believe he was kissing me after my confession. That he still loved me after finding out the truth.

He pulled back, his hand sliding from my hair to my face. "You're crying," he whispered in horror. "Did I hurt you?"

"No. I'm just so scared."

Mason led me over to the bed, and he sat down on the edge of the mattress, bringing me with him. I clung to him while we waited. A minute later, footsteps clomped down the hall, paused, and then walked away.

Mason got up and moved over to the single window. Light filtered through the panes, but I couldn't make out anything outside. The room had been so dark when I made the bed, I hadn't noticed.

"The panes are painted," Mason said, coming back to sit by me. "It's a very effective holding cell."

"Holding cell?"

"No furniture. No curtain rods or lamps. I bet there's not even a light bulb. Nothing to use as a weapon. I'm surprised there's bedding."

Of course it was a holding cell. How could I be so stupid? "There was only a bottom sheet," I said, sounding disheartened. "Jed let me put on fresh linens."

He sighed.

"Mason." The tears were back, and I couldn't stop them this time. "I'm so sorry."

His hand found my face, and he leaned his close to me and whispered, "Shh. We've gotten out of worse scrapes than this one. At least Malcolm is more stable than Crocker. Or is he? You've had more experience with him than I have."

I tried to catch my breath. "He can be a reasonable man, but when he gets something set in his head, it's hard to dissuade him. He doesn't suffer disloyalty."

"And you? How does he treat you? Has he threatened you?"

"He threatened me in the beginning. But I've always stood up to him, and he's not used to that. Bruce Wayne said I was like a new puppy. Skeeter found my disobedience and belligerence cute, but he'd soon get tired of it." I took a deep breath, my voice shaky. "I worried I went too far last night. I've ruined his reputation. I'm afraid he'll never forgive me for that. But he won't hurt me."

He pulled me close.

"But I'm not sorry. I couldn't just stand back and do nothing."

"We'll be okay," he murmured, stroking my head. "He obviously wants you to go through with the meeting tomorrow night. Even though you think he won't hurt you, I know you'll be safe until then. But I can't believe he'll agree to a wiretap. He'll want to hand out his own punishment, and it would be counter-intuitive to involve the police. He'd risk incriminating himself."

"Skeeter was in hiding when I came up with this plan. But Jed agreed to go along with it. He doesn't want me to go to prison, and he knows we need to find evidence against J.R to keep that from happening. It took some convincing, but Jed agreed it was a good plan. Honestly, I think they'd both sooner kill him than meet with him. The meeting is purely for my benefit."

"Why would Jed risk pissing off Malcolm to help you?"

How could I explain this without upsetting him? "Skeeter watched over me in meetings, but he couldn't be there when I questioned his men. He made Jed my bodyguard and told him to put my safety before his own."

"And he just did it?" he asked.

"It's complicated," I sighed, resting my cheek on his shoulder. "I think Jed grew fond of me—"

"He's in love with you?" His tone was harsh.

"No, that's not it. I remind him of his baby sister who drowned when he was a kid. He's always felt responsible for what happened to her. He said he's sure it's why Skeeter assigned him to look after me. Skeeter knows Jed will go above and beyond to keep me safe." I paused. "Jed is loyal to me. Even more so than he is to Skeeter."

"And Skeeter tolerates that?" He sounded incredulous.

"After last week, yes. Skeeter had a conniption after he found me questioning Dirk Picklebie at his pool hall. He told me I was to warn him before I questioned anyone on my own. I told him what I did on my own time was my own business and I quit. He flipped out and sent Merv to find me."

His body tensed. "Carter Hale told me one of Malcolm's men was loitering outside of your office last week."

"That was Merv. But Jed had called to warn me, and when I finally talked to Skeeter, he told me he knew that

Jed had turned on him. He was going to punish Jed, so I convinced him that it was a good thing. That I had to have someone I trusted completely to make sure I was okay. And Skeeter agreed."

"That someone was supposed to be *me*, Rose." The pain in his voice was like a knife in the gut. "Why didn't you tell me any of this?"

"I was in too deep. Besides, I knew you'd make me stop, and while I didn't really want to do it in the first place, I knew it was the best way to save you. Even your momma said so."

"My mother?" He stiffened and leaned away from me. "My mother knows about this?"

I shook my head. "No. But she knows I'm up to something. I snuck out to meet Skeeter while I was staying with her, when you were in protective custody in the hospital."

"Please God, tell me that she tried to talk some sense into you."

I cringed.

"She *didn't*?"

"She loves you, Mason. You're all she has left. It's like I told you, she sensed that you were in danger and your future was tied to someone else. She was sure that I was the one who would save you both."

"So you set up this meeting with Gentry's backer, whom you think is Simmons."

"Yes."

"And Jed? He's been tailing you?"

"I had no idea he was watching me that closely. But if he hadn't been, I would be dead. I'm certain of that."

Mason shuddered and held me closer. "I'm having a hard time buying that Malcolm would give one of his men to protect you. And his right-hand man, at that."

"You know Jed is Skeeter's right-hand man?"

"I make it my business to know as much as possible about the criminal elements in the county."

"Oh."

"So why would Skeeter make his most trusted man your bodyguard?"

"I think it scared him that Lowry figured it out. After that, he became much more careful."

"But why? What makes you so valuable to him?"

"My visions. Working for him has helped me fine-tune them. He said he didn't think I grasped their full potential, and he was right. I've been forcing visions a lot more lately, and I'm learning how to use them to find out what I need to know. I think I've been having a lot fewer spontaneous ones as a result."

"It sounds like he came to trust you and has given you plenty of leeway. Why?"

"I told him I was a woman of my word, and he saw me live up to that again and again, as difficult as it was. But I also have a good head for business. He began to trust my intuition about who to question and what to ask. He tried to intimidate me at first, but I convinced him that fear is a terrible motivator. That our partnership had to be based on mutual need, but maybe I was wrong." I put my hand on his cheek. "Fear is the most powerful motivator in the world."

I lifted my mouth to his, needing to know he still loved me. That he could find it in his heart to forgive me.

He hesitated, but then it was as if I'd opened and unlocked the door to his emotions. Still kissing me, he tugged me backward onto the bed. He quickly dispatched with his pants as I tugged off my panties, but then he slowed down, his hand caressing my cheek.

I could barely make out his face, but his eyes looked haunted as he stared down at me.

"I keep seeing it over and over in my head. That video. I know you're okay, but it could have been real. It almost happened." His voice broke, and he kissed me with a fierceness that stole my breath.

I kissed him back, my hands sliding under his shirt as his reached between my legs. Soon I was whispering his name between pants. "Mason. I need you."

He was inside me in one deep stroke, and I arched up to meet him, desperate to hold onto to him. My need for him wasn't just physical. I loved him with everything inside me, and I couldn't help thinking he was slipping through my fingers, despite the fact that he was here with me now.

# Chapter Twenty-Seven

I fell asleep plastered against Mason's side, his arm around me, protecting me.

But it was an illusion.

I had been the protector all this time, and now I was scared I would fail. Talking about facing J.R. Simmons was a lot different than actually doing it. J.R. had intimidated me the last time we'd encountered each other. Would this time be any different?

When I awoke, I was lying on my side, Mason's stomach pressed against my back, his arm still wrapped tight around me.

The sight of the faded blue wall confused me at first, but then it all came crashing back in. A moment of panic washed over me, and I forced myself to calm down.

I had no idea what time it was, but a faint orange glow filled the opaque windowpanes. I slid out of bed, grabbed my panties off the floor, and pulled them on under my dress, then tucked Mason's under his pants. I had no idea when Skeeter would be back, but I had no desire for him to see our underwear on the floor. It was likely to elicit more antagonistic words toward Mason.

I considered climbing back into bed with Mason, but he'd shifted slightly, and he looked so peaceful that I worried I'd disturb him. Instead, I sat on the floor for a moment and just watched him.

My engagement ring caught my eye. Had that really happened half a day ago? We both had ghosts from our pasts, and I'd always believed we'd overcome them together. But what if we couldn't? Was it even fair to bring Mason into this crazy mess? In truth, I had expected more anger from him. Of course, he was still in shock, and there was no way of knowing how he'd process my revelation with more time.

I suddenly thought about Joe and how badly he must be hurting. According to Jed, Kate had run after him. Evidence suggested she had arranged my kidnapping and planned my murder. Had she done it on J.R.'s orders? Would she hurt her own brother? I couldn't let my mind go there.

Assuming he was safe, where would he go? Who would he turn to for comfort? The thought of him mourning alone brought tears to my eyes.

And what about everyone else? I could only imagine how badly they were hurting. Would they feel betrayed when they found out the truth? Neely Kate. Violet. My aunt and uncle. Jonah. *Bruce Wayne*. Would he feel guilty? But then I reminded myself that I'd been taken as Rose rather than as Lady.

In truth, the lines between us were beginning to blur. I wasn't sure that was a good thing.

Mason stirred, and his arm moved as if to reach for me. Then he bolted upright, panic in his eyes. "Rose!"

"I'm here," I answered softly.

Relief washed over his face when he saw me on the

floor. "What are you doing down there?"

"I couldn't sleep."

He lifted the covers. "Come here."

I got to my feet and climbed in next to him, lying on my side to face him.

He propped up on an elbow and lifted his hand to brush several strands of hair from my cheek. "How are you doing?"

"How can you ask me that after everything I told you last night?"

"Because I love you and you suffered a very traumatic experience. Now that we've both rested, I'm hoping we can make some decisions with a clearer head."

I nodded.

"Rose, you have to see that this is a crazy idea. You have no idea that J.R. Simmons will even show up. And if he does, the likelihood of getting him to admit to anything we can use is slim to none. The man is a criminal genius. Which means he's intelligent enough not to spill his secrets to strangers."

"So then how do we stop him?"

He lay down and snugged me against his side, his arm tight around me. "The problem is two-fold. We need to get the charges against you dropped, and we need to figure out who is behind the order to kill me."

"I can't help thinking Kate is the person behind my kidnapping. It's too big of a coincidence that Neely Kate and I found all her paperwork on you right before this happened."

"You very well might be right."

"That aside, you're forgetting Skeeter."

His arm stiffened. "What *about* Malcolm?"

"He's tied to this too, Mason."

"Then let's talk about Skeeter Malcolm. He hates my guts. In fact, I can't believe he wants me here. I'm too risky. He has no idea which way I'll turn."

"You're here because of me," I said, quietly. "I knew you were in danger, and I wanted you here with me. It was selfish. I should have trusted Randy to watch you. I'm sorry."

"Shh . . ." His thumb brushed my cheek. "I want to be with you so I can make sure you're safe. I'd go crazy at home not knowing where you are or if you were okay." He gave me a soft smile. "But from here on out, you have to tell me everything, okay? We'll deal with how we got here when this is all over."

"Okay."

Men's voices filtered down the hall, and Mason sat upright. He climbed out of bed and put on his underwear, then sat down next to me as I sat up too. He looked down at the deep V of my neckline and straightened it, trying to cover up my cleavage.

"You don't have to worry about that," I whispered. "They don't treat me that way."

Surprise flickered in his eyes, but there wasn't time for either of us to say anything. A knock sounded at the door, and it swung open seconds later. Skeeter filled the doorway . . . or what little I could see of him. Mason was trying to block my view of him with his body.

"I trust you enjoyed your accommodations?"

"Cut the shit, Malcolm," Mason said in a controlled voice. "We want to leave. What do you want from us before that happens?"

I leaned sideways and saw an amused look cross Skeeter's face. "A negotiation before coffee? You picked a real go-getter, Rose."

"Skeeter," I said, exhausted already.

"I sent one of the boys for breakfast. If you want to shower or clean up, you have about twenty minutes."

"I'd rather not wait," Mason said, climbing to his feet. "Let's get right to it."

Skeeter laughed. "That's not how it's done here, boy. You're my guest, so you'll follow my rules. If you want to use the restroom, then I suggest you get in there now. Otherwise I'm going to lock you back in this room."

I stood. "Skeeter!"

He paused. "Fine, but you still have twenty minutes, give or take a few." Then he spun around and stomped down the hall. A door slammed moments later.

Mason turned around to look at me, his eyes guarded. "Do you want to shower?"

"Yeah. I don't have clean clothes to change into, but I feel dirty after what happened last night."

He wrapped his arms around me and pulled me close. "You're not alone now. I'll come stay in there with you."

I didn't argue. He still saw me as their hostage, whereas I was much closer to being their equal. He'd figure it out soon enough. But it only reinforced that I wasn't in the clear. He thought he accepted what I'd done . . . only he couldn't. He didn't understand the extent of it.

About twenty minutes later, the front door opened, and I could hear male voices in the living room. We had already showered and dressed, so Mason took my hand

and started to head down the hall. I stopped him. "Let me take the lead on this. Okay? They're used to working with me."

I saw more surprise on his face, but he nodded slightly. "We'll go that course for now."

"You have to listen to everything we have to say before you make a decision one way or the other."

His jaw hardened. "It looks like I have plenty of time at my disposal to do so."

Not as much as he thought. I led the way, praying Skeeter would behave himself.

Skeeter sat at the kitchen table, unwrapping a breakfast sandwich. A cup of coffee sat in front of him, and there was a paper bag on the table, along with two other hot beverage cups and an assortment of small creamers and sugars. Jed stood by the door, his arm back in a sling. He avoided eye contact, which I took as a very bad sign. No one else was around.

Skeeter grinned. "The boys brought us some breakfast sandwiches and coffee. Sit down, and we'll talk."

Mason pulled out my chair and then sat in the one next to it, all while Skeeter watched with an amused grin. I noticed that Mason placed himself with his back to the wall, leaving both Skeeter and Jed in his line of sight.

Skeeter pulled a wrapped sandwich out of a bag and handed it to me, then tossed another to Mason. "Help yourself to the coffee, but don't be getting any ideas about using it as a weapon." He gestured behind me. "Jed here is ready to step in if necessary."

I looked over at Jed, but he still refused to look at me. My anxiety increased.

Mason grabbed two cups and placed one in front of me, then handed me sugar and creamer packages. While he was usually attentive, he was never this attentive. It was easy to see he was trying to show Skeeter that *he* was the man to protect me.

What a mess.

"Skeeter," I said, doctoring my coffee. "Mason's agreed to listen, but you have to treat him with more respect if we have any chance of getting him to help us."

Mason shot me a questioning glance.

"And we need him," I continued. "You know it."

Skeeter shook his head and picked up a jelly packet. "I've spent the night thinking this over. There's no reason for you to go at all, Rose. You've set up the meeting, we'll establish a place, and then I'll go in and take care of the matter on my own."

I sighed. "That might resolve things for you and Mason, but it wouldn't take care of my own issue. Not to mention you're talking about cold-blooded murder."

Skeeter's voice hardened. "If there was ever a man who deserved cold-blooded murder, it's that man. And as far as *your* charges go, I'll figure out another way to take care of those." He swung his gaze from me to Mason. "She will *not* be going to prison."

I could sense Mason's concern. Why was Skeeter so determined to keep me safe? Why was he going to so much trouble to keep me out of prison? But now I was good and ticked by all of this macho posturing.

I leaned forward. "If that's your plan of action, you don't need either one of us. But don't be stupid. I know you agreed to bring Mason here to keep him safe, but he can help us do this right."

Skeeter slathered jelly on his biscuit. "I think you were right about that part. Deveraux's part of this, and he and I can bring down Simmons together. A two-part process."

Mason had been surprisingly quiet up until now. "If you think I'm participating in a man's murder, then you're crazy."

Skeeter laughed. "I would never expect you to dirty your hands, but if nothing else, I figured you deserve to know why you're part of this. How you're tied to me."

Mason gave him a look of disbelief. "I'm supposed to believe you're just going to give me information for nothing?"

Skeeter took a bite of his biscuit, then said, "Maybe your girlfriend has rubbed off on me."

"Okay, then how is Mason tied to this?" I asked, sneaking a glance at him. His face remained expressionless. He hadn't told me any of this before.

Skeeter shrugged. "Perhaps I should tell you how I'm tied to J.R."

I decided to move this along. "You were one of The Twelve."

Skeeter's eyebrows nearly rose to his hairline, and when he spoke, his voice sounded ominous. "How do you know about The Twelve?"

"I don't know much."

His eyes pierced mine as he snarled, "I didn't ask *what* you knew. I asked *how.*"

Jed shifted his weight behind me, and Mason was just sitting there and taking it all in, ready to pounce into the fray himself.

Crappy doodles.

"Skeeter," I said, trying to keep my anger in check. "*Calm down.* I have my sources, and I promised this person not to say anything. So if I told you, my word would be worthless, and you'd have no reason to trust me whatsoever. Which means I'd be good as dead." I pushed out a breath. "Last night was as close to death as I'd like to come for a long time."

"What else do you know?"

"I told you. Not much. Only that you left Fenton County when you were eighteen and came back when you were twenty-five with enough money to open the pool hall. You told everyone that you made your money in Memphis, but you were probably learning from J.R. You came back as one of The Twelve."

His eyes narrowed to slits.

I forged on anyway. "After you came back, you would disappear for days at a time, and no one knew where you went. You were doin' J.R.'s handiwork, but then five years ago it all stopped. You probably quit, but that's the strange part. You can't quit being one of The Twelve. It's a position for life."

Skeeter released a low growl. "You call that not much? Who the hell told you that?" His gaze swung to Jed, and he jumped to his feet. "Was it you?"

Jed's face contorted with anger. "Are you calling me a traitor?"

"I know you're loyal to her over me," he growled as he stalked toward him. "I've tolerated it until now, but if you—"

I jumped up and stepped in between them. "Skeeter, stop! It wasn't Jed! He didn't tell me a thing!"

"Then who?" Anger radiated off him, and he looked like he was about to explode.

I put both hands on his chest and pushed him back. "Someone who will keep your secret, if that's what you're worried about. Now sit down and let's discuss this."

Skeeter stared down at me, and I noticed Mason had risen from his chair and was standing beside the table, ready to jump in if necessary, but I knew it wouldn't come to that. Skeeter wouldn't physically hurt me. I would bet my life on it.

I lowered my voice. "Look. I was the one who put together the connection between you and Mason. And we both know J.R.'s the common denominator. You should know me well enough to realize I had to piece it together." I worried I had been leading him on a path straight to Carter Hale. Maybe the last statement would send him off my lawyer's trail.

Skeeter rubbed the back of his neck, then headed back to his seat.

I snuck a glance at Jed. His shoulders seemed to relax as I caught his eye. We stared at each other for a long second, and he nodded slightly. He'd proved he would defend me to the death. It went both ways.

"Jed's as much a part of this as the three of us. He needs to be sittin' at this table helpin' make decisions."

"He's guardin' the damn door!" Skeeter bellowed.

"And I'd bet my grandmother's Blue Willow china that Merv or somebody else is on the other side. That's your real threat, not what's going on in here."

Skeeter studied me and then groaned. "Jed, get your ass over here."

Jed took a seat between Skeeter and Mason, and Mason and I sat back down too. It worried me when I saw Mason's expressionless face. What was he thinking?

Once we were all settled, Skeeter pushed back his chair and crossed his legs. "What I'm about to say does not leave this room. If I find out any one of you has told a soul, I will cut out your tongue and feed it to you. Do you understand?"

"Did you really just threaten us?" Mason demanded. "Do you think that's the right way to get our cooperation?"

Skeeter looked vaguely surprised.

"What?" Mason asked in disgust. "Did you expect me to say I was going to bring charges against you?" He shook his head. "I'm not stupid, and I've worked with plenty of informants before." He turned to me. "More than either of you realize." He returned his attention to Skeeter. "Besides, I'll remind you again that I'm currently out of a job. I couldn't press charges against you if I wanted to."

"And what's to stop you from running off and telling someone?"

"Because as Mason Deveraux, private citizen, I could give a rat's ass about your past, and I'm sure as hell not feeding anything to the crooked DA. The only thing I care about is keeping Rose safe, so if telling us about your past will help ensure that, then I'm not only interested in hearing about it, I'll also swear on my life to keep it secret."

Skeeter grinned, eyeing Mason with new appreciation. "You surprise me."

"I told Rose I'd do anything to protect her, even if it means getting my hands dirty. She begged me not to do that, I listened to her, and look where we are now. I'm willing to do whatever it takes, short of murdering someone. Now tell us what we need to know."

"And what about your own life?"

"I don't have a death wish, but protecting Rose takes precedence over my own safety. Otherwise I'd be under twenty-four-hour protection right now."

"What?" I gasped.

Mason offered me an apologetic grimace. "Detective Pearson wanted me to stay in Little Rock and be placed in witness protection."

"Mason!"

"Did you really expect me to stay when I'm following leads to help save you?"

Skeeter groaned. "This is touching and all, but we have another way."

Mason and I turned to look at him.

Skeeter looked me in the eye. "Rose, I take it I have your word."

"I'm insulted you thought you had to ask. I keep your secrets, Skeeter Malcolm, even when it rips my soul apart. I'll keep this one as well."

His jaw tightened and he gave a slight nod, then turned his gaze to Jed.

Jed's eyes narrowed. "I'm not a turncoat."

Skeeter nodded.

He turned his chair to face us, his forearms on the table. "When I was fourteen, I met J.R. Simmons at the Sinclair station where I worked." He nodded to me.

"Where we meet."

Mason shot me a look, but I ignored him.

"I impressed him and he told me to look him up when I grew up. So I did. The day after I graduated, I took the business card he had given me all those years ago and drove to El Dorado. I spent the next six years working my way up his ladder. Until he made me one of his Twelve."

"What's The Twelve?" Mason asked. "I've never heard of them."

Skeeter worked his jaw. "You wouldn't have. It's Simmons' core group of top men, and there's a reason most people don't know about them. They're all successful in their own right, but Simmons played some role in getting them where they are today. Usually with money. It's how he controls them. But some, like me, he trained."

"But he gave you money," I prodded. "Was it a loan?"

"Seed money. Like I said, it came with a price."

"What's the purpose of The Twelve?" Mason asked.

"It allows Simmons to have feelers all over the state. The Twelve are strategically positioned, and they answer only to him. Somehow the person who covered this area was eliminated twenty-five years ago. But after I got to know J.R., I started putting things together. I met him at a gas station in Fenton County around that same time. What was he doing in a nothing county in a nothing gas station only about five miles from a plant that burned down a few weeks later?" He nodded to me. "I suspect he was in town on business with that factory. And I suspect one of The Twelve was eliminated because it all went south."

"Atchison?"

He nodded again. "I have no idea who my predecessor was, but after he was gone, the three neighboring sections covered the area for a while, not that there was much to cover."

"What about Crocker?" Mason asked.

"He was too unstable for Simmons. J.R. was biding his time, waitin' for the right person to take over. He planned for it to be me."

"After you came back from El Dorado, where did you go when you disappeared for days at a time?" I asked.

"I would go do his bidding." He sounded bitter. "Jobs he only trusted to his top men. And since I was the greenhorn, a lot of it fell to me."

"What type of jobs?" Mason asked.

Skeeter released a short laugh. "Most had to do with his son."

My stomach spasmed.

Mason gasped and turned to me. "Rose, he has what we need. You really *don't* need to go through with this meeting. Malcolm can turn state's evidence and testify against both J.R. and Joe. We can use it as leverage to get him to drop your charges."

Skeeter lifted his hands. "Whoa! I'm not testifyin' about anything."

"Are you kidding me?" Mason demanded. "You can destroy this man and save Rose in the process!"

"Do you really think I'd make it to trial?" Skeeter asked, incredulous. "Why the hell do you think you're in Fenton County?"

Mason sat back in his seat. "What are you talking about?"

"You *had* to wonder why you were here, in Fenton County, of all places."

"I've always figured J.R. Simmons orchestrated it, but I could never put together the how or why of it."

"It was a warnin' for me."

"What's that supposed to mean?"

"I was one of The Twelve up until five years ago. J.R. figured out I was gettin' tired of bein' called away from my own work and forced into doin' his. So he called me to El Dorado and gave me a file to look over. I figured out what he wanted me to do, but there was no way in hell I was doin' it."

"Doin' what?" I asked.

He took a long, lingering look at Jed, then turned back to face me, his eyes dark and furious. "There was a hit-and-run case in Little Rock. A guy reneged on his payments to a loan shark after multiple warnings. The loan shark was one of The Twelve. So The Twelve in the area had him taken care of by making it look like an accident." He waved his hand to the side as if that was nothing. "Only Mooney, the moron who was told to take care of it, fucked it up. There was a witness."

"Oh, my God," I gasped. "Mason was the prosecutor. The witness was a kid. An eight-year-old boy."

Skeeter cocked his head, his eyes glittering with suspicion. "How do you know that?"

"Kate Simmons." I cast a glance to Mason, and he stared back at me with a mixture of horror and anger. "I told you. I found a table full of information about Mason in her apartment, which happens to be across from the courthouse and facing the DA's offices."

Skeeter lifted an eyebrow to Mason. "Got yourself a stalker, huh? Pictures plastered on the wall and everything?"

"Not quite," I said. "Stuffed into an envelope. But she had documents and police reports linked to some of his cases in Little Rock. The one she seemed to pay the most attention to was a hit and run from five years ago."

Mason leaned his arm on the table, his hand in a tight fist. "It never went to trial. The kid drowned." His eyes narrowed to slits. "If you tell me you drowned that kid, I will rip you to pieces with my bare hands."

Skeeter scooted his chair back, disgust on his face. "Sorry, Deveraux, but you'll have to find another reason to kill me. Like I said, I wanted no part of that. When I realized what he was askin' me to do, I quit on the spot." He cast another glance to Jed before returning his gaze to Mason. His jaw clenched, and his eyelid ticked. "I saw a kid drown once. Never again, and definitely not by my hand."

"But he died," Mason countered, sounding unimpressed. "Someone still killed that boy, and you could have stopped it."

Skeeter looked like he was about to leap across the table and tear Mason's throat out. "It was such a heinous request, so different from what he normally asked me to do, that I decided it was a test of my loyalty. One I'd failed. I never thought he'd ask someone else to do it." He stared down at his fist, clenching and unclenching his fingers. "But I found out the kid was dead a few days later. I was wrong, and not a day goes by that I don't think about that mistake. My guess is that Mooney ended up murdering the kid to clean up his own mess, but he did it on orders."

"Try telling that to that poor kid's parents," Mason sneered.

"If it makes you feel any better, you got your justice, albeit five years too late. Pete Mooney was beaten to death a few days ago." His gaze shifted to me. "And not by my hands. I wanted him alive." He pushed out a breath. "J.R. must have figured out I was lookin' for him."

Mason looked like he was about to be sick. "I was looking for him too. He was a person of interest in the investigation of the investigator who was supposed to question the DA and instead had me fired."

"So we both got screwed on that one," Skeeter said.

"If you're planning to murder Simmons tonight, I refuse to take any part of it," Mason said, his voice cold. "And like Rose said, if that's your plan, you don't need us. No one knows where we are. Just give us a car, and we'll go hide out somewhere until things blow over."

Skeeter clenched his jaw so tightly I could hear his teeth grinding. "And I'm supposed to believe you'll just let me murder him? That you're not gonna give some warning to the authorities?"

Mason didn't say anything.

Skeeter began to laugh, and the three of us looked at him as if he'd lost his ever-loving mind. "Last night I gave Rose an ultimatum about your response. Is that your final answer?"

My voice didn't sound like my own as I turned to him. "I suggest you give this very careful consideration, Skeeter Malcolm."

He just started to laugh harder.

"I am deadly serious," I said, my blood pressure rising. "You will regret it for the rest of your life if you hurt him."

He stopped laughing. "I know how to hurt him without touching a hair on his head."

Mason got to his feet. "You would hurt Rose? I thought she was valuable to you."

"That's not all you care about, though, is it?" Skeeter's eyes glittered with a secret.

Mason gasped. "Are you threatening my mother?"

Skeeter snorted. "I have some other information you might be interested in knowin'. Something more personal. I was keepin' it under wraps to use as a bargaining tool in case you got your job back and I found myself in need of a get out of jail free card, but I realized it might prove more useful now."

Mason froze.

Oh, God. Did he mean what I thought he did?

"I may have stopped cleanin' up Prince Simmons' messes, but that didn't mean J.R. stopped havin' them scrubbed."

I reached over and took Mason's hand in mine.

Skeeter looked Mason in the eye. "You may have thought you got your justice when you beat Michael Cartwright to a bloody pulp for your sister's murder, but you left the man who orchestrated the entire thing free and clear."

Mason's arm was so tense, it felt like he was about to shatter into a million pieces.

"The man you're lookin' for—" Skeeter said in a slow drawl, "—is none other than J.R. Simmons. How do you feel about killin' him now?"

*Thirty-Five and a Half Conspiracies*

# Chapter Twenty-Eight

Mason took several breaths. "Do you have proof of this, or is it merely a supposition?"

Skeeter grinned, but it was bitter. "Hearsay. It's accurate, but not enough to prove it to anyone in a court of law."

Mason pulled his hand loose from mine and stood, running a hand through his hair. "Goddammit." Grief saturated the word. "That man has stolen or tainted so much of my life, and he gets away with it time and time again."

"Not if we kill him. *Together.* I have a plan. We both want our revenge. We'll mete it out together."

Mason stared at the wall for several seconds, and then shook his head, defeat in his eyes. "No. I can't condone that. Not even for him."

"You'll let this man get away with ordering your sister's murder?" Skeeter asked. "I hear Cartwright stabbed her repeatedly, but he planned it so there'd be some time before she bled out. He pulled up the younger Simmons on her phone and laid it next to her face. Joe's daddy wanted him to hear it. He wanted them both to suffer."

I gasped and grabbed the back of my chair, feeling dangerously close to passing out.

Mason released a loud groan and slammed his fist into the wall, then leaned over his legs. I could tell he was fighting back tears.

"How about now?" Skeeter asked. "You ready to let him skip home now?"

"No." Mason righted himself, his eyes red, and when he turned his gaze to me, the anguish I saw on his face ripped my heart into pieces. "If I help you murder him, I'm no better than he is."

I had to regain some control of this situation. "*No one* is murdering J.R. Simmons."

Skeeter shot me a dark glare. "This is between me and Simmons, Lady. You and Deveraux are simply pawns in the chess game Simmons has been orchestrating for years. The fact that you happen to be his son's last girlfriend is a pure bonus to him. Joe Simmons will never be allowed to marry anyone but that Wilder bitch, so you better be glad you didn't try to follow through on his proposal. Otherwise you would have likely met with the same fate as Deveraux's sister."

I gasped and sat up straighter in my chair. Mason put his hand on my shoulder, and I covered it with my own.

Skeeter stood. "Joe Simmons may have acted the part of a selfish asshole most of his life, but he's capable of real emotions. Trust me, I know. I've watched the man since he was a teen. If he had known Savannah Deveraux was pregnant with his kid, he would have married her in a heartbeat." He glanced at Mason. "Surprises you, huh? Joe Simmons has a soft spot for kids too. He's wanted them since he was barely out of college, even if he's always had the tendency to pick the most unlikely women to give them to him."

"How do you know anything about my sister? How do you know so much about her death?" Mason's voice cracked, but that show of emotion didn't make the look he gave Skeeter any less murderous.

Skeeter fisted his hands. "Not how you think. But I started asking questions when I heard it on the news. Your name came up, Deveraux, and then I found out about her tie to the Simmonses. It was too big of a coincidence. When you showed up in the Fenton County Courthouse, I knew Daddy Simmons had done something extra slimy."

"Who's your source? How do you know their information is accurate?"

Skeeter gave me a sardonic grin. "Well, I can't be revealing my sources, now can I? I wouldn't be a man of my word."

"Cut the crap, Skeeter," I groaned. "What else do you know?"

"That Daddy Simmons realized his baby still had feelings for Savannah even after they broke up. Hilary Wilder put the screws to him big time, but Savannah was still tugging at his heartstrings. Then Daddy Simmons found out she was pregnant and hired Michael Cartwright to kill her. But he wanted to play with her and Joe first. He figured his son would be eaten up with enough guilt that he wouldn't dare stray from that Wilder bitch." He paused. "I've given it some thought over the last few days, and I'm pretty damn sure Daddy Simmons had his son sent to Fenton County to work the Crocker case. He was tired of waiting for the Crocker situation to implode, so he helped roll the ball along."

Mason sat next to me, blinking back tears. "Joe was working for his father when he was undercover with Crocker?"

Skeeter snorted. "Hell no. I'm sure he had no idea. That's all supposin' I'm right . . . and I'm ninety-nine percent sure that I am." He winked at me. "But what J.R. didn't count on was his son fallin' in love again. That was definitely not in his plan." He took a sip of his coffee.

"Why would he send Joe to Fenton County to bring down Crocker?" Mason asked. "What ball did he want to get rolling?"

"So Skeeter would gain control of the county," I said. "Which would put J.R. in the position to take what Skeeter wanted most." I looked at Skeeter. "Which is why I have to go tonight. Killing him outright would be too good for him. We're going to do this right and make him suffer."

Skeeter grinned as he sat back down. "My world has rubbed off on you."

Mason shot him an angry glare.

"*No*," I said. "I'm just tired of seeing so many people hurt by that man."

"You are *not* meeting him," Mason said, turning to face me. "That man is deadly. If you walk in there, you're liable to end up dead."

Skeeter made a face. "As much as I hate to admit it, I think your boyfriend's right. If he's picking off my cherished assets, he won't let you leave that room alive. We're not even sure what good could come of keeping this meeting. It's certainly not worth risking your potential death."

"Skeeter," I said, leaning forward. "You have no plan other than to walk in there and kill him. Don't you think he might be expectin' you to make a move on him?" Something else occurred to me. "Has he even made it clear he's doin' this? If he likes to make people suffer, seems to me that he'd want them to know it's comin' from him. And you're already deep enough in the rat maze."

He nodded, but he didn't look happy as he sat back down. "He's made contact. He made sure I knew where it was comin' from."

"Then Jed and I need to go. We handled Mick Gentry just fine."

Skeeter snorted. "Just fine. I heard you pulled a gun on him."

I lifted my chin. "And it worked out just fine."

"Meeting Gentry wasn't gonna be a church social. Expectin' anything less would have been a fool's errand."

"We didn't go into it with our eyes closed. Jed suspected two of your men, so I used my gift before we left the parking lot behind the station. It's how we figured out they were turncoats."

Jed shifted in his seat. "She forced a vision and saw them waiting for us."

Skeeter scowled. "I heard. And I heard Merv handled the problem. Merv can help handle this one too. There's no need for Rose to risk herself."

I shook my head. "You know darn good and well that your new kingdom isn't the only thing J.R. Simmons is after. He wants the Lady in Black."

Fury flooded Skeeter's face. "*All the more reason for you not to go.*"

382

"All the more reason I *should* go. He's gonna want me to know exactly what he's doin' and all the pies he's got a finger in." I turned to glance at Mason. "I know you said a recording of the meeting wouldn't do squat for us without a court order, but could your detective in Little Rock help us get one?"

Mason shook his head. "You'd be going as the Lady in Black." He paused, as if still shocked by the sound of that statement. "You're going to want to keep your anonymity, but your name would have to be on the court order. That's if we could even get one. No court order, no wire."

"What about Jed?" I looked across the table at him, then at Mason. "He'll be with me. Maybe he could wear it."

Mason looked Jed up and down as though appraising his ability to protect me.

"Jed's not wearing a wire," Skeeter said.

"Why not?" I asked.

"If he goes to the cops, he's gonna have to tell him why he'll be there, as well as a whole host of other things we don't want public."

"Then is this all for nothing?" I asked.

"No," Skeeter said, his eyes hard. "This is between me and Simmons." He shot a glance at Mason. "And if Deveraux wants a piece of his own revenge, I'll let him join me."

One look at Mason told me he was actually considering it.

"No." I stood and banged my fist onto the table. "We need to at least try to make it happen my way." I rubbed my forehead, trying to push away the dull ache in my head. "I'll have a vision of Jed."

Skeeter shook his head. "No."

"Why?" I spat out, bracing my hands on the table as I leaned forward. "Because you're afraid my plan will work and you won't get to see blood?"

He didn't answer.

"Look, you are central to what J.R.'s doin', but he's hurt all of us and so many more. He deserves to rot in prison for the rest of his days. Give him the same fate he wanted you and me to face. Force him to see his whole world go up in a dust storm. Murdering him would be letting him off too easy. Make him sweat. Don't you think it's time?"

He still didn't answer, so I walked over to Jed and put my hand on his shoulder and closed my eyes. I stumbled for a second, trying to decide what to look for, so I asked to see what happened after the meeting. The room disappeared, and I was suddenly in a hotel room. There was a bed at my side, but I was standing behind Vision Rose in a Lady in Black outfit. She was seated in a faded pink chair, her legs crossed, her hands resting primly on her knees. Sitting across from her on a small pink sofa with a tiny white diamond pattern was J.R. and Mick Gentry. There were no other men in the room.

J.R. laughed. "Did you really think you'd leave here alive?"

Then, as if on cue, gunshots rang out, shattering the window to my left. Vision Rose fell to her side, blood splattered on the chair where she had sat. Pain shot through my arm and my chest, and I fell to my knees, taking one last gasp of air as I landed on the large pink and white diamond carpet. Then everything turned to black.

The vision ended, and I said, "We both die."

The uproar from all three men was deafening, but my knees started to buckle, and Mason leapt to his feet to keep me upright. I grasped the back of Jed's chair and pushed his hand away. If I showed any sign of weakness, they'd never let me go through with this. And something told me it was the only way.

"I told you." Skeeter pointed his finger at me. "He'll kill you."

"He didn't do it. It came from outside." I described the vision to them in greater detail, and then said, "We can still make this work. We just need to keep changing the logistics until we get the outcome we want."

"Rose," Mason pleaded. "Can't you see how crazy this is?"

"Yes, but I'm bound and determined to do it anyway." I looked down at Jed. "I'll do my best to make sure you're safe, Jed. But I can't guarantee you'll make it out alive. I'm not sure I can live with that, so I think you should stay with Skeeter and let me go alone."

His face reddened. "And if you think that's gonna happen, you're delirious. If you keep this meeting with J.R. Simmons, I'm goin' with you."

"Okay." I swung my attention between both Skeeter and Mason. "And now we have confirmation that the meeting truly is with J.R. Simmons."

"You can't do this," Mason said, his voice softer.

But Skeeter had the opposite reaction. He was only getting more pissed. He pointed at me again. "I am in charge here, Lady! You've forgotten your place!"

"No, Skeeter Malcolm!" I shouted, letting my temper get the best of me. "Just a week ago you offered me a danged partnership, so that makes us equals! I set this up, so I have more say than you do!"

He got to his feet and advanced toward me. "You never accepted my partnership!"

"Well, in this situation, I accept it!"

"It's too damned late for that!"

"He offered you a partnership in his crime business?" Mason asked, his voice sounding far away.

Oh crap. What had I done? Panic washed through me, but I'd promised him no more secrets from here on out. There was no other way I could hope for a future with him. "I didn't have Skeeter's authority to request a meeting with Mick Gentry. But when I explained it to him later— that I had suggested meeting with him as an emissary to negotiate behind the scenes—Skeeter saw the wisdom of it and offered me a partnership."

Anger and pain washed across Jed's face, and my heart skipped a beat. I could guess what was galling him. Why would Skeeter offer to make me a partner when he had never done the same with Jed, who had been with him since the beginning?

"But I turned down his offer. I've made no secret of the fact that my sole intention has been—and is—to find out who's trying to kill you and stop them."

No one said anything, so I took a breath and turned my attention to Skeeter. "We can make this work. Now let's start with the location." I described all the details of the room. "Where were we?"

"The Henryetta Days Inn," Mason said, sounding distant. "It sounds a lot like the place I stayed when I first came to town. The color scheme and print on the carpet are a giveaway."

"So do we change the place or try to make it work? I said I'd pick the location, so one of you must have suggested it since I have no clue where to go."

"Me," Skeeter said. "It's the place I would have suggested."

"So change locations or stay?"

Mason spoke first. "They attack you from the window, which means it isn't a secure location. If I were sending a plant in to meet an informant, I'd have the windows covered." He looked at Skeeter. "I presume you'd do the same?"

He nodded.

"So that means whoever was watching the outside was eliminated first." Mason leaned forward. "The Days Inn is only one story. We need a higher building, or one with no windows. But the problem with no windows is that it'll keep us from seeing what's goin' on. Obviously closets are out."

"We'll bug the room," Skeeter said, his voice hard, refusing to look at me.

"So where do we meet?" I asked.

"A public location was a good idea," Mason said. "It stands to reason that Simmons would want to keep a low profile here in town. A gunshot burst like that would draw unwanted attention." He started pacing. "But it obviously didn't work."

"We need to figure out a place that has hiding places for my men so they can keep an eye on you," Skeeter said. "A place where the quirks can be used to our advantage."

I looked down at Jed, and then returned my attention to Skeeter. "The factory."

"No," Mason said, shaking his head and continuing to pace. "It's far too remote. Anything and everything could go wrong out there. You and Jed know that firsthand."

"It's perfect, and you know it," I said. "Lots of hiding places."

"He'll never go for it, Rose," Skeeter said. "It's not to his advantage, and he never does anything that doesn't promise a favorable outcome."

"So where do we meet?"

He gave me an exasperated look. "You don't meet him at all."

"And that is not an option." I sat in Mason's vacated chair and turned to look at Jed. "Where should we go, Jed?"

He cast Skeeter a glance, and then looked back at me. "You told Gentry that you refused to meet him in any more hellholes."

"Obviously, I spoke rashly."

"No." His gaze held mine. "You have an image to maintain. So we put you in a nice place. Somewhere rich people would stay."

"And where in Pete's sake are we gonna find a place like that in Fenton County?" I asked.

"The golf course," Skeeter said, getting angry again.

"If you're talking about that vacant house, you're a damn fool."

"What vacant house?" I asked.

Skeeter groaned and shook his head, but Jed ignored him, keeping his gaze pinned on me. "There's a house that's been vacant for a couple of months. Nice place with windows that overlook the golf course and Lake Fenton. Granite counters . . . the works. Fully furnished."

"Why's it vacant?"

A sly grin lit up Jed's face. "It belongs to Mick Gentry."

Anger flashed in Mason's eyes. "Have you completely lost your mind?"

Jed ignored him. "Gentry's charges have been dropped, but he hasn't gone back home, and he won't. Not until he's taken care of me and Skeeter. He knows we want revenge." He grinned. "Meeting him in his own house is like a big F-you from Lady. You took his business. You took his life. He's been sent into hiding since the auction. Now he's about to lose Fenton County to you. He thinks Simmons is coming to eliminate us—and he's probably right if your vision is any indication—but part of him has to worry. If we meet him at his own house, it's going to make him agitated and foolish."

"That seems like a dangerous thing to me," Mason said.

"It would be to our advantage," Skeeter said, grudgingly. "It'll make him sloppy."

"And maybe even more dangerous," Mason said. "Rose's safety comes before everything else."

"No," I said, swinging my gaze to Mason. "I like it."

Skeeter banged the table. "It's another goddamned fool's errand."

"There's only one way to find out." I reached for Jed's hand.

"Wait," Jed said, looking into my face. "We won't tell him the location when we send him the message. That's important to know before you have the vision. We'll do a bait and switch like Gentry did on Tuesday night."

"He'll never go for it," Mason said, sitting in my empty chair. "He'll change his mind and leave."

"Not if we tell him it's a one-time offer," Jed said, looking past me at Mason. "He wants to meet her. Bad. I can taste it."

"No," Skeeter said. "I forbid it!"

"Just let me have the stinkin' vision!" I shouted, then turned back to Jed and took a deep breath. "What place will we give for the original location?"

"The Days Inn," Jed said without hesitation. "We'll give him the room number and watch them enter with hidden cameras. Then we'll notify him that the location has changed and tell him to come without all his men."

"He'll never do it," Skeeter said.

Jed looked him in the eye. "He will. And you know it. He wants her bad enough to do something rash."

A shiver ran down my back. "Why? Why does he want to meet me so badly?"

Mason laughed, but it was a bitter sound. "Rose. Do you really not know?"

I looked over at Skeeter and suddenly I did.

# Chapter Twenty-Nine

I turned back to Jed, refusing to acknowledge what I'd figured out, but the blood rushed to my face as I considered the implications. I couldn't deal with this right now. Our lives were on the line. "It doesn't matter why J.R. Simmons wants to meet me, only that he does. We need to focus on how to survive this. I'm going to force another vision."

"Try to hone in on what will happen if we tell him to meet us at the Days Inn, then switch the meeting place to Gentry's house," Jed said quietly. "Let's see if he goes for it."

I nodded. "Okay."

I closed my eyes, and we were in the back of Jed's car. I was in the driver's seat, and Vision Rose was in the backseat with Skeeter. There was no sign of Mason. We were parked on a neighborhood street, but nicer houses were lined up on either side of us.

I held up my phone, and Skeeter leaned forward as we watched a live feed of Simmons in the hotel room. He was surrounded by four men, while Gentry stood to the side cursing.

"Send the text," Skeeter said, his voice tight with nerves.

"Sent," Vision Rose said.

I tapped my fingers on the steering wheel, about to jump out of my skin with nerves, as I watched Simmons pull out his phone. "It's a direct line to the big man himself," I murmured in Jed's voice. "No middleman."

"You were right," Skeeter said as we watched Simmons type on his screen, but he didn't sound happy about it.

The phone in the backseat vibrated with a text.

"He's agreed," Vision Rose said.

A huge grin spread across J.R.'s face as he looked directly into a tiny camera.

"He's too damn cocky," Skeeter mumbled. "I don't like it."

"His arrogance will be his downfall," Vision Rose said.

The scene faded, and I opened my eyes to stare into Jed's face. "He agreed to go."

We all sat in silence for several seconds. "Okay," I finally said. "Now what?"

"I need some air," Mason said. When Skeeter started to protest, he held up his hands. "I swear to God I'm not going to run off. I just need a clear space to think."

Skeeter nodded, and then walked outside himself. He was gone for several minutes, and when he came back, he held the door open. "You have ten minutes."

Mason burst out the door like he was on fire.

"Where's he goin', Rose?" Skeeter asked, coming back to sit down.

"When he gets upset with me, he usually has to go for a walk. He's not runnin' to tell anyone. He would never risk my safety."

"Is he comin' back?"

"He swore he would." I swallowed. "But he may not help tonight." I told them about my vision.

"That doesn't mean he's out," Skeeter conceded. "I'd prefer it if we all split up."

"But if he sticks with us, I can't imagine he'd leave me alone that close to meeting J.R. Simmons." I looked Skeeter in the eye, choosing to ignore the realization that he was probably in love with me. If I acknowledged it in any way, I risked wounding his pride, and as crazy as our friendship was, I didn't want to lose him.

"You don't know that, Rose," Jed said. "He knows we'd protect you, and we're gonna need someone in charge at the house. That's the more dangerous location. He might plan to be there, waiting."

I didn't answer. "I'm going to have another vision of the meeting."

Jed nodded, and I reached over and grabbed his shoulder, focusing on the meeting this time.

Vision Rose was sitting in an upholstered chair, and I was standing behind her. We were in a dimly lit living room with enormous windows overlooking a lake.

Simmons and Gentry walked through the front door, but Vision Rose remained seated.

"Nice to see you've made yourself at home," Gentry sneered, striding into the living room.

"This place has potential," Vision Rose said. "I'm thinking of relocating. I'll be more than happy to buy it from you since you won't be needing it anymore. At a greatly reduced price, of course."

"You're not getting my house!" He looked like he was about to strangle her.

"Keep your distance, Gentry," I said, making sure he had a good look at the gun strapped to my chest.

Gentry backed up, his hands fisted.

"Enough, Gentry," Simmons said, sounding annoyed as he moved closer to Lady.

She stood and reached out to shake his hand, but he lifted it to his lips instead. "I'm looking forward to finding out what you have hidden," he murmured.

And then he winked.

The vision faded away, and I blurted out, "He wants to know what I'm hiding."

Nausea roiled up in my throat, but I swallowed it down so I could tell them what I'd seen. "This one was entirely different. Why?"

Skeeter sat up. "He thought you were an amateur before. But the way you changed the location on him made him reassess."

"I need to come up with a list of things to ask him. Even if we can't get a court to use it, we'll have some solid leads on what to dig up to find irrefutable proof."

"That sounds like a job for you and your boyfriend," Skeeter grumbled. "I'll go along with your plan, but if he gets off, I'll go for his jugular. Make no bones about it."

I nodded. I was grateful he'd made as many concessions as he had. "At some point, I need to get my Lady in Black clothes. Maybe I can get Neely Kate to bring them."

"Rose," Jed said, getting to his feet. "You can't do that. Neely Kate thinks you're dead."

I grimaced. How had I forgotten? A new wave of anxiety hit me. I couldn't let her keep thinking I was dead. "Let me call her and tell her the truth. Then she can bring my clothes."

"You can't," Skeeter barked. "If you tell anyone— even her—this will all blow to kingdom come." When he saw my distress, he added, "Then take comfort in the fact that you have no say in the matter."

"Are you telling me I'm actually your hostage?"

"The damned locked door didn't already tell you that?"

I sat back down, tears welling in my eyes.

"Right now we're more worried about the fallout of Deveraux going missing," Skeeter said, scrubbing a hand over his head. "I got the latest from Merv. They think you're dead and he's gone."

"They don't think he did it, do they?" I asked, worried.

"No. They think he's met with foul play too. But they're wondering where your body is. They found the burning cabin with the bodies, but none of them was yours."

"Is that a problem?" I asked.

Jed headed for the door. "I'm gonna go check on Deveraux."

I watched him walk toward the door, wondering why he had left so suddenly.

"No," Skeeter drawled, leaning an arm on the table, "but it does give you an option you hadn't considered before."

"What?"

"You don't have to go through with this at all. Let them think you're dead. I can set you up with a new identity by the end of the day. You could go anywhere and be free of all this."

"And Mason?"

He frowned and lifted one shoulder into a shrug. "It's up to him."

"But then I'd just be runnin' away from the problem."

"You'd be *free*."

I shook my head. "No, I wouldn't. Not really."

Skeeter lowered his voice. "If money's a problem, I'll give it to you. The smart thing to do is run. There's no shame in it."

"But I'd lose everything. I'd lose my family and friends and my business. I'd leave you and Jed to deal with this mess."

"We can handle it."

"I know you can. You've been handlin' it for years, but that doesn't mean you have to do it alone." I gave him a soft smile. "It's been a hard lesson for me to learn too, but guess what, Skeeter Malcolm? You do have friends, whether you like it or not."

He sat upright and gave me the saddest smile I'd ever seen. "Arrogance may be J.R. Simmons' downfall, but having friends will end up being mine."

As he got up and walked outside, I found myself wondering if he was right.

# Chapter Thirty

Mason came back from his walk, and we spent several hours working on a list of questions that would help point us toward a paper trail. He was subdued, and he didn't respond to any of my attempts to get him to talk unless it was about the meeting with J.R. I understood his distance, but it made my heart ache.

Jed had returned with Mason. I tried to have several visions showing the outcome of the meeting, but I never came up with anything.

"What's that mean?" Mason asked. "Was Jed dead?"

"No. It's dark and cold when someone's dead. This is gray and hazy. As though what I'm asking doesn't happen . . . or it's too indeterminate to tell."

"So what do you want to do?" Jed asked, worry wrinkling his brow.

"We keep goin'," I said.

After lunch, I said I needed to lie down and rest. Mason came with me, and I nearly cried when he opened his arms, inviting me to snuggle against him.

"Are you ready to talk about Savannah?" I asked.

He hesitated. "Part of me isn't surprised that he's involved. But after the details Malcolm shared with me, I no longer regret beating Cartwright to a pulp. And if that's true, what kind of person does that make me?"

"It makes you human, Mason."

"It may be understandable to think it or wish it, but not to actually follow through." He lay on his back and turned his head to look at me. "And there's a part of me that wanted to help Malcolm kill J.R. Simmons."

"But you didn't. You told him no."

His arm tightened around me. "If he hurts you, I might lose my restraint."

"He won't hurt me. I'm going to be fine."

"He and/or Kate almost killed you last night, Rose."

"But they didn't." I looked up at him. "Skeeter says everyone thinks I'm dead." I ran my finger along his jawline. "And that they suspect you've met with foul play."

"I figured as much."

I stilled my hand. "It doesn't bother you?"

He swallowed. "It hurts like hell that my mother thinks her only living child might be dead and that the woman she loved like a daughter is too." His voice broke. "But there's not a damn thing I can do about it right now."

Something in his voice set me on edge. "Do you blame me?"

He was quiet for so long, I didn't think he was going to answer. "Part of me wants to, but no. Not for this."

I wanted to ask him what he *did* blame me for, but I didn't have the energy. Or the courage. "Skeeter says there's another option. One I hadn't considered. He says I can start over. A new life. A new identity. You could too."

His fingertips lightly stroked my arm, and I couldn't help wondering if he was just doing it out of habit. "And what did you say?"

"I gave him an answer, but I realized that wasn't fair to you. This is your decision too."

"I'm glad you finally see something that way." His words were bitter.

"I know I've made so many mistakes—"

"We're not even going to look at the past two months right now." He shifted to his side to look me in the eye. "At the moment, I'm more upset that you decided to go through with this without asking my opinion or allowing me any say whatsoever."

"I knew you'd never go along with it."

"Did you?" he asked, sounding guarded. "Well, now neither of us will ever know, I guess, because there's no putting that horse back in the barn."

"I'm sorry."

"You keep saying that, but my heart keeps breaking anyway."

Tears swam in my eyes.

"I just found out that you've lived a double life for over two months, and I never had a clue. Do you have any idea how stupid I feel?"

"Mason. No."

He shook his head and looked at the wall. "Watching you with them . . . It's like I don't know you at all."

"How can you say that?"

He closed his eyes. "I'm tired, and I don't want to say anything I'll regret." His eyes opened and met mine. "All I know is that I love you more than I ever thought it possible to love another person. You make me more than I am by myself." He gave me a sad smile. "Does that make sense?"

I nodded, tears leaking from my eyes. "That's how I feel too."

"Do you? I'm not so sure," he said softly. Then he leaned over and kissed me, pulling me close again. "Get some rest, Rose. You need to be on your toes tonight."

"Okay."

*Time*, I assured myself, *he just needs time*. They said time healed all wounds.

But what if these were the type of wounds that didn't heal?

When I woke up, the room was darker, and I sat upright in a panic. "Mason!" He wasn't in the bed, and I tried to scramble to my feet.

"I'm here." He ran down the hall to me and sat beside me on the mattress, gathering me into his arms.

My tears broke loose, and I sobbed my fears and worries into his chest. When I finally calmed down, I rubbed my fingers on the damp cloth, then leaned back and looked up into his shadowy face. "This has become a habit. Me crying into your shirt."

His only answer was to give me a sad smile.

My panic renewed. He must have sensed it, because he brushed his lips against mine. "One way or another, it's going to be okay."

"I'm so scared I'm going to lose you."

"Shh . . ." he murmured against my lips. "I love you. Focus on tonight." He wiped the tears off my cheeks and studied my face. "I need you to be safe."

"Okay." I nodded. "What time is it?"

"After five."

My eyes widened. "You should have woken me up."

He smoothed the damp hair from my cheek. "No. You needed to rest. Jed went by the farm and got your clothes." His voice was tight. "He also brought dinner."

"Clothes?"

"Your Lady in Black clothes. From the back of our bedroom closet." Then he got up. "Come on out whenever you're ready. I'd like to go over the questions again. Skeeter wants you to leave by nine."

A few more tears ran down my cheeks as I stood. Mason came back and pulled me into his arms. He kissed me, but I could taste the sadness on his lips, and it made me even more frightened.

"Mason, I'm so, so sorry."

He cupped my cheek and gave me a sad smile. "I know. I believe you."

I went to the bathroom, and when I came out, I found him at the kitchen table with a pad of paper. He was studying a list, but as soon as he saw me, he pulled the notebook with his questions from earlier on top of it.

"Are you hungry?"

I shook my head. "No. I'm too nervous."

"Okay, but you should eat something before you go. You need your energy. Jed picked up food from Big Bill's."

"Okay."

We spent the next two hours going over the questions and a variety of possible scenarios. Jed came in and out, listening in for a while before he left, but I never saw hide nor hair of Skeeter. After we'd been through every possible question, Jed came back in, looking grim.

"Rose, you need to get dressed so we can get you ready."

Mason turned his head and gave him a hard look. "You said you were bugging the house."

Jed gave him a wary glance. "We are, but we want her to wear a wire too."

"What if he checks?"

"He won't. But if he does, he's still unlikely to find this."

Mason stood. "What is it?"

Jed handed him a small, flat black object. Mason looked it over. "Can she wear it in her bra?"

Jed glanced up at me and looked uncomfortable. "Yeah."

Obviously, he noticed a few of my dresses had been too low cut for me to wear one. Now I was worried to see what he'd packed. "Where are my clothes?"

Jed walked outside and returned with Neely Kate's polka-dotted backpack.

Mason's face hardened when his gaze landed on the backpack. "I see Neely Kate knew. She walked out of our house with that same bag last weekend."

I wanted to say I was sorry, but it had lost its usefulness. I took the bag from Jed.

Skeeter had walked through the doorway after Jed, and he shut the door behind him. "Can it, Deveraux, we need her to stay focused. Heaping a mountain of guilt on her right now is only going to threaten the successfulness of this little field trip."

Jed reached for the device in Mason's hand, but he wouldn't let it go. "The only person going near her chest is me."

Skeeter snickered, but he called out, "I'd like a word with you, Deveraux," as Mason started to follow me down the hall.

I stopped and turned around to face him. "Skeeter."

Mason gave me a look of reassurance. "It's okay, Rose. I want to talk to him too. Go get dressed."

I went into the bathroom and dug through the bag, grateful I had several dress choices, one of which allowed me to wear a bra. I quickly stripped and stepped into the dress. I was still pulling it up when Mason knocked on the door, then opened it a crack. "It's me."

"You can come in."

My back was to him as he shut the door behind him. He reached for the zipper at the base of my spine and slowly zipped it, then pulled my back to his chest. "I don't know if I can watch you do this," he whispered.

I swallowed the lump in my throat. "You mean tonight?"

He lowered his face to my hair. "Yeah. I'm not sure I can watch J.R. Simmons or his minions murder you. Last night was enough."

I turned around and looked up at him, trying to stuff down my disappointment. I understood his decision, but I would feel better knowing he was there with me. "It's okay. It's safer if you're not there."

"Joe's disappeared."

My eyes widened, and I would have taken a step back if Mason's arms hadn't held me in place. "*What?*"

"He left the sheriff's station last night after I watched your video, and no one has seen him since."

"Kate do something to him?" I asked in a panic.

"Kate? No. I'm sure she wouldn't hurt her own brother."

I didn't know what to believe about her.

"I'm sure he's just distraught."

I squeezed my eyes tight. That was only slightly better. So many emotions washed through me I had a hard time separating them out, but first and foremost was grief. I'd caused him this pain. I wasn't sure I could live with the guilt. Still, I wasn't sure there was a better way. "Do you think he's okay?"

"Honestly, Rose, I'm not sure."

I nodded and looked down at the buttons on his shirt. The one he'd worn the night before. How had my life changed so dramatically in such a short period of time?

"Malcolm just told me, but he didn't want you to know. He didn't want it to distract you."

I looked up into his guarded eyes. "So why did you tell me?"

"Because you have a right to know." He cleared his throat and looked down at the front of my dress. "I'm going to pin the mic on you now."

I nodded, the lump in my throat too large to speak. He slid the small flat plastic inside my bra cup, securing it in place.

When he finished, he looked into my eyes. "You should probably take off your ring," he said, sounding distant. "I'll keep it for you until this is over."

Fighting a fresh round of tears, I slipped it off and placed it in his open palm. Part of me wondered if I would get it back.

He slipped it into his pants pocket. "I love you, Rose Gardner. Despite everything." He cupped my cheek and lowered his mouth to mine, giving me the gentlest of kisses. "Promise me you'll be safe."

I nodded, looking away as I blinked back tears.

"Malcolm gave me back my phone with the agreement I don't answer any of my messages until this is all done. Merv's going to drop me off at your landscaping office."

That surprised me. "Oh. Okay."

"Call me as soon as it's done. I'll be there waiting."

"Okay." But some deep selfish part of me thought that if he really cared, he'd stay with me. "I think you should go now."

He looked taken aback by that.

My worry for Joe and the others, combined with the pain of Mason choosing not to stay, was liable to send me over the edge. I knew he'd stay if I broke down, but I didn't want to force his hand. He'd made his decision, just as I'd made mine that cold November afternoon.

Everything had changed, and I only had myself to blame.

I lifted my chin, willing myself not to cry. I had to be strong. "I'm fine. Piece of cake. When I get the recording, I'll bring it to you."

He was clearly surprised by my matter-of-fact tone, but he nodded. "Okay." He started to leave, then turned around. "Rose. Please don't be hurt by this."

I shook my head, my chin quivering. "I have no right to be hurt."

He came back to me and pulled me hard against him, kissing me with a possessive fierceness that stole my breath.

I clung to him, and he lifted me up and sat me on the counter. He cupped my face in his hands, but I averted my gaze. It hurt too much. I choked back a sob.

"Rose." The pain in his voice only stabbed deeper. "Rose. Look at me. Please."

I lifted my eyes to his.

"Sweetheart, don't give up on me, okay?" Tears flooded his eyes. "Leaving you right now is the hardest thing I've ever done."

I released another sob. "Just go, Mason." I tried to pull his hands away from my face, but he held on tight. "If you're not going to help me, just go. I can't do this." I started crying harder, and I heard a hard banging on the door.

"Rose!" Skeeter called out. "What the hell is going on in there, Deveraux?"

Mason gave me another quick kiss, and then the door burst open and Skeeter dragged him out into the hallway.

"I should kill you for this, Deveraux!" Skeeter shouted as he shoved him against the wall.

"Skeeter!" I hopped off the counter. "Let him go!"

Skeeter's eyes burned with anger. "I told him not to upset you!"

"I'm fine. I'm scared, and he was comforting me."

Skeeter looked dubious, but he gave Mason a shove down the hall. "Get. If you can't stay and help your own girlfriend, then what damn good are you?"

Mason gave me one last look before turning and walking out the front door.

"How long do we have before we need to leave?" I asked, wiping my cheeks.

"Twenty minutes."

I nodded. "I can be ready." I turned around and started to shut the door, but Skeeter blocked it.

"Maybe we should call this off."

I looked into his worried eyes and gave him a mischievous grin. "Don't go turncoat on me now, Skeeter Malcolm. One's enough, don't you think?"

"Rose, I'm sorry," he said quietly. "We heard what you said in there."

"How?" Then I knew. I closed my eyes. "The mic."

"Yeah."

I scanned our conversation, cringing at the thought of it being overheard. "I'm surprised you didn't hit him for telling me about Joe."

He shrugged. "I suppose it's better for you to find out now than if Daddy Simmons lets it slip."

I cocked my head. "You set Mason up."

A grin ghosted across his lips. "Guess we'll never know." He looked like he was about to leave, but then he said, "Rose, for what it's worth, I'd never let you do this if I didn't think you were capable of it."

"Thanks. I know."

He walked out and shut the door behind him. I washed my face and put on some makeup I'd found in the bag. Then I pinned up my hair, slid on my shoes, and took a long look at myself in the mirror. My eyes were still red, so it was a good thing I had the veil to cover them. I'd only met J.R. once in person. Several months had passed since that awful dinner in September, but I suspected he was one of those people who remembered everyone. I hoped he wouldn't remember me.

I walked out into the living room. Jed had changed into a black suit, a white shirt, and a black tie. Trying to make light of the situation, I walked over and straightened his tie. "You look very debonair. I feel like I'm going to Homecoming."

Skeeter laughed, but it sounded strained. "We'll save the homecoming for after."

My smile fell, and I looked him in the eye. "Agreed."

"I want you to wear a gun again." He dropped to one knee in front of me, holding the elastic band Jed had given me. He looked up and winked. "Don't be gettin' any ideas about me proposin'."

"I'd never suspected such a thing," I forced out, my heart aching with my new knowledge. How had I been so stupid about that too? "You told me you feared what would happen to your family jewels if you married me."

"That was only if I cheated," he said, holding it open so I could step into it. "And any man who cheated on you would be a fool." He looked up at me and grinned. "Besides, we both know you wouldn't stop with the jewels." He winked and slid the band up to my upper thigh.

Jed handed him a small gun, and Skeeter secured it into the band.

"I can do that myself, Skeeter."

His expression was ornery when he looked up at me. "Can't blame a man for coppin' a feel."

I pushed his hands off my leg. "Enough of that."

"How's it feel?"

I walked around the room. "It still feels strange, but it's secure."

"That's what we're going for." He stood, his seriousness returning. "Ready to go?"

No, but this was happening at my insistence, so I

didn't exactly have room to complain. I started for the door. "Let's do it."

Skeeter opened the door for me, and I shivered as I stepped into the cold night air.

"You need a coat," he said in a low voice.

"Too late for that now," I said, walking past two men on the front porch toward the car that was parked parallel to the house. Another man stood next to the already running car, giving me a grim smile.

Skeeter opened the back door, and I slid into the car. Skeeter shut the door and walked around to the other side as Jed got into the driver's seat.

"Have another vision," Skeeter said as soon as he shut the door.

I nodded and put my hand on Jed's shoulder, forcing a vision of what would happen at the end of the meeting. A room came into view, but it was hazy, and the vision appeared to be unfolding in slow motion. I heard gunshots and shouting, and there were multiple people in the room—far more than the four who were supposed to be present—but I was fine and so was Vision Rose. We were hiding together behind an overturned table.

"There's a gunfight," I said, opening my eyes.

"Were you or Jed injured?"

"No, I don't think so." But my heart was racing as I told them what I saw.

"So you have no idea if you got any usable information from him?" Skeeter asked.

"No, but I can only assume I did."

Skeeter didn't look so certain. "Jed. Your call."

Jed looked back at me. "How are you feelin' about it, Lady?"

"The prospect of a gunfight scares me, but if we know it's comin', at least we'll be prepared." Still, something stank about the whole situation.

Jed nodded. "Let's do it."

"We didn't text J.R. the location," I said, worried anew.

Skeeter pulled out the burner phone. "I already took care of it about an hour ago. They're on their way to the Days Inn, and we have the room under video surveillance, like we discussed."

"We're gonna drive around a bit," Jed explained as he turned a corner. "Then we're gonna head to Gentry's house. We've got men watching it, and the house has been bugged. We've got it covered."

"Okay."

After we drove around for about fifteen minutes, Skeeter pulled out his phone. "Bobby says they've pulled up to the Days Inn."

"They're running ten minutes early," Jed murmured.

"We'd best beat it to the house."

"Agreed."

"Is this a problem?" I asked, starting to worry.

"No," Skeeter said, patting my leg. "Not necessarily. But we need to make a beeline to the house so we're not feelin' rushed."

"He's trying to throw us off," I said.

"Good thing it's not gonna work. Now get a text ready about the change in the meetin' spot."

I did as he asked as Jed handed his phone to Skeeter.

It was linked to the camera planted in the hotel room. It was empty, but then the door burst open and several men entered the room, Mick Gentry and J.R. Simmons trailing behind them.

"Where are they?" Gentry asked.

Simmons grinned and pulled out his phone. "She's a sly little fox."

"Send the text," Skeeter said.

Simmons looked around, then pulled his phone out of his pocket. "Change of plans," he said with a grin. "We're headed someplace else."

"Are you sure you want to do that?" Mick Gentry asked.

"I'm curious as hell to meet the infamous Lady in Black." He looked up into the hidden camera and grinned.

"See you soon, Lady."

I had a sudden urge to get a vial of holy water.

# Chapter Thirty-One

I'm having second thoughts," Skeeter said, jiggling his leg up and down. "I say we abort."

"Why?" I asked. "What's changed?"

"That man is pure evil, Rose."

"You knew that before, Skeeter. What's changed?"

"I think he knows."

"Knows what?"

"That I'm part of this."

Jed pulled into the neighborhood where we were meeting J.R., parking down the block from the house. He re-watched the short video clip.

"What do you think, Jed?" I asked.

"I say you have another vision."

I nodded and put my hand on his shoulder. The vision came almost immediately this time. We were in the living room, and I was standing behind the Lady in Black's chair. J.R. Simmons and Mick Gentry were sitting on the sofa across from us.

There was a smug grin on J.R.'s face as he leaned back on the sofa. "I'm ready to embark on a partnership. Are you?"

Lady moved her hand from her crossed leg to the arm of her chair, then said, "I definitely have what I need." She sounded pleased as she said it.

Then the smile fell from J.R.'s face as he looked behind me. "You. What are you doing here?"

The vision ended, and I said, "I got everything I need." Then I blinked and quickly told them everything I had seen.

Nobody said anything for a moment, and then I finally said, "I'm doin' it." I looked up front. "Jed?"

He glanced back over his shoulder. "No gunfight? No skirmish?"

"It could have happened later, but not in the part I saw. J.R. was too concerned with whoever he saw walkin' in behind us." I turned to glance at Skeeter. "Were you planning on dropping in?"

"While I considered it, no. If I show up, all hell's gonna break loose. I wouldn't risk your life that way."

"So who shows up?" I asked. "He definitely seemed surprised."

"I have no idea," Skeeter responded. "But whoever it was could be the catalyst for the gunfight."

Jed looked over his shoulder. "So when the surprise guest shows up, take my lead and run for cover."

"Have another vision," Skeeter said, his voice low. "Of after."

"Okay," I whispered. I touched Jed again and tried to see what happened after it was all said and done, but all I got was that same gray haze from earlier.

"I don't like it," Skeeter said, looking straight ahead through the windshield. "It's too ambiguous. What's it mean?"

"I don't know," I confessed. "Something like this has happened to me before. When I ask to see things that don't end up happening, I kind of get stuck. But these visions are different. For one, I can leave them without having another vision, and for another, they just *feel* different." I turned to look at him. "Like the future is shapeless and waiting to be formed."

"I don't like it," Skeeter repeated. "I want to know."

"We can't know everything," I said quietly. "Sometimes we have to write our own future."

"Skeeter," Jed said. "Time is tickin'. If we're doin' this, we need to get in there."

Skeeter stared at me for several long seconds. "Rose, if you don't want to do this, I'll give you a new life— money, a new name, anything you need to get away from here and be safe."

"But everything I want is right here," I said with a soft smile. "Besides, I'm tired of hiding and being afraid of my own shadow. I've grown up, and the new me fights for what she wants."

"That's my girl." The corners of his lips lifted, and his eyes twinkled with mischief. "J.R. Simmons won't know what hit him." He leaned over and gave me a lingering kiss on the cheek, then he sat up and was all business again. "Jed's gonna be with you, but I'll be listening in with Bluetooth as long as I'm not too far out of range. If you need to get out of there, just say bananas and we'll get you out."

"Bananas?"

"Yeah." He looked up front. "Jed, I'll get out here and get into position. You move the car up and get Lady inside. We have five minutes tops."

"Will do."

Skeeter opened the back door and grinned. "Knock 'em dead, Lady." Then he hopped out and shut the door behind him.

Before I knew it, Jed had parked a little farther up the road and was opening my door. "Bring your burner phone." He pointed behind me as I started to slide across the seat. "He might text or call you."

"Good thinkin'." I grabbed it in a death grip. It was also my access to 911 should I need it.

"How are you doin'?" he whispered as he led me across the street and up the driveway.

"Nervous. Scared to death."

"That's good," he said. "The adrenaline will make you sharper."

"It only makes me feel clumsy and uncoordinated."

"Focus that fear on your job, and I promise you that you'll be even better at it." He looked down at me with a grin. "But if you get any better, I'll be out of a job. Skeeter'll replace me."

I shook my head as we climbed the few steps to the front porch. "Never gonna happen. After tonight, I'm retirin'. I'll roast my hat in a big ole bonfire."

He cocked his head and grinned at me as he opened the front door. "Never say never. You've got a God-given talent. It would be a shame to waste it."

I released a nervous laugh. "I'll leave the mischief to you and Skeeter. I've had my fill of it to last a lifetime. Now let's get this done."

He looked around for a moment and then entered the house ahead of me. The room was dimly lit, but it was bright enough that I could see from the light of a few lamps scattered across the room. The house had an open floor plan, and the living room was situated next to the open kitchen. It was as nice as Jed had led me to believe. The kitchen had fancy stainless steel appliances and granite counters, along with pendant lights over the island like you see in magazines.

The living room was covered in an off-white carpet. A leather sofa and a couple of upholstered chairs sat in front of a floor-to-ceiling stone fireplace. But the back wall was what was most impressive. Most of it was made of glass, and it overlooked the dark landscape of the lake. I could see a million stars in the sky, and the water was speckled with tiny bright lights from boat docks. It was the dead of winter, but they looked like fireflies.

"We moved the furniture around to optimize our safety," Jed said as we walked into the room, and then he chuckled. "It's liable to piss Gentry off even more."

"Good."

He gave me a look of surprise, then continued. "All of these glass doors lead to a deck, which has stairs to the right. This is escape route one." He pointed to a door by the kitchen. "This is the only open door. The others have been sealed to maximize the effectiveness of our getaway—should we need one—but it's glass, so it won't slow them down for long."

"Got it," I murmured.

"Escape route number two is behind us." He led me through the kitchen and to a short hallway lined with two doors. "This is one of those rare southern Arkansas houses that has a walkout basement. This door will take you downstairs. Once you're down there, there's a door you can use to exit and run to our rendezvous position."

"Which is?" I asked, starting to get nervous.

"In the parking lot behind the country club. We passed it on the way in."

I nodded. It was about a quarter mile to a third of a mile away. I'd never be able to run in these heels, but I'd just kick them off if necessary. "Any other escape routes?"

"If you get truly desperate, you can run up to a bedroom and try to get out a second story window, but I wouldn't recommend it. And of course, there's always the front door."

"Got it."

He pointed to a wine bottle and three wine glasses on the island. "The boys found some of Gentry's wine in his wine cellar." He grinned. "One of them said this was an expensive bottle if you want to play hostess."

"Okay."

He poured me a glass of red wine and set it on the table next to my chair. "It might help add to the illusion."

I needed all the help I could get.

He pulled out his phone, then flinched and gave me a hard look. "They're coming down the street. We need to get into position. We have men hidden around the house, waiting to step in and help if we need them, but their assistance will be in the form of fire-power, and we're hoping to avoid that. Like Skeeter said, the code word is bananas, and as soon as you say it, I'll get us out of here. Got it?"

I nodded, swallowing my nerves. "Do you really think I can do this, Jed?"

He grinned, but his eyes were serious. "I don't have a death wish, but I don't mind taking chances if the odds are in my favor. If anyone can do this, it's you."

He gestured for me to take a seat in the chair. I could see why they had chosen this position. The chair was at a slight angle, and its back was to the kitchen. From here we could see the front door and the hall with the door leading to the basement. The only thing we couldn't see was the door to the deck behind us.

I cast a glance toward it as I sat down.

"We have men covering the back," Jed said, as if reading my mind.

"We know from my vision that somebody gets past them without creating a disturbance." Who was it? Would Skeeter change his mind about coming in?

"Then it must be someone on our side. Skeeter will have beefed up security. I guarantee it." Jed's voice was tight as he hurried to the front window and peeked out of the blinds. "They're here."

I sat down, setting the cell phone on the table next to the wine, then fingered the edge of my veil. I took a deep breath, trying to center myself. I had so much riding on this meeting that I was close to losing my nerve.

Jed's hand rested reassuringly on my shoulder. "One piece at a time. Follow Deveraux's script."

Crappy doodles, I should have been going over it in the car. But it was too late to think of that now.

The front door swung open, banging against the wall, and Gentry stormed into the house.

"Just who the hell do you think you are?" he demanded.

Well, crap. The vision was different right off the bat. Worry followed that realization, but there was no turning back now. The future had already been set into motion. Now we could only live it.

"Ah, Mr. Gentry," I said, trying to sound amused. "I take you didn't have any trouble finding the place."

"It's my own damn house!" he shouted.

"Gentry. That's enough," a cold, genteel male voice commanded.

I swung my gaze to the front door, and my skin started to crawl when I saw J.R. fill the doorway. He paused just outside the threshold, his shrewd gaze taking everything in.

"Are you a vampire?" I asked. "Do you need to be invited in?"

A playful gleam filled his eyes. "I've been accused of being evil, but never a vampire. This evening could prove even more entertaining than expected." He grinned as he walked inside. "Do you often invite evil to your door?"

I shrugged. "It depends. But I suspect you're a whole brand of evil unto yourself, Mr. Simmons." I tried to keep my tone light and playful.

Amusement created crinkles around his eyes as he crossed the room toward me. I'd just added another layer to the game and he was pleased. But his entire life was one long, continuous game. Everyone around him was a disposable object for him to manipulate for his own entertainment.

I despised him even more.

I waited until he stopped several feet in front of me before I stood, as if I were granting him an audience at my throne. I offered him my hand to shake, but he lifted it to his mouth, his lips brushing my knuckles. His eyes darted everywhere, taking in everything, from my shoes, to the doors, to Jed standing sentry behind me.

All within a matter of seconds.

Mick Gentry remained in the center of the room, seething, but he reminded me of a puppy tied to a stake. Despite how much the collar chafed, he knew his master.

J.R. straightened and narrowed his gaze on my veil, still holding my hand. He was close enough that he could probably make out the silhouette of my face. "I'm honored to meet you, Lady. May I call you that?"

I forced myself to remain calm. Jed had said I should focus my fear into doing my job, so I did just that. "Of course."

"Please call me J.R." He released my hand and moved over to the windows. He looked like he was taking in the view, but he was using the glass to study the room.

I sat back down and felt like I was going to be sick. All the preparation in the world couldn't have prepared me to meet this man.

He was Darth Vader, and I was Jar Jar Binks.

What in the world had I been thinking?

Just as I started to panic, Jed's hand squeezed my shoulder, giving me reassurance.

J.R. noticed too, of course.

I gracefully reached up and put my hand on Jed's, stroking it lightly, as J.R. turned and gave us his full attention.

"Malcolm's right-hand man is your lover?" he asked, amused. "Does he know?"

Oh, he was one sick and twisted man, all right. My anger rose up again. I was going to show him pain and suffering, but this time he would be on the receiving end.

I lowered my hand and gave an indifferent sideways wave. "Why would I care whether Mr. Malcolm knows or not?"

J.R. sat on the sofa—in the same exact position he'd taken in my vision—and gestured for Mick to sit next to him. "With pain comes power, Lady. Surely you've learned that by now."

"Some of us have other methods of enforcing our rules."

He grinned. "I'd love to learn all about your methods. I'm excited to learn *everything* about you." His gaze landed on my cleavage before finding its way back up to my veil.

I cocked my head and grinned back. "Some things are better left to the imagination, Mr. Simmons."

"J.R., *please*," he said with a patronizing air. "And while that is true in many situations, I suspect that what you have hidden will far surpass my wildest imaginings."

Could he know who I was?

"I must warn you, J.R., very few people are granted access to my private life. They must earn their way there." I paused. "But I'm sure you follow the same rules."

"I've never been much of a rule-follower, but I suspect I'll break the few I have with you, Lady." His grin turned wicked. "First and foremost, don't mix business with pleasure." He leaned his elbow on the arm of the sofa. "But then I've never understood the reasoning behind that rule. I take pleasure in everything. Particularly business."

It was time to get this show on the road.

"Would you like a drink?" I asked, getting to my feet. I walked to the island and picked up the wine bottle. "This Cabernet is an exceptional treat. The boys found it in the wine cellar."

Mick jumped to his feet. "That's my damn wine! It's worth five hundred dollars!"

J.R. ignored him. "I'd love some."

I poured him a glass of wine and carried it over to him, purposely leaving the second glass on the counter.

"Where's mine?" Mick asked, his face red with anger.

I tilted my head. "You, Mr. Gentry, are forgetting your place. You will wait patiently like Jed." I stared him in the face, which lost some of its effectiveness with the veil, but it was enough to set him off. He moved closer to me, reaching for my neck.

"You touch her and you're a dead man," J.R. said calmly as he swirled his wine, then sniffed it.

Gentry stopped a few inches away from me, towering over me. I had no doubt he would strangle me in a heartbeat. The way he clenched and unclenched his fists was a strong clue.

J.R. took a sip, then gave a half-shrug. "Not bad, but I've had better."

He was good. Damn good. But then, what did I expect from a psychopath?

J.R. set his wine down on the table as I headed back to my chair, but he patted Gentry's vacant seat. "Come join me, Lady. I prefer to keep my friends close." He lifted his eyebrows slightly.

"And your enemies closer?" I added in a teasing tone.

I caught a glimpse of Jed out of the corner of my eye, and he was not happy. I wasn't sitting with J.R. in any of my visions. While I wasn't all that excited about being this close to him, I could see it was a test. He knew the room had been strategically rearranged, and he was trying to tip things to his advantage. But would I call him on it?

His grin deepened, his eyes challenging.

I sat at the end of the opposite end of the sofa, tucking my legs to the side.

"What the hell?" Gentry bellowed.

"Gentry, get Lady's wine," J.R. said, keeping his eyes on me.

"If you think I'm going to—"

J.R. turned to look at the man, his eyes deadly. "You will do as I say or suffer the consequences."

Gentry's nostrils flared with rage. He stomped over to pick up my glass and then strode toward me, pulling his arm back to throw it at me.

In the blink of an eye, J.R. was up to intercept him. They stood chest to chest for several seconds. The glass in Gentry's hand tipped sideways and dribbled the red wine onto the off-white carpet as surprise filled Gentry's eyes. He listed to the side and slumped to his knees.

Jed took several steps toward me, but I remained frozen in my seat, confused by what had just happened.

J.R. pushed Gentry backward and he fell to his back. The wine that spilled onto the carpet almost matched the blood soaking his shirt over his heart. J.R. squatted next to Gentry and wiped his blade clean on the dying man's shirt. Then he lifted his gaze to me, his eyes cold and dark. This man would wipe away an entire town and feel no remorse. He'd probably get off on it.

I was going to die in this room. But I was going to get what I came for first.

# Chapter Thirty-Two

J.R. stood and turned his attention to me, still holding the knife. "Sorry about that. If you really want to purchase this house, I'll be more than happy to pay your carpet cleaning bill."

"No need. I prefer hardwood floors," I heard myself say.

He grinned. "Let me get you another glass." He turned around and walked into the kitchen, setting his knife on the counter.

Oh, Lord Almighty. That was another test.

I was so in over my head I wasn't even sure how to get out. Gentry was gasping for breath, blood oozing from the corner of his mouth.

I cast a sideways glance to Jed, hoping for some direction. I wasn't Gentry's biggest fan, but we couldn't just leave him there. We had to get help.

Jed snuck a glance at J.R., who still had his back to us, then shook his head.

Gentry took one last breath, and his body stilled.

*Focus.*

I pushed away the fear. I had the power to take this man down, but I had to keep it together. "It must be handy having your son as the chief deputy sheriff in situations like this one," I said, gesturing to Gentry's body. "Easier cleanup. No wonder you want in on Fenton County."

"That was a lucky coincidence," he said, bringing my new glass into the living room. He left the knife on the counter, and this time he sat closer to me, in the middle of the couch. "My son has a head of his own and wanted to be a simple deputy. When I realized I could use his position to my advantage, I made sure he had a higher position."

I took the glass and sipped, nearly gagging on the dry, bitter wine. I wasn't sure why anyone would pay so much money for something so disgusting. "And lucky for you, the chief deputy position had just opened up after the former assistant district attorney uncovered the previous chief deputy's alliance with Daniel Crocker."

There was nowhere to set the glass, so I reached out to hand it to Jed, who still stood in between the chair and the sofa, his back to the glass. If nothing else, the move would get him closer to me.

But J.R. saw my gesture and took the glass from me, setting it on the table beside his own.

"Now that my boy is gone, why don't you dispose of your own?" J.R. suggested. "If we're going to talk specifics, I would prefer to have privacy."

Jed's face hardened, leaving me no doubt as to how he felt about the suggestion. But J.R. was a psychopath, and I had no doubt that he would kill Jed if I didn't send him away.

If I were smart, I'd leave with him. But I had come too far to turn back now. "Jed, wait for me outside."

"*No.*"

I looked up at him in surprise.

"I'm not leaving without you."

Anger flooded through me, stealing my senses. He was going to ruin everything. I got to my feet and took a step toward him. "You work for me, Jed Carlisle. You will do as I say." My voice was hard and cold, and it broke my heart to do this to him. Would he hate me later? Better that than risk his life any more than I already had. "Now go wait outside, and I will deal with you later."

He lowered his face, blocking it from J.R.'s view. I could see the question in his eyes. I reached up and patted his cheek. "If you're a good boy, I'll lessen your punishment. Now go."

He hesitated for several long seconds, then stepped over Gentry's body. He shot daggers of hate toward J.R. as he stomped toward the front door.

"You're too soft with him, Lady," J.R. said, his voice silky as soon as the door shut. "If you let them have too much leeway, they will rise up and bite you on the ankle." He paused. "Or the jugular."

I took my seat. "We all have our ways of ensuring our power, J.R. You go your way, and I'll go mine."

"But therein lies a problem. If we are to share the county, then we must agree upon how we rule. And my first order of business will be to dispose of your pet."

"Jed?" I asked, incredulous, as if he'd told me I couldn't have a cookie. "No, I need Jed. He has information about this territory. He helps me keep the men in order."

"But you won't need that with me here," he said, watching me like a hawk.

I cocked my head and gave him a knowing smile. "I like to keep him around for other things. He's *quite* good."

"He can be replaced." His voice took on a husky tone.

"Maybe in bed, but his knowledge of the county is useful. I refuse to dispose of him until I have a firmer handle on how this county works."

"You don't need him for that either."

I released a short laugh. "Your son's been chief deputy about three months and you think you're an expert on the Fenton County underworld? It seems to me he's on the wrong side of the law to give you accurate information."

"He's not my only source."

"Then perhaps you can let me in on how you've been getting your information."

He watched me again, his gaze darting to the window behind me. Damn it, I was fairly certain I'd fallen right into a trap. At least I knew Skeeter was listening, even if he was probably madder than a wet hornet right now. All I had to do was say the code word and he'd send his men in to get me. Hell, he'd probably lead the charge.

J.R. reached up to finger the edge of my veil. "I prefer to keep a few secrets. You obviously feel the same way."

"Mr. Simmons," I said with more force than I felt. "You are much too close for my liking."

"I thought we were getting to know one another." His hand slid down my neck.

I pushed his arm away and stood. "I also like to mix business with pleasure—Jed is proof enough of that—but business always comes first. I would have expected you, of all people, to understand that. Perhaps you're not the man I thought you were."

He was on his feet in an instant, towering over me. "Did you just insult me?"

I was scared to death, but I was also pissed. "I am a woman in a man's world, Mr. Simmons. I did not get where I am today by sleeping my way to the top. I'm sure you didn't either."

He grinned. "No, but I've had my fun."

I lowered my voice. "I like powerful men, J.R. And you certainly intrigue me. But I mean it—for me, business always comes first, and *pleasure*—" I drawled out the word "—comes as my reward for a job well done." I tilted my head slightly. "Will you be part of that reward?"

Surprise flickered in his eyes, followed by what looked like respect. He took a step back, but paused for long enough to run his hand down my bare arm. "I would most *certainly* like to be."

I needed to get him to start confessing. I said the first thing that popped into my head. "I heard how you got the ADA out of office last week. I'm impressed."

He gave me a wicked look. "I have my ways."

Mason had told me I needed him to be as specific as possible. That wasn't nearly specific enough.

"I hear you have sway over many influential people in this county. I heard you used that influence on a judge last summer to get your son's girlfriend out of jail." That wasn't part of Mason's script, but I was looking for anything to stick to him.

I'd made the wrong choice.

He watched me for a moment, as though evaluating me. "So you like powerful men?" he asked, but something was off in his eyes, and I instinctively backed up. "Is that why you hooked up with Malcolm?"

"Malcolm was purely business."

"Oh? Then why hook up with Jed?"

Crap. Why indeed? "Jed was a means to an end."

"So you used him to help you get rid of Malcolm and take over his territory?"

"No. I was willing to bide my time; in fact, I would have preferred it. But you spurred things into motion when you had Gentry kill his two men and set Malcolm up to take the fall. I'd already invested in this county, so I wasn't about to give it up."

"Why reach out to me?"

"Because any fool could see you were making a bid for the county too. I had pieces in play, so it made sense to join forces."

"I don't play well with others."

Unfortunately, that was just about the most incriminating thing he'd said.

Crap. Crap. Crap. I was going about this all wrong.

"You're being dishonest with me, Lady."

My heart leapt into my throat. "And why would you think that?"

He held his hands out to his side. "I'm honest about who I am. I'm J.R. Simmons, the most powerful man in southern Arkansas—soon to be the entire state. You know who *you* are dealing with, but I have no idea who you are. Why would I align myself with a ghost?"

"You want me to take off my hat?"

"Among other things."

Under any other circumstances, I would have thought he meant my clothing, but I was fairly certain that he meant my identity.

"Ah . . ." he murmured after several moments passed. "That's what I thought."

I nearly said the code word, but I suddenly thought of another tactic. "You think I'm being dishonest with you. Who exactly do you think I am?"

"I think you're Malcolm's whore and he's sent you in here as a sacrifice to set up his revenge." His eyes hardened. "He knows I'm coming for him, and that boy's not smart enough to tuck tail and run. So you're here to string me along, and Malcolm's going to come in for the finale."

I slowly lifted my hand to my head, took my hat off, and tossed it to the floor. "No veil now, J.R. Just me." I lifted my chin. "And I'm not Skeeter Malcolm's whore." My voice hardened. "I'm no one's whore. The God's honest truth is that I'm here of my own free will, but you wouldn't know anything about God, would you? You think you're a god in your own right."

Recognition flashed in his eyes. "This *is* a surprise, and those are so rare these days."

He knew who I was. Well, he was in for a bigger surprise. I wasn't the timid woman he'd met at his house five months ago. "No, I suppose it's difficult to be surprised when you're so busy orchestrating so many people's lives."

He laughed. "You're right. I *am* a god."

"I guess you are, aren't you? You hold the power of life and death in your hands. How many people have you killed?"

He grinned. "Countless." He looked around. "And I'm going to kill her too, Malcolm, so you better get in here before I get to work."

I shook my head. "I already told you that he didn't send me. Last I heard, he took off to try and find Pete Mooney so he'd confess to killing that little boy for you."

"Malcolm's a wimp. It was an easy job. Anybody could hold a kid's head underwater."

My stomach churned. "If it was so easy, why didn't you do it yourself?"

A slow smile spread across his face. "I did."

"*What?*"

"I lost two men to that job, so I went and did it myself. I was running out of time."

"So you brought Mason here to torment Malcolm, but why are you trying to kill him? Why kidnap me last night, then plan to kill me?"

He shook his head. "I didn't. I had no part in that, but I have to say I do enjoy watching people suffer. Whoever's orchestrating that scheme is brilliant. If it had been left up to me, I would have sent you to prison. It would have been an effective lesson for my son and Deveraux. There was no way you were going to get out of those trumped-up charges. I paid too many people to make sure that didn't happen."

Had Kate orchestrated my kidnapping on her own? Or was it someone else entirely?

But my momentary shock was all the time he needed.

Before I realized he was moving, he had reached the island and was grabbing his knife. In a quick move, I pulled the gun out of the elastic band on my leg.

I took several steps back, pointing the gun at him.

He grinned, and his eyes sparkled with excitement. He was loving every minute of this. "You won't shoot me."

"You're wrong. I've shot men before."

In my peripheral vision, I saw movement at the back of the house. I nearly fell over when I saw Joe walk in through back door. He had on jeans and a solid green T-shirt under his winter jacket, and he looked like he was ready to kill someone. Did that mean he was here to help his father, or was he here as the chief deputy sheriff?

But it had distracted me enough to give J.R. time to lunge for me, slashing with his knife. Pain tore through my upper arm, but I remained upright, managing to keep from tripping over Mick Gentry's body.

"Dad!" Joe shouted, pointing a gun at his father. "Drop it!"

J.R. stepped over the body and grabbed my injured arm, making me cry out in pain. He pulled my back against his chest and held the knife to my throat.

Mason appeared in the back door, shoving one of Skeeter's men away. Panic filled his face when he saw me, but Joe's expression was stone cold.

Jed had already come through the front door, his gun raised, Skeeter on his heels.

J.R. began to laugh.

"Dad," Joe said, taking a step closer. "Just put down the knife and let her go."

He continued to laugh. "You joined forces with Malcolm, eh? Not so different from your father after all."

"Dad. Just let her go." Desperation saturated his words.

"Rose Gardner is worth more to me dead than alive."

"No!" Mason protested, moving next to Joe. "If we all watch you murder her, you'll get charged with murder in the first degree. You might even find yourself facing the death penalty. You'll only have a chance if you let her go."

J.R. paused. "Malcolm and his lackey will shoot me anyway."

"No! He won't," Mason protested. "Malcolm, tell him!"

Skeeter's face turned so hard he looked like he was made of granite. "Let her go, Simmons. In fact, everyone get out of the room. This is between the two of us."

"That's not going to happen," Joe said, his voice cold. "He's going to let her go, and then I'm going to escort him to the sheriff's station."

J.R. laughed again.

"If you kill her, I will rip you apart limb by limb," Skeeter growled, taking several steps toward us.

J.R. jerked me backward, the knife-edge scraping the delicate skin on my neck. I felt a tiny trickle of blood trail down my neck as Mason's and Joe's eyes widened with fear. Skeeter looked even more murderous, as though it was possible. Jed's expression suggested he'd help Skeeter carry out the deed.

"What has you so fascinated with her?" J.R. laughed. "All the time I've known you, you've never had more than a momentary interest in a woman."

"She's a business asset."

J.R. chuckled. "No. I can see it's more than that."

J.R. was going to make Skeeter admit his feelings for me. I couldn't let this man hurt anyone else I cared about.

The gun was still in my hand, but I had no idea how to use it to get myself free. If I tried to shoot him, he'd slit my throat in a heartbeat. In fact, I had a pretty good feeling he'd slit my throat anyway. I looked around the room filled with men desperate to save me, then decided to spare them the guilt of failing.

I grabbed J.R.'s wrist with my left hand. "J.R.," I said, sounding much tougher than I felt. "This is your last warning to let me go."

"You're threatening me?" He laughed and his arm lifted slightly, preparing to slice. Joe and Mason got a panicked look in their eyes, and I knew it was time for me to make my move.

I held the gun tip against his thigh and pulled the trigger while I yanked his wrist away from my neck with all my might. He cried out in pain and crumpled to the floor, the knife still in his hand, his arm outstretched.

Joe rushed toward me, but I turned and got a good stomp on J.R.'s hand with my stiletto heel, partially embedding the end into his now-open palm. "I told you that you were too close for my liking."

J.R.'s eyes were livid. "I'm going to kill you!"

I started to offer a retort, but J.R. reached for me with his good hand. Joe jerked me away from his father, handing me off to Mason as he kicked the knife across the room.

Joe leaned over his father while J.R. continued to shout a string of threats against me and everyone else in the room.

Mason gathered me into his arms and held me tight against his chest, leading me into the kitchen around the back side of the island while chaos ensued ten feet away. I looked up at him in shock. "You said you weren't coming."

He shook his head. "I'm sorry I had to tell you that. I was worried Skeeter would insist on getting his own brand of justice, and then we might never get your charges dropped. We needed someone from law enforcement to be here. Which meant we needed Joe. If Skeeter had believed I was bringing anyone else into this mix, particularly J.R.'s own son, he would have tied me up. Or worse. And I couldn't tell you in the bathroom because I had the bug in my hand."

"But you said Joe was missing."

"He was. I just had to know where to look."

"And where was that?"

"His old house. I have no idea where he was all day, but tonight he was sitting on the front porch."

"Where we first met," I whispered in dismay.

Sadness filled his eyes. "Yeah."

"How did you know you could trust him?"

"I saw it in his eyes when I was giving him my statement about your kidnapping at the sheriff's station. Then when I got that message . . . I almost told him the truth, Rose. I was worried he would do something harmful to himself."

"How'd you get him to agree to help?"

"I told him your father had set up your kidnapping. He was more than eager to jump on board."

"But J.R. swore he didn't do it."

"Like I'd believe anything that man said," he said in disgust.

"But Kate . . ."

"I mentioned your theory to Joe—without telling him about the incriminating evidence you found in her apartment—I thought I'd leave it up to your discretion. But he assured me she had nothing to do with it. He claims she was nearly as upset as he was when she heard the news."

I pursed my lips. "I still don't trust her. I'm going to tell Joe about goin' into her apartment." Then a new realization hit me. "Joe knows I'm the Lady in Black," I whispered.

He grimaced, lowering his mouth next to my ear. "Not necessarily. I told him you'd come up with the crazy scheme to dress up as her to trap his father and somehow got Malcolm to go along."

I leaned back to face him. "And he bought it?"

He gave me a sad smile. "Do you really think he considers you capable of such a thing?" He pulled his hand off my arm. "You're bleeding. We need to put something on this."

He opened a kitchen drawer, but Jed approached us from the hall and handed him a bath towel. "It's clean. I checked."

I looked around the room. "Where's Skeeter?"

Jed cringed. "He took off."

Mason scowled. "Joe's going to need a statement from him."

Skeeter's pride had to be wounded by all of this. I wasn't surprised he left, but I wished I'd had a chance to talk to him first. "Can it wait until the morning?"

Mason studied my face. "I suppose that's up to Joe."

"Did you hear what J.R. said?" I asked. "Is it enough for Joe to use to get my charges dropped?"

"Once I showed up with Joe and convinced Malcolm that we were working with him and not against him, he gave us access to your mic feed. And the cameras."

"So you saw and heard it all?"

"Yeah." He looked into my eyes, but something was missing. Maybe he was just tired. "You handled yourself very well. You're right. You're good at it."

I wasn't sure how to respond to that, so I said nothing.

"If nothing else, J.R. will face charges for the murder of Mick Gentry. It was captured on tape, and we have eyewitnesses. Maybe if Simmons is in jail, people will be willing to turn state's evidence and confess to setting up your charges."

I turned my attention to the man who had destroyed so many lives. Joe already had his father in handcuffs on the floor, and J.R hadn't lost any steam issuing his threats. "You'll pay for this, Deveraux! I'll destroy you!"

"You can try," Mason said, sounding exhausted. "But you'll find it difficult behind bars."

I had to wonder how difficult it would actually be. J.R. Simmons behind bars could still be a threat.

The towel Joe had wrapped around J.R.'s leg was

already soaked with blood, and a new worry hit me.

"Do you think he'll die?" I asked.

"We wouldn't get so lucky," Jed murmured.

"No," Mason agreed. "But his leg's going to be messed up for some time."

"So if he's gonna make it, what'll happen to him?"

"He'll be arrested for murder and attempted murder and a whole host of other charges, and I suspect there will be a grand jury to investigate the crimes on this tape. They can't press charges from what he said in the tapes, but it can open an investigation. And like I said, people might be willing to turn state's evidence." He paused. "You'll probably have to testify."

"Will people find out I'm the Lady in Black?"

Mason lowered his voice. "Honestly, I'm not sure anyone would believe it. We can stick with the story that you assumed her persona to trap Simmons. We'll need Malcolm and Jed to testify about that."

"We will," Jed said without hesitation.

"But you would have to commit perjury, Mason," I whispered.

His face was expressionless. "I told you I'd do anything to keep you safe. That included."

I might have gotten out of my mess with J.R., but I was still smack in the middle of another. "I love you, Mason."

He searched my eyes, then pulled my cheek to his chest and held me tight. "I love you too."

I closed my eyes, feeling renewed hope we'd work this out.

He just needed time.

# Chapter Thirty-Three

Mason wanted to take me to the hospital for my arm; I refused. It had become a bad routine. Rose gets into danger and someone goes to the E.R.

I was ready for a new chapter in my life.

Besides, I was fairly certain J.R. Simmons would need to go to the E.R. Let him fill the vacant spot.

Joe said he would come by the farmhouse to take our statements in the morning. Since he himself had been an eyewitness to J.R.'s confessions—and crimes—he had everything he needed to press charges. Mason wandered off to talk to a sheriff's deputy, so I took the opportunity to tell Joe about my suspicions about Kate, including the evidence I'd found in her apartment.

Worry filled his eyes. "I know my sister and I don't see eye to eye, but I honestly don't think she's capable of such a thing, Rose."

"But you'll look into it, right?"

"I'll need to deal with this mess first," he said, watching as his father was hauled out of the house on an ambulance stretcher, escorted by two deputies I didn't recognize. "But I promise I'll look into it first chance I get."

"Will you?" I asked, but my words were missing any bite. Instead, they sounded as weary as I felt.

He looked me square in the eye. "No more sweeping anything under the rug. My family's goin' to atone for our misdeeds."

"Thank you." I paused. "I'm sorry you thought I was dead. I . . . I know how hard that must have been."

His eyes clouded. "I want to know more about all of that, but I'll take your statement in the morning when I question you about what happened here."

"Okay."

I started to turn away, but he said softly, "Rose."

I turned back to face him.

"I don't know what I would have done if . . ."

I gave him a determined look. "You would have been just fine, Joe Simmons."

"Maybe so, but Joe McAllister wouldn't have been."

And the sad truth was that Joe McAllister was probably the man Mason had found on Joe's old front porch. I didn't know what to do about that either.

I started to look for Mason, but I saw Jed standing in a corner, taking in the whole scene. I'd worried that he and Skeeter would be in trouble with the law. Joe assured me that neither of them would face charges, at least not for their role in taking J.R. down, but what would be the long-term repercussions? The fact that he and Skeeter had walked into this with eyes wide open didn't make me feel any better. The truth was, all of this had been orchestrated at my insistence.

He smiled and held out my personal cell phone as I approached him. "Skeeter says he'll be in touch."

"Okay." I tried to hide my hurt feelings. I couldn't very well blame him for leaving without a goodbye. He'd said having friends would be his downfall. Did he see tonight as proof of that? Would he cut me out of his life entirely? I was surprised at how much the thought made my heart ache.

"I'm gonna miss you, Rose."

A lump formed in my throat. My Lady in Black days were over. The guilt that accompanied the disappointment was suffocating. "You won't miss all the trouble I've caused."

A wry grin twisted his mouth. "Life's definitely gonna be a whole lot duller."

I threw my arms around his neck, and I didn't care who saw. This man had saved my life countless times, and I owed him my unflinching friendship.

He held me tight for several seconds, then said in a brisk voice, "If you ever need help with anything—anything at all—I'm just a phone call away. Skeeter too."

"Thank you, Jed," I said as I stepped back, wiping the tears off my cheeks. "I owe you more than I can ever repay."

He hesitated, then lowered his voice. "You made Skeeter care about something more than his kingdom. Something I've never been able to manage. That's payment enough right there."

"But I hurt him in the process."

He slowly shook his head. "Sometimes you have to break something to make it stronger. Remember that." Then he turned around and left me alone.

Mason stood across the room, his eyes fixed firmly on me. How much had he seen of our exchange? What did he think of me now?

To my relief, Mason walked toward me and wrapped an arm around my back. "Let's go home."

I nodded. "Okay."

He was subdued on the way to the farmhouse, but he had plenty of reason to be distraught. He'd called Maeve as soon as we got into the car, apologizing over and over again for letting her think the worst. At one point he had even broken into tears, but I couldn't shake the thought that he wasn't himself with her either.

During the drive, I called Violet first and then Neely Kate to assure them I was okay. I gave them an abbreviated explanation of the last twenty-four hours, although the version of events I shared with Violet was condensed to leave out as much about Skeeter as possible. Both went through a rollercoaster of emotions. Violet's reaction to my resurrection was best described as shock followed by overwhelming relief, and while Neely Kate certainly seemed to feel the same way, her voice lacked its usual exuberance. However, there was no denying that my best friend had been through a multitude of traumatic events over the last few months. It killed me that I was now one of them. I knew I had a lot to make up to them, even if *this* part of the situation wasn't my fault.

Mason offered to call Jonah and fill him in on the situation so I could call Bruce Wayne. My business partner sounded wary when he answered, as though he thought he might be picking up a call from a ghost. "Rose?"

"It's really me."

"They said you were dead," he said in a shaky voice. "And that Mason had been kidnapped and probably murdered too."

"We're both okay. I got J.R. Simmons to confess."

"You're kidding."

"And tonight the Lady in Black officially retired. I'm done with my brief foray into the crime world of Fenton County."

He snorted. I wasn't sure why, but I was afraid to ask.

"Listen, I want you to know . . . about that day last November when I convinced you to take me to Skeeter . . . I put you in a terrible position, and I'm so sorry."

"It was a mutual decision, Rose. We did it together."

"But I continued on without you and hurt you in the process. I'm sorry."

"Get some sleep. I'll talk to you tomorrow."

I hung up and caught Mason watching me with that same look he got when he was working out a particularly complex problem.

When we went to bed, Mason held me in his arms, but it felt like he was going through the motions. How could I be in the arms of the man I loved, yet feel so alone? The fact that he hadn't given me my ring back scared the bejiggers out of me, and I was afraid to push my luck and ask.

The next morning I woke up and found Mason standing in the doorway to the nursery. I got up and padded over to him, shivering with cold. "Mason, what are you doin'?"

"Just thinking."

I tugged on his arm. "Come on back to bed."

He looked down at me with a dull look in his eyes. "I'm going to take a shower. I got a text from Detective Pearson. He said the secretary of state's office is sending someone down first thing this morning to question the DA. Looks like he might be out of a job, which means I'll probably get my old one back."

I held onto his arm. "Oh, Mason! That's so wonderful. I'm so happy for you."

"Thanks." He bent over and gave me a light kiss, then walked into the bathroom.

I deserved his aloofness and more, so I shook it off.

I texted Joe to let him know that Mason and I were headed to our separate offices, so he could find us there rather than at the farm. He sent back that he'd drop by to see me later in the morning.

Mason got ready in record time, and it seemed as if he was about to head out the door without a goodbye when he suddenly stopped and walked over to me. He cupped my cheek and gave me a sad smile. "I love you, Rose. Please don't doubt that. I just need time."

"I know." I wrapped my arms around his neck and clung to him. At least he was still here. He was still trying.

I stopped by Maeve's house to get Muffy and was nearly tackled by her and Neely Kate. Maeve was upset that Mason had been so distant. I told her I'd shared her premonition with Mason . . . and how he'd reacted to that and the news of all the things I'd been keeping from him.

"He's upset with me too," I said. "We just need to give him some space."

Neely Kate picked up my left hand. "Where's your ring?"

"I had to give it him to hold before my meeting with J.R."

"He didn't give it back to you?"

I glanced down at my hand again, fear sinking its claws into me. "There was so much going on, he must have forgotten." I forced a smile. "He's meeting with someone from the secretary of state's office. I think he's goin' to get his old job back."

"That's wonderful," Neely Kate said, but I could see the worry in her eyes. Both women were so unlike themselves, talking about everything except for the giant elephant in the room—that Mason might have changed his mind after finding out everything. It became overwhelming, particularly because I didn't know where Mason and I stood with each other. "I need to go to the office. I told Joe I'd meet him there to give my statement."

Maeve pulled me into a hug. "Hang in there, sweet girl. My son can be hardheaded, but he'll come around. He loves you. Love will prevail."

"I hope so."

I was already walking out the front door when she called me back.

"Rose, I've gotten more work done on the journal page." I stopped in my tracks. "Although it might be a moot point now," she added.

I spun around to face her, letting the door close behind me. "No, I don't think it is. What did you find?"

"It says something about a police chief, a shed, and something you were looking for—a key."

I sucked in a breath. The Henryetta police chief had been killed in a break-in days before the fire. Maybe this was another of J.R.'s sins. Anything that could keep him in jail longer was worth pursuing. "That's great. Thank you."

"My shorthand book should be here tomorrow. Do you want me to keep deciphering it?"

I cocked my head. "Would you mind?" I lowered my voice. "But let's still keep this between the four of us—Mason included . . . at least until we know more."

She nodded, a grim look in her eyes. "No problem."

Neely Kate followed me to the office downtown. As we walked into the cozy space together, I asked, "How are things with you and Ronnie?"

She made a face. "The same."

I wondered what would happen with all the people in the county who'd offered their allegiance to Mick Gentry. Would they kiss Skeeter's butt now? What would that mean for Ronnie? I was just as worried about him as I was about my best friend. But I had my own issues to deal with at the moment.

We'd barely gotten settled in the office when Joe dropped in, looking even more exhausted than I felt. Muffy jumped all over him, covering him with licks and kisses.

He scooped her up into his arms. "Good to see you giving me love again after the way you growled at me in the barn. I could use a little affection today."

I put my hands on my hips in an attempt to give him attitude, but my heart wasn't in it. I just wanted answers. "You never did tell me what you were doing out there."

"I *did* tell you—you just chose not to believe me. I was worried about you, so I was checking your land. And I did hear something out there. I'm more positive than ever that it wasn't you."

"Do you think it was the kidnappers?"

A frown creased the lines around his eyes. "Your guess is as good as mine. Why don't you tell me what happened at Jaspers?"

We sat down, and I told him about my kidnapping. I hesitated on the next part, but I told him that Jed saved me and I decided to use it to my advantage. That I suggested I meet his father as the Lady in Black and Skeeter went along with it.

He paused and looked into my face, worry in his eyes. "If it's okay with you, I'd like to leave any mention of the Lady in Black out of this. We'll just say you were dressed up and wearing a hat. If we include anything about the Lady, it will completely blow up. It's bad enough as it is without people thinking you could be her."

"Okay . . ." I said, stunned. "Thank you."

"Can you believe my father truly believes you're her? The *real* Lady in Black?" He laughed, but it sounded forced. "Crazy, I know. But he's agreed to keep it quiet."

My heart skipped a beat. "Why would he do that?"

He refused to look me in the eye. "He just did."

"Joe. What did you do?"

He glanced up, determination making his face rigid. "I got you into this mess. I swear to you I'll get you out of it. I told you the truth that night in your barn. I was working on something. I still am. Just because my father's in police custody in the Henryetta Hospital doesn't mean this is over. We need to make sure he's good and neutered."

I believed he meant it, despite the fact that he was talking about his father, but I couldn't dismiss my lingering fears. "Did you check on Kate's apartment?"

"Yeah, I stopped by for a brotherly visit. There was nothing there, of course. All the things you saw were gone."

"Where do you think it all went?"

He shook his head. "I suspect she was investigating our father. She was definitely happy to find out he's about to be remanded into the Fenton County Jail."

"But that doesn't make any sense. Everything I found was about Mason."

He sighed. "You know she wants you and me back together. Maybe she was hopin' to dig up some dirt on him to sway you." He held up his hands in surrender. "And no. I don't condone her behavior."

"Joe, what I saw was far more than diggin' up dirt. It was a full-on investigation."

He shrugged. "And without any evidence, there's not a dammed thing I can do about it. But I promise to keep an eye on her, okay?"

It wasn't okay, but I wasn't sure what else I could do.

Other than keep an eye on her myself.

"If neither Kate nor your father were behind my kidnapping and the attempts on Mason's life, who was?"

"If you had asked me last week, I would have told you I wasn't sure. But after last night, I *know* my father did it. This is totally his M.O."

I had to agree, except for one little detail that had kept bothering me. "So why did he tell me he didn't do it?"

"So he wouldn't incriminate himself more than he already had? So he'd make you think someone else was out to get you? A million reasons, but the bottom line is that he did it. He's just playing more mind games with us."

More mind games than he even knew. I wondered if I should tell him about his father's involvement in Savannah's murder and how he wanted to hurt Joe while reminding his son of his leash. But he was already hurt over me. I wasn't sure what good it would do, not to mention the fact that it wasn't my place to tell him.

I nodded. "Okay. Thank you. But be careful if you keep digging around with your father, okay?"

He grinned. "I'm the one who's supposed to say that."

Neely Kate and Bruce Wayne had sat quietly on the other side of the room and listened in to our conversation. I didn't mind. I was happy that I wouldn't have to go through the ordeal again. Now I only needed to fill in the details I hadn't given for the record.

Joe stood. "I have a million things I need to do. I better get goin'."

I walked him to the door, and he glanced over at the courthouse. "I was wrong about Mason, Rose. He really does love you. And tell him congratulations on getting his job back. I hated being a part of that, and I told the secretary of state's office everything. I'm not sure how much longer I'll have a job myself."

"I'm sorry, Joe."

He shook his head. "We have to face the consequences of our actions sometime. I've been running from mine for too long." He smiled and ran a finger over the worry lines on my forehead. "Hey, none of that. I'm good with this. It's nice to stop running, you know?"

I nodded. "I do know." I needed to give myself the same pep talk.

"Look, I know you love Mason, and he's one damn lucky guy. I gave a lot of thought to what you said the other day, about me still seeing you as the inexperienced woman I met on my front porch. There's a lot of truth to that. But watching you last night . . ." His eyes filled with awe. "You're right. You're not that woman anymore. But I'd love to be friends with the woman you've become. If you would let me."

I smiled, tears filling my eyes. "Of course. I'd like that too."

He gave me a sad smile, and as I watched him walk away I wondered what the future held for him. If he would lose his job. How much longer he'd stay in Fenton County.

I turned my gaze to the courthouse, feeling like the life I wanted so badly was slipping through my fingers. Why hadn't Mason let me know about his job? The truth was, I *knew* why, and it made me feel more helpless than ever.

I was tired of waiting for life to sort itself out. I was going to take matters into my own hands.

I hurried over to my desk and grabbed my purse and my coat. "I'll be right back. I'm gonna pick up some lunch at Merilee's and take it over to Mason."

Worry filled Neely Kate's eyes, but she said, "That's a good idea."

Bruce Wayne only watched in silence.

I bolted out the door and into the cold. As I started across the street, I thought I saw a suspicious man out of the corner of my eye. When I turned back to look, I slammed into someone.

"Oh!" I exclaimed. "I'm so—" I paused when I realized I'd run into Hilary. "Sorry."

Indignation covered her face. "Haven't you caused enough trouble, Rose Gardner? I heard that you brought false charges against J.R. Simmons. Do you really think he'll stand for that?"

"He won't be standing anytime soon, considering that I shot him in the leg."

She gasped in disgust. "I'm not surprised you'd joke about such a thing. It only shows your true character." She pinned her gaze on me. "You may very well have disabled him for life. I'm sure he'll be suing you."

Fear shot down my spine at that thought, but suing me would be like squeezing blood out of a turnip. "Well, good luck and Godspeed to him."

I started to walk around her, but she blocked my path.

Anger filled her eyes. "Do you know what you put poor Joe through? He was overcome with grief."

I didn't need to be reminded of my guilt, particularly not by her. Besides, how could she have the audacity to chastise me for getting kidnapped? "I've already talked with Joe, but perhaps I should call him to apologize again for letting someone accost me in Jaspers, haul me off to a cabin in the woods, and almost kill me. How incredibly thoughtless of me."

Her mouth pursed into a thin line, and her cheeks tinged pink.

I released a sigh. "I've had a very exhausting week, and I'm really tired of this thing we do, so I think I'll be on my way."

I started to step around her again, but she blocked my path.

"Hilary. What the Sam Hill do you want?"

She opened her mouth to answer, but someone behind me interrupted.

"Rose Gardner," Carter Hale drawled behind me. "Just the person I was looking for."

I spun around to face him.

He shot a glance to Hilary. "Sorry to steal her away from you, Ms. Wilder, but my client and I have important things to discuss."

Hilary looked like she'd just swallowed a toad. Then she took a breath and a serene look covered her face. "Rose, you're one of the unluckiest people I know. You really do need to be more careful and stop worrying everyone in town."

"What just happened?" Carter asked as he watched her sashay away. "She looked like she was about to rip your head off, then she turned all peaches and cream."

"That's Hilary." I watched her turn into Merilee's and shook my head. She was probably the unhappiest person I knew, including Miss Mildred. Given my own current situation, I couldn't help feeling a tiny bit sorry for her.

A grin plastered across Carter's face. "You sure know how to make friends."

"Ha. Ha," I muttered. "You just keep findin' me with unpleasant people."

"Be mindful of the company you keep. You keep jumping deeper into the cesspool."

His meaning wasn't lost on me. "Did you really need to see me, or were you playing white knight?"

"I just left the courthouse, so I really was on my way to see you." He winked. "Rest assured. I only play white knight if I have ulterior motives."

I considered calling him on his statement—he'd helped Neely Kate before without ulterior motives—but I was more interested in what he had to say. "Do you want to head into your office?"

"No need. This will be quick." He grinned. "All your charges were dropped."

"*What?*"

"I just left your boyfriend and the state investigator. When one of the DA's cohorts heard J.R. is facing big time charges, he admitted to knowing the judge was bribed by the big guy to put you away." He shifted his weight. "The thing about living at the top is that people are often eager to see you fall, and once you do, they'll turn into piranhas. I suspect this assistant is the first of many."

"But why didn't Mason tell me himself?"

He shrugged, oblivious to the drama of my love life. "He was busy with the investigator. So he asked me to tell you."

I felt the blood go rushing to my toes. Before Tuesday night Mason would have never left that errand to Carter Hale.

Carter blinked in surprise. "Why don't you look more excited about this?"

"Oh! I am!" I said, forcing myself to recover. "I'm just in shock is all. I didn't expect it to happen so fast. Thank you."

He leaned closer and lowered his voice. "Skeeter informed me about everything that happened over the last forty-eight hours. I'm glad it all worked out."

I nodded. "And Glenn Stout? What happens to the bail money?"

"He'll get it all back. But you can bet we'll be keeping an eye on who picks it up."

I knew exactly who he meant by *we*, and it had nothing to do with anyone in law enforcement. "Tell Skeeter not to do something stupid on my behalf."

"Skeeter Malcolm doesn't do stupid, Rose. He's trying to rebuild his shattered empire." He saw my concern and tapped my nose. "Now don't you be worrying about Skeeter. He's tough as the hide on a bull. He's gonna rebuild it all bigger and better than it was before." A grin twisted his lips. "If you ever need help again, whether Skeeter's involved or not, give me a call. You've been one of my most entertaining clients to date. And that's saying something."

I muttered thanks as he ambled toward his office. Hilary was still in Merilee's, and after talking to Carter, I was fairly certain I was the last person Mason wanted to see.

I headed back toward the landscape office, defeat and worry slowing my footsteps. Neely Kate met me at the door. "What happened with Hilary?"

I started to answer her, but I noticed a man coming around the corner of the courthouse. He crossed to my side of the street, then stopped on the sidewalk not far from the office. Watching me, he pulled the stocking cap on his head down the side of his face.

"Who is that?" I asked, walking out onto the sidewalk. Something about him set off bells in my head.

"He looks familiar." But I wasn't sure how. Almost every part of him was covered up, including his cheek.

"Who?" Neely Kate asked, following behind me.

When he realized I was watching, his eyes widened and he tugged harder on the cap.

It was lunchtime, which meant there were more people on the sidewalks than there would be later in the day. He ducked around two elderly women headed into the antique store.

"Who are you talking about?"

"That man—" I turned around to find him, but he was gone. I shook my head. "I'm paranoid." I was seeing suspicious folks everywhere.

She wrapped her arm around my shoulders. "After everything you've been through over the last week or so, you're entitled. Now let's get back inside. It's freezing out here."

I let her lead me back into the warm office, wondering if I really had lost it.

After I told Neely Kate and Bruce Wayne the good news I'd received about my charges, Neely Kate went and picked up lunch for all three of us. She knew not to ask why I'd changed my mind about visiting Mason. When she got back, I only took a few nibbles of my sandwich as I filled my friends in on all the details I'd glossed over in my police report.

When I was done, Neely Kate asked, "Why do you think you'll still need the journal page? Seems like Joe's got enough evidence stacked up to put his daddy away for a long time."

"I'm not sure," I said. "J.R. Simmons is a pretty sneaky guy. They might need all the help they can get to put him away for good. Besides, for all I know, the original journal's gone."

"What about those two keys?" she asked.

I sighed. "Maybe some mysteries are better left in the past."

A dark shadow crossed over her face. "I agree."

I didn't hear from Mason until mid-afternoon. He appeared at the front door of the landscaping office as I was showing Neely Kate how to use the landscape software on my computer. Bruce Wayne had gone to bid on a commercial job.

As soon as Muffy saw him, she started to run for him, but then she stopped and hurried back to her bed under Bruce Wayne's desk. I took that as a bad omen.

Mason shut the door behind him, his face pale. "Neely Kate, could you give us a bit? Maybe fifteen minutes." He pulled out his wallet and started to grab some money. "Why don't you go grab something at Dena's Bakery? My treat."

She gave me a worried look, then stood and grabbed her coat. "Put your money away, Mason. I don't mind giving you and your fiancée a few minutes alone." She stopped next to him, looking like she was about to say something, then hurried out the door.

A guilty look washed across Mason's face.

My stomach fell to my feet as I stood next to my chair, unsure of what to do.

"Joe told me about your job. Congratulations. When do you start again?" I'd hoped he would text me with the news, but he hadn't. He was angry with me. I deserved that. And more.

"I'm not sure yet." He moved closer and stopped several feet in front of me. "Carter told you about your charges?"

I nodded, not trusting myself to speak past the lump in my throat.

"Can we sit and talk?"

I nodded again, fighting tears. I wasn't sure I could do this.

But I sat in my desk chair, and he sat in the one Neely Kate had vacated. He looked down at his hands before lifting his gaze. "I told them I'd fill in temporarily until I've made a decision."

"Did they kick out the DA? Are they offering you *his* job?"

"No." He rubbed the back of his neck, glancing down at Muffy under Bruce Wayne's desk. "After his assistant caved, they're almost certainly going to boot him out of office, but there's been no official decision yet."

"Oh." Then it hit me, and I struggled to take a breath. "*Oh.*"

He stared into my eyes. "Rose, I love you. You have to know that."

I remained frozen for several agonizing seconds, then my terror burst free like water from a busted dam. "I'm so sorry, Mason," I forced out, trying to hold back my tears. "I'm so sorry."

"I know you are, sweetheart. I know."

Hearing him call me sweetheart broke me, and the tears started flowing. "I did it for you, Mason. I hated lying, but I had to save you. I had to do it." I was nearly hysterical. The thought of life without him was unthinkable.

He pulled me to his chest, running a hand over my hair. "I know you did, sweetheart. I know. And you will never know how much I love you for that."

I pulled away from him, searching his face. "Please, Mason," I begged. "I know I've hurt you, and I know you don't trust me, but I'll tell you everything from now on. I promise." A sob burst from me. "*Please* don't leave me."

He broke down and tears fell down his cheeks as he got to his feet. "I've been thinking about this non-stop since I found out about it Tuesday night." He knelt in front of me with anguish in his eyes. "I can forgive you for doing this to save me. What kind of bastard would I be if I didn't? And I'm sure I can eventually get over the hurt and the distrust, but there's one thing I just can't get over." He paused, and I forced myself to calm down and listen to him.

"What?"

His eyes hardened. "The first time you went to him, you weren't doing it to save my life or even yours. You went to get your money back. Money I tried to give you." He got to his feet. "And I can forgive you for that too. I know how stubborn and pigheaded and . . ." He released a loud groan and pushed out a sob. "But you went to that damned auction, Rose. You went there thinking you were pregnant with our baby!"

*Oh, God.* I clambered to my feet and grabbed his arm, frantic. "I was desperate, Mason. I know it's no excuse. None."

He looked down at me, his face twisted with heartbreak. "I was the assistant district attorney, Rose," he said, his voice cold. "I was your boyfriend. Why wouldn't you come to me?"

I took a step back. "I don't know."

He broke down again, covering his forehead with his hands and crying for several seconds before he dropped them and stared at me. "I can forgive you for everything else, but I don't know if I can forgive you for that."

"Mason!" I broke down, anew. "I'm so sorry."

"You keep saying that, Rose." He put his clenched fist over his chest, trying to catch his breath. "You keep saying you're sorry, but my heart is still broken."

I fell into my chair, trying to settle down. "Mason. *Please.* I'll do anything. I don't want to lose you."

He shook his head. "I think it's too late."

"No." I stood again and grabbed his arm with new determination. "Don't say that. You said you love me. Remember?" I smiled through my tears. "It *can't* be too late."

He gently pushed my hand off his arm and took a step back. "Maybe love isn't enough."

I broke down again. "Mason, just please give me another chance. I can't lose you. *Please.*"

He started to cry. "I need time. I need more time to think this through."

I grabbed onto the sliver of hope he gave me like a drowning man to a log. I nodded, trying to catch my breath. "Okay. Time is good."

He stared at Bruce Wayne's desk. "I'm going by the farm to pick up some of my things."

His words sunk deep into my bones. This was really happening.

But maybe Joe was right. Maybe it was time for me to face the consequences of my actions. And maybe Jed was right too. Something better would be built from the pieces. Even if it ripped my soul to shreds. "Will you stay with your mother?"

"That might be kind of awkward with Neely Kate there."

"She can stay with me." To my chagrin, I started to cry again.

"No," he said quietly. "I'll just stay in a motel for a few days. I'm upset with my mother too." He turned to face me, looking like he was about to say something, then shook his head. "I need to go," he said, wiping his face. "If you need me, you know you can call me. And if you find yourself in a dangerous situation, call Joe."

I didn't answer. I just watched him walk out the door. He needed time, and I'd give it to him.

For once, I hoped time was on my side.

Thirty-Six and a Half Motives
May 17, 2016

\*\*\*\*

Center Stage: A Magnolia Steele Mystery
March 15, 2016

The first book in the new mystery series by Denise Grover
Swank

If you like Rose, then you should try
The Wedding Pact Series!

Start with the New York Times and multiple USA Today
Bestseller—The Substitute!

Then continue with the USA Today bestselling The Player
and The Gambler.

*Quirks accepted. Family protected.*
*Ghosts expected.*
*Welcome to the Lowcountry.*

Try the 1<sup>st</sup> installment, *Not Quite Dead*,
for FREE on eBook!

In the *Lowcountry Mystery* series, by Lyla Payne, Graciela Harper returns to small town Heron Creek, SC to get her life back on track. What she finds is that while it's not *technically* true that you can't go home again, things won't be the same when you do.

With her first love married to one of her childhood best friends, her estranged cousin trapped in a dangerous relationship, her grandfather navigating his final days and unwanted attention from the town's sexy new mayor, the last thing Gracie needs is a ghost begging her to solve a centuries old mystery.

But that's just what she's going to get.

# ABOUT THE AUTHOR

New York Times and USA Today bestselling author Denise Grover Swank was born in Kansas City, Missouri and lived in the area until she was nineteen. Then she became a nomadic gypsy, living in five cities, four states and ten houses over the course of ten years before she moved back to her roots. She speaks English and smattering of Spanish and Chinese which she learned through an intensive Nick Jr. immersion period. Her hobbies include witty Facebook comments (in own her mind) and dancing in her kitchen with her children. (Quite badly if you believe her offspring.) Hidden talents include the gift of justification and the ability to drink massive amounts of caffeine and still fall asleep within two minutes. Her lack of the sense of smell allows her to perform many unspeakable tasks. She has six children and hasn't lost her sanity. Or so she leads you to believe.

www.denisegroverswank.com
Twitter: @denisemswank
Facebook: DeniseGroverSwank
Instagram: DeniseGroverSwank

25608309R00264

Made in the USA
San Bernardino, CA
05 November 2015